The Blind Goddess

All the characters and the storyline in this book, are entirely fictional and any resemblance to anyone alive or deceased or real events is entirely coincidental.

This book is sold subject to the condition that it shall not, by way of trade or otherwise be lent, resold, hired out or otherwise circulated without the author's prior consent. Nor in any form of binding or cover other than in which it is published and without a similar condition, including this condition being imposed on the subsequent purchaser.

The series so far:

The Lost Gorillas
Knife of the Sun
The Last train to Nowhere
Jade
The Blind Goddess

Meet the 6ix

Ben Damo has given up his job as a National Park ranger in Congo to work for Ong Thakkrani in his orangutan sanctuary in Indonesia. He is also involved with the WWF programme to transfer gorillas to Venezuela. His uncanny tracking skills have proven invaluable to the 6ix.

Izi Uhuru is enjoying life at her new school, the CEA for Talented Children in England. She has discovered a new skill as a researcher and problem solver. Her mother Betta is slowly getting used to her being away from their home in Gambia for much of the year.

Jannie Pietersen is still avoiding the Johannesburg street gang, the Takers, who have been chasing him all over the world. His wealthy benefactor, Johann Prinsloo, continues to assist the subterfuge, by finding him work placements within his vast industrial organisation. Jannie is currently in Darwin, Australia but dreams of returning to his orphanage.

Laura Dalton, has changed a lot over the last 12 months, primarily due to her involvement in all sorts of dangerous adventures with her new friends. She loves spending time in luxury shopping malls but almost despite herself, has developed new computer skills with Izi.

Sam Ascanio is used to being at the CEA School, far from her father's farm in the deep south of Venezuela. She has demonstrated her remarkable skills as a microlight pilot during the recent escapades. She keeps her favourite horse, Nimby in the school's stables.

Stan Ogenko, is already used to being apart from his parents due to their busy work schedules, so his new life at boarding school isn't such a change. His skills as a computer hacker are well balanced by his ability to climb sheer rock faces like a spider. He still enjoys playing computer chess against his acquaintances from all over the world.

Supporting characters

Brenda Kinney, admin assistant in the Ministry of Defence archives
Turner, senior conservator at MOD
Arkan Vaduga, leader of thuggees, The Master
Dharmesh Vaduga, Arkan's son
Abdul Khan, criminal mastermind hunting for Jannie
Butcher, assassin for hire
Johann Prinsloo, billionaire industrialist
Ade Bambang, Warden on the orangutan sanctuary
Bonn Thakkrani, school friend of the 6ix
Christopher Perez Ascanio, Sam's father
Esther Ogenko, Stan's mother
Ong Thakkrani, Bonn's father
Spencer Ogenko, Stan's father
James McCloud, owner of the Trident dive boat
Jasmine Banjudie, James' girlfriend.
George Abrahams, Head of Special Branch
Joseph Stein, leader of Bonn's security team
Lawrence, Joseph Stein's deputy
Owen Strasser, Head of Prinsloo Industries' Special Operations
Dan, Roger, Sandra and Charlie, Bonn's personal security team.
Sadeeb Deburwani, Chief of Detectives, Colombo
Sanjit Singh, bank manager, Blackman Brothers bank

PART ONE

Chapter 1

Sri Lanka, 1940

As the knotted garrotte bit into his neck, the courier desperately tried to force his bony fingers beneath it, in a futile attempt to take another life-saving breath. The blood supply to his brain had been cut off by the stained old rope and as the blackness of death squeezed his conscious mind, his feet drummed in an irregular staccato on the surface of the empty street.
Less than a minute after the noose had first bit into his wrinkled neck, the callous attacker dropped the old man's limp body onto the dusty road surface.
"That was easy" the attacker said quietly, as he recovered the rope and re-tied the garrotte around his waist, as a belt.
"That's only half the job done" his brother replied as he approached the body. He glanced briefly at the bulging eyes and protruding tongue, before crouching down and opening the old man's canvas satchel that was slung across his chest. "Getting the money is the other half..."
"How much do you think?" his brother asked, as he nervously glanced up and down the gloomy alleyway.
"The Goddess is good..." came the automatic response.
"She will provide" his brother completed the chant, as the other withdrew a thick wad of £5 notes from the satchel. "And she has!"
"There must be a fortune there. Why would an old man be carrying so much cash?"

"The Master knew. That's why he sent us after him. Maybe he had a vision from the Goddess..."

Watching from behind the half-closed shutters of a first-floor window, two cloaked figures had watched the deadly attack.

"You have done well" the Master said quietly.

"Thank you father" Dharmesh replied in a crisp English accent. "Who are those men? I don't recognise them."

"They have only been with us for a few weeks." the Master replied as he watched the brothers stripping the corpse. "This is their first sacrifice to the Goddess. Tonight, they will be presented to Her in the temple, to make their blood bond."

"And their tattoos?"

"Once they dispose of the body, they will return to the caverns to prepare themselves for tonight's ceremony and receive the eyes of the Goddess. As we all did in our time."

As Dharmesh recalled his own initiation into the cult of the Goddess many years ago, he absently felt under his right arm, to the site of his tattoo. The ancient design consisting of two, bright red orbs set in a figure of eight, were only visible to others if he raised his right arm high enough to reveal his arm pit. Every one of the Goddess' followers carried the mark which was branded into them after their first murderous robbery, as a sacrifice carried out in Her name.

"You are sure you don't want me to be at the ceremony tonight?" Dharmesh asked.

"The Goddess will understand your absence my son. The disappearance of the courier, so soon after leaving your bank, may become a Police matter. You need to work late at the bank to deal with any possible enquiries into his disappearance. I will not risk your position being endangered when we have worked so long and hard to establish you within the bank."

"I understand, father. The Goddess guides us on the road to Her greatness."

"And what of the war? You told me that the British authorities appear to be nervous?"

"My manager has had several late-night meetings in the last few weeks, with the deputy Ambassador from the British Consulate. I have had to attend to keep notes of the meetings, since my manager doesn't trust his Secretary to do it. The matters discussed are too sensitive."

"And...?"

"It seems that despite the news in the papers and on the radio, the British and her Allies are losing the war. The Japanese seem to be unstoppable. The deputy Ambassador made it clear in their last meeting, that the garrison here in Colombo will not be reinforced. Which means that they won't have enough troops to defend the capital never mind the rest of Sri Lanka, if we are attacked."

"Did he say when they expect the Japanese to invade?"

"He would not say for sure but he officially advised the manager, as the representative of Blackman Brothers bank, to prepare plans to evacuate his staff and all deposits. I assume he has had similar meetings with all the other banks in the city."

"Evacuate? To where? They can't expect to hide in the mountains."

"No. It seems that the advice from the foreign office is to go to India. He insisted that the mainland would be much safer.

They have more troops there and the Indian Army is being reinforced every day with new recruits from around the rest of the British Commonwealth."

"And you told me that they want this information to be kept secret?"

"They don't want a panic on their hands. If people suspected the real level of danger they are in, there would be a riot. Any ship arriving in the harbour would soon be swamped with desperate people."

"I must think on this." the Master replied slowly. "If the Japanese come, we would have to retreat to the mountain and our caverns, to protect the Goddess. If what they think comes true, we must organise food, water and supplies for a long siege. But before that day comes, there may be many opportunities for us to take advantage of the situation."

"To take advantage?"

"If all the banks have been advised to prepare to evacuate, we can assume that there will be others too, so it's quite likely that this secret will get out. Once word spreads, a lot of people will want to escape from the city and they will obviously want to take their valuables with them. You are in an ideal position to watch the withdrawals from your bank's vaults and safe deposit boxes. Then the Goddess, with your help, will guide our assassins to them."

"You are wise, father. The Goddess will be pleased with the offerings."

"That blade is double edged. What you tell me about the real threat from the Japanese comes only as a little surprise, my son. I have to tell you that I had another vision last night" the Master replied and closed his eyes.

"What did the Goddess reveal to you?"

"The Goddess was in danger. She was surrounded by Japanese soldiers who had invaded the cavern."

"Inside the cavern...?" Dharmesh whispered. "Surely that's impossible. Did she tell you what to do?"

"The visions do not work that way, my son. Maybe it is time for me to explain something to you." the Master's eyes flickered open to stare deeply into the eyes of his son, before they drooped closed again as he cast his mind back in time. "When I had my first insight, I was only seven years old and it really frightened me. I tried to tell my father the details but he insisted that I should speak to my grandfather about it. His instruction confused me. I was very close to my father and he had always understood me, so I thought it was a strange suggestion. Clearly, since I was still much too young to be inducted into the sect, I didn't know that my grandfather was the Master at that time.

"Your father did not have the Sight?"

"The Gift often skips a generation, as it did with my father before me. And thus far, also with you, it seems" the Master admitted sadly.

"I'm sorry to disappoint you."

"It is the will of the Goddess...you serve her in a different way, Dharmesh. Each of us works to honour Her."

"Yes father"

"When my grandfather visited later that day, he told me that my dream meant that the Goddess was simply reaching out to me, as She had done when he was a boy. He listened carefully, as I told him exactly what I had dreamed. He sat silent for many minutes considering what I had told him. Eventually he admitted that he could not tell me exactly what the dream meant. He explained that the Goddess' messages were rarely simple or easy to interpret. But with experience, it became easier to recall the visions and to understand them better. He finished by telling me to come to him if I ever had any other strange dreams."

"Did the Goddess speak to you often? When you were a boy, I mean?"

"In the early years, no. I did not have another one until I was 10 or 11 years old. But they came more regularly after that. Whenever I had one of the special dreams, I told my grandfather about it and he helped me to learn how to recall the details and how to interpret them. The Goddess has blessed me with Her guidance on many occasions since then."

"And your vision last night? What did it mean?"

"I have not had enough time to consider it fully. But from what you say, it seems clear that the Goddess is aware of the coming Japanese invasion. The soldiers attacking her were glowing with a strange green light, almost like demons...It was clearly a warning that we must be fully prepared for their arrival. And to ensure the cavern's location remains unknown to them."

"The Japanese have already gained a vicious reputation in this war. Murdering and mutilating any who oppose them..."

"The Goddess will be protected from them. And she will guard us in return" the Master replied with a steely voice. "We will disappear into the mountain and fight them like shadows if they are a threat to Her. They will never overcome us. We will be like vengeful ghosts to them. Now go. I have to return to the caverns to prepare for tonight's ceremony."

After the Master had concluded their induction into the cult, the two brothers who had killed the old courier were granted the honour to pass the night as part of the Goddess' personal guard. Four men were chosen every day to guard Her candle-lit cavern, for each 24-hour period. The Goddess' statue was located at the rear of the echoing space, which was the largest of the dozens of caves and tunnels which riddled the mountain and had been the home of all the Masters and the Goddess' followers for the last 150 years.

"Are you sure you want to do this?" one brother whispered to the other as he glanced nervously left and right.

"It is exactly as I planned" his older and more reckless brother replied. "We will never have a better chance to do it. The other guards are almost asleep, just look at them..."

"But the Goddess never sleeps. Those red eyes blazed as I smeared my blood on her feet in the ceremony. I am sure that She knows!"

"Keep your voice down, you fool. You can't back down now. The Englishman is expecting us tonight. And the ship to Madras leaves at dawn. Those rubies will make us as rich as princes."

"I know She is watching...we will never escape. She will have warned the Master..."

"The Master suspects nothing. He left hours ago. I saw him take the tunnel to the gateway with my own eyes. And everyone else is sound asleep by now."

"This is madness. We will never escape..."

"We will be out of the country before they're even awake. We must do it now, we have planned this for months, from the first time we saw the Goddess. And you agreed..."

"I'm not sure that I can do this."

"You take the guard to the right, he is half asleep anyway. Give me a minute to get around the other side. Then watch for my signal. And do it silently."

The two brothers stood up casually and moving on silent feet, they approached the other two guards. The older brother gave a slight nod to his sibling, before he clamped his hand over the guard's mouth and rammed the blade of his knife between his ribs. The steel drove deep into the guard's heart, killing him instantly. The other brother copied him in the shadows on the other side and suddenly they were both committed to the crime.

Without a word, the older brother stepped over the bleeding corpse and approached the statue of the Goddess. The eight-foot-tall figure's shiny black surface flickered in the candle light and the numerous shadows around it moved in an eerie dance. As his brother watched in awed silence, he reached up with his dagger and pushed the point into the socket beneath her left eye. The flaming red jewel, almost two inches across, popped out of its obsidian socket and dropped into his outstretched palm. As he moved to the other side of the statue, he slid the giant ruby into his trouser pocket, before repeating the process with the other eye.

"I hear footsteps" his brother hissed, as he turned from the Goddess. "Someone is coming."

"Take the back stairs, as we planned. We need to get past the door guard before they raise the alarm here."

The two brothers ran out of the Goddess' chamber and taking the stairs two at a time, raced up the ancient corridor towards the exit door. Moments later they saw the startled guard who stood blocking the closed door.

"What are you doing?" he asked as he placed his hand on the hilt of a curved machete hanging from over his hip. "You should be guarding the Goddess."

"Have they been this way?" the older brother asked breathlessly. "We must find them."

The confused guard looked left and right and asked. "What are you talking about? Who came this way? I've seen no one."

"The thieves" the brother replied as he moved slowly forward. Excited voices rose from the stairway behind them. "Have you checked the door? Is it still locked?" He asked innocently, casually moving towards the guard.

"Of course it's locked" the guard snapped, but he automatically turned his head towards the door. He immediately paid the price for his error, as the brother's knife arced forward and sliced across the guard's unprotected neck. Hot, dark red blood spurted across the passage as the guard fell sideways and then crumpled to the floor with a clatter of metal on stone.

"We are doomed" his brother urged, as footsteps pounded up the stairs behind him.

"Block the stairs, slow them down while I unlock the door. Use that table..."

The younger brother seized the guard's heavy wooden table and threw it down the corridor into the pursuers. More shouts echoed up the passage as the table crashed into them.

"Come on!" his brother called as he leapt through the open door and ran into the forest beyond.

As his younger brother turned to follow, he slipped in the large pool of the guard's blood that now covered the stone floor and he fell heavily onto his knees. As he scrambled to regain his footing, the first of the pursuers burst out of the corridor and threw himself headlong on top of the brother. As the two men grappled, the other thuggees arrived and the brother was soon overpowered and dragged back to the caverns below.

"We have the thief, Master" one of them proclaimed proudly.

"Where is the other one?" Arkan asked darkly.

"The other one?" the man asked obviously confused.

"His brother...They were both guarding the Goddess. Surely you don't think one man could kill two guards in silence, do you?"

"There was only one, Master. We caught him before he could get through the open door."

"The open door?" Arkan advanced on the man and struck him across the face. "You didn't think it was strange that he opened the door and then waited for you to catch him?"

"No....Master. I didn't. Forgive my stupidity."

"Have you searched him?"

"Yes, Master. We did that immediately. He does not have the Goddess' eyes."

"More stupidity...You didn't think that was strange?"

"As we had caught him..."

The Master's face showed his fury as he turned to one of his lieutenants. "Find the other brother and bring him back to me. Alive. The Goddess will want to witness both their deaths."

"Immediately" the lieutenant replied before he rushed away.

The Master swung his eyes to another of his followers and said "You...Bashir. Torture this one. Here, in front of the

Her Mightiness. Find out everything he knows. Where his brother is. And what they intend doing with them."

"Doing with them?" Bashir asked.

"I know what he is planning!" the brother stuttered aloud, cutting off Bashir's question. "The Englishman is buying them. My brother is selling them to the Englishman in the city. He told me tonight. Please don't hurt me Master. I will tell you everything I know. You don't need to torture me."

"Indeed, you will tell me" Arkan replied. "But I need to be sure that you speak the truth. Bashir, once he has told you everything that I need, don't let him die quickly. The Goddess has been deeply offended by the desecration of Her image. And now she demands retribution. A bloody sacrifice must be made."

Chapter 2

London, Present day

"Don't you just love London, Bob?" Tracy asked as she looked out of the tall window of their luxury hotel suite. "These last few days have been fantastic."

"Darling, I really couldn't be happier" Bob Dalton said, as he relaxed in one of the dark velvet covered armchairs that were dotted around the large lounge, situated high above the busy streets of Mayfair. "I love London and I love travelling anywhere with you. But now I can finally relax. Since Laura got interested in doing the historical research I love so much, we finally have something in common. Since they discovered the wreck of the Diadem, she's a different girl."

"I really hope she keeps it up" Tracy replied. "It's been quite a turnaround, I agree. Remember that her teachers told us that she had studied a lot for her end-of-year exams too. In fact, Laura admitted to me that she has never worked so hard for an exam."

"Let's be honest, that wouldn't have been difficult" Bob laughed. "But you're right. The head of year at her school phoned to tell me about the massive improvement in her attitude last term. I have high hopes for the exam results when they come out in a few weeks' time."

"So, now we can relax and have fun for the whole summer. Unless you have to work...again!"

"Are you talking about me, by any chance" Laura asked, as she walked out of bedroom into the huge lounge.

"Why, were your ears burning?" Bob asked with a smile.

"Nope. But I heard you talking about a fun summer..."

"For all of us that meant." Tracy replied. "And then Bob was telling me about you having an interest in common..."

"What do you mean?" she asked defensively.

"Just the research thing, darling. You know how I much I enjoy my research..."

"Oh, right. Research....yeah. Fascinating."

"And talking about summer fun" Tracey quickly changed the subject. "What time are Izi and her family arriving? Have you heard anything from them today?"

"Yes. Funnily enough, I just got a text from Izi. They had a wonderful time exploring the Lake District with their guide and they arrived back in London on their train, a few minutes ago."

"I thought you told me that their train had been delayed?" Bob asked.

"Only by thirty minutes, apparently." Laura replied. "So, after checking in at their hotel they should be with us before lunch time."

"Perfect" Tracy replied. "A nice catch up over lunch and then Knightsbridge for shopping. It will probably be Izi's last chance to do some proper shopping before they all head back home to Gambia."

"I'm sure she will love that" Laura replied dubiously. "I keep trying to get her excited about clothes and shoes...but she still just doesn't get it!"

"I'm sure that you are desperate to have me with you too but I am going to have to cry off" Bob replied with a shrug. "I need to go over to the Ministry of Defence building again, honey. It's actually rather important. And it's got to be done today. You won't mind too much will you...?"

"Of course we don't mind, Dad." Laura interrupted with a smile. "I know you only come along to keep us happy."
"And we both know that you just hate shopping, Bob Dalton. So you may as well admit it!" Tracy added.

Two hours later, Bob passed through the towering bomb-proof doors of the public entrance to the Ministry of Defence Headquarters. The classic, pre-war building squatted on the banks of the river Thames, just 5 minutes' walk from the Houses of Parliament in central London.
The four rifle-carrying soldiers who watched Bob as he made his way through the metal detector arch, were only the first and most obvious layer of protection which secured the building. As Bob looked around, his professional eye picked out the array of cameras mounted on the walls and ceiling of the entrance concourse. The second layer, Bob thought to himself.
"Are you Mr Dalton, by any chance?" a voice asked.
Bob turned his head and looked down to find himself confronted by a glum faced, grey haired man standing next to him. "Yes, that's me." he answered.
"Perfect timing. My name's Turner. I am one of the senior conservators here at the Ministry. I have been asked to assist you with the documents you requested."
"The documents which I should have been given the last time I was here..."
"Yes, indeed. I understand there was some minor mix-up?"
"Not minor to me. The documents relating to the voyage of the Diadem are now public access, Mr Turner...all of them. And I should have been given all of them."

"I wasn't given all of the details of your, erm...previous visit...My staff have the relevant details..."

"Well, let me explain them for you. The HMS Diadem was part of a British naval fleet which sailed around the beginning of the 20th century carrying a cargo of Chinese bullion. Her captain handed his ship's log to the Commodore of the fleet when he was sent on a secret mission. Unfortunately, the Diadem was lost at sea so without that log book we would never have known what happened to her."

"So what are the other documents you are looking for?"

"The logs of the rest of the fleet should also have been released at the same time. The disclosure law is very straightforward. *'Open government'* Mr Turner...the public has a right to know what our Government and our armed forces are up to. Even if we have to wait 100 years for that information."

"I am sure we can sort it all out today for you, Mr Dalton. You have to appreciate we have numerous requests like yours under the public disclosure legislation. That means thousands of documents to copy, in readiness for their release each year. It puts a lot of pressure on the staff in the Archive section. We are under-staffed...funding cut backs etc... budgets reduced..."

"All I am interested in is the documents that *I should have been given last time.* I have had to travel a long way to collect them, so I want to make sure that I get everything this time."

"My staff are completing the work as we speak. We are doing our level best to correct the slight misunderstanding of your requirements from last time. I have instructed them to rush it through the copiers for you. As a top priority, you understand. Please attach this Visitor's badge to your jacket and follow me. It's only a short walk."

Bob did as he was told and followed the uncomfortable seeming civil servant out of the concourse and through a series of corridors deeper into the building.

"Here we are" Turner said as they reached an unmarked, ordinary looking doorway. He placed his hand on an illuminated panel positioned at head height on the wall next to the door.

"Fingerprint reader?" Bob asked.

"It takes the full palm print too. The whole building has the latest security technology. Perhaps you noticed the overhead cameras everywhere? Sadly, no money for librarians though..." Turner replied as the door slid open with a hiss of escaping air to reveal a short corridor on the other side.

"An air lock too?" Bob asked as he walked forward through the doorway.

"The humidity of the air inside the archives is significantly reduced and maintained at a higher, positive pressure, to maintain air quality and help with the document preservation requirements. The inner door won't open until the outer one is completely closed."

"Safer too. Security wise, I mean" Bob suggested.

"I assume so. But that's not really my field of interest. Preservation is my main concern"

The two men passed through the second door as soon as it slid open. "It's huge" Bob said as he looked down one of the long corridors which lead towards the far end of the huge library.

"I'm sure you know that the Military keeps records of everything" Turner replied with pride. "Of course, these days everything is digital, but we are still in the process of trying to get all the paper documents computerised. It's a massive task, especially as we are so short staffed. We still have millions of documents in this building alone."

"But you have enough staff to do my copying?" Bob suggested.

"Absolutely Mr Dalton. I am sure that the documents you requested will be ready for you by now. My manager made it clear that I should rush your Release Request through the appropriate channels. Even though there seems to be quite a few documents..."

"I am leaving the country again, first thing tomorrow. So I can't come back *again,* Mr Turner."

"Everything is ready, Mr Turner" a young woman interrupted them. "I put them in these two boxes...to make it easier for you to carry. I hope that helps?"

"I don't think I know your name, Miss...?" Turner asked.

"Kinney" she replied. "I'm new in the Department. It's actually my first day in the Records section. I'm very excited to be working here."

"That's excellent Miss... Kinney. But you can leave it with me now. Is that the Record Release instruction you have there?"

"Yes, it is" she replied with a smile.

"Give it to me, if you please, so that I can check through it. He ran his figure down the long checklist and then turning his attention to Bob he said. "It's all here. The full record of the voyage of the Chinese bullion fleet as you requested. I'm sure it's a fascinating piece of military history."

"It should be. If it's complete. I really don't want to have to come back again, but looking at those two full boxes there's too much to go through all of it now."

"I'm positive Miss Kinney will have given you everything you requested, our staff are very efficient and the Release sheet is quite detailed."

"Miss Kinney seems keen enough. I'm sure she will be a useful addition to your team."

"I just need a couple of signatures, Mr Dalton and then you can take the documents away with you."

"A job's not done until the paperwork is finished...eh?"

"Exactly, Mr Dalton. Exactly."

Ten minutes later, Bob was standing on the footway. He hailed a black cab that was cruising past the MOD building and he clambered inside placing the two boxes onto the cab's floor space. He gave the driver his hotel's name and dropped down on the wide seat with a grunt. A satisfied smile crept across his face as he gazed at the boxes. Laura and Izi will have some more reading to do when they got back from shopping, he thought to himself as the cab accelerated forward.

Chapter 3

Darwin, Australia

"Owen Strasser and Johann Prinsloo are with me in Reception." the Hotel receptionist said into the phone. "They say that they have an appointment to see Mr Thakkrani?" She apparently then listened to the reply. "Ok. Yes, yes. I will send them right up." Replacing the handset, she turned her attention back to the visitors. "You're expected, gentlemen. Room 1201. It's on the twelfth floor. The elevators are over there..." she finished, pointing to her right.

"Thank you" Johann replied with a smile before following the directions and heading to the bank of elevators which, he had noticed on arrival at the hotel, flew up and down the exterior facade of the brand-new structure.

"Top floor?" Owen asked moments later, as he looked at the control panel inside the elevator.

"That's where the best views are" Johann replied as the doors slid silently shut.

"And the best suites too, I'm sure."

"Ong doesn't strike me as a poor man. The Black Marlin alone must have cost millions."

"It takes one to know one" Owen replied with a wide smile, as the elevator came to a halt. "Maybe you should buy a boat JP..."

"I can't pay your wages *and* buy a boat" Johann replied. "So, unless you want to work for free...?"

"Maybe you don't really *need* a boat then. And you know that you would miss me too much if I had to leave."

"That's settled then" Johann replied as the elevator came to a halt. "No luxury yachts for me!" They exited the elevator and walked along the deep pile carpet which lined the floor towards the double doors to 1201, Ong's suite. Owen pressed the door bell and they heard the chimes ringing inside.

Owen had noticed the tiny camera mounted to the top right of the door, as they had approached the doors and had assumed they were being monitored by someone inside the suite.

"Johann...Owen, lovely to see you again" Ong said as he swung open the door. "Please...come inside."

They stepped inside the suite to find themselves in a fabulous room with floor to ceiling windows overlooking the ocean. "Nice view" Owen said as he walked towards the windows.

"The best in the city, I am told." Ong replied warmly. "I've got fresh coffee on the table. We can enjoy both as we chat, can't we. I want to apologise in advance if our meeting is going to seem rushed, but I did warn you that I've only got an hour before I need to leave, didn't I?"

"That should be plenty of time, Ong" Johann replied as they sat down at the table. "I assume we can speak freely in here?"

"I've taken Owen's suggestion to increase my protection seriously since we last spoke about our mutual friend. The whole suite was swept again this morning, by my own team. They didn't find any listening devices of any kind. Anywhere. So, what we say here will remain between us."

"I think Owen has made me a little bit paranoid too." Johann replied. "But industrial espionage is very common now and if our suspicions are correct, Abdul Khan is not a man I want to under estimate or give any possible advantages in terms of information gathering."

"When we first started discussing him and Asia Resources, it was hard to believe he could actually be a criminal mastermind." Ong replied. "But once my people started digging properly we also found a few, shall we call them...*inconsistencies* in his business practices."

"Nothing you can prove though?" Owen asked.

"Asia Resources and my businesses have only overlapped on a few occasions over the last few years but even so they have won every one of those contract bids. That in itself is unusual because I am very competitive so you would expect to win at least one out of every three."

"It's a similar story with Prinsloo Industries" Johann replied. "Asia are just a little bit too successful in winning contracts. So as we discussed before, Owen and his team started looking much deeper into Asia Resources."

"And the shadowy Mr. Khan" Owen added. "And to think that we almost caught him red-handed at the centre of that smuggling operation in Gambia. Well before we started looking into Asia's *good luck*."

"It *might* have been him, Owen. You always tell me that I shouldn't jump to conclusions without proper intelligence, so maybe it wasn't him. Don't forget we couldn't find a single document connecting him to anything. Remember, that lawyer presented us with plenty of proof to the contrary."

"It was all far too convincing, Johann and you know that."

"Too convincing?" Ong asked.

"Yes, too convincing." Owen replied forcefully. "If I gave you 30 minutes to prove to me that you owned all the companies that you own...could you do that, Ong."

"I'm sure that if I asked my lawyer, I'm sure he could dig up the necessary documents..."

"In 30 minutes?" Owen asked.

"In all honesty, probably not. It might take me 30 minutes just to track him down. And he works full time as my 'in-house' counsellor."

"And yet, this lawyer just happens to be on scene at the poachers' warehouse when the raid goes down. And coincidentally he just happens to hold every relevant ownership document proving that Khan's name is nowhere on the official record. "

"Owen and I both agree that it was just too pat" Johann added.

"Someone had tipped Khan off that we were coming. I'm sure of that" Owen insisted.

"That's hardly conclusive Owen." Ong suggested.

"You're right but since then we've been slowly piecing data together." Owen told Ong. "Khan keeps a very low profile, even in his legal businesses. He uses layers of shell companies, lawyers and bankers to keep the real ownership of them hidden. My guys are the best at investigating these things and even they were hard pressed to track Khan's connections. But his criminal involvement is even better hidden."

"Owen is modest about what his team has achieved. From what they managed to find out we are sure Khan was behind the sabotage of our pipeline in Siberia and the slave trade we discovered here in Australia." Johann insisted. "Nothing that we could take to a prosecutor, of course since Owen's team had to breach a whole raft of laws, restrictions and guidelines to obtain the data. But it was him. For sure."

"And we are pretty sure he is funding gangs to carry out kidnappings around the globe too."

"Do you think he was responsible for the kidnapping of Bonn's friends? In Venezuela?" Ong asked.

"Yes. Almost certainly." Johann replied. "If we hadn't used Owen's Specialist Operations team...well, it would have been a lot worse. I don't think the Police would have ever found them, never mind rescued them."

"Which brings us to today." Ong replied with a sigh. "Kidnapping..."

"Yes. We know that you've got a full team guarding Bonn. Even at the CEA School while she is in England..." Owen pointed out. "And it seems you are very careful about your own security too. Cameras on your doors, security sweeps, armoured vehicles to take you around..."

"All necessary precautions Owen. I can assure you." Ong replied heavily. "Like you, Johann, I am a very wealthy man. I worked long and hard to get to that position but even so, some people get resentful, especially in a poor country like Thailand. And I have probably made some enemies in the business community over the years..."

"Which makes you a target..." Owen suggested.

"I believe so. But also, my daughter. About a year ago there was an explosion near Bonn's school in Bangkok. The city has more than its fair share of them, sadly. Luckily, on this occasion no one was killed or injured and the police decided it was the work of one of the usual fanatical political groups. But no one was ever convicted or even arrested."

"But you disagree?" Johann asked. "You think Bonn was the reason?"

"Yes. Let me explain why. My admin office receives all sorts of junk mail, every day, which they filter them for me. There have even been a few crazy threats over the years, which they normally pass to my security people to decide what, if anything, they need to do. But this was different. The day after the explosion a package arrived through the post."

"Another bomb?" Owen asked.

"No. It was a video of them planting the one that had just exploded. The commentary on the tape pointed out that they knew the location was near Bonn's school and listed her school schedule. They said it would have been easy to kill her. And they threatened to do so...unless I gave them money."

"But you sent her to England instead" Johann said.

"It took me a few weeks to organise but, yes. In the interim I sent her to our country home where she was home-schooled while I recruited her own security detail that would accompany her to England. She wasn't very happy when I tried to explain to her the need for close personal protection officers but eventually she accepted the very real need for them. Then I had to persuade the CEA Headmaster to accept the bodyguards too. I couldn't risk my only daughter. Once that was all done I hired detectives to track down the bombers or kidnappers or whatever they were, who had sent the video."

"Why didn't you go to the Police?" Owen asked.

"The Police in Thailand fall into two groups, Owen. Those who are worth bribing and those who aren't. Corruption is rife in my country. From the lowest of street cops right up to the most senior officers. Trust me, I know. I've had to deal with that fact as part of doing business there. I quickly decided that I was not going to put my daughter's safety into their hands."

"And did your detectives find out who planted the bomb or sent the video?" Johann asked.

"No, they didn't. But I didn't hear anything more from the bombers either. I began to assume that it was all some kind of clever hoax or that moving Bonn had solved the problem or maybe the detective's investigation had frightened them off."

"But something changed your mind recently?" Johann asked, leaning forward in his chair.

"One of the detectives that I hired to track down the bombers was murdered in a bar in Bangkok and his apartment was broken into and trashed."

"I'm sure he made enemies in his line of work." Owen pointed out. "Jealous husbands, angry debtors..."

"Possibly. But he had only been working on my case. For more than a year now. I suspect that the bombers killed him when he got too close to finding them."

"That's a big conclusion to jump to, Ong" Johann said.

"I don't believe it is. He sent an envelope to my office in Bangkok. It must have been sent on the same day that he was killed. The envelope contained three things. A photocopy of a hawala money transaction dated the day before the bombing took place. It was from someone in Saudi, for ten thousand dollars. There was also a memory stick with a telephone recording. The detective had had the recording compared by expert analysts to the voice in the video of the bombing and it was made by the same voice. The voice was talking to a man who called himself Rhino,

Rhino told the voice that he had contacted a gang in London, who had agreed to kidnap Bonn. This Rhino pointed out that the London gang expected to receive the money before they did the job. And lastly, the envelope contained a scribbled note from the detective himself."

"A hand-written note? Bit unusual in an official report. What did it say?" Owen asked.

"He must have written it in the Post Office where he posted the envelope. It said that he was being followed and he was sure that they were going to kill him. He wrote that an informant he used regularly had just called him and warned him to disappear. To get out of the country. Immediately. The informant had said that the enquires he had been making had upset someone powerful. Consequently, a huge bounty had been put on his head. And the man who had issued the contract was called...Abdul Khan."

"It's not a particularly unusual name Ong but...we don't believe in coincidences. Do we Owen?"

"It cost my detective his life" Ong replied sadly. Ong's private phone buzzed quietly at that point and he glanced at his watch. "I lost track of the time but I need to take this call...please relax" he added as the two men automatically rose from their seats. "You don't need to leave..."

Owen and Johann were surprised but nodded their understanding as Ong began to speak.

"Hello Bob. I understand from my secretary that you've got some good news for us? Actually, Johann and Owen are still with me...so I'm just going to put you on the loudspeaker."

"Oh right" Bob Dalton's voice sounded clear and calm from the loudspeaker. "Hello Owen, and Johann"

"Hello Bob" they both replied at the same time. "We could do with some good news" Johann said.

"Has Laura passed all her exams by any chance?" Owen asked playfully.

"Ha! I certainly hope so. But we won't find out for a few more weeks yet. No, I am calling about the treasure trove. I don't know if Ong has told you that he asked me to check around a bit? As a follow-up to the discovery of the Diadem?"

"I haven't had a chance to brief them yet Bob." Ong replied. "But I'm sure they will catch on."

"Well, I wondered if the MoD had any more information...on the Diadem or the rest of the treasure fleet from China, which could give us a lead on what happened to the other statues. And my persistence seems to have paid off. I think I've got a line on the rest of the jade statues. The ones that weren't aboard the Diadem when she sank."

"I knew you would track them down for me" Ong interrupted. "I had a funny feeling the rest of the figures from the Chinese army had survived somehow. Well done Bob."

"I can't claim all the glory actually. As soon as I arrived with the copies of the documents, Laura and Izi both started reading through them. I couldn't have done it without their help in this short a time scale to be honest. As you can imagine, with the ship's logs from half a dozen ships of the line and assorted support vessels, it's a lot of paperwork."

"Like father...like daughter" Johann suggested with a smile.

"And Izi is fast showing her talents as a diligent researcher" Owen added.

"Well, the Royal Navy scribes didn't let us down either." Bob replied from the speaker. "We haven't managed to go through all of it yet. But fortunately, the first bundle we opened up makes it clear that the crate with the rest of the statues in, was off loaded in Colombo, in Ceylon. It seems that they got instructions to put the crate into a vault there. In a private bank called Blackman Brothers..."

"You have to go there, Bob" Ong replied excitedly. "Can you leave today?"

"This all happened a very long time ago, Ong. It's a very cold trail by now..."

"I don't care about that Bob. It's the only clue we've got to go on. And I really want to get my hands on the rest of the statues. I know you're on holiday with your family in London..."

"I thought that you might insist on a rapid follow-up, Ong. So, I've already booked the flights. I will obviously have to take the girls with me. It's the start of the school holidays here, but I'm sure they won't mind a week's holiday on a tropical island."

"I think that you had better make that two weeks Bob" Owen suggested. "There's bound to be some nice shops for Laura and Tracey to look around too."

"I don't think Izi will though!"

"Izi?" Johann asked.

"Yes, she's here in London with her family at the moment. When I was explaining to Laura and Tracey about my new plan to go to Colombo, Izi was hanging onto every word."

"She's got the adventure bug" Owen pointed out.

"Indeed she has. But she's also been involved with the Diadem right from the beginning so I asked her if she would like to come with us instead of going back to Gambia with her Mum."

"And she snatched your hand off?"

"Almost" Bob replied with a laugh. "She actually got straight on the phone to her Mum and begged her to let her come with us."

"And it seems that Betta agreed?" Ong asked.

"Yes, she did. On the one condition that I don't let her get involved in anything dangerous!"

"I can't imagine anyone describing a luxury holiday in Sri Lanka as dangerous" Owen said.

"Do you think that it's possible that Khan really is ultimately behind the threat to Bonn?" Owen asked Johann, as they drove away from the water-side hotel.

"Of course, anything is possible but that would be a stretch. Ong admits that he's made a lot of enemies over the years."

"Someone called Abdul Khan took out the contract that got his investigator killed." Owen pointed out.

"Which may or may not have been the result of his investigation into the bombing."

"But if that gang in London has already been paid to kidnap her...? Ong will definitely have to take her out of the CEA school."

"And probably out of the country too." Johann replied.

"As Bob pointed out, the UK schools are on holiday now for a few weeks. So Ong's got time to decide what to do next."

"We've given him even more things to play on his mind now" Johann pointed out.

"Bonn's situation is a bit like the problem we had with Jannie. Which, fortunately we've now sorted out."

"You really want him to go back to South Africa?"

"It's his home, Johann. He misses the other boys. He needs friends. He told me that sometimes he even misses old Theo."

"That bad, eh?" Johann asked half humorously.

"And it will also give William and Miriam a break too. It can't have been easy for them to act as parents and bodyguard for him for all this time. They would never admit it, but I'm sure that they must need a break by now."

Chapter 4

Jannie

Jannie Pietersen was sitting quietly in one of Darwin's quaint waterside cafes which overlooked the still aquamarine waters of the natural harbour.

"Day-dreaming again?" Sam asked as she sat back down next to him.

"I suppose so. Just looking at the boats out there. It made me think about James Macloud and the Trident actually." Jannie replied as he stared at the assorted vessels bobbing in the busy harbour.

"I'm sure he's out there somewhere. Anchored off some hidden reef, diving for a long-forgotten wreck with Jasmine. I'm sure he still hopes to find that long lost Spanish galleon he told us about, he's the modern-day Cousteau."

"I don't remember Jacques Cousteau or his son ever looking for Spanish galleons, Sam. They are more like conservationists."

"Well, one thing's for sure, Sam replied ignoring his sarcastic rebuke. "We will never see him in Darwin again. Those gangsters who were after him, were scary people...from what we heard."

"I'm sure you're right, he's much too smart to come back here now. But after Bonn told us about the Black Marlin coming back to Darwin for repairs.... well, it just made me think about the last time it was here. That's all."

"I know. When my Mum and Dad said we were coming back to Australia for the holidays, I was the same. Then we discussed it all on the plane, on the way here. It's a very long flight for us to get here from home too. As well as finding the Diadem and the treasure we talked all about seeing the city again and the harbour. Of course, Dad is particularly keen about coming to see Arnie's new cocoa farm. If this scheme with Arnie works, it will almost double the amount of chocolate we can produce.

"I actually fly over Arnie's place sometimes. When I am having my lessons on the Predator, I mean. To be honest, it doesn't look like much has changed since you were here last."

"The cocoa plants don't grow overnight!" Sam laughed. "You're always in such a hurry, Jannie. But Arnie told my Dad last week that the plants are doing fine. Dad told me that he is very happy with the farm's progress so far."

"I'm sure they know more about it than me."

"Actually, Arnie has asked me to fly his microlight during the roundup of the horses, so I will be able to check out the progress myself."

"Roundup? What roundup?"

"The bi-annual roundup? I told you all about it on our last trip here. Arnie organises it to collect the wild horses living on the farms that adjoin his. You could come too if you want to...Bonn and I will look after you."

"Riding a horse? I don't think I would be very good at that so I will leave that to Bonn. But I suppose I could use my buggy to help. I get more time off from my studies now that official schools are closed for the holidays. But I will have to check in with Miriam and Bill before I can say it's Ok."

"You're scared of horses. Admit it you Petrol Head!"

"That may be true. But my parents tell me that discretion is the better part of valour."

"Oh, they do, do they? And speaking of your parents...where are they? They don't normally let you out of their sight."

"They haven't. Look across the terrace...over there. Just on the corner" Jannie replied and pointed across the restaurant to where his parents sat enjoying the sunshine. "The other day I accused them of stalking me!"

"You're terrible, Jannie Pietersen. You know they are only looking out for you."

"I know that. But it's been a very long time since the Takers managed to track me down. I'm sure they've given up looking for me by now."

"Safety first." Sam replied dramatically. "As our friend Stan would say."

"And he would tell me that horse riding is very dangerous."

"You should come out with us girls when we go riding at School. Bonn has a spare horse at the stables."

"Unlikely" Jannie replied before subtly changing the subject. "But speaking of horse riding with Bonn, didn't you say that she was going to be joining us for lunch today?" He asked with a smile.

"She told me that her Dad is really busy today, so she did actually warn me earlier that she might be a few minutes late.

"Not that late it seems...because here she is...along with her entourage." Jannie replied with a nod of his head towards the restaurant entrance.

"Hello strangers" Bonn laughed as she strolled across the restaurant trailed by her ever-present security detail.

"Lovely to see you again, Bonn" Jannie replied. "And your *friends*."

"I just invited him to join us on the roundup" Sam said as Bonn sat down at the table. "But he is scared of horses."

"You said that, not me" Jannie replied quickly.

"I'm not one hundred percent sure we will be doing the round-up" Bonn told them.

"Why not?" Sam asked. "I thought it was all agreed?"

"Something has come up" Bonn replied mysteriously. "But it's a good something, so don't worry."

"What sort of good something?" Jannie asked.

"I can't tell you just yet. But you can ask my Dad yourself, if you like. He is making some last-minute phone calls right now, but he said he will join us for dessert. He said he wants to talk to all of us about another little trip!"

"On the Black Marlin?" Jannie asked immediately. "Is she here?"

"Not on the Marlin. No. I think she's going to be out of action for the next few days, having a refit and overhaul in the marine yards. But it's almost as good..."

"Tell us" Sam insisted.

"Nope, I'm sworn to secrecy. You will have to wait for your dessert! But I *will* tell you all about my surfing lessons."

"You can't just leave us hanging like that" Jannie insisted.

"Patience Jannie." Bonn grinned before continuing. "It's the best thing ever. I'm sure it's my Dad's way of trying to soften the news about him getting me a personal tutor for the summer holidays."

"A tutor?" Sam asked.

"I suppose that he wants to make sure that you're top of the class all through sixth form." Jannie suggested.

"The competition at our School is far too tough for that. I doubt I will beat you or Sam to the top spot, never mind super geek."

"Stan's not a geek" Jannie replied. "Have you seen him climbing? He's just like a spider on a wall."

"I'm only joking, silly...we all love him really."

"So... tell me, what is your surf instructor like?" Sam asked. "Tall, blond and gorgeous I suppose?"

"One track minds..." Jannie replied huffily as the girls laughed.

Just as their desserts arrived, Bonn's father strode into the restaurant. "I hope you enjoyed your lunch" he said as he sat down. "It's going to be your last one in Darwin."

"What's happened?" Bonn asked excitedly.

"It's all good news." Ong smiled broadly. "Bob Dalton and Laura and Izi are going to meet us in Sri Lanka for a fantastic holiday."

"Us?" Bonn asked.

"Yes, Sam is coming too."

"I am?" Sam asked.

"But unfortunately, Jannie can't join us. Sorry young man. Your parents told me that you have to stay here to finish your flying lessons.

"I've only got a few hours training left before I pass." Jannie replied slowly.

"But luckily your parents, Sam, have agreed that you can come with us. If you want to? Obviously" Ong asked looking directly at Sam.

"You have? I mean, if they say its Ok...Sri Lanka...another trip of a lifetime...?" Sam said unbelievably. "Are you sure that Mum and Dad are Ok about it? I thought we were supposed to be here in Darwin for another couple of weeks..."

"It will all work out I'm sure. Our trip has to begin tomorrow. It's urgent that I get to the island as soon as possible. Obviously, your Mum and Dad will discuss it with you this afternoon, once we finish lunch, I assume. But they seemed to think you would enjoy it, when I told them what I had planned."

"You'll miss Arnie's roundup." Jannie reminded her, half smiling.

"Oh, right. Yes, I forgot about that...you will have to go now, Jannie. Arnie said he needs all the help he can get."

"There will always be another round up to go on" Ong replied. "I'm sure Arnie can manage without you two girls this time around. especially if Jannie has volunteered now..."

"It's very short notice" Sam said as her mind whirred.

"All you need to worry about is your clothes and your passport" Ong replied. "Ask Bonn. She will tell you how good my secretary is at making sure everything runs smoothly..."

"That's true" Bonn confirmed. "She's a fantastic organiser. Wow, what a great surprise Dad. I wasn't sure what was going on when you were so secretive...and I've never been to Sri Lanka. Didn't it used to be called Ceylon?"

"A long time ago. When the British ruled the island" Ong replied. "But now it's a modern, independent nation."

"What about the civil war they have going on?" Sam asked. "I read about terrorist attacks there, didn't I."

"The Tamil Tigers" Jannie added.

"That's all finished now. The Government sorted it all out a year or so ago." Ong replied. "It's an idyllic holiday destination now."

"And anyway, don't forget we will have Joseph and my protection team with us." Bonn added, as she glanced around the restaurant at the assortment of sunglass-wearing bodyguards. "They will definitely scare off any terrorists."

"Exactly darling. So everyone can relax and enjoy the holiday."

"Are we flying in your jet, Dad?" Bonn asked.

"It's not *my jet*, Bonn. The company owns it. But yes, as it's a business trip, we will be using it to fly to Colombo, once I finish my business here in Darwin tomorrow."

"A business trip to a paradise island...?" Bonn replied innocently.

"I told you. I'm meeting Bob Dalton. Laura's father?" Ong asked. "He and I have some urgent matters to sort out, so for me, it is a business trip."

"Will Laura and Tracey be there too?"

"Yes, they are coming with Bob and I think Izi will be there too."

"Laura told me that she was looking forward to London's shops" Bonn said. "I hope she had time to get some new clothes."

"I thought Izi was supposed to fly home to Gambia with her Mum after they completed their holiday in the UK?"

"Bob didn't tell me about that. But I'm sure you can text or call her and get all the details once we finish here" Ong replied.

"It's a shame that you can't come " Sam said to Jannie sincerely. "It's always more fun when we do stuff together."

"It would be great to go with you guys, but really, I can't. Mr. Prinsloo wants me to concentrate on my flying lessons with the Predator this week. And he says he's got a nice surprise planned for me if I pass with flying colours."

"I'm sure you will ace it. Just like your exams." Sam said with a grin.

"Let's hope we all ace our School exams." Jannie replied. "Then we can all do 6th form together."

Chapter 5

The Trident

Since he had slipped away from Darwin many weeks ago to recover the rest of the silver bullion bars from the reef, James McCloud had deliberately kept a very low profile. He wasn't sure whether the gang from Darwin would bother to try to track him down again but he didn't want to take any chances, or risk the lives of his girlfriend, Jasmine or his new partner, the Padre.

He had only visited the smallest of sleepy harbours to refuel the Trident's tanks as he made his way west along the Indonesian archipelago towards his final destination. An unmarked tropical reef, 15 miles off the north coast of Java.

"That boat is coming straight at us" Jasmine pointed out nervously, as she joined the Padre at the stern rail of the Trident.

"I'm surprised to see anyone else out here" the Padre replied, whilst looking in the direction of the oncoming vessel. "We haven't seen another boat for days."

"Should we bring James up?" Jasmine asked, glancing at the bright yellow safety line which the Padre was holding securely in his hand.

"James is safe enough darling. He's more than sixty feet down. And the crew on that boat must have seen the warning flags we've got up" The Padre unconsciously glanced up at the Trident's flying bridge, towering twenty feet about them at the bright orange warning flags flapping in the light breeze which indicated that there were scuba divers in the water nearby. "They are probably just going to wave us a friendly hello and then steer a wide berth."

"Well, they better veer away soon" Jasmine's reply didn't sound convinced.

"I'll keep a close eye on them, don't you worry."

For the next few minutes they both watched as the approaching vessel loomed ever larger as it continued its straight-line course towards them across the otherwise empty sea.

"I can see a lot of smoke coming from the stern..." the Padre observed. "I think they're in trouble. Might be a fire..."

As he spoke, the boat slowed its approach and a lone figure emerged from the boat's wheelhouse and began waving his arm.

"Looks like he's injured too. See? He's got his arm in a sling" Jasmine noted.

"Your young eyes see better than mine. But it does look like he's going to come right alongside..."

"What about James?"

"James is a clever lad. He will have heard the other boat's engine by now. He's probably looking up at us right now, deciding whether it's worth him coming to surface or not..."

"I need help" the man on the boat shouted as he drew ever nearer to the Trident.

"We've got a diver down" the Padre shouted back. "Stay away from our stern."

"I fell in the engine bay, trying to stop the fire" the stranger shouted back as his boat drew level with the Trident. "Think my arm's broken...and I got a bang on the head too." The boat's rubber fenders kissed the side of the Trident with a gentle thump as they met.

"We saw the smoke..." the Padre began but his reply was cut off when a fast-moving projectile hit him in the middle of the chest and flung him backwards across the deck to strike the far gunwale with an audible crash.

"What?" Jasmine stammered in shocked response as she looked at the Padre's fallen figure.

"Riot gun" the stranger replied calmly, as he dropped the short-barrelled weapon which had moments before been hidden within the sling on his arm. He nimbly jumped across the narrow gap between the two vessels and landed lightly on the Trident's deck holding a mooring line. "But this has thirteen shots" he added, as he pulled a handgun from the waist of his trousers.

"What do you want?" she asked as her eyes flickered between the silver barrel of the weapon and the stranger's features.

"I just want to talk to you, Jasmine" he replied as he quickly looped the line to one of the Trident's cleats. "You, me and my old friend the Padre are going to have a nice chat while we wait for your boyfriend to surface. I assume Mr Macloud is below us? I bet he's wondering about my unexpected arrival too"

"How do you know our names? Who are you?"

The stranger took off his large floppy hat and dark sunglasses.

"Oh no." the Padre said as he roused himself and rubbed his chest. "It's him. The guy who shot me in the Dream Bar."

"I told you I would be back to see you. Didn't I?" the Butcher replied grimly pointing the gun at the Padre. "Help him up...Jasmine. And then we will move into the shade. We are going to make ourselves comfy while we wait for lover boy to join us. I'm sure he won't keep us waiting for long."

"Do as he says Jasmine." the Padre insisted as he painfully levered himself onto his feet. "He enjoys hurting people."

"I'm so glad that you said that Padre. It saves me giving you another lesson. I want you to sit on this side" the Butcher pointed at the helmsman's seat. "Put your hands on the arm rests so that Jasmine can tie you up for me." The Butcher produced a bundle of cable ties from his pocket. "You can use these." he told jasmine. "And make sure they are tight. If you don't do it right, I will have to put another bullet in him. And he wouldn't like that, would you, old man?"

The Padre remained silent as he moved slowly to the chair and sat down and finally said softly. "Don't try anything. Don't give him an excuse to hurt us."

"Very good advice" the Butcher said as he carefully watched Jasmine's actions.

Jasmine followed the instructions to the letter and soon the Padre was securely tied, hand and foot to the chair.

"Now it's your turn young lady. Sit in the other chair. Quickly now. I don't want to have to tell you twice" the Butcher snapped.

Jasmine briefly considered her options of escape but glancing at the Padre and seeing his shake of the head, she sat heavily in the other sturdy chair opposite. "Tie your feet first, then your right hand just like you did with the Padre. I will do the last one myself..." the Butcher instructed her as he held the barrel of his gun to the Padre's uninjured knee.

Beneath the Trident, James had indeed noticed the arrival of the other boat and when his safety line went slack, he decided to return to the surface to investigate. He now hovered ten feet below the surface, passing a compulsory five-minute decompression stop, blissfully unaware of the vicious killer who had commandeered his friends.

"I think it's best if you stay quiet when Jimbo comes aboard" the Butcher told them as he pulled the last cable tie tight around Jasmine's wrist. "You might be tempted to call out a warning and I don't want that. If he gets all brave, I might have to shoot him first and I actually have other plans for him...so just to be sure..." The Butcher produced a roll of masking tape and stuck a piece across Jasmine's mouth and then moved to stand next to the Padre. "You too Grandpa" he added before repeating the process. "But don't worry, you'll have time to chat soon. You disappointed me last time, remember? And you paid for that mistake..."

The Padre's eyes blazed back at the Butcher as he recalled their previous meeting.

"Hey...what's going on?" James was invisible from the wheelhouse where the others were waiting but his voice carried from the landing deck at the stern. "I saw the other boat, so I came up. Give me a hand with my gear will you."

"They're a bit tied up at the moment, James" the Butcher shouted back. "You'll have to manage yourself."

"Who's that? Padre...Jasmine, where are you?"

In the silence that followed, the Butcher listened as James feverishly removed his fins and heavy air tanks and dropped them onto the landing platform on the stern. Eventually, his head appeared above the railing as he climbed the five steps up onto the main deck. He stopped mid-stride as he saw the Butcher holding a gun to Jasmine's temple.

"Mr Macloud. How nice of you to join us" the Butcher's voice was like ice.

"If you've hurt them..." James replied as he took several steps towards the Butcher.

"Stop right there. Or I will spray you with your darling Jasmine's brains. I don't actually need to keep her alive but I assume you would prefer that I did?"

James stood rigid. His body visibly shaking from the tension he felt as his mind controlled the automatic urge to rush forward.

"If you behave yourself and tell me what I need to know, she may well survive the day. Not forgetting your friend over there. Do you want them to live or die?"

"Take whatever you want. Just don't hurt them."

"Take a seat over there. And tie yourself to it." The Butcher threw the remaining cables ties across the wooden deck, to land at James' feet. "Nice and tight. Or Jasmine here will have to be... *punished*."

Two minutes later, James was also securely bound to a seat. The Butcher walked away from Jasmine and secured the last of the cable ties to James wrist. "Very good James. All nice and tight just as I asked. Now I am going to ask you questions and you are going to answer them as fully and honestly as you can. Ok?"

"I told you already. Take whatever you want and then leave. All the cash is in a box in the galley. There's almost a thousand dollars, I think..."

"A thousand dollars? Oh, no, no, no, James. I didn't spend weeks tracking you all the way to this isolated island for a thousand dollars. No, I want the rest of my silver bars. I know you didn't put them all in your locker in Darwin."

"You're the one broke into the warehouse?"

"Of course it was me. Who else? Did you think it was Mirrors perhaps?"

"No. I saw what you did to him."

"Technically I didn't break in. The security guard let us in.

"And you killed him too..."

"That's called *collateral damage* in the Army, Jimbo. I killed your stupid minder, Mirrors as a favour to his boss. But the security guard was watching when I did it, so he had to go too. I can't leave loose ends like that, can I?

"You're a monster" James snapped back.

"Just business. So now I need to get the rest of those silver bars.

"That was all I had" James quickly replied.

"Really? I've found in the past, that people are greedy and don't like to tell me the truth. People lie to me. Especially when they are trying to protect their money. So, I had to find ways to make sure they told me the truth...the whole truth as they like to say in Court."

The Butcher walked back to stand next to the Padre and ripped off his gagging tape. "Padre. Where is the rest of my silver?"

"I don't know..." the rest of Padre's answer was cut short as the Butcher fired a bullet into his uninjured knee cap. The Padre's screams sent a shiver down the spines of both the other captives.

"You see. That was the wrong answer, old man" the Butcher said aloud before he leaned down and whispered in his ear. " I have to tell you something.... I like it when you lie because then I get to show your friends how unpleasant things are going to get. I was very disappointed when I couldn't find you in Dream Bar. I was really looking forward to poking my knife into your smashed knee. I understand that is very painful. But you'd run off. But now here we are, all back together again."

"You will pay for that" James snarled as he desperately tried to think of a means to escape his bonds and launch himself at their attacker.

"I'm going to pay for it, am I? Is that what you think James? Really? I don't think you're in any position to threaten me..." The Butcher raised his voice again so he could be clearly heard above the sobs of the Padre as he approached James' seat.

"You see James, it's like this. Maybe the Padre doesn't know where you've stashed my silver. But you do. The difference between him and you, is that if *you* tell me a lie, I won't hurt you. Oh no, no, no. You would expect that now, wouldn't you? You fancy yourself as the hero, don't you? Overall, I think it's better if your friends here are punished for your lies. The Padre's knee is never going to work properly again now. So, now he's got two useless knees. And that's your fault. *He* might not know where you hid my silver bars but I am going to keep hurting him...or Jasmine, until you tell me the truth. Got it? The whole truth, Jimbo. Jasmine's turn next, I think."

"I sold them" James said immediately.

"For a thousand dollars? No, I don't think so Jimbo. They're worth a whole lot more than that. That's not the whole truth, is it Jasmine?" He asked her as he raked the blade of his knife down the soft skin of her arm.

"That's not all the money. The rest of the cash is in our safety deposit box."

"Oh really...that was much too easy Jimbo. And I never believe people when it's too easy. Perhaps I should ask Jasmine where my silver is?"

"Don't hurt her. Please..." James pleadings were cut off when the Butcher pulled another piece of tape out and sealed it across James' mouth.

"I don't hurt ladies, James. I'm not an animal." he added, shaking his head and then strolled calmly back to where Jasmine sat. "Now Jasmine, I am going to ask you to tell me everything you know about my bars. If you hold anything back I am going to put some more bullets into the old man. I won't kill him but it will hurt him...a lot. And that will be your fault as well as Jimbo's. I'm sure you don't want that, do you?"

Jasmine shook her head violently in reply.

"You see that Padre?" the Butcher asked. "Jasmine is going to keep you safe. So, stop that blubbering while I talk to her. And just to make sure you don't interrupt me..." The Butcher said as he re-applied the tape to the Padre's mouth and then returned to Jasmine's side, smiling broadly.

"I am going to take your tape off. All I want to hear from you are the answers to my questions. Or the Padre is going to pay for it. Do you understand that?"

For the next ten minutes Jasmine willingly told the Butcher all about finding the wreck of the Diadem. She told him about the hoard of silver bars, which had been divided up between the people on the Black Marlin. She even told him about the teak case containing the jade figures and how Ong had taken all of them away from Darwin on the Black Marlin. Finally, she gushed out the details of how James, the

Padre and herself had returned on the Trident to the hidden reef and collected more bars from the sandy shelf.

"That's everything I know. Please believe me."

"Actually, for the moment, I do" the Butcher replied as his mind absorbed all the new information and began to plan how best to use it to his advantage. "I'm sure the Padre is very pleased with you. But tell me, what did you do with the silver bars you recovered the second time?"

"We sold most of them to get the money to finance this trip. The others are still in the bank's vault, with our emergency cash."

"Where's the bank?"

"In Jakarta. We rented a safety deposit box. But you need us to get it out. The security there is very good...They won't let you get to it without us being there."

"Oh really? I *need* you to get into the bank, do I? A valiant attempt to keep you all alive Jasmine. But trust me, I know *everything* about bank security. So, I will decide *if* I need to keep any of you alive or not. I need a moment to think about this." He replaced the tape over her mouth and then began to pace up and down the deck.

The three hostages watched him silently. James watched as blood from the Padre's wounded knee began to drip onto the wooden deck to form a deep red pool, which quickly congealed in the heat. The Padre's face was turning grey as shock and blood loss pushed him towards a state of shock. The plastic ties around James' ankles and wrists were reducing the blood flow to his extremities and he was beginning to lose all feeling in his hands and feet as a result. As he looked across at Jasmine he could see tears rolling down her cheeks as her eyes pleaded to him to save them.

The Butcher ceased his pacing and returned to the Padre. "I like the sound of what Jasmine has told me. I guess she really likes you, old man. Do you agree?

Through the haze of shock and pain that had dulled his thoughts, somehow the Padre managed to respond with two nods of his head.

"Still with me then.... How's that knee feeling now?" The Butcher asked just before he squeezed the bloody wound on the Padre's leg. The resulting screams were muffled by the tape covering his mouth but his whole-body spasm'd against his bindings as the pain engulfed him. "I bet that's sore, isn't it?" The Butcher laughed as he walked back to James.

"Ok. You're turn again Jimbo. Just got to give the padre a few minutes to get his breath back, you understand...Now, why don't you tell me all about your safety deposit box? And remember, even though the Padre is feeling a bit sorry for himself at the moment, I haven't touched a hair on Jasmine's lovely head.... Well not yet."

The Butcher pulled the tape slowly from James' face. "The safety deposit vault is open between 10am and noon, but only on weekdays" James said as soon as the tape came off. "We have to show our passports to get inside. And have the account number and our key to the box."

"We? You and Jasmine you mean?"

"Yes, it's a joint account. We have to go there together to get access."

"You both have to be there eh? Don't you trust each other?" The Butcher asked sarcastically.

"The bank suggested it." James replied through gritted teeth.

"Really. That's a nuisance isn't it. Where do you keep your passports?"

James paused as he considered the question before he slowly replied. "In the galley. There's a flat silver box in the drawer next to the sink. It contains all the cash we've got onboard and all of our documents."

"Very organised of you Jimbo" the Butcher said and replaced the tape on James' mouth before he disappeared inside the galley. James watched him disappear below deck and he listened intently as he stared once again at Jasmine. A few minutes later the Butcher returned to the deck holding three passports.

"You don't look a bit like your passport photo, Jimbo." he said as he held the passport pages open. "You really should have updated it you know. It's the little details. Life is all about the details. You should know that by now. And I have to tell you that having an old passport photo is going to be really bad news for you I'm afraid. And also for your good friend the Padre, of course."

James violent response was masked by the tape over his mouth and the bonds on his wrists and ankles, which remained firmly in place despite his straining muscles.

"Don't worry about your little lady though Jimbo. I told you I would look after her...And I will."

The Butcher walked across to Jasmine and without warning struck the back of her head with his gun, knocking her instantly unconscious. He produced a small knife and quickly cut all the cable ties securing her to the seat. He bent down in front of her and in a smooth motion swung her up and across his broad shoulders before he spun on his heels and strolled back along the deck. As he walked past James he said "She's coming with me for a little trip to Jakarta. I hope you don't mind."

Out of sight of James or the Padre, the Butcher crossed the length of the Trident's deck and swung his leg over the stern rail before lightly jumping onto his own vessel and disappearing into the wheelhouse. Moments later James heard footfalls on the wooden deck as the Butcher returned to stand in front of James. "She's a lovely girl...Sleeping like a baby in my bed. Shame you didn't have time to say goodbye..." He stared into James eyes. "Nothing to say now Jimbo? Oh well...Just wait here will you...I've got one more job to do before I leave you two alone again."

Once again, the Butcher disappeared from sight to go below decks. After ten long minutes James watched as he returned to the deck, a broad grin across his face.

"You really should pay more attention to your ship maintenance Jimbo. Details again, you see? It took me ages to get the stop-cocks fully open. They really should have been greased regularly. You never know when you might want to sink your own ship, do you?"

He paused as he stood in front of James shaking his head then said. "Tape on or tape off? I wonder, would you like to chat while the water level rises?" He raised his eyebrows as he talked. "A few last words with your old friend over there?" He paused again but James made no sound. "The strong silent type eh? Fair enough. Tape on it is then."

He walked across to the Padre. "What about you? Anything to say before I go Padre? But you better make it quick because I can't stay long" He pulled off the Padre's gag.

"Rot in hell" the Padre snarled.

"Oh, I think I will. But before that I am going to have some fun with Jasmine and all your hard-earned cash. How long do you think it will take, Jimbo?" he called across the deck.

"Another little detail you ought to know. Fifteen? Maybe twenty minutes before she fills up and sinks? After that...Well, how long can you hold your breath old man?" He asked as he swung his gaze back to the Padre. "Probably not as long as scuba pro Jimbo over there."

The Padre gritted his teeth but remained silent as he recognised that the Butcher was enjoying his threats.

"Mind you. There's probably a lot of hungry sharks around here too...Maybe they will find you before you run out of air? Especially with all that blood on you..."

The Butcher walked over to James and removed his tape again. "How about you Jimbo? Any last words? A prayer maybe."

"You're scum. You won't get away with it."

"Oh, I'm fairly sure that I will actually. All your clever misdirection and your cloak and dagger antics at the port to avoid fellow treasure hunters finding out what you were up to. That will only help to cover my tracks. No one is going to know where to look for you, even if they ever realised that you had gone missing. No one is going find the wreck of the Trident in a thousand feet of water. You will simply and effectively disappear from this life. Then once I've got the money out of your bank, I really don't think Jasmine and I would work out in the long run, so I will probably send her to join you."

"You said you wouldn't hurt her..."

"Yeah, I did, didn't I? But I lied. What can I say? I did warn you that people lie. Weren't you listening?"

"You bastard."

"It also seems really unfair that a young man like you, should have an unfair advantage over poor old Padre over there...He paused as he watched a look of confusion passed across James' face. "When it comes to running out of breath, versus becoming shark bait, I mean. Don't you agree?"

"What are you talking about...?" James asked.

The sharp blade, which the Butcher had slipped back into his hand, slashed back and forth across James' right thigh leaving two, deep bloody gashes across the unprotected skin below his shorts. "Now...that's much fairer, isn't it?"

James looked down at his leg as the pain hit him and bellowed "I will see you in hell" As he once again fought against his restraints he suddenly felt the Trident shift under him, as the sea water continued rushing into the engine room below the deck.

"Perhaps, but I don't plan on going there for a long, long time, Jimbo."

"Somebody will pay you back..." James replied desperately.

"From the feel of it, I think it's time for me to get going." As he walked past the Padre he once again ripped the tape from his face. "You two have a few minutes to chat before the fun with the sharks starts. I'm going to go to get better acquainted to the beautiful Jasmine before we go to the bank to pick up my money" the Butcher replied, as he strolled casually back along the deck towards his own craft.

As soon as the Butcher reached the bridge of his boat he reversed quickly away from the Trident before putting it into a tight turn to head back to the distant shoreline.

Moments later the Trident was sinking fast by the stern and the sea started to lap over the stern rail. The padre and James both watched in fascinated horror as the water quickly flowed up the deck towards them. As the first wave licked at the pool of congealed blood beneath the Padre a red stain bloomed across the surface.

"Can you slip out of your bonds?" James asked, trying to keep the desperation out of his voice.

"No chance. Jasmine pulled them all tight. You?"

"The same" James replied as he looked around the deck for any possible means of escape.

"My blood's in the water now" the Padre pointed out. "The sharks will smell it for miles around. They will be waiting for us as we go under."

"Better to drown before then Padre. Try to resist the urge to take a deep breath when we go under. I don't want to wait for the sharks to do his dirty work."

As he finished speaking a gurgling groan boomed from below as the water burst into another compartment and the Trident lurched sideways.

"I think she's going to roll over" James said as the vessel began her deadly plunge into the ocean depths.

Chapter 6

The Sanctuary

Ben Damo was sweating heavily in the tropical heat as it pressed down on the dense forest which covered the mountainous island in the far east of the island kingdom of Indonesia. It didn't help that he was hanging upside down, almost seventy feet above the fetid leaf-covered forest floor of the orangutans' secret island sanctuary.

Finally catching his breath, he managed to shout "Why do things always go wrong when you get here, Stan? I've been up and down dozens of trees since you left and I assumed that I would go the whole day without needing your help."

"It's a common mistake people make once they have mastered the primary climbing skills." Stan replied as he smiled at his friend. "You just relaxed a little too much, that's all. You know that you have to concentrate all the time up here. Or things go wrong very quickly. Remember what my Dad always says? *Safety first*."

"I'm fully aware of what your Dad always says...you tell me often enough. And I'm perfectly safe. Just the wrong way up. Now swing over here and give me a hand to get upright again...please."

An hour later, having completed another carefully constructed section of the canopy walkway, they dropped all their climbing equipment at the Sanctuary's base camp with the warden, Ade Bambang. The camp huts, constructed with locally felled logs, were concealed amongst the thick forest close to the island's only beach. In fact, the camp, guest rooms and walkways for the sanctuary had all been carefully positioned so that nothing could be seen from the seas surrounding the isolated island. In that way, any passing boats who scrutinised the inaccessible walls of the island, would simply assume it was another uninhabited rock, amongst the 17000 islands which made up the sprawling country of Indonesia. Ong Thakkrani had insisted that the team on the island did everything possible to keep the island's location hidden and the Warden and every member of his small team, had worked hard to comply with that instruction.

As the blazing tropical sun slid towards the western horizon, Stan and Ben made their way to the far end of the small, narrow beach to recover their canoe from its hiding place. They placed small log rollers on the sand to help them drag it out of the thick undergrowth towards the water's edge. Slowly but surely, they eventually pushed the heavy dug-out into the peaceful waters of the shallow lagoon and clambered aboard.

Once Stan was seated in the bow he picked up a paddle and said "You know what? I've had the best times of my life since we met up in Gambia."

"Really?" Ben replied as he pushed the canoe off the sandy bottom.

"It's been a roller coaster ride that's for sure but my life was...well a bit boring, before then."

"Before you got involved with poachers, kidnappers, drug dealers and killers you mean?"

"Exactly." Stan replied with a laugh. "And now look at us. Canoeing in the tropics around our own secret island"

"I think Mr Thakkrani would probably like us to refer to it as Bonn's secret island..."

"You know what I mean, Ben. And I'm sure Bonn wouldn't mind me saying it at all. She hasn't got that kind of ego."

"You're right. Considering her upbringing she's very modest about her lifestyle. Private plane and all..."

"We've done a fair amount of flying all over the world too. Just think about all the exotic locations we've been to with the rest of the gang."

"You will soon have more air-miles than your parents!"

"Don't be so evasive." Stan replied as the canoe surged forward across the lagoon. "Meeting up with the others has changed your life a lot too."

"I'm only playing with you..."

"I would be stuck in Moscow if it wasn't for your call. Funnily enough just before you phoned, my dad was packing to go back to the Prinsloo nickel mine in Venezuela. He told me that since Mum and him couldn't spend the start of the summer holidays with me, I might as well get a well-paid job to keep me busy and out of my Grandmother's way. But I don't think this is quite what he had in mind when he suggested it."

"When you told me that your parents were going to have to leave you in Moscow, to return to their jobs abroad, it seemed like a perfect solution to my problems here." Ben replied, as he thrust his paddle deep into the clear water below them "And I figured that spending the whole of the summer holidays with your Nan wasn't ideal."

"No. Not ideal. I couldn't call it that. Nor would getting a job stacking shelves at the local supermarket" Stan agreed as he mirrored Ben's paddling action.

"So, when I explained the situation to Mr Thakkrani, he agreed immediately. I just handed the phone to Ade, who was sitting next to me in the camp office, to make it all official and that was that."

"You and Ade's team have achieved so much since I was here last. It's all really impressive. The new guest rooms are just beautiful. All that polished mahogany. I'm pretty sure we will finish all the canopy walkways and everything else Ade wants to get done, long before I have to go back to School in September."

"You'll have your exam results by then too, won't you? How do you think you did? Ten A stars, I assume?"

"I doubt that but I did do a lot of studying for them. We will have to find out at the end of August. To be honest everyone has been working hard since we got back to School. I am sure that all the others will do really well too."

"I'm surprised that the latest adventure of the group didn't put you all totally off your studies. Not that I know much about studying for exams. I left school around 13 years old when I went to live with my Grandfather. I don't have any qualifications at all."

"Maybe not. But you've got lots of skills. Which are more useful in the jobs you've had."

"I suppose so" Ben replied wistfully. "I assume all your friends at school wanted to hear all the details about Australia when you got back there?"

"It was all a bit embarrassing actually. We were treated like celebrities when we first got back. Luckily that only lasted for a week or so, but then it died down a bit. To be honest, you can only tell the story so many times before it gets tiresome." Stan replied with a smile.

"It must all have sounded a bit like a film script. A tale of a fabulous treasure on a sunken warship, human trafficking by a dangerous gang of slavers."

"It did make for quite a story..."

"Did anyone ask what happened to the statues and all the silver bars?" Ben asked as he steered the canoe towards the protective coral reef surrounding the lagoon.

"Of course. Everyone wanted to know if we were rich now."

"We didn't get that many bars each" Ben pointed out.

"I haven't spent any of my share yet. Dad insisted that I invested the money instead."

"Very sensible. But what about the statues?"

"We just told them that Mr. Thakkrani had kept the statues, because he owns the boat."

"A reasonable explanation in the circumstances. I would have accepted that."

"It helped when Bonn explained to them that her Dad would be giving us all a cash reward for helping recover the treasure, once he had it properly evaluated."

"I bet you those statues are worth a lot of money. Millions perhaps." Ben suggested.

"Which is why he told us to go out to the cave, to check they are still safe."

"Obviously, the motion detectors in the cave that we set up would have triggered an alarm if someone had managed to find and enter the cave. But there's nothing like seeing it with your own eyes...just to be totally sure."

"I suppose you're right. Particularly if the statues really are worth millions..."

"It's the perfect hiding place. You and I are the only people who know exactly where the cave is. It was a miracle I found it in the first place."

"Following the bats, you mean?

"That really was a stroke of good fortune for me again."

"That was going to be your last time searching the cliffs for access points, wasn't it?" Stan asked, wiping the sweat from his forehead before it ran into his eyes.

"I'd been around the whole island and found just three places where someone with your kind of supernatural climbing skills could possibly access the island."

"And we've got cameras at each of them now."

"Correct. But as I was paddling back to the lagoon at the end of the day I saw hundreds of bats streaming out of a crevice in the cliff face."

"And of course, you had to find out where they were coming from..."

"Obviously!" Ben replied with a laugh. "I managed to steer the canoe into the crevice and then I saw the bats flying out of the mouth of the cave."

"And don't forget the smell!"

"Rotting bat dung...not my favourite aroma."

"As we are about to be reminded..."

"When you agreed to come back here Mr. Thakkrani said we should do it the first chance we got. Dependent on the tides, of course."

"And it has to be this evening because it's a really high tide?"

"Yes. The moon is very close to us right now, so the tidal rise is enormous. You remember last time. Getting into the cave from the canoe when the water is really high was hard enough, then passing all the statues in the cases up into it. But that would be basically impossible when the water is three foot lower at its normal height. So, it's got to be done in the next hour."

"It also means that we can paddle right over the coral reef which is currently covered by the waters of the high tide. That saves us going through the hidden channel and then back to the cliffs. Must save us at least a mile of extra paddling."

"And once we've checked the cases and the changed the batteries in the cameras and then paddled all the way back to report back to Mr Thakkrani, you want me to spend several more hours walking around the jungle with you. In the dark."

"You got it! All part of your summer holiday adventure, remember!"

"I almost forgot..." Stan replied sarcastically.

"It will only take a few minutes to call him on the satellite phone. And then we can move out again."

"When it's pitch black..."

"It's the only way to check the infra-red systems and motion detectors are working correctly. You'll love it."

"Unless we walk into a 300lb orangutan who is trying to get to get to sleep..."

"You know full well that they sleep in the tree tops."

"Or a ten-foot python. They move along the forest floor and I know they often hunt at night."

"We don't have any pythons on the island, Stan."

"Well, cobras then...Indonesia is famous for king cobras..."

"The only poisonous thing on this island is that spicy stew Ade makes every Wednesday. You may as well give up

Stan...you're coming with me! Now paddle harder, I don't want to be out here too long. We've got a night of adventure ahead of us."

"I can't wait" Stan replied sarcastically but unseen by Ben, a wide grin split his face demonstrating his real feelings on the subject.

PART TWO

Chapter 7

Colombo, Sri Lanka

Bob Dalton sat in a circle with Tracey, Laura and Izi on the highly polished mahogany floor of their beachside villa. The villa was one of the largest at the five-star resort and was positioned at the far end of the hotel's private beach allowing the total privacy. The hotel itself had been built just a mile away from the hectic centre of the Sri Lankan capital city, Colombo, thereby combining the best of easy access to the city's hot spots with the tranquillity of the palm fringed bay in which it had been built.

Bob and the ladies each had a swath of photocopied documents spread in front of them. The pages occasionally flapping from the warm tropical breeze which was gently blowing through the open patio doors.

"You've read the most pages Laura" Bob said to her. "What you think of it?"

"Izi has read loads too, Dad" she replied protectively. "Especially the bits that have been blanked out. She is much better at guessing what they said.

"Redacted" Izi replied without raising her eyes from the page she was currently reading.

"Yes...that" Laura said with a smile. "And you're much better at it than I am."

"Maybe." Izi looked up thoughtfully. "But they don't seem to have done so much of it this time."

"This time?" Tracey asked.

"When we got the Diadem's log, there was lots and lots of redacted lines" Izi informed her.

"I think they were rushing to get it all done in time for my arrival" Bob said.

"Well, I'm really impressed. You girls spent most of the flight here reading through all this. "Tracey added and waved her arm towards the papers spread before them.

"We couldn't put it down!" The two teens replied at the same time.

"Just imagine it. All that silver bullion travelling thousands of miles across pirate infested oceans." Laura said.

"The fleet was actually attacked by them outside Singapore harbour, you know." Izi added.

"Really...what happened exactly" Bob asked

"The record shows that the Commodore and his fleet stopped for more fuel in Singapore. Apparently once they were fully re-supplied they left the harbour just before dawn, headed towards the southern tip of India." Izi said.

"And once past that, they were going onwards towards Suez." Laura added.

"The navigators knew that the water just outside the harbour was quite shallow, so the fleet was travelling slowly to avoid any collisions with the underwater rocks." Izi explained as she recalled the story which she and Laura had pieced together from various ship's logs. "Suddenly they were attacked by 40 or 50 small pirate vessels which were invisible against the black sky and dark waters."

"The boats were all crammed with heavily armed pirates." Laura added, as she took over telling the tale. "They used grappling irons and ropes to swarm up onto the ships' decks. Fortunately, the Commodore had heard rumours about the imminent attack on his fleet whilst they were in port and he had posted all of his highly-trained Marines on the decks of every one of his ships. They were reinforced by the veteran sailors all of whom had been armed with cutlasses or staves. As the first wave of the pirates scrambled onto a ship's deck they were met with a devastating rifle volley from the Marine's rifles, which smashed through their massed ranks. From then on fighting was hand-to-hand, vicious and deadly but after only 15 minutes the fight was over and the surviving pirates were fleeing back to their vessels.

"One of the logs described how the dawn was just breaking over the eastern horizon." Izi interrupted. "Giving enough light for the heavy cannons of the Commodores battleships to open fire and many of the pirate vessels were sunk before they had the chance to escape.

"It must have been terrible" Tracey said.

"Hand to hand battles are the worst" Bob replied, as he imagined the carnage.

"It must have been frightening, even for the Commodore's soldiers." Izi suggested.

"It was 1901." Bob reminded them. "Soldiers and sailors in those days were hard men living a very tough life."

"I'm glad we live in the 21st century." Laura said. "Life isn't quite so cheap nowadays."

"It's a great story ladies, but did you find anything relating to the Jade figures? I'm sure that's what Ong will want to know about when he gets here."

"I'm getting to that bit Dad." Laura scolded him and pulled a face before continuing. "You remember the Diadem's log told us that they were supposed to deliver the other 500 statues to one of the British government's men? Laura asked.

"Yes, I do. But I can't remember his name" Bob replied.

"Albright" Laura announced proudly. "Your memory is going Dad!"

"I knew his name, darling...I was just testing you" Bob reassured her.

"Of course you were..." Laura paused theatrically before she said. "Well, even though big chunks of his personal log had been *redacted,* Izi managed to figure out that the Commodore received a change of orders just before he arrived in India. In the log that he wrote, I've got it right here." Laura said as she picked up one of the numerous packs on the floor. "He was ordered to off load the anonymous crate in Colombo."

"He didn't actually say 'jade figures' then?" Bob asked.

"I'm not sure the Commodore even knew what was in the case." Laura replied. "There was no sign that the contents had been redacted. He never wrote 'jade' anywhere that I could see."

"But it was the only case offloaded. It must have been the jade figures." Izi pointed out.

"But why Colombo? I thought the Commodore was due to offload the crate in India? Tracey asked.

"Maybe a change of government policy? Bob suggested. "The treasure fleet had been at sea for weeks by then. Things were changing rapidly in India around that date. What with the East India Company falling out of favour with the British Government. It must have caused all sorts of problems locally.

"Reading around the redacting at that point was very annoying" Laura said. "It was basically every other word. I couldn't make any sense of it this morning, so I asked the crossword expert over there to see if she could make any sense of it."

"I'm not a crossword expert" Izi replied indignantly. "It's just that my mind works slightly differently to yours, so I can fill in the gaps more easily."

"A bit like those pictures where you have to stare at them and suddenly you can see what's really behind them? Tracey asked.

"Precisely." Izi said. "Remember that private bank the log talked about? And we guessed that they meant Blackman Brothers? Well, this time the whole of the name was redacted but it's clear that the Commodore was ordered to secretly offload the crate and deposit it in a bank pending the arrival of a government official."

"But we can't find the words *jade statues* in any of the logs." Laura pointed out.

"I guess the British government didn't trust the Commodore with all the information either." Bob suggested.

"I'm sure they were worth a lot, even in those days" Tracey pointed out.

"There's no mention of offloading the case in any of the logs that I read" Bob said.

"I only found it in the Commodore's personal log" Laura agreed. "For some reason, the other Captain's logs made no mention of it."

"Maybe he kept it secret from them?" Bob asked.

"Reading between the lines, it was clear from his log that he wasn't happy with the orders to do everything himself." Izi suggested. "There were even a couple of scribbled notes in the margins, which were obviously his only way of complaining about his part in the operation.

"And then what happened?" Tracey asked

"The Commodore and his war fleet left Colombo the next day and continued on their journey back to London with the bullion." Laura informed them.

"No other mention of what was in the case or what happened to it afterwards?" Bob asked

"Once the case was offloaded to the bank I suppose that the fleet had nothing more to do with it." Tracey said slowly. "They had other things to worry about."

"Like keeping millions of pounds' worth of silver from getting stolen by pirates." Izi reminded them. "There were still plenty of miles at sea to go before they arrived safely in London."

"It's annoying that we don't know the final story about what happened in the end though." Tracey said sadly.

"That's all we could find in the documents Dad brought back from the MoD. Between us, we've read everything now."

"Actually, I've got a small admission to make" Bob replied thoughtfully. "To be honest I've still got one more, small bundle to go through in my pile." Bob admitted. "Unlike you youngsters, I actually needed to get some sleep on the plane. But it doesn't look too promising. It's the ship's log from one of their support vessels, which only played a very minor role, so I'm not hopeful. I think we've now found out everything we can from the Admiralty documents."

"Maybe I can do some more research on the Internet?" Izi offered enthusiastically. "Now that we've got the full details on the fleet's voyage. You know, see what else I can find out about the Blackman Brothers bank back in those days or see if there were any rumours of the jade soldiers being sold around that time?"

"That's a great idea" Laura added. "The hotel's Wi-Fi is really fast so I will do that too. It will be fun to see which one of us finds out the most."

"I had better ring Ong." Bob said. "Although he told me that they would all be here tomorrow he told me to keep him informed if we found out anything definitive in the meantime."

Chapter 8

Colombo

As it was high season, Colombo's international airport was even more chaotic than normal. Consequently, the newly completed car park was virtually full but fortune smiled on them when a small saloon pulled out of a space on the ground floor just as the minivan containing Bob, Laura and Izi entered. The other van in their convoy was less fortunate and Bob watched somewhat concerned, as it turned left onto the ramp to climb to the next floor.

"I will find him, don't worry, Sir" his driver said confidently. "We will both be here when you come back. You can rely on me."

"Ok. If you're sure..." Bob replied as he glanced at his watch. "The flight should be landing about now..."

Even though Bob had anticipated the increased traffic congestion, he knew that they now only had a few minutes before Ong's flight was estimated to arrive.

"Come on ladies" he said to Izi and Laura, as he stepped from the van. "Don't dilly dally."

"Dilly, dally?" Laura said. "Nobody says that anymore Dad."

"Are we going to be late?" Izi asked as they walked quickly out of the car park and into the bustling Arrivals building.

"We will never find them in this crowd" Laura complained. "We need to be right at the front to see them."

"I'm the smallest. I will squeeze through to the front." Izi replied helpfully.

"I think it's best if we all stick together, Izi" Bob insisted, as he pressed through the crowd towards the large EXIT sign which was visible high over the double doors where arriving flight passengers emerged from the Customs control point.

It took them several minutes to work their way to the front of the waiting crowds but eventually the two teens were pressed up against the chrome barriers with Bob standing protectively behind them.

"Are you sure this is the right place Dad?"

"Yes, absolutely. I spoke to the concierge at our hotel. This is definitely the best spot."

"What are you two doing here? Izi shouted aloud as Ben and Stan appeared through the Arrivals door.

"What are you guys doing here?" Ben replied as he approached the barrier with his canvas bag slung over a shoulder. "It was supposed to be a big surprise for you. I guess Ong told you we were coming after all."

"Actually, we didn't know you were coming at all." Laura replied. "Or did you know dad?" Laura asked suspiciously.

"Not a word. I thought we were here to meet Bonn."

"And her Dad" Izi added.

"Oh, right. Haven't they come out yet? Stan asked. "They were well ahead of us. But we got separated in the passport queues."

"Hang on" Izi said. "You saw Bonn and her Dad in the passport queue?

"And Sam as well." Ben added helpfully

"And Sam too? Are you sure you didn't know about them all coming here, Dad?" Laura asked even more disbelievingly.

Before he had a chance to reply, Izi let out a loud whoop said "Look. Look. They're here. Perfect timing."

Bob waved his arms in the air and caught the attention of the two bodyguards who preceded Ong and the two teens who were happily walking alongside the porters pushing their luggage trolleys.

"It's very good of you to come and meet us." Ong said as he shook Bob's outstretched hand. "I'm sure it wasn't necessary. But very kind nonetheless."

"We came out in one of the vehicles that your secretary ordered." Bob said. "We even managed to find parking space. Surprising as the island is very busy at the moment."

"But the weather is perfect" Laura pointed out to Sam and Bonn as they all hugged each other. "Sunshine and blue skies and all our friends in one place. The summer holidays have really begun now."

"Well I think we should get out of the airport first" Ong pointed out. Then with the wave of his arm the whole group moved forward again.

As they slowly inched through the milling crowds, Izi quickly manoeuvred herself to stand at Ben's side. "It's so lovely to see you again Ben. Have you got some stories for me? We really weren't expecting to see you again so soon. Bonn didn't tell us..."

"It's not really a story" Ben replied. "But after Bonn and Sam left Darwin with Ong his plane flew north and picked us up from a small airstrip on an island not far from the sanctuary. Ong wanted an update on what we had been doing and he also thought it would be nice for us to have a week's holiday with all you guys."

"Of course it will." Izi replied with a grin. "Now we are all back together again, well except for Jannie of course."

"Yes, it was shame he couldn't make it too. But he had to stay in Darwin. He is doing really well flying the predator. I think he had to stay to pass some test flight or something like that. But I'm sure he will see you again soon. He loves you just like the rest of us."

"I know he does but it's always the best when there's all six of us."

Once they walked outside into the tropical atmosphere Bob lead the group back into the car park to find the two minivans waiting for them as promised. Then as the bodyguards hovered protectively around them, the porters loaded all the baggage into the aluminium trailer while the passengers climbed into the two luxury minivans.

Once they were all seated in the vehicles and the luggage was secure, the security team joined the other passengers and the convoy set off towards their hotel.

"I thought we could all have brunch together" Bob explained to Ong. "We've got some news to tell you about the statues. While we are all together."

"All together?" Ong asked.

"Laura and Izi have booked an open-air bus for a sightseeing tour around the city for all of them.

"No old people allowed? Ong asked with a laugh.

"Precisely. I'm afraid you're going to miss out on the history lesson." Bob said. "So, if you have any other matters you want to discuss, we can do it privately while they are away. Plus, we've got an appointment with the bank.

"It's going to be really informative" Izi pointed out to her friends in the other minivan.

"It's going to be fun, actually" Laura insisted and shook her head theatrically.

"We've got our own English-speaking guide." Izi continued smoothly. "He will tell us all about Colombo's fantastic history.

"But he won't point out the big shopping Mall." Laura interrupted. "because there isn't one! In fact, they actually don't have many nice shops at all."

"You two never change" Sam said with a smile.

Two hours later, after a sumptuous brunch at their hotel, their tour bus arrived outside the hotel to collect them. It looked a bit like a London double-decker bus but the roof had been removed to be replaced with gauze netting to keep the sun off tourists on the top deck. The rest of the bus had been painted an assortment of colours in an apparently random design reminiscent of the hippy designs of the 60s.

Two of Bonn's bodyguard team had climbed aboard when the bus first arrived. They surreptitiously signalled to their team leader, Joseph Stein who was standing inside the hotel's entrance, that it was safe for everyone to board. Joseph lead the small group through the entrance doors onto the ornate marble forecourt.

"All aboard the fun bus" Sam shouted in a loud voice.

"Everyone upstairs." Izi insisted. "The best views will be from up there."

"This is going to be terrible" Laura predicted to her friends as she clambered up the metal staircase.

"We will certainly know all about Colombo and its history by the end of the trip." Sam replied as she followed her upwards. "I'm sure Izi will make sure of that"

Moments after they had taken their seats, the engine roared into life in a belch of blue/black diesel smoke. Crunching into first gear, the bus pulled away from the hotel's doors and the voice of the guide burst forth from the speakers strategically positioned around the bus.

For the next hour, the brightly coloured bus wound through the congested streets of the capital, with their knowledgeable guide pointing out the most interesting buildings and linking them to the long and often violent history of the tropical island.

"In 1857, the Sepoy Revolt took place all across India" the guide told them. "The uprising by the native soldiers marked the beginning of the end for the East India Company's absolute control of the Indian subcontinent. A year later the British government removed the company's trade monopoly and took over control.

"I was reading all about the EIC" Izi whispered to Sam who had taken the seat next to her at the front of the bus. "They were the first real international conglomerate the world had seen. And they had a complete monopoly. They made millions and millions of pounds' profits from trade, even back in those days. They even had their own armed forces. Like a private army."

"Unfortunately, the waning control of the EIC was not all good news for Sri Lanka." The guide's voice told them. "With the withdrawal of so many military personnel, the criminal gangs resurfaced. These bands of murderous thieves had been operating in India for hundreds of years but the EIC soldiers had forced them underground. When the soldiers left, they appeared all over our country to rob and pillage at will. You see, back then the local police were not equipped or trained to take over from the soldiers so quickly.

"The same sort of thing happen in Africa when the colonial powers withdrew." Ben told Stan, who was sitting next to him, directly behind Izi. "Whoever lead the strongest tribe or had the best armed group, just took whatever they wanted from the weak or powerless."

"Human history is full of stories like that" Stan replied. "And it's always the normal people who suffer. Farmers, shop workers, women and children. All the same to these bullies."

"The Indian mainland..." the guide's voice rose again, "was also plagued by highly organised gangs who called themselves thuggee. At about the time of the downfall of the EIC one of those thuggee bands migrated to our beautiful island. Rumour had it that they found a base in the mountains surrounding Colombo where they worshipped an ancient goddess with flaming red eyes and demanded blood sacrifices. They were led by a fanatic known as the Master who had mystical powers..."

"Now it's getting more interesting" Laura said aloud to Bonn.

"I didn't know you were so bloodthirsty, Laura." Ben replied with a grin.

"You don't have to be a boy to be bloodthirsty" she replied with a smirk. "And anyway...it's only history. We read about worse things happening on the treasure fleet."

"Really?" Bonn asked.

"Unlike the other robbers and thieves around then..." The guide continued. "The thuggees used a particularly gruesome method to dispatch their victims. Strangulation!"

"That's not gruesome" Laura insisted to Bonn.

"A rope garrotte was dropped over the head of their unsuspecting victim and the rope was snapped taut. The victim quickly strangled to death." The guide concluded dramatically.

"Happy now Laura? Ben asked

"Not very bloody." She replied. "The Commodore massacred hundreds of pirates..."

"You're terrible." Izi insisted.

"It was hundreds of years ago Izi. Life was harder back then, remember? History is just informative you know." Laura smiled knowingly.

"With the loss of control of the East India Company and the breakdown of the Mogul dynasties..." their knowledgeable guide informed them. "Many wealthy individuals, terrified of the thuggee threat hid their wealth in deep cellars or placed them in the hands of one of the few English banks, some of which are still to be found in our fair city."

"Like Blackman Brothers, for instance..." Izi suggested with a smile at Laura.

"The power of the thuggees continued for a hundred years and it wasn't until the start of the century that the local police finally stamped out the worshippers of the mysterious goddess so that the people of Colombo could go about their business safely."

"So we won't be strangled in our beds then" Laura told them.

"We all love a happy ending, to a scary story." Sam replied.

"It doesn't mean there aren't thieves still wandering around out there" Ben insisted. "Wherever there are tourists, there will be someone willing to snatch a camera or unattended purse. Isn't that right, Joseph?" Ben turned in his seat to address Bonn's personal protection officer.

"My team won't allow that, I can assure you, Ben" he replied sternly.

"Joseph and his team are very professional Ben" Bonn pointed out. "Dad only employs the best people. Isn't that right, Joseph?"

"I'm sure you know your Father best, Bonn." Joseph replied diplomatically.

"We are now going to take you on a short drive into the hills surrounding Colombo. I will be able to show you one of the world-famous tea plantations which actually produce the best tea in the world."

"Not that he is in the least bit biased in any way." Stan said quietly to Ben.

"Better than the tea growers in Russia though..." Ben replied.

"We grow the best snow storms..." Stan replied and laughed loudly.

Whilst the teenagers were enjoying their sightseeing trip on the bus, Bob and Ong had arrived for their appointment with the manager of Blackburn Brothers bank in the city's business centre.

"I'm terribly sorry for keeping you waiting gentleman" the smartly dressed man said as he approached them. "My name is Singh and I am the manager. I understand that you wish to make a significant deposit with us?"

"That's correct. Ong Thakkrani at your service and this is my associate, Bob Dalton. I assume that your headquarters have been in touch to confirm my bona fides?"

"Indeed they have Mr Thakkrani. You come with the highest of reputations. However, I must say that your request to see inside our main vault is to say the least, highly unusual."

"Although Mr Dalton's report assures me that your bank is the most secure in Sri Lanka and I trust his judgement implicitly I had one query. His assessment of your protective arrangements had one glaring omission, that being your main vault."

"I can understand that. Details of our security systems, like most organisations, are restricted on a need-to-know basis. We do not generally release any information about any of our defensive capabilities, even to our most trusted customers."

"Which in itself, is highly commendable" Bob reassured him. "And normally that would be perfectly acceptable. However, in this particular case, those procedures need to be adapted so that Mr. Thakkrani can reassure himself of the absolute safety of his possessions. And as I assume you know, your London headquarters agreed with that requirement."

"Yes, they did Mr Dalton and I have already made the necessary arrangements for the visit." The manager replied. "If you would please follow me this way Mr Thakkrani? Mr Dalton if you wait here, my secretary will provide you with any refreshments you desire."

"That's very kind of you." Bob replied with a nod as he sat down in one of comfortable chairs.

The manager turned on his heel and Bob watched as he and Ong walked through an ornate steel mesh gate at the far end of the bank's vestibule. As they passed through the gate, under the baleful glare of the armed guard who stood on one side of the entrance, Ong said "Human and electronic surveillance, I see."

"Both have their own advantages, Mr Thakkrani. This doorway leads to the vault area. The only way to access the vault is via the dedicated freight elevator, to which only I have the key." The manager explained as he placed an intricately carved key in an illuminated lock in the elevator's facade. As he turned it Ong heard an engine start somewhere beneath his feet and he also noticed the floor light illuminate a large letter 'B'.

"The elevator automatically returns to the basement level when not in use" the manager explained when he noticed Ong looking at the glowing indicator. "The system locks down when my key is not in the lock, making access to the vault totally impossible."

"Doesn't that mean you will have to be constantly employed going up and down from the vault?"

"The bank's daily routines are very well organised so that usually I only need to access the vault, with the relevant personnel two or three times each day. Your visit of course, is additional to my normal schedule."

As he finished speaking, the elevator door slid smoothly open. Ong could see an identical set of doors at the far end of the elevator. "Two entrances?" Ong asked.

"The other doors lead to our loading dock. They only open when I put my key in the corresponding lock on the other side. I only need to do that twice per week, when the security vans enter bank's outer precincts or when a customer like yourself is making a bulk deposit. On the other side of the doors are an assortment of armed guards who are on duty 24 hours a day."

"You continue to impress me, Mr Singh"

"Please step inside the elevator. The vault is almost 30 feet below street level. Built of reinforced concrete more than three feet thick."

Ong entered the freight elevator and waited for the descent to begin.

The doors slid smoothly closed behind them. "Railway tracks?" Ong asked as he examined the twin rails running the length of the elevator.

"Some of the valuables held in the vault are extremely heavy. Gold bullion, for example" the manager explained. "When the bank was designed and built, the architects anticipated such deposits and the loading dock elevator and secure vaults are all fitted with these mini rails to make the process smoother."

"Very clever" Ong replied as the elevator slowly descended. "Some of the valuables I intend to deposit with you are both heavy and bulky so these arrangements will suit me perfectly."

"We try to meet all of our customer's needs" the manager replied smugly before the elevator doors opened to reveal the subterranean vault. "Here we are. As you can see the floor of the vault has a matching set of rails."

"This is where you intend to store my valuables? Ong asked as he looked around the room before him.

"No, no. This area is another secure zone. As you can see, in each one of the walls, there are a series of time controlled vault doors."

"I wish my goods to be stored in the most secure of your vaults. Mr Singh."

"So I have been informed Mr Thakkrani. And that vault is the one at the far end of this chamber, please follow me."

"I see you have numerous cameras mounted in the ceilings and walls and yet you also have armed guards in those booths?"

"Blackman Brothers use state-of-the-art camera systems which are monitored 24 hours a day, from another secure remote location. But as my father always used to tell me, belt and braces is the way to go, so we also have live guards to support the array of infrared and motion detector devices deployed within the vaults."

"I can see the gun barrel protruding from the armoured glass, but those booths have no doors that I can see."

"Correct. They have no direct access into the vault. The two booths are accessed through a series of separate tunnels through a secure entrance in the bank above us. If anyone enters this area without me they are instructed to open fire. A combination of human observation supported by technology gives us the most reassurance against attack."

"Open fire?" Ong's voice indicated his thoughts on the matter.

"Anyone attempting to rob us, puts their life at risk..."

"But surely the Police...?"

"We have the full support of the local Police Chief, who is fully aware of that part of our security arrangements."

"Good to have him on your side."

"This will be the vault we would use for your property Mr Thakkrani." Mr Singh informed him as they stopped in front of the massive steel door. "I will open the vault door for you to look inside but you cannot enter the vault itself."

"I can't go inside?"

"Nobody enters this particular vault, except the bank manager. No exceptions. And that is a rule that Blackburn Brothers never breaks. There are certain *features* inside which prevent any individual, other than myself, entering this particular vault safely."

"A final layer of security..." Ong replied having reluctantly accepted the manager's explanation. He then watched as Singh spun the combination lock before the massive steel door glided silently open to reveal the brightly illuminated space beyond.

"As you can see, the transport tracks continue inside this vault as with the other vaults. We can handle your large and heavy valuables as easily as other banks deal with your cash."

From his position, Ong could see the racks and assorted steel containers which were positioned around the perfectly white room. "I am reassured that your bank would be an ideal location for my valuables Mr Singh. And I also appreciate the personal tour."

"It has been a pleasure, Mr Thakkrani. I'm very proud of my bank's facilities. But I need to close the vault and return you upstairs to continue with my other duties." As the massive steel door hissed close once again the manager and Ong retraced their steps to the elevator "You may be interested to know that the bank has stood in this very spot for more than a hundred years and we have never been robbed."

"An amazing fact, considering the history of other banks around the world. And especially in view of the civil unrest with the Tamil Tigers etc, in Sri Lanka." Ong said as they walked back into the elevator.

"Even when the second world war was raging and we were warned that the Japanese army could invade us at any moment, the bank remained open to its customers."

"I didn't know that the Japanese invaded Sri Lanka." Ong remarked.

"No they didn't. But I understand from the newspaper records around that time that it was highly likely. I've always had an interest in the history of our island, you see."

"I know they were sweeping all through the Far East, virtually unstoppable. They even overcame Britain's supposedly impregnable fortress at Singapore."

"I was told that the manager at that time, was given a contingency plan to evacuate the bank if necessary. Taking all of the contents with him of course."

"I would hope so too." Ong replied with a grin as the elevator slowly rose to the bank's ground floor.

"I hope to see you again soon." The manager said as he shook hands with Ong before adding. "And you too, Mr Dalton. I hope my secretary looked after you?"

"Oh yes. Yes, indeed Mr Singh. Very attentive." Bob replied before he and Ong left the manager's office and strode towards the bank's exit.

"Another dead end I'm afraid" Ong whispered as they walked through the doors and into the sunshine beyond.

"What do you mean?" Bob asked.

"The crate. The crate the jade statues were in? I managed to have a good long look into the top security vault and there's nothing like it in there. I'm afraid that I have wasted your time Bob."

"It was always a long shot. Anything could have happened to the case in the last hundred years. But we wanted to be sure, so we had to look inside."

"I suppose you're right, it's just that I had a really good feeling about this. How about a drink to drown my sorrows? I'm sure Bonn and the others won't be back yet." Ong suggested as they climbed back into the minivan which had waited for them outside the bank.

"Always happy to have a drink with you Ong." Bob replied as they settled into the comfortable leather seats. "And it may taste a bit better because I've got some good news for you too" Bob replied smugly

"You did? An email from one of your numerous informants perhaps?"

"Not on this occasion...But even if your visit with Mr Singh may not have been very helpful, his secretary was. I think she's been here since the bank was built...well, she looked like she has been anyway. When she brought me a cup of tea I got talking to her, some investigators forget to talk to secretaries but they often know a lot more than you would expect."

"The power behind the throne...?"

"It's often the case. Anyway, amongst other things I was asking her about where they kept the old bank records. She said there weren't any really old ones they were all destroyed sometime during the Second World War. Instructions from headquarters apparently, so that was another dead end for me."

"Yes, Singh told me they were expecting to be overrun by the Japanese. But I don't see how a lack of records constitutes good news for us, Bob."

"No, it doesn't, you're absolutely right. But it will probably interest you to know that she told me about an old man who was the Blackman Brothers bank manager after the Second World War and who is still alive today. His father was also the bank manager before him, almost a family business it seems. Apparently, he was a friend of her own grandfather. Well, the old man still lives in Colombo. And last but not least she gave me his address, so maybe the trial is not completely cold get."

"Bob, you really are a marvel. I think you just earned yourself a glass of champagne."

"I completely agree." Bob laughed. "Put your foot down driver. I want to get there before you change your mind Ong."

Chapter 9

The Butcher

From his vantage point on the waterfront, the Butcher watched the Black Marlin through his powerful binoculars. His underworld contact had told him that she had been sent to Darwin and was now moored in the harbour awaiting her repairs. As he gazed at his target, the Butcher was reassessing the details of his recent plan, which had allowed Jasmine to slip through his fingers.

The day after sinking the Trident, he had stridden confidently into the bank in central Jakarta with Jasmine walking demurely beside him. Before they had entered the bank, the Butcher had made it very clear to Jasmine what would happen to her if she raised the alarm or even appeared nervous during their visit.

As soon as they stepped through the bank's entrance door, following the Butcher's carefully worded instructions, Jasmine had led him over to a desk close to the security vault entrance, where the friendly manager fondly remembered Jasmine's last visit with James.

"Good morning, Miss Banjudie. How lovely to see you again." He said while glancing towards the Butcher, who was wearing dark sunglasses and a broad-brimmed Panama hat. "And may I ask... Is Mr MacLeod well?"

"Actually, he's feeling a bit under the weather today. That's why Mr Smith here, is accompanying me. Extra security, so to speak." She replied smoothly.

"Oh, sorry to hear that. Please give him my best wishes when you return to him." He slid a form across the desk top to Jasmine and said. "Just sign in the usual place and I'll show you through."

Jasmine signed the form as indicated and slid it back to the manager, along with the silver biro he had lent her.

"Please follow me" he said as he stood up from his desk. Jasmine and the Butcher both stood up and began to follow the manager.

"I'm terribly sorry Mr Smith. But only security box owners are allowed in the vault. You are welcome to wait here for Miss Banjudie. I'm sure she will only be a few minutes. There are no other customers at the moment."

As the manager and Jasmine continued to walk away from him the Butcher almost called out to her but decided that discretion would work just as well. Where could she go? He sat in the seat as directed, which gave him the clear view of the door to the security vault. This had not been part of his plan with Jasmine but he was well aware that sometimes plans needed to be flexible he thought to himself. He was confident that she would not betray his confidence to the vault manager as he had made it clear to her that many innocent people would die if she told anyone his real identity or purpose at the bank.

Two minutes later, the Butcher's confidence in his position was shattered when a Plexiglas security shutter dropped from the ceiling and slammed into the floor, sealing off the doorway to the security box vault and a wailing alarm shattered the bank's previously quiet atmosphere.

"Please evacuate the bank immediately" an automated voice rang out. "Security shutdown in progress. Please evacuate the bank quietly and quickly. Thank you for your cooperation."

The Butcher leapt to his feet as the rest of the bank's customers began to obediently file out of the bank's entrance doors. One of the armed security guards noticed that the Butcher was not complying with the automated message and quickly approached him. "You have to leave sir. Immediately!" the guard told him. "Please leave now. We have a security situation occurring."

"My friend is in the security vault." The Butcher replied without moving.

"You will have to wait for them outside Sir. The bank is being evacuated."

"But the security screen..." the Butcher began.

"I must insist that you leave. Now!" the guard said as he swung the muzzle of his gun so that it pointed directly at the Butcher's chest.

The Butcher briefly considered attacking the guard. He had no doubt that with his reactions and skills he would easily overcome the guard but doing it in full sight of the rest of the guards and in sight of numerous security cameras, would place him in an even more difficult situation. "Ok. Ok. I'm leaving. Right now." The Butcher snapped.

As the Butcher slowly walked towards the bank exit, closely followed by the nervous security guard, he was trying to decide what had happened and considering his best options. If the security vault was being robbed, Jasmine would probably be detained as a suspect as soon as the Police arrived. He assumed that they would soon be arriving in force, in response to the activation of the attack alarm and he had no wish to be caught up in a police scoop. His work required absolute anonymity, which was one of the reasons that he had obscured his features with the big hat and glasses before entering the bank. Simple but effective he thought to himself as he walked through the doors. He never took an uncalculated risk and he had long ago assumed that Abdul Khan's intelligence capabilities included facial recognition software. He had no intention of being recognised by the Police and even more so, by Khan when the bank's camera recordings were examined. Appearing in one of Khan's complex daily reports would be problematic. Even best case, he was sure that Khan would wonder what he was doing involved in a bank robbery in Jakarta, hundreds of miles from where he should have been at that time.

Inside the security vault Jasmine was shaking uncontrollably. When the Butcher told her what he would do to the customers in the bank if she betrayed him, she had decided to stick to the letter of his instructions. But while she was alone in the bank's security vault she saw the panic alarm set in the wall and without fully considering her actions, slammed her hand into it causing the response which the Butcher had witnessed. Now, as she sat in the small room she wondered what was happening outside. She hadn't heard any gunshots and wondered if perhaps the Butcher had not carried out his threat to open fire inside the bank. As she looked down at her shaking hands, she decided she had to go outside and tell the vault manager everything that had happened since the Butcher had attacked the Trident. She could only hope that the local police would be able to identify and capture the Butcher before he could escape from the city. If he was arrested, maybe she could then avoid the terrible punishments he had promised her that she would suffer, if his plan was thwarted.

By the time the Butcher had descended the bank's marble stairway and reached the footway outside, he had made his decision. He casually melted into the growing crowd that was now gathering outside to see what all the fuss was about and then strolled nonchalantly towards the approaching Police cars. He had decided that Jasmine and her cache of money and silver bars would have to wait for another day. Obviously, he wouldn't forget her and he smiled grimly to himself, confident that Jasmine knew it too. With one more backward glance at the bank's glass facade, he shrugged his shoulders and looked for a taxi to take him to the grubby hotel he was booked into. His few belongings and fake ID were packed in a small canvas bag which he had left in his room there. He only intended to be there for a few minutes. It was time to get out of the country.

When the Butcher entered Jakarta's hectic International airport, his first destination was the 24-hour Chemist. It was situated in the row of convenience stores which were plying their trades with the assorted nationalities who used the airport. Once inside he purchased a packet of light brown hair dye and an assortment of other domestic essentials, all purchased with cash and all without removing his hat or glasses, so that the in-store cameras would be unable to record his identity in any way. He then made his way to the nearby toilet block and entered one of the polished-aluminium stalls inside.

Twenty minutes later he emerged from the shower cubicle, looking completely different to the man who had entered. His hat had been discarded showing his new hair-cut and colour which matched the theatrical moustache which now covered his top lip. His new features now perfectly matched the photograph in his recently acquired Australian passport. His belongings had been transferred to a new lightweight Sports bag, which he had bought the previous day and had hidden inside the old canvas bag. The old bag was now discarded inside the large waste bin in the toilets along with the shirt and trousers he had been wearing in the bank. He confidently approached the ticket booth of Qantas airlines where he purchased an economy fare to Darwin, using a handful of used Australian dollars. The salesman informed him that the flight was not full and that it was due to depart on time in less than three hours, which suited the Butcher perfectly. He was confident that even if Jasmine had told the police about his recent activities, her physical description of him would no longer help to identify him at the airport. He smiled menacingly as he considered his future plans and promised himself that Jasmine would not get rid of him that easily.

Once he had arrived in Darwin he immediately headed to the harbour where it only took an hour to track down the berth where the Black Marlin had been moored.
He now sat, patient as a leopard, watching the crew aboard the Marlin going about their usual business. Glancing at his watch he calculated that it would be dark in a few hours and he anticipated that at least some of the crew would then take

advantage of the local hostelries, many of which were scattered amongst the waterfront properties.

His suspicions proved correct when, as the sun was setting in an orange blaze on the western horizon, three crew members in their easily identifiable uniforms, stepped off the Marlin and strolled past the Butcher's vantage point. He calmly took some cash from his wallet and dropped it onto the table as he stood up to follow the crewmen. Ten minutes later, the three crew men entered one of the three rowdy bars which the Butcher had checked out before taking up his observation post. The bar was already half full with a friendly mixture of off-duty boat crews, holiday makers and business people. The Butcher followed them into the bar only a few paces behind, unseen and unnoticed. He confidently made his way through the crowd to an empty seat on the far side of the bar. From there he had a partial view of the bar area where the crewmen had positioned themselves to order their drinks. A bored waitress approached the Butcher and took his order for a cold lager without even glancing at him.

As he slowly sipped his beer, his patience was soon rewarded when one of the crewmen left his friends to weave his way across the bar. He passed within a few feet of the Butcher on his way to use the bar's toilets. The Butcher silently eased himself upright and followed the crewman through the toilet door and immediately struck him on the side of the neck with the calloused edge of his right hand. Before the crewmen could crumple to the floor the Butcher slipped his arm around the crewmen's waist and half carried, half led him, through the rear door of the bar into the dark alley behind. To any unsuspecting observer, it looked like one friend helping his drunken companion outside for some fresh air. The Butcher's sharp eyesight rapidly searched the nearby buildings for any surveillance cameras or infrared lighting, which might have caught him in its view, with a negative outcome. Satisfied, he continued dragging the unconscious crewmen to the other end of the alley from where he hailed a taxi as it cruised by looking for fares.

Ten minutes later, the somewhat bemused taxi driver dropped his two passengers on a small industrial estate on the outskirts of the city. The Butcher had passed him a few crumpled notes before they left the vehicle to pay the fare and he now stood on the side of the road, supporting his 'friend' as he watched the taillights disappearing back towards harbour front. He felt sure that the taxi driver would naturally assume that his unresponsive passengers were simply two friends, one of whom had gotten far too drunk in one of Darwin's numerous drinking establishments. The Butcher hoped they were both unremarkable and easily forgotten.

The location the Butcher had directed him to was not as random as the taxi driver had assumed. The Butcher had found this area the last time he was in Darwin. He had discovered that for the most part the industrial units on this estate were unattended at this time of day and the empty warehouse that he had selected earlier today would be perfect for the upcoming interrogation. The Butcher was looking forward to squeezing the information from his latest victim. He hoped it would assuage some of the tension which losing Jasmine had caused him.

Twenty minutes later the groggy crewmen woke to find himself stripped naked and tied to an ancient cast iron office

chair. A blinding light was shining directly into his eyes.
"Where am I? What happened?" He asked aloud.
"You went to the wrong bar" the Butcher replied calmly.
"Where are my friends? Why am I tied up?" The crewman's well-developed muscles bulged as he tried to free himself.
"No friends. It's just you and me now."
"Who are you? Untie me..."
"No. That's not going to happen."
"Where am I? What's going on? Is this a joke? Is that you Johnnie? This isn't funny...
The crewman stopped speaking as he felt liquid splash across his legs and stomach.
"I will ask you questions." The Butcher replied menacingly. "You answer them. Clear?"
"What questions. I don't understand what's going on here...The crewmen closed his mouth as he felt a burning sensation spreading from where the liquid was on his body.
"It's burning. What have you done?"
"It's just sulphuric acid. Car battery acid to be exact. Nothing too concentrated. It won't kill you."
"Battery acid? Oh, my God. It's burning. Get it off. Please..."
"Listen very carefully. I'm going to kill you sometime in the next hour. That's guaranteed. You need to believe that." The Butcher informed him casually. "You only have one choice to make in this matter. If you tell me everything you know, about the jade statues and silver bars that you fished out of the ocean with James McLeod and his girlfriend, your death will be fairly quick and relatively painless. If you tell me lies or refuse to answer my questions the next hour will be the most agonising and longest of your miserable life. Am I clear?"

"What are you talking about? You can't just kill me. I haven't done anything.... The crewmen's pleading stopped suddenly as he felt more acid splash onto his arms and legs.

"I have lots of acid and you have lots of sensitive skin. You should believe me when I tell you that I really enjoy hurting people."

"Put water on me...it's burning through me! Please...."

"You will give me the answers I want. Sooner or later, so either way I will get what I want. It's just a question of how much agony you want to go through before I end your pathetic life."

"I want to tell you whatever you want to know. Give me a chance. Just don't hurt me."

"You're not listening.... Are you? I *am* going to hurt you. A lot. And I'm going to enjoy doing it. So, the sooner you tell me exactly what I want to know, the sooner I will kill you and end your pain." The Butcher stepped out from behind the bright light and the crewmen saw that he held a plastic watering can in one hand and a small knife in the other.

"Maybe I should start on your eyes? You don't need them to tell me what I need to know. So…left, or right?"

"The jade statues. Yes, I was there. I can tell you everything that you want to know. We brought them up in a huge box. Mr Thakkrani paid us all double salary as a bonus."

"Where are they now?" The Butcher asked as he stood poised with the watering can held aloft.

"They're not on the Marlin now. We offloaded them a few days after we brought them onboard."

"Where to?"

"They're on an uninhabited island."

"And the name of this mysterious island?" The Butcher asked as he sprinkled acid across the shoulders and back of the crewmen.

"Please stop." The crewman screamed again as the acid burned into his skin. "I'm telling you the truth. I'm helping. I'm doing what you asked." He sobbed.

"And I'm doing what I said I would do. Hurting you and enjoying it. Now...the name of the island?

"Get it off...It's burning. Crewmen screamed.

"The name of the island...?" The Butcher asked again as his knife began to carve a large circle on the crewman's chest.

"We weren't told the name. There was rumour amongst the crew that it didn't even have a name."

"Really? I think maybe this acid isn't hurting enough..."

"No. I know the navigator told me that he had to delete the GPS satellite data. It's Mr. Thakkrani's secret sanctuary, his charity for the orangutans. Please that's all I know. Please...don't hurt me anymore...."

"Orangutan sanctuary? What are you talking about?"

"Just chit chat on the boat. By the crew. If we want to keep your jobs we have to be discreet about what we see and hear onboard."

"Not today you don't. I think the left eye... The crewmen watched in terrified fascination as the butcher slowly raised the knife towards his face. He tried in vain to crane his neck backwards to avoid the point. "Or maybe an ear.... The razor-sharp knife flashed forward to slice off most of the crewman's left ear. "I saw them do that in a film once..."

The crewmen screamed again and thrashed against the bonds holding him to the chair, as the blood ran down his neck and back and then feinted.

The Butcher walked back behind the flood lights he was using to blind his victim. He returned moments later carrying a small bottle in his hand which he waved under the crewman's nostrils. The strong ammonia smell roused him back to consciousness and he sat up abruptly.

"The name of the island...?"

"I don't know the name of the island. If I did, I would tell you. Please. That's all I know."

"How can I find an island with no name? That's no help to me."

"The charity. The orangutan charity. They do trips for VIPs. To see the apes. They must know where the island is. They can tell you."

"And where did they put the jade statues on the island. I can't search an island..."

"I don't know. Honestly, we just put the statues in a small boat and they took them to the beach. It wasn't even me doing it."

"But you saw them doing it?"

No, my friend told me about it though. They definitely put them in a small boat to go to the island. There were a lot of them. That's everything. That's all I know. You should be able to find them. So, you can let me go now. I need to get to a hospital. I won't tell anyone what happened. I don't even know who you are or where I am. You can just go and leave me here. You don't have to kill me. I won't tell anyone..."

"You expect me to believe that told me everything you know?"

"It's the truth. I've told you everything I know. Please. Just don't kill me."

"What about the silver bars?"

"They were unloaded in Thailand. When Mr Thakkrani got off. A big security van was waiting for us. We unloaded them by hand, a conga line of all the crew, into the back of the van. Then they closed the door and drove off. I don't know where they took it, I guess it went into Bangkok? Honestly, I don't know. That's everything. The statues and the silver bars. We got paid a bonus on our salary."

"Probably in some bank vault by now." The Butcher said aloud as he pondered the information. "I wonder why he didn't put the statues in the same place? I think your Mr Thakkrani may be avoiding the authorities. Avoiding taxes, maybe. He's a thief. And as you know there is no honour amongst thieves...

"Look, I have a wife...and a young daughter. They depend on me...Please... Just let me go, I won't say anything. I don't know who you are... Please I've told you everything I know."

"You know maybe you're right..." The Butcher picked up the watering can and took it back to the flood lights.

"Yes. Yes. Just leave me here. You can be far away before I get out. You'll be totally safe."

"Yes, totally safe and far away, my thoughts exactly." The Butcher replied slowly before turning and switching off the bright lights. He then walked slowly back towards the crewmen. "But I gave you my word, and I never break my word."

"You gave me your word?" The crewman asked. His face showed his confusion.

"Yes. I told you that if you told me everything you knew that I would kill you quickly..." The Butcher's right arm swung in an arc and the sharp blade in his hand sliced the crewmen's neck open from one side to the other, opening both major arteries in his neck. The crewmen's partially severed head lolled back and his lifeblood pumped high into the air.

"I need another shower." The Butcher thought, as he examined the numerous blood splatters covering his rippling arm muscles. "And then I will pay a visit to my old gangster friend in Darwin and get myself another Australian passport. I need to be here for a few more days anyway since I need to send Abdul Khan the report he is expecting. It shouldn't take too long to provide an update on the Authorities' pathetic investigations into both the explosion at the nuclear test site and the aircraft crash just off the coast of Adelaide.

Chapter 10

Colombo

Bob and Izi were sitting in the back seat of one of Colombo's colourfully-painted city taxis. The driver was swerving left and right, trying to avoid the worst pot-holes in the unmade dirt track which they were bumping along, many miles from his usual routes.

"This is *so exciting*" Izi said. "I'm so glad you invited me along, Mr Dalton."

"I had hoped the three of us would go together, but unfortunately my daughter does not agree with your point of view as regards this particular journey." Bob replied with a snort.

"She can be difficult to persuade sometimes, can't she? Izi smiled to herself. "I think she was really disappointed when we failed to find the statues in the bank."

"Really? She didn't say that to me."

"She worked really hard on this. She actually read *all* of the documents that you brought back from the MoD, which was more than even I did. And then we spent hours searching fruitlessly for news of the statues on the Internet."

"And you think that made her lose heart?" Bob asked. "But you didn't."

"Oh, she hasn't lost heart. Not at all, despite the impression she gave you at breakfast. We had already agreed that I would come with you while she went back to the Internet search. She told me that she had had a few ideas overnight. She kept waking up apparently..."

"She could have told me..."

"She's very determined to do this. I think secretly, that she wants to impress you."

"Impress me...?"

"She knows that she's been a bit...difficult, at times."

"She's often too stubborn for her own good."

"I wonder where she gets that from?" Izi asked innocently.

"Touche" Bob replied with a smile. "But she's turned around this last year at School. Since you guys got involved with all your adventures."

"I think today is just like real detective work, a bit like when we were searching through all those old records to discover the truth about the Diadem and then the new documents about the rest of the convoy."

"But she will regret not coming with us, particularly if we solve the mystery today. I've got a good feeling about this already. If the old man remembers anything about the jade statues we will have another trail to follow."

"Did you explain to him why we were coming to see him?"

"No. Apparently, he doesn't have a phone. So, I assume that we are going to be something of a surprise for him."

"What if he isn't home?"

"In that case, this will be a very short visit" Bob laughed.

The taxi unexpectedly came to an abrupt skidding stop, causing a cloud of red dust to blossom around the car. "This is the address you gave me, Sir" the driver advised them.

"It doesn't look like much" Izi replied as she looked out of the grimy window and through the dust cloud towards the building the driver was pointing at.

"That's great" Bob told the driver. "Please wait here. I doubt we will be more than an hour."

"Or a lot less, if he's not home" Izi added.

"Of course, Sir. That won't be a problem" the driver replied. "But I will have to charge you more."

"I understand" Bob replied. "I will have to put it on my expense bill" Bob explained to Izi as he climbed out from the taxi.

Izi followed him out of the taxi and the pair looked at the small lonely house on the side of the road. "Come on Mr Dalton. Let's get detecting!" She instructed. Bob followed Izi's confident stride as they walked towards the house.

Before they had a chance to knock, the door swung open to reveal an elderly man leaning on a small bamboo cane. "Can I help you?" the man asked in a crisp English accent.

"I hope so" Bob replied. "We were hoping to speak to a Mr Sanjit Singh?"

"That is my name. Who are you?"

"I'm Bob Dalton and this little lady is Izi Uhuru" Bob replied formally. "Are you the same Sanjit Singh, who used to work for Blackman Brothers bank?"

"I am indeed. I was the manager there for many years. As was my father before me."

"Excellent. In that case, you're the man we came to see." Bob replied. "I wonder if we could come inside? We have a few questions for you."

"Of course," he replied with a friendly smile. "I don't get many visitors these days. Please come inside." He finished with a smile.

"You have a lovely English accent" Izi told him as she stepped through the doorway.

"Thank you, Izi. It's hardly perfect, but I do try." He replied as he closed the door behind them. "Can I offer you both some tea?"

"That would be lovely" Izi said.

"If you could manage some sugar too?" Bob added.

"I always have sugar in my tea, Mr Dalton" he replied. "It gives me extra energy. Please take a seat. It won't take me long..."

Whilst Bob and Izi made themselves comfortable in the small front room, they could hear Mr Singh as he busied himself in his kitchen next door.

"He looks too young to have been in charge of the bank during the war" Izi whispered to Bob.

"Of course he does. It was his Dad who was the manager during the war" Bob replied. "If what the secretary told me is correct, he took over from his father twenty years later on."

Five minutes later, Mr Singh returned to the cosy front room and poured out hot tea with milk for everyone. Once he had settled into the other chair, Bob began to speak. "We visited your old bank yesterday, as we are doing some historical research into war-time Colombo. The current manager was as helpful as he could be, but unfortunately the records we were interested in were all destroyed or lost during the Second World War."

"My Dad would have known all about that. He was the manager during the war years you know. They were worrying times for all of us back then" Mr Singh told them.

"Funnily enough, one of the secretaries told us the same thing. Which is what brought us to see you today. Since your father was the manager during that time, we thought that you might be able to assist us. I admit it's a bit of a long shot. I don't know if you remember much about that time. I realise it was a very long time ago."

"I may be very old now Mr Dalton. But I am pleased to say that my memory is as sharp now as it ever was. I was still very young during the war years but I was very close to my father who had high hopes of me eventually joining him in the bank. He and my mother always hoped that perhaps I might even to rise to the position of manager, as I grew older."

"And I understand that's exactly what you did do" Bob replied with a smile.

"My mother was a very strong woman. She usually got what she wanted!" Singh told them with a smile.

"My mum has ambitions for me too" Izi informed them.

"But do you have ambitions for yourself?" Mr Singh asked. "At the end of the day, that's actually what counts."

"I think I'm ambitious but I'm not sure exactly what I want to do yet. Right now, this research I'm doing with Mr Dalton is absolutely fascinating."

"That's good" Singh said "So ask me your questions."

"We've been trying to trace a large teak case, as tall as a man and weighing five or six hundred pounds, which we think was deposited in your bank vault at the beginning of the century."

"The beginning of the century? That's well before my father's time" Mr Singh interrupted with a quizzical look on his face.

"Indeed it was." Bob replied. "But the records that we have about the case, clearly state that it was deposited in Blackmans. Unfortunately, the trail we have been following comes to a dead end with your bank. Unless you can help us, that is?"

"Do you know what was in the case" Mr Singh asked slowly.

"If our information is correct" Izi said. "The case contained 500 rare jade soldiers, which were a gift from the Chinese government."

"Rare jade soldiers? That was a very honest answer, Izi. It's refreshing to hear the truth about such things."

"My Mum told me that I should always tell the truth."

"Indeed...that's good advice. For the most part" Singh replied, as he rubbed his chin thoughtfully. "It seems that you are looking for a very valuable case then, Mr Dalton. Are you treasure hunters? Is there a reward for recovering them?"

"To be honest with you Mr Singh, at the moment we are working for a private individual who wishes to track down the current whereabouts of the statues, if they still exist. Any reward would be the responsibility of the owner and ownership of the statues will probably take lawyers and the courts a long time to decide. If we eventually find them..."

"Another honest answer" Singh said. "So, I will be honest with you. For many years after I took over at the bank, I wondered if anyone would ever ask me about the case and those jade soldiers."

"What? You actually know about the case? Izi asked.

"I do. But I'm sorry to have to tell you that I'm not going to be as helpful as you might have hoped. The case and the statues *were* in the bank's vault during the war but they aren't in the bank any more, I can assure you of that. When I was promoted to manager and was allowed personal access to the vault I confirmed my suspicions that the case was missing. But I am happy to tell you what I know for myself. Please relax and drink your tea. I think that you will find that it's an interesting story."

"But why would you be looking for the case in the first place?" Izi asked him.

"If you give me a little more of your time, I will explain it all to you."

Bob and Izi leaned back in their chairs and concentrated on Mr Singh's words.

"Some of what I am going to tell you, you may already know. But some things, you definitely won't."

"We are all ears, Mr Singh" Izi said before gulping another mouthful of lukewarm tea.

"You probably know that the war against the Japanese was not going very well for the Allies in the early years. Singapore had been overrun and the Japanese armies seemed unstoppable. My father told me that he had received orders from our headquarters in London to prepare the bank for evacuation. I was only a skinny kid at that time, but he had brought me into the bank for a few weeks work experience. The staff were all obviously stressed by the war but also by the sudden change of manager. You see, my Father had only been promoted to manager for a few weeks following the sudden death of his boss, the branch manager. He was still going through all the paperwork in his new office and trying to do a full inventory of the vaults in preparation for any evacuation.

"His boss had just died? Izi asked. "A Japanese attack?"

"Nothing so dramatic. He had a heart attack. I remember he was very old. My Father told me that he should have retired years before. My father had been his deputy for far too many years in my Mother's opinion.

"And the jade soldiers?" Bob asked

"Patience, Mr Dalton. I'm coming to that. I haven't spoken about this to anyone ever before and I told you it's a good story."

"I like historical stories" Izi replied. "Especially if they are factual."

"I'm sure that you will enjoy this one then" he replied with a friendly smile. "My father had to go through all the Manager's confidential files and on this particular day I was sitting in his office, while he did so. Apparently, one of the files in the private safe in the manager's office, related to a crate being stored in our top-security vault, for one of our clients. The file related to one of the bank's oldest accounts which had been set up around the time the bank was opened but the account had been dormant for many years. My father finished reading the file and then suddenly stood up and told me to follow him. As we left his office he asked the new deputy manager to accompany us to the vault floor. To be honest I never liked the man. He was sly. I always felt that he was listening to other people's conversations and he generally stood much too close for comfort when he was talking to you. He encroached on people's personal space, you understand? He was creepy. Especially to my young eyes."

"I know exactly what you mean." Izi replied. "Creepy!"

"The world is full of all sorts of people Izi" Bob pointed out.

"He was sly, Mr Dalton. I never trusted him." Mr Singh repeated before continuing with his story. "The three of us descended to the vault floor and my father and Mr Sly opened the vault door. It took two keys to access the high security vault back in those days. We have different security processes now as you may have found out when you visited my bank, Mr Dalton?"

"It's very, very secure." Bob replied. "Did you go into the vault with your father too?"

"No. Only the Manager is allowed to go into that particular vault. I doubt they've changed that rule even today. It's one of those ancient traditions at the bank."

"So I understand" Bob replied.

"My father entered the vault to look for the case, whilst Mr Sly and myself stood near the open door. We could clearly see my father as he approached an old wooden crate which he then opened with the aid of a crowbar. I remember Mr Sly was craning his neck for a better view, even though he was considerably taller than myself. Once he had loosened the lid on the case, my father had to stand on a box to see inside the case. My view was slightly blocked by Mr Sly but even so I could see my father pull out a bright green statuette. Maybe 12 inches in length. I heard Mr Sly gasp loudly and then say something under his breath, which smelt horribly by the way. I still remember it to this day. But I also remember that bright jade statuette. There was something eerie about the light coming from it. A few minutes later my father came out of the vault and we all returned upstairs. He never discussed it with me and I never asked him about it. I guess I felt a bit guilty about looking inside..."

"But eventually you joined the bank and worked your way up to manager, didn't you?" Izi asked. "Couldn't you go into the vault when you were the Manager? To look for the case, I mean?"

"By the time my father retired and I took over, the crate was no longer in the vault. You have to realise that many years had passed since I saw it. In actual fact, it was one of the first things I looked for when I took over from my father. Not very professional perhaps. But I remembered it even after all those years."

"Do you know who came to claim the case?" Bob asked. "There must have been a record of it in those secret files in the Manager's office..."

"I was only very young so I was only at the bank for a few weeks as I explained to you but I didn't see or hear anything about the case while I was doing my work experience. And since my father rarely discussed business at home with my mother, that was the end of the matter as far as I was concerned until I began work at the bank many years later."

"What about when you evacuated the bank?" Izi asked. "Maybe there are records of that?"

"It didn't happen. The staff packed up all our records and sent them for storage off-shore as they had been directed by HQ, in preparation for the evacuation. But then we didn't leave. It was very strange time for the whole world. Full of uncertainty, which made everyone even more nervous than usual."

"Well, maybe there was a bank robbery and the case was stolen during all the confusion of war?" Izi suggested.

"Impossible. At that time during the war, the streets of the city were being patrolled by squads of armed soldiers as part of the preparations for defence or evacuation of the city. Consequently, street crime was at an all-time low and the criminals kept a very low profile. The troops had orders to shoot on sight, you see. I remember that before the war started and the troops arrived, there was a particularly notorious gang, called thuggees who terrorised the city. They were supposed to worshipped a mysterious goddess who had eyes that fired laser beams at her enemies. Sounds ridiculous now, but those were the stories I heard."

"Seems very odd how a valuable case could just disappear from the bank" Bob pointed out.

"Owners often removed their valuables from the vaults. Maybe that's what happened. I'm sorry I can't be more helpful. I would have liked to have known what happened to the statues myself. Idle curiosity I suppose. I did try to raise the subject with my father once I started working at the bank but he always cut me off. Which was not unusual for him even after he retired. He took his responsibilities at Blackman Brothers very seriously."

"So it seems" Bob replied.

"I suppose we had better head back to the hotel to tell Laura what we found out." Izi said

"Laura?" Mr Singh asked.

"That's my daughter. I left her back at the villa doing some more research for us. I'm sure that she will be intrigued by your story too."

"I just wish that I could have been more helpful to you. More tea before you go? I don't get many visitors these days. Unfortunately, my own children died before me. A parent should never have to bury their own children. Should they Mr Dalton?"

"No, indeed not. That's very sad, Mr Singh" Bob replied. "I appreciate the offer of tea and you've been really helpful to our research, but I think it's time we left."

"I'm glad that I could be of some help. It's been many years since I thought about those war years. Terrible times...." Mr Singh said.

"And thank you for the tea" Izi added as they all stood up to leave.

Once outside Bob and Izi walked across the road to the waiting taxi and Bob tapped on the window to awaken the sleeping driver.

"We want to go back to the hotel now" Bob said as the driver quickly wound the window down.

"Right. Yes. Of course," the taxi driver replied between yawns. He turned the ignition key and the ancient engine rumbled into life.

Bob swung the rear door open and then he and Izi resumed their seats in the back of the vehicle as the driver began a multipoint turn in the road to head back into the city. Before he completed the manoeuvre Izi saw Mr Singh open his front door and wave frantically at them.

"Can you wait a moment?" She asked the driver.

"What is it Mr Singh" Bob asked as he approached the taxi on his walking stick.

"I've been thinking about what I told you and another memory came back to me. You must appreciate that it was a very long time ago but something else came back to me as soon as you left."

"Anything would be helpful" Izi replied.

"It may be irrelevant. It's more like just a snippet of conversation I heard when I was doing my work experience at the bank. One day, maybe a week after my father had opened the case, I heard the secretaries whispering about the bank being opened in the middle of the night on secret government orders and armed troops carrying valuables from the vaults. They were discussing us being evacuated and the bank being shut up but several days passed without anything happening. Eventually I spoke to my father about the evacuation but he insisted that he was waiting for further instructions from headquarters and he completely denied all knowledge of the bank being opened in the middle of the night. Ridiculous, was the word he actually used."

When they finally returned to their luxury villa on the beach. Bob and Izi were surprised to find Bonn and Ong waiting for them inside.
"Your hard-working daughter has found another clue Bob." Ong said proudly as soon as they had walked through the door.
"Really?" Bob replied. "What have you found out darling?"
"Before I tell you what I discovered." Laura insisted. "I want to hear all about your meeting with Mr Singh."
"You've got your investigator head back on then." Izi suggested.
"It's a team problem" Laura replied with a smile. "So... tell us how you got on..."
Izi and Bob quickly recounted the story Mr Singh had told them.
"It seems safe to assume that the Commodore did as he was ordered and offloaded the crate in Colombo." Ong summarised.
"And it then sat in the bank vault for the next 40 years apparently forgotten until Mr Singh's father looked in the crate." Bob replied.

"Which may have triggered its disappearance" Ong suggested.

"Or maybe not" Bob replied. "It may have been moved years later. The only definitive timeframe we have, is that it was gone by the time Singh Junior took over as Manager."

"What about the secretary's gossip?" Izi asked.

"That soldiers came in the middle of the night and robbed the bank?" Bob replied. "And then Mr Singh Senior covered it up? That would have to be one heck of a conspiracy."

"Which Blackman Brothers headquarters in London would soon have uncovered." Ong suggested.

"It's a bit strange that all the records disappeared at the same time." Laura pointed out. "So, we don't have any clues as to where it went to."

"Which I think means we have reached another dead end" Izi concluded glumly.

"Or maybe not!" Laura replied triumphantly. "That's what I need to tell you and Dad. Remember that last bundle you didn't have time to go through Dad? The one with ship's log from the supply vessel?"

"Yes, of course I do." Bob replied defensively. "I was going to read it when I got back."

"Well it seems that you were unwittingly saving the best till last Bob." Ong interrupted. "Wait until you hear what your clever daughter discovered."

"As you guessed Dad, the ship's log wasn't very helpful I think it had the least to tell us about the voyage of the convoy. But as I turned over the very last page, I found a copy of a very different sort of document."

"What do you mean?" Bob asked.

"As soon as I saw it, I knew it was an important. And even though I didn't know what it meant I called Bonn in her room straightaway and then she and Ong came over here to have a look themselves."

"And she was right, Bob." Ong interrupted again. "Especially since you drew a blank with the bank manager."

"Can you show it to me then?" Bob asked.

"Of course!" Laura said as she reached behind her and proudly handed him a single sheet of photocopy paper.

CLASSIFIED

ULTRA

Date: 20.2.42
To: PM
From:1st SL

Re: Operation Double Bravo
Update
Following the meeting of the JC's, I immediately spoke to the Commissioner. He has now seconded Cmdr SB to MoD indefinitely.
Bomber Command have released an appropriate aircraft for his use and he will leave today. ETA +68 hrs.
Local rep of HMG has been read into op. Will take no action prior to CSB.
HM PO read in.

Bob read through the document twice before looking up and handing the document to Izi. "It's a shame about the smearing all over the bottom half of the sheet. It means we can only see the top half.

"I said exactly the same thing when I read it." Ong replied. "It's clear that there was more writing lower down."

"It looks to me like the copy got stuck in the photocopy machine." Laura suggested. "I've done it myself at school. And it comes out just like that one."

"And it's usually the most important page too." Bonn added.

"I don't really understand what is says." Izi said as she looked up from the page.

"People in the Armed Forces and in Government love to use their abbreviations." Bob explained helpfully. "Coincidentally it makes it quite difficult for outsiders to understand what they're saying."

"The word Commissioner stood out for me." Laura said. "Isn't the top policeman in London called the Commissioner?"

"He is indeed darling" Bob said. "Which might help us. But it looks more like some sort of interdepartmental Forces memorandum rather than Police. Not that we should exclude that possibility yet. The reference to Bomber Command probably means it came from the Air Force. And what has it got to do with a supply ship travelling in the Commodores fleet before the RAF was even formed?

"But it is a classified document." Ong pointed out.

"The word Ultra at the top means nothing to me. They usually classify documents as Secret or Top Secret, depending on what they contain. So I don't know why that's there."

"But it says it's about Operation Double Bravo" Laura reminded them. "That has to be the code name for the Commodore's fleet."

"It's possible" Bob's voice revealed his scepticism.

"This single sheet may mean nothing." Ong suggested. "But since all other leads have come to a dead end, this is all we have. Joseph?" Ong called to Bonn's personal bodyguard who was standing nearby. "You worked with the Metropolitan Police, didn't you? Do you recognise any of this jargon?"

Joseph approached the group and Izi handed him the photocopy which he quickly read.

"Well, if this was a Police memo, reading this first section I would say that it means that the Commander of Special Branch had been seconded to the Ministry of Defence. Unfortunately, that would literally be unheard-of. So it can't mean that. Having the word Ultra written across the top below Classified, would normally be where the Police would have their document security classification. Like Secret or Eyes Only as Mr Dalton explained. But without seeing the bottom of the document, I'm just guessing."

"On the other hand, if this was a Naval memorandum, '1st SL' might mean it comes from the First Sea Lord, which would make some sense if it related to the Commodore's voyage."

"But the date shown is much later than the Diadem's voyage." Laura pointed out.

"Maybe Double Bravo is the operation to find the wreck site of the Diadem?" Izi suggested.

"That's a great suggestion Izi" Ong replied.

"And JC could mean the Joint Chiefs." Bob suggested. "They are the very top of the command structure of the British Armed Forces."

"Could PM refer to the Prime Minister then?" Laura asked.

"It could be..." Bob suggested. "The Joint Chiefs would only refer up the chain of command to the Prime Minister. So that could be the PM."

"What about the other abbreviations?" Izi asked. Does anybody have any ideas." She looked around the group and everyone shook their heads.

"HMG could be Her Majesty's Government, couldn't it?" Joseph offered.

"Their representative in Northern Australia. Yes, that would make sense" Ong replied.

"But if Operation Double Bravo was the codename for recovering the wreck of the Diadem, why is it in with logs from the supply vessel in the Commodores fleet? Laura asked.

"Maybe it's just a mistake." Izi said. "Maybe somehow the photocopies got mixed up? You did say they were very busy when you collected the box of documents, didn't you Mr Dalton?"

"It did all look fairly hectic. So maybe you're right."

"So it's another dead end." Izi said sadly.

"Perhaps I could make a suggestion?" Joseph asked.

"Of course, Joseph." Ong replied immediately. "Any suggestion is a good one at this point."

"My best friend from my days in the Met is now the head of Special Branch in London. If you agree, I could give him a ring and talk to him about the memorandum. It's a long shot, so if anyone has a better idea..."

Ong looked around the group for a few moments but hearing no dissenters or better offers he said, "It seems like you're our best shot Joseph. Please call your friend and let us know what he says."

20 minutes later, as the group of friends were sipping their cool drinks and enjoying the sea breeze on the villa's wide veranda, Joseph re-joined them.

"I've got some good news. And I've got some bad news." He informed them.

"Let's have the good news first then, please Joseph." Ong replied.

"The good news is that I think the memorandum is not a complete dead-end. My friend told me that he recognised some of the language in the memorandum."

"That's good. And now the bad news... Ong suggested.

"He won't talk about it on the telephone. At all."

"That sounds like a complete dead-end to me" Laura pointed out abruptly.

"Not completely." Joseph countered.

"Why not?" Izi asked when she saw the smile on Joseph's face.

"He will talk to me about it. But only if he can do so face-to-face."

"And I assume he doesn't want to come out to Colombo today?" Bob asked

"I'm sure he would love to. But he's a very busy man."

"So?" Laura asked.

"So, as the good book says" Ong interrupted. "If the mountain won't come to Mohammed...

"Ha! It looks like you're going to London, Joseph..." Bob said.

"But my protection duties with Bonn? Joseph asked as he considered Ong's statement.

"I'm sure the rest of your team will manage without you for a few days Joseph. You've trained them very well. And since this is the only clue we have to go on. And since your friend will only speak to you about it...As you know, I really want to find the rest of those statues."

"Yes Sir. I understand that. But..." Joseph replied.

"No 'Buts' Joseph. You're going" Ong insisted with finality. "I also suggest that it would be a good idea if you went too, Bob. Ong said. I hope Tracey and Laura won't mind me breaking up your holiday. But the fact is that you have lots of information and knowledge about the statues and the Diadem which we don't have time to brief Joseph upon. Once he has spoken to his friend, you will be perfectly placed to fit the new information into what we already know. I really don't want to leave any stone unturned and I don't know why, but I feel like this investigation is time sensitive for some reason."

"I follow your logic." Bob said. "What do you girls think?" He asked Tracey and Laura.

"I'm sure we can manage without you for a couple of days Bob." Tracey replied.

"Only if we can go to do some proper shopping while you are away..." Laura suggested.

"I would be surprised if you didn't" Bob answered her with a warm smile.

"If you take my jet rather than relying on commercial planes, you can be there and back in less than 48 hours." Ong offered.

"It's not *your* jet, remember Dad?" Bonn replied and everyone laughed.

"I will ring the crew and have them prepare the plane before I brief Lawrence to take over for me here with Bonn." Joseph replied before approaching Bob. "I can be ready in an hour if that suits you Mr Dalton?"

"I can be packed and ready by then." Bob replied. "I will meet you in Reception in an hour."

Chapter 11

Darwin

A hundred miles south and west from where the Black Marlin was moored in Darwin harbour, a dusty airstrip had been marked out on the surface of the hard, red desert surface of the desert outback. As part of Prinsloo Industries latest venture to recover oil and gas from a large offshore field, the small team of engineers and scientists who had been assigned to initiate the project, had set up their base camp alongside the makeshift runway.

After many weeks working at the site, the entire project team were used to the noise of the Predator's twice-daily take offs and landings, along the perfectly straight and gently undulating runway. The Predator was an ex-USAF model, which Johann had managed to acquire through a contact at the Pentagon more than a year previous. The Unmanned Aerial Vehicle had proven essential to the successful completion of their project, to survey a route for the oil and gas pipelines which would carry the products from the well head far out at sea to the planned refinery plants on shore. Several of the project team watched the graceful arrival of the UAV at the end of its flight. Her highly polished white surfaces gleamed brightly in the afternoon sunshine as the small aircraft taxied towards the side of the runway where it's self-contained control unit was located. Moments later, the high-pitched whine of its powerful engine dropped lower and the spinning propeller blades began to slow as the flight controller inside the control cabin cut the power.

As the ground crew walked towards the UAV, Jannie followed Mike Stoney and Pablo Moreno, as they all stepped out of the Predator's control room. All three of them were grinning widely, as they walked across the runway towards the dust-covered car waiting near the base's Portacabins.

"From the look on their faces, I am willing to bet that he passed" Owen said to Johann, as they sat on the hood of the car.

"Mr. Prinsloo!" Jannie shouted as soon as he recognised the two men waiting for him. "I passed" he added as he walked swiftly towards them.

"I'm sure you wouldn't tell me a bald lie like that but I would like to hear that from Mike and Pablo too" Johann replied light heartedly.

"Just to be sure" Owen added quietly.

"No, Mr. Prinsloo. He's not lying." Mike replied as he joined them. "He passed with flying colours. You know that not everybody could have done what he has. Learning and passing after such a short time, I mean. I have to say that I'm thoroughly impressed with the lad."

"After his first few lessons, he picked it up really quickly." Pablo added with a grin. "I think he might be after my job."

"Don't worry Pabs" Owen replied. "Your job's safe enough. JP has other plans for young Jannie."

"Other plans?" Jannie asked. "Is that the surprise you told me about? If I passed my flying test today, I mean?" he gabbled.

"Come over to the office" Johann replied, placing a friendly hand on Jannie's shoulder. "Then Owen and I will tell you all about it."

"If we can get a word in sideways..." Owen added sarcastically. Jannie swung his head towards Owen, about to make a response, but when he saw the look on Owen's face he realised he was once again joking with him.

"Really well done, Jannie." Owen said, as they sat at the table in the relative cool of the small office Portakabin with a cooling drink. "You've worked really hard since you arrived here after your School exams. I've been getting regular reports from Mike about your progress. Almost every day in fact.

"Occasionally, Owen told me what was going on too" Johann added with a smile.

" I don't need to tell you everything boss. You've got an empire to run."

"I understand that. But Jannie's important." Johann replied. "Anyway, congratulations all round. You've passed. While we've got time, I also want to tell you about your meteorite."

"*His* meteorite? Owen sounded surprised.

"I did help a lot to get it back to camp in Siberia, Owen." Jannie replied defensively.

"He's only playing with you, Jannie. Take no notice. We both know how much you helped. Just ignore him. He's just being grumpy today."

"*His* meteorite." Owen muttered again.

"My geologists have finished analysing it" Johann began again. "And it seems that Owen's dubious methods to get it back to Johannesburg were worthwhile."

"That translates as 'Well done, Owen and team. You did a fantastic job' getting Jannie's meteorite back to Jo'Burg" Owen suggested with a grin.

"Modest as usual" Johann replied. "But on balance, you and the team did a fantastic job Owen. So well done to you too. Ok?"

"So those sparkly bits all over it...they really were valuable?" Jannie asked without waiting for Owen's response.

"Very valuable actually. The rock is crammed full of rare metals which we can use in our complex industrial processes. The unusual metals which we will recover from the meteorite will probably net several million pounds' profit for Prinsloo Industries."

"Wow...Millions? Really? That's amazing."

"I didn't appreciate the possibilities myself." Johann admitted. "I now understand from the geologists that some of the metals in the meteorite are virtually impossible to find here on earth. So even tiny amounts are phenomenally valuable."

"That's great news for you" Jannie replied as he tried to imagine that much money.

"And for Jannie, ace meteorite hunter..." Owen said dramatically.

"A substantial finder's fee." Johann replied.

"A finder's fee?" Jannie asked.

"Just like the one Stan got for finding the nickel on the tepuy." Owen reminded Jannie.

"And also for the others who helped to find and recover it" Johann added.

"Oh, thank you so much Mr Prinsloo. Can I pay it into the bank account you set up for me?"

"I hoped you would say that, Jannie. Always save for a rainy day." Johann replied. "But that's only half of what I want to tell you. Owen... Why don't you tell him the good news as you suggested it."

"You're going home to South Africa" Owen added.

"South Africa. Do you mean another work experience? Or am I really going home, home?" Jannie asked.

"Home, home. It's all planned out for you. My people haven't had any information to make us think you are still in mortal danger. We think that the Takers have finally given up their strange grudge against you."

"That's even better news than the meteorite. Thanks Owen. You know I've missed all my friends at the orphanage. It's been years..."

"But just to be super safe..." Johann interrupted. "You won't be travelling directly to Johannesburg on a commercial route. I've decided that we are going to fly you from Darwin on a company cargo plane into Zaire and then cross the border from there into South Africa."

"You know how JP likes to complicate my straightforward plans" Owen interjected

"From the border, you can drive across country to Jo'Burg and the orphanage."

"With my parents?" Jannie asked.

"Actually, we've decided that this would be a perfect time for Bill and Miriam to get a well-earned rest while you are in S.A.." Owen told him.

"You want me to drive through Zaire and South Africa on my own?" Jannie's normally confident voice trembled a little.

"Even Owen wouldn't suggest that" Johann informed him.

"Of course not." Owen replied. "Travelling on your own is boring. So, just to keep you entertained I have asked Mr Smith and Mr White to travel with you. I'm sure you will enjoy listening to all their war stories."

"Oh right. Yes, that will be fantastic. They're both really interesting to talk to. Thank you so much Mr Prinsloo....and Owen, of course."

"You're welcome. I'm sure you will enjoy this trip more than the others." Johann suggested.

"Finally going *home*. I hope Theo will be pleased to see me again...considering why I left..."

"I'm sure he will do. And all the boys too." Owen reassured him.

"And since you will be travelling in one of the Company cargo planes, you can take that crazy buggy of yours with you too." Johann said.

"Really? That's even better. It sounds like another great plan, Owen."

"You know that all of my plans are great Jannie...they just vary in brilliance!"

"But what about the Predator? Jannie asked.

"She's staying right here for now." Owen replied. "There's a lot more work to be done still. But I'm sure that Mike and Pablo will somehow manage without your flying skills."

"I'm going home at last..." Jannie spoke wistfully. "Can I tell them I'm coming home?"

"Owen and I agree that it's best if your arrival comes as a surprise to the orphanage boys and Theo. Just to be on the safe side. I'm sure they will enjoy the surprise too."

"Especially since we're not sure exactly when you'll be getting there." Owen said soothingly. "To be honest, the roads in Zaire and North S.A. are not famous for their high-quality surfaces. Plus, you can't even leave here until Smith and White arrive which might not be until late tonight."

"Where are they coming from?" Jannie asked

"Not far" Owen replied unhelpfully. "In the meantime, you just worry about packing your bags, saying goodbye to Bill and Miriam and checking that dodgy buggy of yours. You don't want it breaking down in the desert do you."

"What do you mean dodgy?" Jannie challenged him. "She runs like a Swiss watch."

"You've never even seen a Swiss watch..." Owen relied with a laugh. "Now off you go, I need to talk to Mike and Pabs about how they are going to cope without their new 'Ace' pilot."

As soon as Jannie had left the office, Owen's smile vanished as he turned to face Johann. "My team have been looking into the explosion at the old atomic bomb test site at Woomera as you asked."

"I was wondering when you were going to give me an update."

"Obviously the Australian and UK governments are trying to keep it all secret. There's no way you can spin this to look good for either of them..."

"Is that code for 'you haven't been able to find out much'?"

"You're such a cynic, JP"

"Must be from working with you for too long, Mr. Strasser."

"Unlikely..." Owen replied with a snort. "However, I'm pleased to tell you that because the whole place is now in the middle of Aboriginal land, the Authorities are legally required to keep the tribes informed of their investigation and all findings."

"And you, of course, have an informant within the aborigines?"

"You know I never reveal my sources JP. Not even to you."

"Accepted. So, what did he tell you?"

"*He* might be a *she*..." Owen replied mysteriously. "But either way...My informant told me that they haven't been able to get to the bottom of the mine to examine it at all. Too much damage was caused during the explosion. But the UK side have convinced the Aussie's that they definitely didn't leave any practical explosives within the mine after they left it."

"Which means someone else did. What about the clean-up company? What was it called?"

"Blue Moon Environmental Services." Owen reminded him. "It seems that the investigating team quickly made the same suggestion to their bosses. And now we come to their real dilemma. Considering the sensitivity of this type of contract, you know, clearing up a highly radioactive site in the middle of a civilized country, you would expect that it would be fairly important to be able to ask the company doing it, what had happened."

"Of course."

"Well they couldn't. BMES has disappeared."

"A multimillion dollar operation doesn't just disappear overnight, Owen."

"This one did. The investigation team have drawn a complete blank. And they've got some good people on their team."

"That's not going to go down well with their bosses. Or the Press either, I'm sure." Johann pointed out. "Even though there's always a current news story, they won't just forget about an explosion at a nuclear site."

"Right on all counts, JP. Some senior heads are going to roll over this, for sure."

"So what's happened to BMES? You told me it was a huge operation. And that sort of company must leave a big corporate footprint. They had their own security army, Government contracts, a private airfield...the works."

"And private aircraft. Which brings me to something that the official team haven't found out yet?"

"What do you know, that they don't?"

"Do you remember the plane that crashed off the coast of Adelaide?"

"Vaguely..."

"It's connected to the mine explosion."

"How do you mean?"

"I don't know if the official investigation teams will join the dots, like my team have done on this, especially since they told me it has all been covered up very well. Not unlike the disappearance of BMES actually. Someone has gone to a lot of effort to muddy the waters over this."

"Muddy waters don't usually stop your team, Owen."

"But it made it much more difficult to be sure of their findings..."

"Which were?"

"Contrary to what was on the official flight plan, the downed plane actually started its journey from the airfield at the mine site. We managed to access some time lapse satellite images..."

"You just happened to find some satellite images...just laying around on your desk, were they?"

"Not exactly, JP." Owen replied slowly.

"I'm sure I don't want to know..."

"Probably not. Anyway, once it had passed over the coast near Adelaide, it changed course significantly which then put it directly over a very deep part of the ocean when it crashed, making it effectively impossible to recover the aircraft."

"You think it was sabotaged?"

"I actually think that someone went to a lot of trouble to make sure that whatever, or whoever was on that plane never saw the light of day again."

"BMES tying up loose ends?"

"That would be my guess."

"But neither of the Governments have come to the same conclusion?"

"The Australian Civil Aviation Authority investigation is getting nowhere. Without the flight recorders, or the plane itself, they've got nothing to examine. Their team are stalled."

"And the Press will be having similar problems. Unless they can find some useful satellite images of course."

"I think that's unlikely. They don't have my sources."

"Have your team also been able to find out who's behind BMES?"

"That's the last thing I need to tell you. The answer is a huge 'NO'. BMES is a ghost company. Layer upon layer of shadowy holding companies and well-hidden offshore boards of directors. It all looks real enough to a casual check but now things have gone wrong...nothing and nobody to blame or even talk to. And it was all done very professionally. My team leader told me he couldn't have done it better himself."

"So we've drawn a blank. Just like the real owners of the opal mine we raided."

"Funnily enough, that was exactly the same phrase that my team leader used."

Chapter 12

Colombo

Early the next morning, Izi and Sam were sitting in their hotel room in Colombo, pouring over the Internet once again.

"Look at this review" Izi said. "It's called Bliss. It says it's surrounded by lush tropical gardens and unspoiled forests. *This luxury retreat and day spa gets five stars from us*."

"It sounds exactly like what we need." Sam replied. "The perfect getaway for a day, I'm sure Bonn and Laura will enjoy a day's pampering. The complete opposite to yesterday's bus trip."

"What about Stan and Ben? I can't imagine Ben is really the spa type."

"But you think Stan would be?"

"Of course. I think we all know he would like it."

"Why don't we just go and ask them. It's well past the time they were up and about."

"I'm going to order fresh fruit and a coconut milkshake for breakfast...this place is amazing."

Once they were all gathered in the hotel's open-air beachside restaurant, Izi described the spa in great detail to them as they were sitting around the large round table.

"I think I will let you guys go on your own today." Tracey replied when Sam asked who wanted to go to the spa. "Ong has kindly offered to escort me for today. Since he sent Bob away to London. He has even promised me some civilised shopping and then a long leisurely lunch somewhere. So I'm fine, if you want to go without me."

Ben was less gracious when Sam invited him. "A day at the spa?" Maybe I could get a manicure too?"

"You make it sound like you've never been to a spa" Stan said, his voice clearly displaying the surprise he felt.

"Have you then?" Ben asked indignantly

"Of course. Everyone in Moscow uses the hot spa baths. It's the only way to warm up during the winter months."

"Well it never gets cold in the Congo...or here, for that matter. I'm warm enough, thank you."

"They do sea-salt body wraps too." Izi added as she remembered the facilities described. "And hot stone massages."

"Have they also got a herbal steam room or a sauna?" Stan asked.

"They do." Sam informed him. "And the whole place is set in tropical gardens with running streams and waterfalls."

"This just gets better and better" Ben said sarcastically.

"Just come with us Ben" Sam pleaded. "Then make a decision once you've seen the place. It sounds like a stunning location.

"Okay. I'll come with you. I don't want to spoil the party."

"Good. That's decided then." Bonn said quickly. "As soon as we finish breakfast we should collect our swimwear and then meet in the lobby. Ok?"

" I assume your bodyguards will be coming too?" Sam asked

"They're just like my shoes and handbags" Bonn replied with a smile. "I never travel anywhere without them!"

Half an hour later the six teenagers met in the hotel lobby and once there Bonn's security team hustled them all outside and onto two minivans which the hotel had supplied for their VIP guests.

"Do you know a day spa called Bliss." Izi asked the driver of the first vehicle as soon as she clambered aboard.

"Did you say Bliss?" He asked in a friendly voice.

"Yes, Bliss. Apparently, it's on the road to Adam's Peak? About halfway up the mountain? Their website said there's a big sign outside with a picture of a waterfall on it?

"Oh yes Miss" the driver replied. "I know exactly the one you mean. I took some guests there a few weeks ago. They told me it was very beautiful."

"Will it take long to get there?" Sam asked.

"It all depends on the traffic to get out of the city. And sometimes the mountain road can be full too." The driver replied as he started the engine. "I am sure that we will get there when we get there."

"That's very helpful" Ben whispered to Stan who was sitting next to him.

"Don't be such a grouch" Stan replied. "It will be fun. Trust me."

"Fun? Wrapped up in sea salt while someone messes up my hair...?"

Sam who was sitting right behind them laughed out loud. "You will be fine Ben. She suggested, as the convoy set off.

The taxi driver's prediction of city traffic proved to be correct. But eventually they made their way out of the city limits and began to climb on one of the many roads leading towards the forest covered foothills, which surrounded Colombo.

As they drove further from the city, the road surface deteriorated as it began to climb through dozens of winding curves which suffered through alternating cycles of torrential rain from thunder storms and blistering daytime heat.

"I hope he's got spare tyres" Ben suggested as they bounced through another deep pothole.

"He knows what he's doing" Stan reassured him.

"Really? That's not my experience of taxi drivers in the Congo. And the roads there are just like these ones."

"These drivers were recommended by the hotel, remember?" Izi relied.

"I admire your confidence" Lawrence replied from his seat next to the driver. Since taking over from Joseph as team leader of the bodyguards, he had taken his new role very seriously. "But I'm glad we've got a spare vehicle...just in case."

"The scenery is amazing..." Bonn said as she gazed out the window.

"Lots of rain" Ben informed her.

"But today it's nothing but sunshine" Izi told him.

The group fell silent as they all watched the changing scene through the windows as the altitude increased. They passed several small villages along the route, many of which were advertising goods for sale on trestle tables set up outside.

Thirty minutes later the passengers were all surprised from their thoughts when Laura shouted "Microlights" and pointed to a hand-painted sign on the side of the road.

"Oh wow, who would have thought we would see them." Bonn replied.

"They are very popular with the tourists." The taxi driver informed them before adding "But very, very dangerous."

"They're not at all dangerous. Sam has one of her own." Izi replied proudly.

"But not in Colombo, of course." Sam replied defensively.

"And she's given us all rides in it." Izi informed the driver to convince him.

"Not all of us..." Ben pointed out grumpily.

"That wasn't my fault. You were in Africa at the time." Sam replied as Stan elbowed Ben in the ribs.

"Well I'm just saying that not all of us have been in Sam's microlight. That's all."

"You should come to visit me on the farm then" Sam offered.

"My next trip that I make to the tepuy in Venezuela I might take you up on that offer." He replied with a smile.

"Ohhh.... I see. *You* get special treatment from *my* big sister." Izi said raising her eyebrows

"Are you getting jealous Izi? Laura asked.

"I'm just saying..." Izi replied quietly.

Ten minutes later the casual conversations in the taxi were interrupted again when Izi shouted with glee. "That's it! There's the sign."

"There's another one...see they've got BLISS SPA printed on an archway over the little path too." Bonn pointed out.

"I told you I knew where it was." The van driver said smugly. "As you can see the road to the spa isn't as good as this one. And it gets much steeper and bumpier from now on. So hang on tight!"

"Worse than this one?" Stan asked Ben. "Is that even possible?"

"Welcome to my world" Ben replied.

The taxi driver was proven correct. The friends watched as the road became narrower and more winding as they slowly climbed higher and higher through the forest towards the unseen spa ahead.

"It's very remote." Lawrence remarked quietly.

"I understand it is very relaxing, Sir." The driver replied. "The guests I took last week said it was very tranquil. Apparently, they never heard a sound apart from the tinkling of the wind chimes and the splashing of the waterfalls.

"I'm sure it's idyllic, but I want you and the other taxi to wait at the spa for us. Just in case we need to change locations."

"I will have to call to my manager about that, Sir. Normally we just drop the guests here and the spa calls us when they need picking up."

"Well these guests are different" Lawrence replied. "I will talk to your manager myself to clear it."

"Yes sir of course. Whatever you prefer. Do you need to use my phone?"

Lawrence depressed the small button in his palm which was attached to his covert radio set and spoke rapidly. "Two from one. I have told my driver that he will be required to remain at the spa during our visit. Please confirm with yours."

"One from two" came the reply in his earpiece. "Understood. Will do."

"If you dial up your boss and pass me the phone" Lawrence said to the driver. "I will get his agreement for you to stay, before we arrive at the spa."

The narrow road eventually made one more turn to finally reveal the Spa entrance set amongst the verdant jungle backdrop. As soon as the minivans stopped at the entrance, Bonn's security team disgorged from the second minivan to take up their usual protective positions around the vans before Lawrence allowed anyone out of his van. Picking up their swimwear the teens piled out of the front van and then Lawrence strode through the glass entrance doors, a few steps ahead of Bonn and her friends.

"It's just like the photos" Laura announced.

"Flowers everywhere" Izi added.

"And look at the view..." Bonn pointed through the open sides of the reception area at the jungle covered valley spread out below them. "You can see for miles."

"And listen...you can hear the waterfalls" Izi said.

Ben and Sam were the last ones through the doors, closely followed by the rest of the security detail. "Sam... I've been thinking" Ben said.

"Really? Sam replied. "You think you might like a massage after all?"

"Not that" Ben replied with a smile. "I was actually thinking about the sign we passed at the bottom of the hill? The one about the microlights?"

"I'm not with you" Sam replied as she stopped walking.

"Microlights...Everyone else has been for a flight in your one. And even though I have a healthy fear of heights, which Stan finds most amusing, I really would like to go up in one."

"And?" Sam asked, as a thought began to blossom in her mind

"Well...I was thinking about it in the taxi...If you don't mind missing out on the spa today... Maybe we could... You know... Rent one of those microlights and you could take me up for a flight." He finished in a rush.

"I thought you had gotten very quiet on the minibus Ben Damo. I should have guessed you were up to something."

"It would save me travelling all the way down to your farm in Venezuela..."

"But I would miss out on the spa..."

"You can go to a spa any day and I would be very grateful..."

"How grateful?" Sam asked with a frown.

"Maybe I could organise a trip to the orangutan sanctuary for you and your parents when we get back?"

"But I thought, Ong only wanted VIPs to visit the island?"

"I think I could persuade him that you all qualify as VIP. Would that make it worth your while, to miss your spa experience?"

"You drive a hard bargain." Sam replied whilst trying to keep a straight face. "But I know my parents would love to see the orangutans..."

"And maybe a night's accommodation in the treetop cabins...?"

"If they are available, I'm sure Ade won't mind that..."

"Great. So it's a deal." Sam said and held out her hand to seal the agreement.

"Come on you two slow coaches." Izi called out. "We're waiting for you. We need to get changed."

Ben and Sam strolled over to join the rest of the group to explain what they had agreed.

"To be honest" Sam told them. "I'm sure we will go to the spa another day before we leave the island. It actually seems too good a chance to pass up to take Ben for a flight I mean."

"I think you just miss flying yourself" Bonn suggested.

"We'll be back before you know it." Ben replied hopefully.

"I assume the taxi driver won't mind taking us back down the mountain?" Sam asked Lawrence.

"I will get one of my guys to go with you in their van. I don't want the driver deciding to go for a lunch break while he's down there."

"Thank you." Ben replied. "Is it OK if we call you when we need picking up again?"

"That will work" Lawrence replied before walking across to one of his team and saying, "Charlie. I want you to run Sam and Ben back down to that sign we saw about the microlights. And then get straight back here. Okay?"

"Understood." Charlie replied.

"Be as quick as you can." Lawrence said quietly. "I don't like relying on just one vehicle. We're a long way from civilisation up here. Call me on the radio when you are back on station outside."

"Roger that." Charlie replied before walking towards the exit. "Come on Sam... Ben. Your chariot awaits." He told them with a smile.

Back in the city centre, Ong and Tracey were strolling casually along the tree-lined boulevard when Ong's mobile phone began to buzz in his breast pocket.

"Sorry...It's my secretary in Bangkok" he explained. "She has instructions to only call me if it's urgent, do you mind if I take it?" Ong asked.

"No, of course not" Tracey replied. "I'm used to Bob and urgent phone calls and I'm sure your business never sleeps."

"Indeed, it doesn't" he replied as he lifted the phone to his ear. "Yes?" was all he said. There was a long pause as he listened to his secretary for several minutes, making only occasional yes and no responses.

"Problem?" Tracey asked when he finally switched his phone off again and thoughtfully put it back inside his jacket.

"Possibly...I'm not sure if I told you but the Black Marlin is in Darwin again. She needed some work done to one of her engines."

"No I don't think you mentioned it."

"Well it appears that some of the crew went out last night for drinks and one of them didn't make it back to the ship."

"Is that unusual?" she asked. "Darwin has lots of attractions for a young crewman."

"Going out for drinks is perfectly usual but staying away from the ship overnight in a foreign port is very much against ships rules. The crew of the Marlin are very well paid and very disciplined. The captain runs a tight ship so for one of them not to come back to the ship is especially unusual. They have made the usual enquiries at hospitals and with the police but to no avail."

"And your secretary thought that was important enough to bring to your attention?"

"Since the events in Darwin last time we were there, I gave her instructions that any incident involving the ship, should be reported to me immediately."

"I'm sure it's nothing to worry about" Tracey tried to reassure him. "You know what these young people are like when they've had a few drinks too many."

"I hope that's the case but I usually plan for the worst."

"What will happen now?"

"The Captain has reported the crew member as missing in mysterious circumstances and the police are looking into it. Also, my head of security in Bangkok, has already opened channels with the local Chief of Police, so I expect to get an update later today."

"Do you think Bob could help?" Tracey asked

"No, I want him to concentrate on his current task. And I'm sure it will all turn out to be something mundane. But in the meantime, how about some lunch? I know a lovely restaurant near here. My treat obviously!"

Chapter 13

London

As Bob and Joseph's plane was landing at London's city airport in the heart of Docklands, Commander George Abrahams was sitting in the office of his opposite number, Rear Admiral Reginald Fleming, in his plush office within the Ministry of Defence building in Westminster.

"It sounds like someone's dropped the ball in your records department, Reggie."

"I wouldn't go so far as to say that George." He replied confidently. "Even if your friend has got a copy of an Ultra document. There's nothing in there which tells the story. I've already checked the copy here."

"It's enough for them to fly all the way from Sri Lanka to see me."

"Which gives you the perfect opportunity to cut them off. And conclude the matter today."

"Whilst I am happy to help you clear up this mess, I have to say that I worked with Joseph Stein for a good few years. He won't be fobbed off easily."

"I'm sure he was a very competent officer when he worked with you but I am confident that you can spin your way out of this with him easily enough. Would you care for tea? Or perhaps coffee? I seem to remember you prefer that?"

"Coffee would be good. You're request for an early meeting has thrown my normal routine."

"Terribly sorry about that old chap. But I thought face to face on this one would be best."

"Never know who's listening into our calls these days..."

"Exactly. My security man tries to reassure me that all our systems are infallible. But the Chinese and Koreans have been pouring millions into their techies for years now."

"And the Americans are doing them same. They are our Allies, but even so..."

"Speaking of Americans. This Bob Dalton, who is involved in this thing. I've made some enquiries about him with our guys over in MI5 and 6. They knew his name straightaway. For some reason I can't quite fathom, he is very well respected amongst the intelligence community. So, I think he's the one we need to keep an eye on. He is the brains behind this enquiry, I'm sure."

"In that case, they will make a formidable team."

"I don't care." The Admiral replied forcefully. "They are poking their fingers into business which her Majesty's Government does not wish them to poke in. I strongly suggest you make it clear your friend Stein that the matter is closed and he should back off. And take his friend Dalton with him."

"What is this all about Reggie? You aren't really telling me much. Apart from you telling me to shut their enquiries down because it has national security interests."

"I'm afraid that's all I'm really allowed to tell you George. You going to have to take this one completely on trust. The Ultra classification is even above my pay grade. But word has come down from my boss that even this long after the event we don't want any outsiders looking into that Ultra memorandum. The best I can do is give you a copy of the document which they have, so you are not completely in the dark when they come to speak to you."

The Rear Admiral handed in a single sheet of paper with the word 'ULTRA' in bold type face across the top of it. Most of the words on the document had been redacted, apart from the first half-dozen lines.

"I don't think this is going to help me very much Reggie." George complained as he quickly read the copy. "Most of it is missing."

"That's all I've got old chap. As I told you it's above my pay grade. But word from on high is that this investigation of theirs stops today. That has been made abundantly clear to me."

"And if they don't want to stop their investigation?"

"If you can't persuade them George, I got the definite impression that the whole matter will be taken out of our hands. If you get my drift..."

"Really? That serious?"

"It seems so. Even though I haven't been given any more information than what I've told you, I'm pretty sure that your friends are poking their noses into a hornets' nest. If you can lean on your friendship with Mr Stein you might save him and Bob Dalton a good deal of inconvenience."

"Well I've cleared my diary for the rest of this morning. Then, once they arrive at the Yard I will use all my charm and persuasion. But like I said, unless Joseph has changed considerably this will not be an easy sell. And you told me that Dalton might be worse."

"When was the last time anyone gave you an *easy sell* George? They never give people like us the easy jobs to do. That's why we get paid the really big bucks. Isn't it?" He pointed out with a smile.

Two hours after landing in Docklands and following a slow taxi ride through the heavy morning traffic in London's congested streets, Bob and Joseph finally arrived outside the glittering tower block which housed New Scotland Yard.

"We're here to meet Commander Abrahams. He is expecting us" Joseph explained to the receptionist inside the heavily fortified lobby as he passed his business card across the desk.

"One moment, Mr...err...Stein" the receptionist replied as he glanced at the card. "I will need to speak to his office."

As the receptionist made the call, Bob and Joseph glanced left and right to take in the details surrounding them.

"Busy place" Bob noted.

"This is where all the Admin is done for the Met. Plus, most of the senior officers are based here too." Joseph explained as they watched the constant stream of staff passing through the security doors to access the buildings high speed elevators.

"Commander Abrahams is indeed expecting you gentlemen. If you would please take a seat over there, his secretary will come down to collect you shortly." The receptionist briefly pointed to a plastic bench near the outside windows before turning her attention to the next enquirer.

"Ok. Thank you very much" Joseph replied. Bob and he followed the instruction and turned from the desk to perch on one of the uncomfortable plastic sofas which populated the reception area.

Ten minutes later a young man approached them and asked.

"Mr Dalton and Mr Stein?"

"Yes" they replied together.

"If you would please affix these visitor badges to your lapel and follow me."

The young man led them through the security airlock, enroute to the elevators, whilst being carefully scrutinised by the heavily armed security officers standing nearby.

"Are we at a high alert status?" Joseph asked as they waited for a elevator.

"No more than usual, sir." he replied nonchalantly. "If you read all the security bulletins, they make it sound like every terrorist group in the world wants to blow us up in our offices or shoot us down as we leave the building. It's just the way life here is now. You get used to it."

"Very reassuring. I hope we don't look like Policemen." Bob whispered to Joseph as they stepped into the express elevator to the 12th floor.

"I'm afraid to tell you that we do, actually" Joseph replied with a smile. "But I'll keep you safe, Bob."

The elevator rose rapidly and when the doors opened on the 12th floor their escort said. "I must ask you to leave any and all electronic devices at this desk. The entire floor is classified as Secret. So, you have to leave everything here. Tablets, phones plus any sort of recording device. I hope that's okay..."

"It's fast becoming standard procedure these days." Bob said to Joseph as he took his two telephones from his pockets.

"It's the world we live in I suppose" Joseph replied.

"If that's everything gentleman? Please follow me this way." The young man instructed them as he swung open another heavy security door to reveal a long corridor beyond.

"You're very trusting" Joseph said to the escort as he passed through the doorway.

"I'm not actually. The door has a scanner built in. If you have any electronic devices an alarm would have gone off."

"That told you" Bob whispered as he walked alongside Joseph in the corridor.

"The Commander's office is right at the end of the corridor."

"With the best views, I assume?" Bob asked their guide.

"Actually no. All of the windows on the floor have been blocked off. Even the Commanders. Security, you see. He added over his shoulder as he walked along the corridor in front of them.

"I hope George hasn't been waiting for us long. Traffic was terrible on the way here" Joseph explained.

"He's only just arrived himself actually. But I understand that the Commander has cleared his diary for you for the rest of the morning. Would you like a tea or coffee to take in with you?" The secretary asked as they stepped through the door indicated and found themselves in a small windowless office. "This is my office" he explained when he saw the confused expressions they wore. "The Commander is through the other door."

"Oh, right. Yes... Coffee would be perfect." Bob replied.

"Still water for me" Joseph added.

"You can go straight in. I will bring your drinks through in a moment."

Following the secretary's instruction, Joseph opened the indicated door to reveal his old friend seated at a large desk. "Hello Joseph" Abrahams said as they walked into his office. "And this must be Mr Dalton?"

"Please call me Bob" he replied.

"Yes, Bob then. Of course, keeps it friendly. And you can call me George. So, Bob and Joseph please take a seat. I assume you've been offered tea or coffee?"

"Yes your... secretary is kindly getting us some."

"Good. Well while we are waiting for that to arrive I just need to get you to sign a copy of the Official Secrets Act."

"Pardon?" Bob spat out in a surprised voice.

"Just standard operating procedure you understand, Bob." Abrahams explained. "Since we are going to be discussing an Ultra Classified document."

"Which is what exactly?" Bob asked.

"As soon as you sign the forms I will tell you what I can. How does that sound?"

"It sounds like a normal bureaucratic nonsense." Bob replied tensely.

"Possibly. But you want to speak to me about a confidential document, and I need to be sure that the answers I give you, go no further than you two. So bureaucratic or otherwise I need you to sign the forms."

"Fair enough." Bob said with a shrug as he glanced at Joseph. "Rules are rules."

"Hopefully you can clear this all up quickly and easily." Joseph added.

"I hope so too." Abrahams said as he slid the documents towards them. "Ahh... And here's your drinks. Perfect timing."

"Did you bring your copy of the document with you? Abrahams asked, as he slid the signed documents into a folder and the secretary left his office.

"Yes, I have it here" Bob replied before taking an envelope from his inside jacket pocket. He removed the single sheet and carefully unfolded it before he passed the photocopy to Abrahams who quickly scanned through it.

"Yes. Right. It looks like somehow you have laid your hands on one of her Majesty's Government's secret documents.

"That much we had already figured out ourselves" Bob said.

"I don't recognise the 'Ultra' classification though. Joseph pointed out before Abrahams could respond to Bob.

"Indeed" Abrahams replied without moving his eyes from Bob. "Apparently, it was something they used during the war years. We don't use it these days which is why you wouldn't have seen it Joseph."

"But I don't really understand what it was doing in the bundle of documentation I picked up about the voyage of the treasure fleet that sailed in 1900. Can you explain that?"

"I'm not sure that I can Bob. I was over at the Ministry of Defence building this morning trying to find out exactly what this was all about. Just between the three of us, it's all a bit of an embarrassment for them. There's no way that document should have been released to you. Or anybody else actually."

"That's hard to believe, George." Bob replied. "I'm sure you are fully aware of the instructions about open government. It can't be necessary to keep it secret after all this time. Surely?"

"As I understand it from my friend in the MoD. All documents classified as Ultra are still excluded from public disclosure. Even having innocent possession of it is probably still a criminal offence."

"Bob didn't steal the document." Joseph pointed out. The MoD just gave it to him in amongst all the other papers that they had to give him. In accordance with the Public Disclosure guidance.

"I can guarantee you that I won't be pressing any kinds of charges against you or Bob for having the document. Especially now that I have reclaimed it on behalf of the MoD. But they have been doing some internal house cleaning over this matter. The supervisor who dealt with Bob has been placed on administrative leave, pending a full disciplinary procedure. And I understand that the young lady who actually did the photocopying, has already been fired. They are taking this breach of their security protocols very seriously, I can assure you that."

"But you are going to tell us what the document was about aren't you George? Joseph asked.

"I'm going to go out on a limb here, Joseph. As a big favour for when we worked together in the protection department. I still remember how you covered my arse on several occasions back then. So I will tell you this. The memorandum is from the First Sea Lord to the Prime Minister, Winston Churchill. I can also tell you that it concerns a secret operation that even to this day, very few people are aware of. Even the Admiral that I spoke to this morning, doesn't know the details. But I have it on the highest possible authority that the Ultra document has nothing to do with your search for the Commodore's fleet or anything it was carrying. That was made very clear to me and you can see for yourself that the date on the memorandum excludes any possible connection. Lastly, I want to impress upon you that any disclosure concerning the Ultra operation, would embarrass her Majesty's Government, so I must ask that you two to accept the facts and let the matter lie."

"That really isn't very helpful George." Bob replied. "We have very pressing reasons for tracking down all the information we can find about the Diadem and the treasure fleet. And that memorandum is the only clue that we have left to follow. My client has spent a lot of time and money trying to track down the cargo, which included a packing case full of jade statues. Our enquiries have led us all the way to Colombo and this memorandum is the last piece of the puzzle."

In that case, I'm afraid your clue is a dead end. I have been reassured that the Ultra memorandum has nothing to do with this *Diadem* or your treasure fleet. Or even jade statues. To be honest my man at the MoD knows nothing about any of those things. I'm afraid you've been led off course by this secret document, which you should never have had access to in the first place."

"Can you at least tell us what was on the rest of the memorandum?" Joseph asked. "Just in case the MoD is wrong? As you can see the bottom half is all blurred. We assume the copy got stuck in the machine, hence us only having the top half of the document. If you can tell us anything, it would be really helpful George." Joseph pleaded.

"As I said Joseph, the document has absolutely nothing to do with your enquiries. It was a complete fluke it was included with the other documents. I told you, people are getting the sack over this. It was a mistake. That's all. Hence, I don't have any more information to give you. But if I were to guess, it is something that Churchill did during the war which even after all these years, the Establishment wants to keep under wraps. As you know, for about a year it was touch and go whether the Allies were going to be overwhelmed. It's possible that Churchill overstepped his authority or issued some questionable orders. Did you know that he had an unenviable reputation for cutting corners?"

"I heard that" Bob replied. "But if we knew which corner he was cutting, maybe we can solve our own problem."

"There's nothing else I can tell you Bob. Honestly. So. unless you have any other questions I think our business here is concluded."

"Okay George." Bob replied. "I can see where you're going with this. But it would be really helpful if you could speak to your friend the Admiral, to see if we can get a full copy of the memorandum. Especially now that we've signed your official secrets document. If I can see the whole document, it will put my mind to rest and then I can tell my client, in all honesty, that I have made every and all possible enquiries, in relation to it.

"It's an unusual request, Bob. But in an effort to put your mind at rest, I will ask the Admiral and see what he says. Why don't we meet for lunch tomorrow at my club in Pall Mall. You've been their Joseph, haven't you? They do a fabulous beef Wellington."

"That would be splendid, George" Joseph replied. "Which should give you time to talk to the Admiral about Bob's request. We've have flown a long way to track this down and I don't want to go back empty handed."

"That's settled then" George said as he stood up and held out his hand. "Shall we say 12 noon for cocktails? If you make your way back to the reception desk they will give you your phones back. It's really good to see you again Joseph. Hopefully we can catch up and swap some old war stories tomorrow over a relaxed lunch. I'm sure you'll enjoy that too Bob."

As soon as Joseph and Bob had left his office the commander sat back in his desk and opened the file he was using. He took out the photocopy that Bob had given him and then another sheet of paper which the Admiral had given him and put them both side-by-side. Although the bottom half of Bob's copy was completely blurred the document still held more information than the one which the Admiral had given to George for his information. George's copy had been heavily redacted with only the two and from sections still legible.

"What is it that you are so afraid of Reggie? George asked aloud as he compared the two copies. "It looks like Joseph and Bob have gotten themselves into something seriously unpleasant. I know Winston Churchill came up with some very strange plans and decisions while he was in charge, which maybe the Establishment still don't wish to come to light. An assassination of Hitler maybe?" George shook his head and then replacing the documents inside the file, stood up and replaced it inside his personal safe in the office. He had been assured that one of the Admiral's lackeys would collect it from him later that afternoon. Then it would be the Admiral's problem. George had enough to worry about running his own department.

Chapter 14

Colombo

As soon as Sam, Ben and Charlie were seated back in the taxi, the driver shunted the van backwards and forwards until he was able to point it back downhill.

"This could be as exciting as flying your microlight" Charlie suggested as the van began the steep descent from the spa.

"You obviously haven't been up in one!" Sam replied as they bounced through the first monstrous pothole.

"But it's going to be totally safe, isn't it?" Ben asked Sam.

"I've been flying for years Ben. So yes, you will be totally safe."

"But you're in Sri Lanka." The driver interrupted them. "We have different standards from what you are used to. So, it's probably best to give all the equipment a very thorough check before you take off."

"Now he tells us!" Ben replied.

"He's right, guys" Charlie added. "I've seen a few sights in my time."

"Ha! You sound just like my father." Sam replied

"I prefer to get advice like that." Ben said. "I'm sure Stan would tell us that safety comes first every time. Just like when we're climbing."

"Stop worrying Ben. I will look after you. I know how to check the aircraft, my Dad made sure of that."

Ten minutes later Charlie said, "There's the sign for the microlights again."

"This is the place! Turn right here please." Sam told the driver. "Nearly there, Ben."

As it turned out, Sam was half right. It wasn't far in distance but the roadway was so uneven driver had to drive very, very slowly in order to avoid damaging the vehicle's suspension. "It would probably have been quicker on horseback." Charlie suggested as he looked at his watch.

"That would have suited me perfectly." Sam replied. "I am already missing my horse Nimby back at School."

"Horse riding is *not* one of my favourite activities either." Ben grumbled.

"You can't always have your own way Ben." Sam replied and gave him a friendly shove.

"This looks like the place" Sam said as they turned around yet another sharp bend in the road to see two microlight wings leaning casually in the grass of a manicured oblong field.

"I thought we would never find it" Charlie sounded exasperated. "Lawrence will think I've taken a long tea break."

The driver pulled to a stop next to the roadway where a wooden hut had been constructed. They noticed the sign on the roof which read 'Sunshine Flyers. Private runway. Customers only. Keep Out.'

"Private runway?" Ben asked aloud as he looked around the area. "Where?"

"I think you're looking at it Ben." Sam replied as she slid open the passenger door. "Come on let's go find out how much it costs."

"Listen," Charlie called to them as they walked away from the van. "I've really got to get back. I've already been gone a lot longer than I expected as it is. Just get them to call the spa when you're finished and I will come back to pick you up. Okay?"

"Yes that suits us perfectly" Sam replied. "We will be a couple of hours at least. Come on Ben it's a lovely day for a flight." She added as she looked up at the clear blue sky.

"You're sure about this Sam?" Ben asked as the minivan turned around and headed back along the trail. "If that's really the runway, I mean?"

"You don't need a concrete runway. Microlights are.... light. Trust me, you'll love it."

"Maybe they're fully booked..."

"Looking around I don't think they're that busy" Sam laughed as she walked towards the open door of the office. "But if they are, we can always go horse riding instead!"

Thirty minutes later, Sam had satisfied the manager and head mechanic of her qualifications to fly the microlight and carried out a thorough examination of the aircraft, explaining each check to Ben, who had followed her around like a faithful dog.

"Right! Time to get you a helmet and some overalls" Sam said to Ben at the end of the inspection and walked back to the hut.

"That was professionally done. The shop manager told them from his position sitting in a deck chair on the veranda which surrounded the hut containing the Sunshine Flyers office.

"Almost as if our lives depended on it..." Ben pointed out as they stepped onto the veranda.

"I never realised he was such a pessimist." Sam said to the manager.

"You'll be totally safe in her hands." The manager replied as he stood to his feet. "Your friend seems very competent." Looking Ben up and down he added "I guess you're a large..."

"And I'm a small" Sam said and then asked. "I don't suppose your helmets have intercom, do they?"

"Nothing but the best at Sunshine Flyers young lady." The manager replied with a grin as he handed her one of them.

In no time at all Sam and Ben had donned their matching yellow overalls and dark blue helmets and returned to the Microlight outside.

"Testing. Testing" Sam said into the helmet microphone.

"Loud and clear, Captain." Ben replied with a smile and a thumb's up sign.

"Climb aboard then shipmate. It's time we were airborne. You obviously take the back seat."

"Perfect place for me to keep an eye on you." Ben replied as he carefully took his seat behind the Pilot's position.

Sam took her place and they both settled themselves into the narrow fibreglass seats and attached the multipoint seat belts. Sam took hold of the microlight's control arm and swung it to lift the microlight's broad wing into horizontal. The manager pulled the chocks away from the microlight's undercarriage in preparation for their departure and then stood by the engine block.

"Ignition on" he shouted.

"Ignition on" Sam shouted back and held her thumb aloft to signal that she was ready. The manager placed both hands on the gleaming propeller blade and with a heave spun the blade around. The engine immediately coughed into life and the propeller blades became a silver blur as a blast of wind flattened the grass behind them. The manager quickly walked away from the aircraft as Sam pushed forward on the accelerator making the pitch of the engine's wine climb higher.

"Here we go" she said happily as the aircraft rolled forwards. "To the sky and beyond!"

"I'm as ready as I will ever be" he replied just before the microlight accelerated across the field towards the tall trees on the other side of the oblong.

As the microlight's speed rapidly increased across the surface of the grass, Sam pushed gently forward on the control arm. Seconds later the aircraft left the ground and climbed in a graceful arc to pass safely over the treetops on the outskirts of the airfield.

"That was easier than I expected" Ben said as he breathed a deep sigh.

"You haven't seen anything yet" Sam replied as she banked heavily to the right.

"Ooohhh..." Ben said as the aircraft leaned dramatically.

As they flew higher and higher, they could see the hundreds of terraces of the tea plantations which had been carved into the steep mountainside. They also flew over numerous winding trails and small roads which meandered through the plantations and the remaining forested land connecting the small villages which dotted the mountain.

After half an hour Ben said "I wonder what's on the other side of the mountain? More tea plantations perhaps?"

"Why don't we just find out" Sam replied.

"You're going to fly over the top?" Ben sounded surprised.

"We could go much higher than that if we wanted to."

"I think we are high enough already."

"Chicken" Sam replied as she once again accelerated the engine to climb higher and higher until they were level with the mountain peak.

"Look over there" Ben said as he tapped her on the shoulder

"A waterfall. It's beautiful" Sam replied.

"Can we go closer?"

"Of course," Sam replied as she swung the aircraft towards waterfall.

As they approached closer they both saw a huge expanse of water glinting at the base of the waterfall.

"Do you think it's a reservoir for the city?" Sam asked

"Unlikely. It's on the wrong side of the mountain. I can't imagine why they would put it on this side. No, I think it's just a natural lake. Very isolated up here of course. I can't see a village or even a house for miles around.

"It looks very tranquil" Sam replied as they flew high above the glittering surface of the water.

"Just like the spa I suppose."

"Oh my goodness. I totally lost track of the time" Sam said rapidly. "I think it's time we headed back. We've been gone hours."

"I'm sure the others are in any sort of hurry. Probably still having their sea salt body wraps." Ben suggested mischievously.

"You're terrible Ben Damo."

"But I suppose you're right. Come on we'd better turn back." Ben reluctantly agreed.

The decision made Sam put the microlight into a long sweeping turn, back towards the way they had come.

"Hang on!" Ben said suddenly as he stared downwards during the turn. "I can see something in the lake."

"Don't tell me...it's the Loch Ness monster?" Sam joked before she also looked downwards.

"Hardly. But have you ever seen anything natural shaped like that down there?" he replied pointing downwards.

"I can see it. You're right. There is something glinting below the surface."

"That's what I mean. It can't be anything natural."

"I'm going to drop down lower for a better look. Hold onto your helmet."

Sam put the aircraft into a steep turning dive and the airspeed picked up dramatically.

"You don't scare easily do you Sam."

"It's perfectly safe Ben. We're not going that fast."

"This is fast enough for me" he replied as they raced down towards the water surface.

Moments later, Sam pushed firmly forward on the control arm and reduced the engine speed so that the microlight slowed significantly as it levelled out and was then cruising at stall speed only 50 feet over the surface of the lake.

"It was somewhere around here, I think" Ben suggested as they retraced their bearing across the lake. "It's going to be hard to find it though... there's obviously no landmarks on a lake."

"There, there." Sam replied as they passed near the same spot.

"Amazing. You found it again. I saw it glinting" Ben replied, as Sam put the aircraft into a steeply banked turn for another pass over the sunken object.

As soon as they passed over it a second time, Sam put the aircraft into a tight flat loop to come back on an opposing bearing of 180 degrees.

"I'm not a hundred percent sure" Ben said after the third pass. "But if I was a gambling man, I would bet that there's a small plane sitting on the bottom of this lake."

"If the lake water wasn't so clear we would never have seen it."

"If we hadn't flown over the mountain to see the waterfall, we wouldn't have seen it."

"This is amazing. I wonder how long it's been down there?" Sam asked as she pulled the aircraft into a shallow climb away from the lake surface.

"A long time, I would guess since I haven't heard of many aeroplanes crashing in Sri Lanka lately.

"I bet James and Jasmine would love to know about a sunken aeroplane, don't you?"

"Only if it's filled with Spanish doubloons" Ben replied with a laugh. "But I think you've forgotten something..."

"I have?"

"Duhhh...we need to get back! Remember the sea salt wraps?"

"Oh right. Yes, of course you're right" Sam replied and once again turned the microlight around and began to climb rapidly towards the mountain's peak. "I suppose the mystery of the plane will have to wait for another day." Sam decided as she accelerated the motor again and the microlight gained height and speed away from the water. "Don't worry, I will have us back in no time. "

"Why don't you fly over the spa on the way back and we can give them a wave as we go by" Ben suggested.

"I think that's a great idea. So, yes sir, Captain." Sam replied and gave Ben a salute.

In the Bliss Spa two of Bonn's bodyguards, Dan and Lawrence, were speaking in hushed tones.
"I'm telling you that if Joseph was here, he would not be happy." Dan said.
"I'm not happy either" Lawrence replied. "But it's the best plan I can come up with."
"There simply aren't enough of us now. If anything happened..."
"Who are you worried about, Dan. The two old guys snoring by the pool or maybe the honeymoon couple. I can't see any of them hiding an AK-47 under their bathrobe."
"This whole place is wide open. Admit it, if we had sent a recce team here first, we wouldn't have come here. All those little pathways, secluded hidden alcoves and trees and bushes everywhere. And then Charlie taking Sam and Stan to the microlight place..."
"I couldn't send the taxi driver down there on his own, he would have wandered off somewhere for a cuppa. But if we do have a medical emergency our driver knows the roads around here like the back of his hand, or so he tells me anyway. He can get us to the hospital or back to the hotel in a hurry. Which is lucky, because the maps that I downloaded from the Internet only show half of these little trails through the forest. We're a bit off the beaten track up here."
"I know you've made the best of it Larry, I'm just saying it isn't ideal. Not that it often is..."
"We'll just have to cope. I must admit that Charlie getting a flat tyre on the way back from the microlight place wasn't

part of my plan. It leaves us one short to cover these gardens properly. But I've got to leave Roger in the lobby where he can cover our minivan and also monitor who arrives. So you and I are it out here, and Sandy is close in. Speaking of which I'd better check in with her. Pressing the small radio switch in the palm of his hand. " Sandy this is Lawrence. How you doing?"

"The massages have finished." Sandy responded calmly. "We are all going over to the sauna and steam rooms next. It's all very quiet. I haven't even seen any other guests."

"It looks like they have only got four other visitors at the moment." Lawrence told her. "Two at the pool, two in the snack bar. The gardens are empty apart from the staff."

"Will the radios work in the steam room?" Dan asked.

"I assume she will stay outside." Lawrence replied. "There's only one entrance door. As long as she's got a clear view of the doorway, Bonn will be safe enough.

"If we just had one more pair of eyes out here..."

"Well we don't! So off you go on your rounds. I will meet you back here in 15 minutes and then you can swap over with Roger okay?"

"You're the boss, Larry" Dan replied with a grin.

"Thanks for reminding me." He said before turning on his heel and heading back towards the lobby.

"My Dad's birthday is coming up in a few weeks' time and I want to do something really nice for him. Has anyone got any great ideas?" Bonn announced to the others sitting around her in the steam room. "He works all the time so he needs a break."

"Do you think he will be enjoying going out shopping with Tracey?" Izi replied.

"I'm sure he is. He often goes with me. But I bet he's got his phone with him. And I'm fairly sure that he will have had several calls from his secretary which just *had to be dealt with by him straightaway*."

"My Dad's just the same." Laura admitted

"And my Mum and Dad..." Stan added.

"I don't think my Mum gets any calls." Izi pointed out. "Apart from me of course."

"Do you think we will all be like that?" Bonn asked. "Once we leave school and start our own careers, I mean."

"I think it's the way things work nowadays." Stan replied. "If you want to succeed..."

"I don't intend to spend every waking hour working." Laura said firmly.

"I think I will have to since I'm going to run my own business." Izi said proudly.

"What sort of business?" Bonn asked.

"I'm going to set up a family business. Like your Dad and Sam's have done. And I will employ all my family, so that they all have good wages and nice homes."

"That sounds like a good plan, Izi." Bonn told her. "My dad's business started out really small. I think he and his brother had one stall selling T-shirts in Bangkok when he first started."

"And now look at him..." Izi replied dreamily. "We will have a company jet too."

"You certainly don't lack ambition, do you?" Stan asked with a smile.

"Ong told me I had to think big if I wanted to succeed. So I am. Are you going to help your Dad with his business Bonn?"

"I haven't really thought about it too much. He tried to talk to me about it last Christmas, but it's too far away for me to think about it to be honest. I need to pass my A-levels first and then I want me to go on to university."

"You could do a degree in business." Stan suggested.

"Maybe I will..." Bonn replied.

"I might do fashion." Laura suggested. "Or maybe performing arts. There are a couple of great universities in London that I was looking at."

"You're going to university? Izi asked.

"Of course. Why not? Aren't you?"

"I hadn't given it any thought. I guess it depends how successful my business is." Izi laughed loudly.

"I'm getting too hot." Bonn announced as she stood up. "I'm going to have an icy shower to cool off. But don't talk about me while I'm gone." She added with a grin as she stepped out the door.

"Sandy from Lawrence. Can you give me an update?" Lawrence asked on his radio. He waited a few seconds for a reply before saying. "Sandy, can you hear me?" he waited another few seconds before saying. "Dan from Lawrence."

"Yes, go ahead." Dan said.

"Can you go down to the sauna. Looks like Sandy's radio has packed up."

"I did tell you that they wouldn't work in there." Dan said smugly.

"Alright Smartass. I will congratulate you later but for now get down to the sauna and give me a SitRep."

"Understood. I'm not far away."

As Bonn followed the stone pathway around the corner to the showers, she failed to notice that Sandy was no longer in her position outside the door to the sauna. Bonn hummed quietly to herself as she turned on the shower and a cascade of cool water splashed over her head cooling her immediately. She closed her eyes and tilted her face skywards as the water rained down upon her.

As the water splashed noisily onto the tiled floor, it covered the almost silent footsteps of the two men who approached her. She was shocked when a pair of strong arms suddenly wrapped around her chest, pinning her arms to her sides. Then, before she had a chance to cry out a thick wad of cloth was clamped over her mouth and nose. She struggled vainly to loosen the grip and barely had the chance to think about the strange smell before the fumes from the noxious liquid-soaked cloth, filtered into her lungs and the chloroform rendered her unconscious. Moments later she slumped against the man who was holding her so tightly.

The second man bent down in front of her and Bonn's unconscious form was slumped across his slender shoulders. With a slight grunt, he then straightened up and turned on his heel before both men walked out of the back of the shower area and into the lush jungle beyond.

Thirty seconds later, Dan arrived outside the steam room and spoke rapidly into his radio. "She's not here Lawrence."

"Dan from Lawrence. Is that you?" Lawrence asked, confused by the incorrect radio syntax Dan had used.

"Yes. Sorry. But Sandy is not at her post outside the steam room."

"Check inside. Now!" Lawrence instructed him.

Dan pulled open the door to the steam room and stepped into the clouded room. "Is Bonn in here?" He asked the shadowy figures seated on the benches inside.

"No. She stepped out to go for a shower." Laura replied. "Why? What's wrong?"

"Nothing to worry about." Dan replied. "Just wait here a minute okay." He closed the door and ran along the short path to the shower area.

"Lawrence from Dan. I can't find Bonn either."

"Lawrence to team. We have a situation. Everyone stay off the air" He said into the radio. "Dan. Stay where you are. I'm coming to you. Charlie get the van ready for departure."

"Lawrence from Roger. I've just got back. Where do you want me?"

"Check the changing rooms. Maybe Bonn and Sandy went back there."

"Roger that" came the simple reply.

"Lawrence from Dan. Meet me behind the sauna. Not the steam room."

"I'm almost there Dan." Lawrence replied as he ran.

As Lawrence ran around the corner of the sauna, he found Dan kneeling down next to the lifeless form of Sandy.

"She's dead." Dan announced flatly as he heard Lawrence arrive behind him.

"Bonn?" Lawrence asked.

"They must have taken her."

"Who's that?" Lawrence asked pointing at another body half laying in the flowering border.

"I guess there must have been two of them. Maybe more. She killed that one though." Dan replied without changing his position. "Must have taken her from behind."

"Fast and silent" Lawrence said as he looked down at her body. "She didn't get a chance to push the Emergency button on her radio before they killed her."

"Looking at the marks around her neck, I'd say she was strangled. The guy who did this is very strong. She got the first one though."

"What about Bonn?" Lawrence asked, scanning the surrounding ground for signs of her struggle.

"No sign of her here or the showers. I checked there first."

"Shit." Lawrence said before pressing his radio button. "All units. Sandy is down. Charlie, have you checked the changing rooms yet?"

"They're empty" Charlie replied immediately.

At that moment, the sound of an aircraft passing overhead broke the tense atmosphere. Lawrence and Dan automatically looked up to see the bright yellow wing of a microlight pass above them. As they watched the aircraft tilted to perform along slow turn above the spa and both the occupants began to wave vigorously.

"It's Ben and Sam" Lawrence said. "They've got a perfect view from up there."

Dan's mind whirred then he said. "If only we could contact them. They might be able to see who's taken Bonn."

"I was thinking the same thing. Maybe we can override their helmet comms." Lawrence replied. "Try to contact them. Go through all the channels on your radio. Quick before they fly away." Lawrence told him before he then spoke into his radio. "Charlie meet us at the rear of the sauna. Bonn's been snatched by an unknown number of kidnappers."

Moments later Stan walked around the corner and quickly scanned the scene. "Is she dead?" He asked as he stared down at Sandy's body.

"I'm afraid so." Lawrence replied and positioned himself between Stan and the bodies. "You and the others need to get changed..."

"What about the man in the bushes?" Stan asked trying to peer around Lawrence.

"He's dead too."

"Did he have a fight with your bodyguard?"

"I'm sorry Stan, but we're really busy now. Can you do me a favour and organise the others and get them back to the changing rooms. I will meet all of you in there and explain everything, okay?"

"Do you want me to call the police?" Stan asked.

"Not right now. Just get everyone back into their street clothes and I will meet you outside the changing rooms."

"You know that Bonn isn't in the sauna, don't you?"

"Yes, I know. Now off you go. I will meet you in a few minutes."

A range of emotions passed across Stan's face before he did as Lawrence had asked and returned to the sauna to collect his friends.

As Stan disappeared, Dan tapped Lawrence on the shoulder. "I've got them. On channel 52. But the signal is really bad."

Lawrence pulled out his radio and quickly changed the channel setting. "Hello Sam, can you hear me?" he said into his radio.

"Just about" Sam's cheerful voice replied.

"I don't know how to say this to you. But we think some men have taken Bonn. We can't find her in the spa. Can you do a few circles around the spa area and let me know if you see anyone running away. Or a vehicle nearby?"

"Can you repeat that? I think I misunderstood." Ben replied sternly.

"Bonn's been kidnapped and I want you to look for her from up there. Understand?"

"What are we looking for?" Sam asked her voice fading in and out as the signal changed.

"I assume they have a car nearby. They can't be expecting to take her far on foot. Can you see any other roads from up there."

"I wasn't really paying any attention before. But we will do it now."

"The radio signal probably won't reach very far, so if you see anything at all, fly back over where the spa building is, so you can talk to me."

"Understood" Sam said. "I'll be right back." Then as Lawrence watched, the Microlight banked sharply left and began to turn a lazy circle in the sky above him.

"What you want me to do?" Dan asked.

"You wait here. Charlie and I will search the rest the gardens and the buildings just in case. But I don't hold out much hope for it. My gut tells me she's been taken into the jungle, back at the showers. Plus, I've got to organise the rest of the kids."

Two hundred feet above the spa, Sam and Ben began their frantic search of the surrounding forest, looking for any sign of Bonn and her attackers or the vehicle Lawrence had anticipated. It was on their second loop high above the treetops that Ben's sharp eyes found what they were looking for. "Look there. Right below us. He called into the headset and pointed downwards. "It's a small van or maybe a car. I saw the sunshine glinting off the roof."

"Hang on. I will swing us around again. I didn't see a road..."

"Nor did I. But there has to be one. Because I definitely saw a car down there. It's probably covered over by the thick tree coverage."

"There it is!" Ben said, as Sam flew over the same spot again. "It's a brown van. And there's people getting into it right now. That could be them."

"Hello, hello, Lawrence. Can you hear me?" Sam said into the radio and waited nervously for his reply.

"We must be too far away, Sam" Ben said when there was no immediate reply. As he spoke he craned his neck to keep an eye on the getaway vehicle.

"I'll have to fly closer to the spa to tell them we've spotted them."

"Then we will lose sight of the car when it moves off. We won't know where they take Bonn."

"But Lawrence said..."

"I think we should try to follow them if we can. Can you do that? Maybe go much higher to make sure they don't hear us? Lawrence will soon figure out what we are doing, when he sees you stop circling."

"And then what? It's not like they can drive through the jungle to catch up to them. I can't see a road running from the spa to the van...can you?"

"No, I can't. But we will have to play it by ear Sam. The important thing is for us to stay with the van. They probably don't even know that we are up here watching them. Then if we get an idea which direction they are going on the road, we could come back to tell Lawrence that."

"I agree. But we'd better not lose them."
"Come on. It's up to us now."

"I can't see the microlight anymore." Dan said into the radio.
"They'll be back around in a few minutes." Lawrence replied. "I've given Ong the bad news and he's calling the police. We are to stay here and secure the scene unless our flying friends find the kidnappers. They're Bonn's only chance now."
"Where can they be going?" Sam asked, as she guided the Microlight high above the van. I thought they would head back towards the city. There's nothing up here but jungle."
"Maybe they have a stash house up here in the middle of nowhere...or maybe they've got a helicopter up here. They're certainly in a hurry and seem to know where they're going."
"That looks like the end of the road." Sam pointed downwards.
"And the van has stopped." Ben replied
"I can't see a helicopter waiting for them. This must be where they are taking her."
"They are carrying somebody out of the car. That's got to be Bonn. There must be a property hidden down there."
"I think we should tell Lawrence where they are." Sam insisted.
"I agree. We won't see much more through this thick tree cover and we don't want them looking up and seeing us, now we know where they are."
"Let's get back to the spa quickly and see what he wants us to do." Then she put the microlight into a sharp turn, back towards the Bliss Spa.

"Hello Lawrence. Can you hear me?" Ben asked.

"Yes, just about. Go ahead" Lawrence replied.

"We've found her." Ben said. "They put Bonn into a van and drove further up the mountain to their hideaway. There's a small dirt track at the rear of the spa. We saw them take her out of the van and carry her into the jungle. Then we came straight back to tell you."

"How far is the van from the spa and what direction?" Lawrence asked as he ran to the minivan to check his maps.

"It's probably only about 2 miles from the spa. Almost due north from you."

"Well done you guys. I can see the road you're talking about on my map. We'll take it from here. You had better take the microlight back to the runway. We will pick you up from there."

"I found this rag in the undergrowth near the showers." Dan said as he walked up to Lawrence. "It still stinks of chloroform. That must be why no one heard her cry out."

"After they took out Sandy. It must have taken at least two of them to attack her. She killed the guy in the bushes, but didn't see the one that came up behind and strangled her. And then one or two to take Bonn in the showers. It might have been the same guys."

"Had to be. We couldn't have missed four or five guys following us into the Spa, could we? It's a single road..."

"They must have come up through the jungle and been in the bushes near the steam room waiting for Bonn to come out."

"But nobody knew we were coming here. Not even us, until this morning. That's not enough time to organise a kidnapping."

"I agree. And they must have killed Sandy before Bonn came outside. How would they know she would come out to use the showers alone? It doesn't add up that Bonn was the target..."

"Maybe she wasn't. Could it have been a random snatch? And Bonn just happened to be in the wrong place at the wrong time?"

"I'm not jumping to any conclusions right now." Lawrence decided. "Either way, we need to find them and get her back. Right now." At that moment, Charlie and Roger arrived in the lobby and Lawrence filled them in, on what Ben had told him. "Dan and I are going to go with the taxi driver to see if we can find this van and hopefully where they are holding Bonn. I want you to guys to secure this scene until the police arrive and keep an eye on the rest of our guests. Stay in radio contact. We will call you once we find the car."

"I don't like the idea of just flying away and leaving Bonn with those men." Ben said into his head set.

"Me neither" Sam said. "But what else can we do?"

"Have we got enough fuel to fly us back to where the van is parked? I've got an idea."

Sam looked at the fuel gauge, which was hovering just about the red warning line. "Only just." She replied. "But then we have to head straight back to the landing field."

"A few minutes later they found the spot where the van was parked, again.

"Here's my idea" Ben said as they passed high over the spot. "If you could land on the road behind the van, I could follow their trial through the jungle to find the house. You could wait by the car van when bodyguards arrive you could tell them what I was doing. How does that sound to you?"

"You want me to land on that bit of dirt track?"

"The others all told me you're a fantastic pilot. And that you can land anywhere. You managed to land on the tepuy easily enough, they said."

"The first time was the scariest landing I have ever done."

"So, landing on a road must be much easier..."

"On a real road, yes. But that's not much more than a stony path. At least on the tepuy I had plenty of space..."

"I'm sure you can do it Sam. I really think we should try to do it..."

"Alright. Let's go back around so I can have a better look at it."

A few minutes later, the microlight was flying above the dense green canopy which partially obscured the small road. Sam examined the roadway, looking for a possible landing spot.

"There's just not enough room to get the microlight down there, Ben." She assured him. "The branches are overhanging the road too much. I simply can't land down there. It's impossible."

"Take us back around again" Ben insisted. "I've got another idea."

"I can't wait..." Sam replied, as she once again banked the aircraft in a steep turn.

"Look back down the road. See that section over there...where the trees have just been chopped down?"

"They're probably going to have another tea plantation there."

"Yes, but right now it's the only bit of flat ground for miles around. Is that little patch of open ground big enough for you to land on."

"It might just be big enough." Sam admitted. "You need much more space to take off than land. But if I put it down there, we could never take off again."

"We can worry about that later. I'm sure the company won't mind in the circumstances. They will just have to come and tow it away somehow."

"It is a real emergency, I suppose." Sam replied absently as she tried to assess the length of the field. "I will only get one go at this you realise" she warned Ben.

"I'm ready when you are" he said tightening is seatbelt. "Oh, one more thing...I want you to turn off the engine..." Ben asked quietly.

"Turn off the engine?" Sam's voice had risen an octave.

"They are bound to hear us, if we don't..."

Sam shrugged and flipped the 'kill' switch before she had a chance to reconsider. The engine died immediately and the only sound was the wind as their speed dropped. Putting the aircraft into a glide slope she headed straight at the open area. The undercarriage barely brushed through the leaves of the last of the tree tops, before she pointed the microlight downwards and the ground rushed up to meet them. At the very last second, she flared the wing to make a perfect landing on the patch of ground not much bigger than a garden. The landing gear had no brakes and the small aircraft slid and bounced as it hurtled towards the trees on the other side of the clearing. Ben gripped the sides of the seat fiercely, his eyes fixed on the fast approaching tree line.

"I don't think we're going to make it." Sam squeaked.

Suddenly the microlight's undercarriage struck a wet, muddy section of ground and stopped dead, pitching the wing forward so that its tip buried in the ground, throwing Sam and Ben hard against their safety belts.

"Sam. You did it." Ben gasped as he quickly unclipped his belt. "Are you okay?"

"I think so. But I don't think the owners are going to be happy with the state of their aircraft."

"It was an emergency landing Sam. I'm sure they will understand."

"Well we're hear now. Let's get after Bonn."

"I told you. You have to stay here Sam, so you can point Lawrence in the right direction when he arrives."

"Whilst you do the dangerous bit of catching the criminals, I suppose."

"I'm not going to confront them. And I have done this sort of thing before Sam." He said as he took his helmet off and handed it to her. "You do your bit and I'll do mine. And he set off at a fast trot back towards the roadway. Sam watched him disappear along the road and then around the trees. She took one more glance at the microlight before she too set off towards the road to intercept Lawrence.

She actually had to wait longer than the expected ten minutes, it was almost half an hour before Lawrence arrived in the minivan to find her waiting at the side of the track.

"You didn't go back to the runway like I told you then?" Lawrence asked as they drew to a stop. His anger was evident. "Where's the van?"

"The van is a couple of hundred yards further up the road. I had to make an emergency landing.

"Where's Ben? Don't tell me he's hurt?"

"No. He's fine in fact he's gone after the kidnappers."

"What?" Lawrence snapped. "I don't believe this." he added shaking his head. "Just jump in and show us exactly where the van is."

Sam did as she was asked and the minivan set off once again uphill.

"I had to turn the engine off. Ben didn't want to alert them that we had found them."

"The only sensible thing you've done" Lawrence replied without looking at her.

"We're almost there...I think" Sam informed him.

"Ok. Stop here." Lawrence told the driver. "We will go on foot. And no noise. Ben's right, they could be nearby still."

Lawrence, Sam and Dan exited the minivan and jogged along the track. They turned left and right following the narrow track through the forest. All eyes were fixed ahead. After a few minutes, they found the van abandoned in the middle of the track. "This is the car we followed" Sam said.

"So where is Ben?" Dan asked as he carefully opened the van's door to peer inside.

"I'm guessing he followed them into the forest." Sam said from behind them.

"But which way did he go? I can't see any paths leading from here. It's a dead end." Lawrence pointed out.

"I have no idea" Sam replied. "But if anyone can follow them through these trees it will be Ben. That's his job."

"His job?" Lawrence asked.

"He's a wildlife ranger. In the Congo. He has to track poachers in the National park. So I guess he's following the kidnappers tracks."

"But where is he now?" Lawrence's frustration was evident in his voice. "I need to tell Ong what's going on." Lawrence added as he pulled his telephone from his pocket.

As soon as he had finished updating Ong, Lawrence then dialled Joseph Stein in London.

"Hello boss. I know it's late there, but I knew you would want the bad news straightaway."

"Oh. Hello Lawrence. What's happened?"

"Bonn's been kidnapped..." Lawrence went on to give a full explanation of everything that had happened at the spa as far as he understood it.

"And they killed Sandy?" Joseph asked as he tried to control his emotions.

"Strangled, we think. But it looks like she managed to kill one of them too before she died."

"I don't think we'll be able to get out of London until first thing in the morning." Joseph replied as his thoughts churned.

"The sooner you can get here the better, Boss. I know the contingency plan to deal with a kidnapping was to keep it amongst ourselves. But with two murders, the police obviously had to get involved. Ong's called them himself."

"Yes, you're right. But I will ring Ong now and discuss it with him. Keep it tight until I can get back there, Larry. I think the airport opens at 6am, so with any luck the plane's crew can have the jet ready to take off before seven. Either way I will call you once I know."

"We have to go back to Sri Lanka." Joseph explained to Bob, as soon as he finished the call and then explained why.

"Chasing down lost documents just became totally irrelevant." Bob replied. "We will need to call the Commander too and cancel our lunch appointment. After you've called Ong. Better put it on speaker, he will probably want to speak to both of us about this."

"I should have been there..."

"No point trying to second guess what might have been at this stage. Let's get Bonn back first. We can start worrying about blaming people once she's safe."

PART THREE

Chapter 15

Jakarta

Having seen Jannie off on the Prinsloo Industries cargo plane, Bill and Miriam had boarded their own flight. As soon as they landed, they had gratefully begun their well-earned holiday by driving to a small villa overlooking the bright blue sea just north of Brisbane, Queensland. Unexpectedly, soon after unpacking their suitcases, Bill's phone buzzed on the table next to him.

"Is that Bill Phillips? A strange voice asked

"Yes, it is. Who is this?" Bill asked.

"It's James McLeod. From the Trident in Darwin. I hope you remember me?"

"Yes of course I do James. How are you?"

"Actually, I'm not good. Not very good at all to be honest with you. Which is why I'm ringing you. To warn you that you are probably in serious danger."

"Danger?" Bill asked as he automatically looked around his luxury surroundings. "Me? What are you talking about?"

"Yes. You, Miriam and Jannie. And probably the others on the boat too."

"The boat? I don't understand…"

"Okay. Yes, I'm not making myself very clear. I should have started at the beginning."

"That's usually the best place..."

"Yeah, I know. Sorry. Do you remember that I had to hide my silver bars from the Black Marlin in a warehouse? So that those gangsters wouldn't rob me?"

"Yes I remember that."

"Well I got robbed anyway. And the guy that stole them, killed Mr Sunglasses and a security guard to do it."

"Mr Sunglasses? You mean your crewmen that we didn't like?"

"Yes, him. He was killed by the same guy that broke into the Dream Bar and shot my friend the Padre in the knee. I think I told you about that?"

"Yes, you did" Bill replied, obviously still confused. "But why does that put us in danger?"

"I think the same killer is coming after you next. To steal your bars and the jade statues too.

"Why do you think that? I haven't heard anything about him..."

"I think that's because he tracked us down first. The Padre, Jasmine and me, I mean. And he sank the Trident."

"Slowdown James. This doesn't make any sense. He tracked you down and sank the Trident?"

"Yes. I'm sorry. I need to explain myself better. I'm a bit shaken up, to be honest. It's like this, a few days ago this killer attacked us on the Trident. We were diving off the north coast of Java. I don't know how he found us but he tortured the Padre for information and once he had all the answers he wanted, he scuppered the Trident with the Padre and me still onboard."

"What about Jasmine?" Bill asked.

"He kidnapped her and took her away with him on his boat. And I haven't been able to contact her since…"

"Oh my God. But you're okay now?"

"Only just. Luckily, the water where he sank us wasn't very deep, so the stern of Trident struck the bottom. So that she was standing straight upright. I was in the stateroom, which meant that I was only thirty or so feet below the surface when we struck the bottom. I managed to break myself free just before I ran out of air. Sadly, I couldn't save the Padre..."

"The Padre? He's dead?"

"He drowned. I watched him struggling right to the very end. Right before my eyes. I eventually broke the arm off the chair that I was tied too and escaped just before the sharks arrived. Luckily, one of the emergency rafts had floated to the surface and I managed to climb into that."

"I can't believe it...you're lucky to be alive by the sounds of it...But why do you think that we're in danger too?"

"This maniac tortured us to tell him what he wanted to know. He wanted information about what we had recovered from the Diadem. And about the Black Marlin. and everybody involved. He wants everything for himself. It seems logical that he could be coming after you next. He might even be in Darwin already. You have to warn everybody else for me. Yours was the only number I could remember, so I rang you as soon as I could get to a phone. To warn you."

"Stop right there James. I'm going to connect us to Owen Strasser. He's my boss and he needs to hear this too." Bill tapped a few buttons on his phone and Owen's voice came on the line.

"Hello Bill. I'm surprised to hear from you so soon. I hope you're enjoying your holiday..."

"Owen, I've got some serious news. James McLeod is on this conference call and he just told me that there is a vicious killer searching for the Diadem's silver and jade. A couple of days ago, he kidnapped Jasmine and tried to kill James. His friend the Padre was murdered. James thinks that the killer may be trying to track down everyone else involved, because he wants to steal all the treasure that we found aboard the Diadem."

"Okay Bill. You've got my attention. I'm listening."

"Right...Ok. Now James, continue with your story, will you." Bill asked him.

"Once we had told him what he wanted to know, the guy opened the stopcocks on the Trident and left me and Padre to drown. He left us tied to a couple of chairs while he took Jasmine with him on his boat. I think he intends to use her to gain access to our safety deposit box in Jakarta, where we left the money we got from selling the bars. He may already have done it. Like I told Bill, I've been unable to reach her by phone."

"When did this all happen?" Owen asked.

"A couple of days ago..." James replied as he remembered the time he spent in the life raft. "I managed to get myself free from my bonds and swim to the surface but I couldn't get to the Padre before his breath ran out. I had to watch him die. But once I'd clambered into my life raft I was still stuck in the middle of an empty ocean. Far off most shipping routes. I was very lucky to be picked up by a passing freighter who happened to see me when it did. Then, as soon as I could get a phone I knew I had to ring you. This guy is a killer. Stone cold. And he wants to get the rest of the treasure. I'm sure he will be looking for Jannie and his parents. And all the others too."

"Have you informed the police about what happened?" Owen asked.

"Bill was my first call, after I failed to get hold of Jasmine. They are going to be my very next call. But how much help they will be, I'm not that sure."

"I'm not sure either." Owen replied. "Dealing with murder, torture and kidnapping is a specialist operation. I don't know if the Indonesian Police are up to that. Can you give us a detailed description of this killer."

"Nothing that is going to be helpful. He looks very normal. He doesn't have any tattoos or scars on his face."

"Anything you can remember might be helpful" Owen reassured him.

"I suppose he was about my height, a little under 6 feet." James replied. "Slim, but muscular. Not overdeveloped. More athletic looking. Light brown hair, shortish. Ordinary, like I said. He would blend in amongst any Eurasian crowd."

"Well if you think of anything distinctive tell Bill straightaway." Owen replied. "I need to make some phone calls myself now. Bill, can you get a number where we can contact James and I will ring you both back in an hour. Good luck with the Police, James. And hopefully Jasmine is fine." And with that, Owen left the conference call.

"Where are you right now by the way?" Bill asked. "I need to be able to ring you back in an hour."

"I'm in the docks, outside Jakarta city. But I need to get to the bank to see if he's been there with Jasmine. I'm going there before I try to involve the Police."

"I understand that. Call me from there before Owen rings back. Can you do that for me?"

"I should be able to. Gotta go now..."

As soon as he had cut off the call to Bill and James, Owen quickly considered the new information and how it might affect his plans for the safety of Jannie, who was currently driving his buggy with Mr. Smith and Mr White somewhere near the Zaire border. Having decided that Jannie was currently almost untraceable he first dialled the number for Bob Dalton.

"Hello Owen." Bob said as he picked up the phone. "I'm afraid you've caught me at an awkward time."

"Possibly, but I'm sure you're going to want to hear what I have to tell you Bob. You're in Colombo right now with the kids, aren't you?"

"The kids are. But I had to come back to London. With Joseph Stein.

"Bonn's bodyguard?"

"Yes, he's with me right now."

"In London?" Owen sounded confused. "That's probably not a good thing."

"You don't know the half of it." Bob replied. "But I really can't talk at the moment. We're in the middle of a bit of a crisis."

"Even so, you have to hear this Bob. Because Laura and the others may be in considerable danger."

"What? Why?"

"I've just been speaking to James McLeod. Remember the diving guy from the Trident? Seems he was attacked on his boat by a professional killer who left him for dead. The guy kidnapped Jasmine and James thinks he might be coming after the Black Marlin next and everyone who was on board."

"Jasmine's been kidnapped? When did this happen?"

"A few days ago. James was only just picked up from the ocean. He's lucky to still be alive. He phoned to warn Bill and Miriam as soon as he could reach a phone."

"I'm afraid your warning is an hour too late Owen. We've just heard that Bonn Thakkrani has been kidnapped on the island. And one of her bodyguards was killed at the same time. From what you've just told me, it's got to be the same guy behind it..."

"Is there anything I can do?" Owen asked as he considered this new information and how it might affect Jannie.

"I'm not sure. We have to get the first flight back there in the morning. It's going to take most of the day to fly back there. But I will call you when I can. I will need to update Ong about what you just told me. So, I've got to go Owen."

"Good luck to you." Owen managed to reply before Bob switched off. He thought for a few moments before dialling Johann's private number to tell him the bad news.

Chapter 16

Republic of South Africa

After several hundred miles of rough roads, Jannie's brightly coloured buggy was now covered in a thick layer of dust. They were happily speeding along another section of countryside road, heading roughly South and East, when Mr Smith's telephone unexpectedly burst into a loud version of Wagner's Ride of the Valkyrie.

"Hello Owen." Smith said as he had recognised the caller ID. "Since we agreed that I would call you once we got to the orphanage, I assume you've got some bad news for me?"

"It may be nothing." Owen replied through the satellite phone. "Can you hear me Ok? I can hear a lot of road and wind noise."

"We are making the most of the good roads" Smith answered sarcastically as Mr White steered around another huge dip in the road. "And there's nothing wrong with my ears. Just don't try whispering."

"I won't" Owen replied, raising his voice automatically anyway. "I just received some information and I thought I should pass on to you. Just in case."

"I'm listening..."

"When Jannie and his friends were in Darwin a while back, they were involved with a man called James McLeod, on a treasure hunt."

"Yes, I know the name. Jannie told us all about his adventures finding silver and some jade statues. McLeod sounds like a real old-fashioned adventurer."

"Well it seems that James has recently picked up a very bad enemy too. And there's a connection to Jannie and all of the people who were on board the Black Marlin."

"How is this guy a threat to us?"

"This enemy tracked down McLeod's boat in the middle of nowhere, murdered his partner, sank the Trident and almost drowned McLeod while he was doing it. Plus, he kidnapped McCloud's girlfriend. Who is still missing. That's where my guesswork comes in. I think that there's a good chance that the guy will now be coming after the other people involved in recovering the treasure.

"Including Jannie...?" Smith suggested.

"Including Jannie. In your present circumstances, I think it's a long shot. But I think in view of this guy's obvious ruthlessness and talents, it's best that I informed you in any event."

"What's the guy look like?"

"I'm afraid I can't help you very much with a description that would be of any help to you. Primarily because McLeod described the killer as being of ordinary height, weight and age. No distinguishing marks whatsoever. From what McLeod told us happened, the guy sounds like a professional too, so he can probably change his appearance to suit himself, anyway."

"That's really not very helpful Owen. You want me to be on the lookout for a man who fits the description of 25% of the population..."

"I understand that. But something in my bones told me to pass it on to you anyway."

"Okay Owen. Consider it passed on."

"Where are you now, exactly?"

"About a hundred miles south of the border. Our plane landed without incident in Zaire yesterday and we drove south to the border post. Jannie has been his usual inquisitive self, so White and I have almost run out of war stories to tell him."

"I doubt that." Owen replied with a laugh. "Any problems at the border?"

"The only problem we had, was waking up the guards."

"I like those kind of problems."

"They made a fuss of carefully checking our passports and noting down all the details. But I'm not sure any of them could actually read."

"Still no computer system, I assume?"

"Nope. It was just as we discussed. Apart from the fact that they didn't even have biros. Pencil and paper was the best they could manage."

"I love it when a plan comes together." Owen reminded him. "No chance of anyone crosschecking your details on a central database...just like the old days."

"Jannie's old passport worked a treat too. We looked the part. Just three dust covered guys crossing over to find work in South Africa."

"How is the buggy holding up?"

"Surprisingly well on these unmade roads. Our boy Jannie did a great job constructing it. And the extra fuel tank you put in for us, means we are not worried about running out of fuel in between petrol stations. They are a bit sparse in this part of the world, you know."

"Another of my brilliant ideas." Owen responded proudly.

"Well I wouldn't go that far... And we did have to pay a 500 Rand fine."

"Why?"

"You know the guards have to come up with some way of extracting cash from anyone passing through their outpost."

"500 Rand? They must have thought you looked rich."

"It's just the price of doing business, Owen. We kind of expected it actually. And this route was much safer than coming through one of the major entry points."

"I'm sure will be on your expense account" Owen laughed. "When do you think you will reach the orphanage?"

"If we keep going the way we are, will be there sometime late tonight. I assume you still haven't told them we are coming?"

"No. I still want to keep it on a need-to-know basis."

"Fair enough. I will have to tell White about this new guy on our trail at our next stop, but for now going I'm to pass you across to Jannie, he wanted to talk to about something anyway."

"Hello Owen." Jannie's voice sounded cheerful.

"I hope you're not driving." Owen responded reprovingly.

"No Mr White is taking his turn at the moment. Always safety first, Owen."

"You're sounding like Stan again. But I haven't got time to idle chitchat, this call is costing me a fortune."

"Okay, I'll be quick. I was wondering... I know you want to keep my trip to Jo'Burg a secret, but once I am there will it be okay for me to ring my friends in Colombo? I want to catch up with all the news and how their tropical holiday is going."

"Well since you brought it up. That might be a problem." Owen replied ominously. "I'm afraid your friends have got themselves wrapped up in a serious problem."

"What's happened? Is somebody hurt?"

"I'm not sure of all the details yet. Obviously, I can only pass on what I have been told. But it appears that your friend Bonn has been kidnapped."

"Kidnapped? Surely that's impossible. She's got bodyguards..."

"I gather there was some breakdown in the protection. Not sure exactly. But one of the bodyguards was killed by the kidnappers."

"I can't believe it..."

"But the rest of your friends are fine."

"But Bonn...? That's terrible Owen. Are you going to help get her back? You know, like you did in Venezuela? Do you need Mr Smith and Mr White to go there? is that why you called? I'm sure I will be safe in the orphanage with Theo."

"No, I don't think that will be necessary. I'm sure that a man like Mr Thakkrani has access to all the resources he might need. I think it's better to leave your two companions with you while you are in Jo'Burg. JP will feel better if we leave arrangements just the way they are at the moment."

"Is that what you were talking to Mr Smith about?

"Yes. Even though there's no danger to you, I like to keep all my people informed of what's going on. And to get his views on the incident."

"I didn't hear him say much" Jannie queried.

"Once he's had time to think about what I told him, I'm sure we will have a longer discussion once you arrive at the orphanage, probably while you are telling the boys all about your own adventures around the world."

"I'm really looking forward to it, Owen. And I'm sure there are some new arrivals to meet too. You know that Theo has a constant stream of boys who need his help, arriving at the orphanage."

"Indeed I do. But that's enough chatting for now. Enjoy your drive to Jo'Burg, I remember the scenery across the veldt as being spectacular. Particularly at this time of year. Another chance of a lifetime for you."

"The view would be much better if my goggles weren't constantly covered in dust." Jannie replied.

"That's all part of the experience." Owen joked. "I will talk to you again tomorrow."

"Okay. Bye Owen. Do you want to speak to Mr Smith again?"

"No that's fine. I will talk to him tomorrow too. So just hang up the phone."

Jannie handed the phone back to Smith and immediately began to interrogate him and White about how they would plan a hostage rescue operation for Bonn.

"It's complicated..." Smith replied with a shrug.

"But it will give us something to talk about" Jannie insisted. "We've still got a long way to go before I get home."

Chapter 17

The Tracker

As Lawrence waited with Dan and Sam by the suspects van, his frustration and impatience began to show.
"I know it's hard to wait" Sam said to him.
"I feel I should be doing something. Not just standing in the middle of nowhere, doing nothing. Once the police arrived at the spa, I should be there to brief them." Lawrence replied as he looked at his watch.
"Charlie and Roger can handle that Larry" Dan reminded him. "This is where we need to be right now."
"It's going to be dark soon. Sam said as she looked towards the setting sun. "Just wait until then. I'm sure Ben will be back with some good news."
As soon as she finished speaking, Ben stepped silently from the bushes in front of them.
"You're back" Sam said unnecessarily
"Did you find her. Lawrence asked. "Is she alive?"
"No. I didn't." Ben replied as he walked up to them. "Their trail through the jungle was easy to follow though. It continued almost straight upwards from here. There were at least three of them I think. One in front to force the route, one carrying Bonn and one following behind. I lost the trail at a deep ravine with no way across it. It looks like they cut the rope bridge which spanned the chasm from the far side. To stop anyone following them I would guess. Which it did. I couldn't see another bridge in either direction and there was no way to know which way they went on the other side

either. So, I turned around at that point to tell you what I had found. I guessed you would be here waiting..."

"I don't know how helpful that information will be" Lawrence replied. "But thank you for trying. And you Sam. Without your activities, we wouldn't have any idea where they had taken her. We need to get back to the spa now and discuss this with the Police. Maybe they know where this ravine is and what's on the other side. It might be a useful clue as to where they took Bonn. Jump in the van, time is slipping away. Quickly now."

When the minivan arrived back at the spa, they found the approach road crowded with police vehicles. In the gathering gloom of sunset, the spinning blue lights sent flickering shadows across the surrounding trees.

Having identified themselves to the police officer blocking off the road, Lawrence and the others strode into the spa lobby to find Laura, Stan and Izi seated together to one side, with Roger, standing nearby.

"Did you find her?" Izi asked as soon as she saw them enter the lobby.

"We thought you might have crashed." Stan added. "You were gone so long."

"We didn't see Bonn and we didn't crash." Ben informed them. "But I don't think the microlight will be flying again anytime soon."

"I had to make an emergency landing..." Sam explained quickly when she saw the looks on their faces.

"But you didn't find Bonn?" Izi insisted again.

"No. I followed her trail through the jungle to a dead end." Ben replied.

"It could have been very dangerous." Lawrence interrupted. "Best to leave it to the Police and us now. I will get the taxi driver to take you all back to the hotel right away. I'm sure you will need a rest. Roger, can you organise that for me? I need to go and speak to whoever is in charge from the Police. Have you met him yet, Roger?"

"It's the tall guy over there" Roger pointed to him. "He's already spoken to all of us here. Not that we could tell him much, to be honest."

"He's brought most of his force up here too, by the looks of the road outside." Lawrence pointed out.

"He's taking it very seriously, Larry. As you'd expect."

"Ok. Well you sort the kids out and then get back here as soon as you can."

"No problem. Leave it with me." He replied then turned and said. "Come on you guys. You must be exhausted. If the police have any more questions, they can talk to you at the hotel. I am sure they will probably want to talk to Ong and Tracey too."

The teens followed him back outside and climbed back into the minivan once again. Ben and Sam told the others about what they had done during the bumpy journey back to the hotel but eventually they fell into a stony silence, as each of them kept their thoughts to themselves. Once they returned to the hotel Tracey insisted that they told her everything that had happened.

"Ong has left to go to the spa." She explained once they had finished with their stories. "You must have passed him on the way."

"There were lots of police at the spa when we left. Laura pointed out.

"I'm sure they will find Bonn quickly." Izi said.

"I'm not so sure" Ben replied gloomily. "Unless they can work out where they took her after they cut the rope bridge."

"The Police seem very well organised." Stan added. "And the bodyguards have lots of experience too."

"I'm supposed to ring Bob, as soon as you get back." Tracey said. "He's obviously worried about all of you guys too. I will leave you here for now while I do that, if that's okay. Plus, we need to organise some dinner or something. I bet you haven't eaten anything..." She added as she left the room.

"I don't think I can just sit here and pretend to go back to normal." Stan said as he stood up and began to pace the room. "They could have taken anyone of us. Whoever went to the showers first..."

"It's best to leave it up to the police and the bodyguards. Don't you think?" Izi replied.

"I think they wanted Bonn specifically. The kidnappers seem very well organised" Ben said thoughtfully.

"Why do you say that?" Stan asked.

"They killed a highly-trained bodyguard and then took Bonn without a sound. The car was well hidden and they only used it for a short drive and they knew exactly where they were going to get to that ravine after they abandoned the van. Once there they took an almost perfectly straight-line walking through thick jungle, which is hard for amateurs to do. Trust me."

"They didn't expect an eye in the sky though, did they?" Izi pointed out.

"Especially one prepared to crash into the jungle to keep up with them." Stan reminded them.

"What about the ravine though? Laura asked.

"That's where I actually lost the trail. I think they walked across to the other side using an old rope bridge which is now hanging down the ravine wall. I also found a climbing rope, like the ones Stan and I use on the island. It was still attached to a post on this side of the ravine but the other end of it had been cut with a sharp knife. Stan will tell you, those ropes don't just break."

"He's right" Stan said. "It might have been used for extra safety. If the other ropes are old..."

"Then the police can start tracking them from the other side then." Izi suggested.

"If they can get to the other side." Ben replied. "I don't know how they'll manage that with the rope bridge cut. The far side is covered in more thick jungle seventy feet high. Sam will tell you how difficult we found it trying to land."

"A helicopter could land in a smaller space, couldn't it? The Police must have one." Stan added.

"Possibly." Ben said slowly. "But then where did they go? I don't remember seeing any roads nearby. Did you Sam."

"I don't think so" Sam replied. "But to be honest I was really concentrating on flying at that point."

"The local police must be used to getting around up there on the mountain." Izi insisted. "So they'll know the best places to look for her."

"Perhaps" Ben replied. "We will have to see what happens tomorrow. I don't think they will get much done tonight in the dark."

"But they can't just leave her out there all night without doing *something*..." Izi replied with a catch in her voice.

In the spa's lobby, Ong had gathered the bodyguards together on one side to update them about the phone call from James McLeod. He finished by saying, "I've also been told that the Police have found the missing crewman from the Marlin, in an abandoned warehouse in Darwin. I haven't got all the details but it's clear that he had been tortured to death."

"This killer is ruthless and efficient." Roger said. "McCloud, Jakarta then Darwin and now here..."

"Assuming it's all connected to the same man…" Lawrence queried.

"It looks fairly straightforward." Roger replied. "After torturing McCloud, he tracked down the Marlin to Darwin, got the information about Bonn's whereabouts from the crewman and then flew here to snatch her. He's going to use her to force us to give him the jade statues."

"He has to be working with a local gang here though." Dan suggested. "He must have had two or three men to help him take Bonn. The body we found next to Sandy wasn't the guy who attacked McCloud. He looks like a local. I also noticed that he had a tattoo under his arm, two bright red orbs in an infinity figure '8'. It looked very unusual. Maybe a gang affiliation mark. Hopefully the Police will be able to tell us what it means."

"I don't want to jump to any conclusions just yet." Ong replied thoughtfully. The senior police officer over there admitted to me that they have had a number of kidnappings in the last five years. Always rich tourists. Maybe Bonn has been taken by a local gang and this professional killer has nothing to do with it. I think I prefer that scenario."

"That would have to be a huge coincidence Mr Thakkrani." Lawrence replied. "Usually the simple answer, is the right answer."

"Possibly. But I want to leave all options open for now. I don't know how good the local police are. I want to get our own people out here. I'm going to make some phone calls to get that sorted. Whatever it takes I'm going to get my daughter back. And then once she is safe, we will track down whoever is responsible...and deal with them."

"We would normally expect to hear from the kidnappers within 24 hours. According to the Police Chief. "If it's the same gang that took the other tourists..."

"I'm not going to sit on my hands for 24 hours." Ong told them.

"The van they used was stolen from the city yesterday." Roger said. "There may be some forensics from that."

"What about this ravine?" Ong asked. Any clues as to where they went from there?"

"It's already too dark to get anything useful there." Lawrence replied

"What about Joseph?" Ong asked.

"He will be on the jet with Bob first thing tomorrow. He told me that the airport is closed overnight so that's all he can do."

"Okay Lawrence. We can't do anything else here now. Get everybody back to the hotel. You need to set up some sort of communications centre there, so I can stay in touch with the Police, local government and any specialists that we bring in. Let's go."

In their hotel room, Izi and Laura were both crouched over their laptops whilst Sam, Ben and Stan watched on.

"You're getting really good at doing this Laura" Sam informed her proudly.

"It's like Izi told you, you can find anything on the Internet these days?" Laura replied without raising her eyes from the screen.

"You're sure about the description of the tattoo, Stan? Izi asked as she scrolled through the pages she was reading.

"I only got a brief look at it." Stan replied. "Lawrence was trying to get me out of there as quickly as possible. But I could see it clearly because of the way the guy was lying up against the bush. I thought at the time that it was an unusual place to have a tattoo. I don't think I've ever heard of a tattoo in someone's armpit."

"But if you didn't want anybody else to see it, it's a perfect place." Laura pointed out.

"Why would you have a tattoo that you didn't want other people to see?" Sam asked. "That would be pointless."

"Not if you were part of a secret or illegal gang." Laura suggested with a smile as she sat back from her laptop.

"A secret illegal gang?" Stan asked.

"Yep. Look at this photo Stan. It looks just as you described doesn't it. Laura said as she pointed at her screen. "A black figure of eight, filled in with bright red ink?"

"That's it! It looked just like that." Stan replied excitedly. "What does it mean?"

"Just hang on and I will read what it says." Laura replied as the others crowded round the screen. "It says that it was the sign of membership of a criminal gang, infamous for robbery and murder."

"But it says the gang was operating a hundred years ago." Sam added, as she read the article quickly.

"So these ones are copycats." Laura theorised.

"It says here that the tattoo represented the blazing red eyes of the goddess they worshipped..." Sam continued.

"Criminals don't worship goddesses." Ben said. "They worship money."

"Well these ones did. And they carried out blood sacrifices in her name." Laura told them as she continued to read the article.

"Don't be so gruesome Laura" Izi insisted. "That could have been Bonn you're talking about."

"I'm just reading what it says in the article." Laura replied defensively.

"But the article is about a gang from a hundred years ago remember." Izi pointed out

"Who just happen to use the same tattoo as the man who killed Sandy." Sam reminded them.

"Coincidences do happen." Izi pointed out.

"They were called thuggees. They killed victims while strangling them with a garrotte." Laura read aloud.

They haven't strangled Bonn. She's been kidnapped. I don't think is a connection really.

"Actually, I think they might have strangled Sandy..." Ben said slowly.

"And I think the tattoo is identical." Stan insisted.

"Why would anyone copy an ancient tattoo and then keep it secret? I don't get that." Izi asked.

"We need to tell Ong about this" Ben said.

"They will send a ransom demand in the morning, won't they?" Laura asked. "That's what kidnappers do, right? Ong is rich. He can just pay it and we can get Bonn back. Then the police will track down the murderers after that."

"As long as Bonn can't identify them." Ben said quietly.

"What do you mean?" Izi asked.

"Well I don't want to sound pessimistic. But this isn't a standard kidnapping like you see on TV. They are now wanted for murder as well as kidnapping. If Bonn has seen their faces...."

"Oh. don't say that, Ben." Izi said. "They simply have to let her go..."

Chapter 18

Colombo

The following morning everybody had gathered on the veranda outside Tracey's villa, for breakfast.

"I need to ask you a favour" Sam said to Tracey as she sipped her black coffee.

"Sure, what is it Sam?"

"I know we are all supposed to stay in the hotel's grounds while we wait for them to find Bonn, but I really do have to go back to Sunshine Flyers."

"Sorry? Sunshine Flyers?"

"That's the place where I rented the microlight yesterday? I used my Dads credit card to put down a deposit, so I need to tell them where it is now. Or they will send him a huge bill. I forgot all about it in the excitement last night."

"Oh right. Yes, I understand now." Tracey replied. "But obviously, you can't go alone. And I think I need to stay here. maybe you can take Ben with you. Would that be Ok with you, Ben?"

"Yes, it is. In fact, I've already volunteered...and Stan says he will come as well since he can't do anything useful here."

"Thank you, Ben. I won't need to worry then. Izi and Laura can stay at the hotel with me and once you all get back, we can organise some lunch or something. I'm sure we will have Bonn back by then."

"Of course, we will" Izi added between mouthfuls of her muesli.

"Which gives us two more time to research the secret gang and the jade statues" Laura pointed out.

"All okay" Stan asked when Sam joined them in the hotel lobby.
"Yep all sorted. I've got the credit card receipt and contract. How about you? Did you get the hire car alright?"
"Yes, we were really lucky actually." Ben replied. "I went to the agent's desk just over there. A 4x4 had just been returned by the previous hirer. Since I told him we will have it back here in just a few hours, he's done it for half the usual price."
"As long as you can find the place where you crashed microlight." Stan added.
"I didn't crash" Sam insisted. "It was almost a perfect Emergency Landing, actually."
"Almost perfect?" Stan asked with a smile. "That sounds like a 'crash' to me!"
"I know exactly where it is" Ben replied seriously. "But we had better get going if we are going to get back here in time."

After another long bumpy drive, they eventually arrived outside the Sunshine Flyers office again. As they pulled to a stop, the manager stepped out from his small office and then walked rapidly towards their car.
"What have you done with my microlight." He asked as soon as they stepped out of the car. "I've already reported you to the police. You're in big trouble young lady!"
"Look, I'm really, really sorry" Sam said quickly. "We had to make an emergency landing in the forest. Our friend has been kidnapped."

"Kidnapped? What are you talking about? Where is my microlight? Your deposit won't cover the cost you know. I'm calling the police. They will arrest you."

"If you just wait two minutes" Ben interrupted. "I'm sure we can explain everything."

It eventually took more than five minutes to explain what had happened the previous day and as he listened to their story the manager's anger drained away completely.

"That's terrible. But it all makes sense now" he said after Ben finished speaking. "When I reported you for stealing the microlight, the officer told me they had a major incident running and that no one was available to deal with my complaint until tomorrow. But no one has been here yet. Now after what you've said, I assume the major incident was about your friend."

"I guess so." Sam replied. "But as Ben just told you we haven't stolen the microlight. That's why we're back here now. To show you where it is. I'm afraid you'll have to recover it on a trailer though. There isn't enough room for me to take off again."

"Or enough petrol either" Stan added thoughtfully as he remembered the fuel gauge reading.

"That's alright. We've got a trailer out back. But you three will have to help me disassemble the aircraft. My engineer hasn't turned up for work yet today."

"Of course, we'll help." Stan replied with a smile. "And then you can tell the police that we haven't stolen it. We don't want to get arrested on the way back to the city."

"I will call them." The manager replied. "But not till we've got it back here. Give me five minutes to hook up the trailer and then I will follow you to the crash site. I hope there isn't too much damage, you understand that this is going to come out of your security deposit. Don't you?"

"I'm sure my father will understand. I told him all about Bonn last night" Sam responded before they all trooped out of his office to return to their hire car.

"I hope there's not *too* much damage" Stan said as they drove up the small track towards the crash site. "For your Dad's sake."

"The ground was very soft." Sam replied. "There must have been lots of rain up here the last few days. That's the main reason we managed to stop before we reached the treeline, so hopefully it cushioned the impact of the wing hitting the ground."

"We'll find out soon enough." Ben informed them. "I think we will find it just around the next bend."

"If it hasn't been stolen." Stan suggested unhelpfully.

"Thank you, Mr Optimistic." Sam replied.

"I was just trying to be funny. I'm sure it will be there really."

"And how right you are" Ben said as they drove around the bend, to reveal the brightly coloured microlight wing sitting at the far end of the small clearing near the track. He turned off the roadway onto the clearing, followed by the manager with his truck and trailer. The two vehicles stopped just short of the microlight and everybody got out of the vehicles.

"How on earth did you manage to put it down here?" The manager asked looking around the small field as he approached the microlight. "You must be a really good pilot. I don't think I could have put her down here."

"I did tell you she was really good, when we hired the microlight" Ben reminded him.

"It looks like you've twisted the landing gear." The manager said as he crouched down to examine the wheels.

"The ground was a lot softer than I had hoped." Sam replied. "I think that's why we stopped so suddenly."

"Saved us crashing into the trees though" Ben added.

"The frame of the wing looks to be intact. Which is good." The manager said as he ran his experienced hands over the tubing which formed the wing. "But I can't be sure until I get it back to the workshop."

"So where do we start?" Stan asked.

"I will get some tools from the trailer." The manager replied. "If someone could start undoing the lashing for the wing fabric..."

"Do what?" Stan asked.

"You need to undo that nylon rope." Sam replied pointing out the loops all along the edge of the fabric. "It secures the fabric of the wing onto the frame. You're good with knots so that can be your job Stan."

"I can help you" Ben suggested. "There are an awful lot of knots to undo."

For the next hour, the four of them worked together to dismantle the aircraft and arrange the various components in the manager's trailer. As they worked they retold the details of Bonn's disappearance from the spa.

The manager was undoing the last of bolts on the undercarriage when he suddenly stopped, stood upright and looked at Stan. "Can you describe that tattoo again? He asked.

"It was a figure-of-eight. With the two halves filled in with a bright red ink. Why do you ask?"

"I feel really sorry for your friend. They are in the worst kind of trouble."

"I think we already know that." Sam replied.

"No, I think it might be even more serious than you've guessed." The manager insisted. "The tattoo that you describe is the mark of the Goddess."

"You recognise it?" Sam asked.

"I'm sure the police will have done so as well." The manager replied.

"I don't think they mentioned a goddess...why do you say that."

"The figure of eight represents infinity. The goddess is supposed to live forever you see. And the bright red infill is said to represent the Goddess' eyes from which deadly beams lash out onto her enemies. Those who carry the mark of the Goddess belong to a secret cult. A very dangerous cult. If your friend has been kidnapped by them, you may never see your friend again."

"So it's true then. We searched the Internet and found the same stories. But we kind of hoped they were just that... Stories. The article said the cult died out 100 years ago." Sam told him.

"Surely you're making this up." Stan said "It's got to be some kind of copycat gang. This is the 20th century, we don't have blood sacrificing goddesses with lasers eyes. These days it's the Mafia, Chinese tongs and street gangs."

"I'm only repeating what I have heard." He replied defensively. "Which admittedly, is very little but this is happening today. Not a hundred years ago. The Police know about them. More than I care to know that's for sure. People who have crossed paths with the Goddess' followers have died. Strangled usually."

"You're serious?" Ben Said. "You think this cult still exists."

"I'm afraid so. If the dead man at the spa is one of the Goddess' acolytes. Then I fear for your friend's life."

"No, you're wrong. I'm sure she's safe." Sam said. "Her Father is very wealthy and will pay any ransom they ask for."

"If they do indeed ransom her." The manager replied gloomily.

"What else could they do with her. They won't just hand her back without getting paid, will they?"

"I don't want to scare you but my grandfather once told me a very grim story about the Goddess when I was just a small boy."

"A small boy?" Sam asked incredulously

"Oh yes. Your research was right in that respect. The Goddess and her followers have plagued Colombo and the surrounding area for more than a hundred years, so the rumours go. My grandfather's story described how a band of thuggees, on the run from the police in India, arrived in Sri Lanka at the beginning of the 20th century and then terrorised the land from one end to the other.

"You're saying they've been doing this for a hundred years? Sam asked.

"And before that in India too." The manager added. "The whispered stories have been around so long that nobody knows what is truth, what is myth and what is guesswork. My grandfather told me that their leader was supposed to be some kind of witchdoctor or shaman, who could communicate with the Goddess who has no name. As you might know we have dozens of gods in our country both good and evil. Their particular Goddess was said to have blazing red eyes that fired laser beams to kill her victims."

"A mysterious goddess who kills people with laser beams from her eyes? Stan asked unbelievingly.

"That's the story my grandfather told me. And over the 50 years since I have heard a few similar rumours."

"And the police know all about this goddess and her followers?" Ben asked.

"I don't think the police have ever found any hard evidence, at least, I've never seen anything in the papers about it. But that isn't surprising. This whole country depends more and more upon the tourists that arrive. Without them and the hard currency they spend in the hotels and shops and even my microlights, the entire economy would collapse. So the police, local authorities and the tourist offices try to hush up any serious crimes that happen here."

"You can't hush up murders and kidnappings... Can you? Sam asked.

"They don't happen every day of the week, obviously" the manager replied. "And as long as nobody rich or famous get killed, it's in everyone's interest to keep it quiet. Then life just goes on as usual.

"Well Bonn may not be famous, but her father is rich and powerful. There is no way they can hush this up." Ben replied.

"Hopefully, this isn't connected to the Goddess." The manager said. "The ransom will get paid and your friend will be released and we can all go on about our business again, as if nothing has happened."

"What you're saying is unbelievable." Stan said.

"You come from a modern civilised country Stan." Ben told him. "I can assure you that I have heard similar rumours of crimes being covered up in the Congo. And I bet Izi could tell you similar stories of life in Gambia. Tourists are easily scared away and without tourism the economy of many Third World countries could easily collapse."

"But if what he said about the cult is true, they might kill Bonn as a sacrifice to this Goddess." Sam said.

"I'm sure that won't happen, Sam." Stan tried to reassure her. "Ong won't let anything happen to her. He's very rich, so they will just make him pay a big ransom to get her back."

"I'm sure your friend's going to be fine, Sam." The manager said. "I probably shouldn't have said anything really. It's just rumour and gossip after all. So, if that's everything done and loaded up? I had better be getting back." He added wiping his hands on a cloth. "I'm going to take it all back down to the office and find out exactly what the damage is. My engineer should have arrived by now, so he can get on with that."

"And remember to tell the police that we didn't steal it." Ben reminded him.

"Yes. I must do that straightaway. I don't want you to get arrested by mistake."

"Nor do we." Sam agreed as the manager climbed into his truck and then slowly drove back across the muddy field and onto the mountain trial.

"Well that's one less thing to worry about." Sam said. "I suppose we will head back to the hotel now."

"Actually, Ben and I thought we might have a look at the ravine."

"You want to go to the ravine? Sam asked.

"While you were getting your documents this morning. I told Stan about the ravine and the cut rope and he said he would like to see it. So, as we are so close now anyway, I thought we would have another look. Now that it's full daylight."

"Shouldn't we leave it to the police to deal with? Lawrence and Mr Thakkrani made it very clear that they and the police would deal with it. Didn't they?" Sam reminded them.

"We're just going to have a look Sam." Stan insisted.

"The police have probably already been there to look around." Ben added.

"Well I suppose that just looking couldn't hurt. Could it?"

"That's what I said" Stan replied. "Come on Ben. Show us some of your famous tracking skills."

It only took a few minutes for Ben to lead them back up the roadway then through the jungle to the ravine where he had lost Bonn's trail.

"Lawrence must have brought the police up here at first light." Ben informed them as he examined the ground close to the ravine.

"He did?" Sam asked.

"Probably half a dozen people have walked all over this area since I was here yesterday. Completely obliterating all the footprints which I'd followed through the jungle to here."

"I wonder if they got to the other side. Stan asked as he gazed across the chasm.

"Not unless they grew wings." Sam suggested as she moved to stand next to Stan and looked down into the ravine.

"Or they had their own Spiderman." Ben replied. "What you think Stan, is there any way you can get across to the other side? Ben asked as he pulled up the climbing rope to show Stan the other end which had been cut.

"Sliced clean through" Stan said. "No way that was an accidental break. It would be frayed at the end, not a bit like this."

"It's strange" Sam said slowly. "I thought we might have found the police still here. Trying to find a way across, or something."

"It would have been a dead-end for them. There's no way they could get across from this side and look at the jungle on the far side." Ben said. "There's no room for them to could get a helicopter to land over there."

"So now what?" Sam asked.

"I think I have an idea." Stan replied unexpectedly.

"I hoped you were going to say that" Ben replied

"Why do I think you two are up to something." Sam asked. "Is there something you want to tell me?"

"When Ben was telling me about this ravine and about the climbing rope that had been cut. I suggested to him that maybe we had skills which the police don't."

"We've got skills they don't?" Sam asked

"Climbing skills." Ben replied.

"You're not thinking of climbing across the ravine, are you?" Sam asked incredulously as she looked down into the gloomy depths. "The ropes have all been cut through..."

"Which is why I borrowed that length of rope from the microlight's wing." Stan replied whilst pulling out a tangle of nylon rope, which had previously been used to attach the material of the microlight's wing.

"You stole that?" Sam said. "He's going to blame me..."

"No, I just forgot to put in the trailer. We can give it back to him on our way back down the mountain."

"Your unbelievable." Sam told him.

"Look, if we can get across to the other side, Ben can pick up the trail of the thuggees on the far side of the ravine. Then maybe we can find where they took Bonn to..."

Chapter 19

London City Airport

Bob and Joseph had checked out of their central London hotel as the summer sun was just starting to brighten the far horizon. The taxi driver had made easy work of the light traffic and they were some of the first people to enter the executive airport, in the heart of the Docklands.

With so few passengers they quickly passed through the security scanners but were surprised when they were approached by two uniformed police officers on the other side. Both officers were carrying Heckler and Koch submachine guns across their chests.

"Mr Dalton? Mr Stein?" One of the officers asked.

"Yes. that's us" Bob replied defensively. "Is there a problem?"

"If you two gentlemen could follow us please..."

"We've got a private jet waiting for us." Joseph interrupted. "What's wrong?"

"This will only take a few moments sir." The officer said sternly. "I'm afraid that I have to insist..." and placed his hand on the butt of his weapon.

Bob and Joseph exchanged a look and with a shrug of their shoulders, picked up their hand luggage and followed the officer who had spoken to them. His colleague took up a position behind them, as they all walked across the large room towards the far wall. Joseph noticed that it was equipped with two large polished windows which he assumed were two way mirrors. These would allow those inside to observe the passengers as they passed through the security scanning area.

As they stepped through the office door, Joseph was surprised to see Commander Abrahams sitting behind the battered metal desk. "Thank you, officer." He said in a friendly voice. "If you could wait outside while I speak to the gentleman."

"Yes Sir." The officer replied, before he disappeared back through the open doorway.

"What are you doing here George" Joseph asked.

"We've got a flight to catch" Bob added.

The commander paused until the officer had closed the door before he replied. "Well since we couldn't meet for lunch today, I thought it was only fair that I came send you off."

"At six o'clock in the morning? Joseph asked

"Well after our meeting yesterday and what you told me what had happened in Sri Lanka, I felt that I had to tell you something. But what I'm about to tell you is strictly off the record. If the Admiral even got a hint of me being here, he would definitely smell a rat. That's why I had to use this little bit of cloak and dagger to talk to you before you left. It's better for all of us this way, I can assure you."

"I know we've been friends for a long time, George. But meeting the Head of Special Branch at 6am in a Security Room at City Airport, is unusual to say the least. I have a feeling this is going to be even more bad news."

"I realise that and you've got a lot on your plate with this kidnapping thing but for your own good I thought it was important that I met you again. In short, I have to officially tell you to let this Ultra thing drop, Joseph."

"Well, right now we have other priorities as you say." Bob replied quickly. "But you could have phoned to tell us that."

"As I expected the Admiral refused your request of getting a complete copy of the document. In fact, he laughed when I asked him. Then reminded me to warn you off again."

"I kind of expected that response." Bob replied. "Bearing in mind what you told us about what happened to the curator and the clerk involved in giving us the copy in the first place."

"Exactly. Let sleeping dogs as they say. I'm sure that if the Admiral even suspects that you were still poking around in it you're going to find yourselves in very hot water. So please drop it. Whoever your rich client is... Just tell him to forget the Ultra document and look elsewhere for information about his statues."

"I will definitely be passing on your warning." Bob said. "So if that's everything? Because we've got a plane to catch."

"I was hoping you'd see it that way Bob. But when you left me yesterday, I remembered a story my grandmother once told me. And knowing Joseph as I do and his curious nature, I thought you might like to hear it."

"A story your grandmother told you?" Joseph sounded as surprised as he felt. "Maybe another time George..."

"It will only take a couple of minutes. And I'm fairly sure you will want to hear it, so bear with me." The Commander paused as he looked from Joseph to Bob before continuing. "Few people remember that my grandfather was Head of SB during the second world war. Like me, he never talked about what he did exactly, as you would expect. But when you were talking about the events surrounding the Ultra document, I suddenly remembered my grandmother talking to me when I was a small boy, about how they never had time to take holidays."

"Holidays?" Bob sounded exasperated. "We don't have time for this Joseph."

The Commander held up his hand and said, "Almost there Bob. She was complaining because my grandfather had taken a six-week holiday in India without her. And it was about the same time as the date on the Ultra document."

"Sorry I really don't follow you" Bob said.

"I'm telling you this purely as a family matter you understand. Completely off the record. But what if he wasn't in India at all, but in Sri Lanka? The Commander paused to let the premise sink in. "What if the initials CSB on your photo copy could have been his rank, Commander Special Branch and this Ultra document refers to his mysterious holiday? HMG is obviously His Majesty's Government. The whole thing has got to be something fantastical. For Bomber Command to release a plane for his personal use? At that time in the war? That would have been simply unheard of. Aircraft were worth their weight in gold back then."

"An interesting grandfather you have" Joseph replied as he thought about the possibilities.

"He never told me any of this, of course." Abrahams said.

"But why tell us now?"

"Officially, I haven't. Unofficially, it's an old family story, which I can tell anyone about. And if you want to believe any of it, you can. I don't know if that will help you in your quest Bob but if they did second my grandfather to the MoD and then flew him all the way there... It would be a great story to tell my grandchildren one day."

"It would be one hell of a coincidence" Joseph said.

"And maybe it has nothing whatsoever to do with my enquiries." Bob added.

"Well its guaranteed that you're never going to find out for sure from the MoD. But either way, I can't imagine anything that would have justified such an operation." Abrahams said.

"We really have to get going George." Joseph said as he glanced at his watch. "I appreciate you coming all this way, but we have to take off before we lose our take-off slot."

"Yes, yes, I understand. I just thought it was a least I could do, particularly in view of the kidnapping and all that."

Bob and Joseph stood up and shook hands with the Commander who added. "The two officers outside will take you straight onto the air side so you can get on your plane quicker and be on your way."

"That would be really helpful George. Thanks." Joseph replied. "I will call you next time I'm in London for that lunch appointment."

"Yes, I'd enjoy that. And you too Bob. If you can make it."

As they left the office they found the two uniformed officers waiting for them outside, as described. "You just need to follow me sir." One of the officers said. "You're clear to go straight out to your plane."

Bob and Joseph followed the officers as they strode quickly out of the security area then through a series of doors and stairs, all marked with 'Staff Only' signs, to finally arrive at the bottom of the stairway to Ong's private plane.

"I've got to ring Lawrence and let him know that we are about to take off." Joseph told Bob as they dropped into their wide leather seats.

"And I've got to call Tracey too" Bob replied as he fastened his seatbelt. "That was strange, don't you think? George coming all this way to tell us about his grandfather, I mean."
"I agree. Completely. Something isn't right about it. But for now, I need to worry about getting Bonn back. His old wives' tale will have to wait till another day."

Chapter 20

Darwin

Once the Butcher had finished interrogating the Black Marlin's crewman the previous day, he had cleaned himself up and eaten a good meal. While he was finishing an exquisite dessert, he had decided to approach his latest contact in the Darwin underworld, a rising Boss who owed him a favour.

He had entered the Boss' smoky office around midnight, while the strip club which laundered the cash from the Boss' criminal activities, was in full swing.

"Busy night...?" the Butcher asked as he sat down opposite the Boss.

"It will be like this until about 4am. But if you want a private booth, I'm sure I can get you one."

"Not interested tonight. I'm here to ask you for a small favour."

"Sure. I owe you one for getting rid of Mirrors for me."

"That was my pleasure. He was a complete waster. I can't believe he lost McCloud and the Trident for you."

"That dive boat was just what I was looking for to bring in my...err...*merchandise*."

"I'm sure you found something else without too much trouble. Darwin harbour's full of them for a start off."

"Not at the price I was going to get the Trident for...but there's no point worrying about that now. What can I do for you tonight?"

"I need a new passport. Preferably Australian, plus a driver's licence in the same name."

"No problem. I assume you brought your own photos?"

"Naturally" he replied and taking an envelope from inside his jacket, slid a set of four photos across the desk.

"Anything else?" the Boss asked.

"I need to get my hands on a pair of baby orangutans. For a friend of mine. I heard that there's an island sanctuary near here where I could pick them up easily. But I can't find anyone who knows exactly where it is."

"It's not around here, that's definite. Somebody's given you bad info." The Boss replied confidently. "You need to try Indonesia, where they come from. But even up there, they're hard to get. And you know they won't be cheap, right? Endangered species and all that crap. But I can ask around for you if you want?"

"Nah. I don't want to put a lot of effort into it. He's not that good a friend!" As the Butcher didn't want to push the point and arouse the Boss's street-wise instincts, he smoothly changed the subject, to discuss new drug distribution possibilities on Darwin's city streets and how he might help the Boss with any supply problems.

Twenty minutes later, having accepted the offer of a large whisky, he left the club and strolled the two city blocks back to where he had parked his car, unobtrusively making sure he hadn't been followed from the club. The Butcher had learned long ago never to trust anyone and it had kept him alive in a business where people usually didn't see their old age.

Early the following morning he had made a call to the charity which ran the orangutan sanctuary using another burner phone, to try to arrange for a visit to the mysterious island. Unfortunately, the friendly secretary that he had spoken to had made it clear that the charity carefully controlled access to the island. She advised him that all visitors were carefully selected by the charity itself and even those few guests were thoroughly screened before being invited to visit. At that point, the Butcher cut off the call having realised that a straightforward approach to gaining access to the island would be more difficult than he had anticipated.

Glancing at his watch, he swallowed the rest of his strong, black coffee and made his way to his morning appointment.

Inspector Brian Hayes of the Darwin Police, had arrived just a few minutes earlier at the small coffee shop, which was just a short walk from his office. He had waited as he had been instructed, nervously drumming his fingers on the surface of one of the bright blue tables which had been placed on the pavement outside. His drumming was finally interrupted by the arrival of his blackmailing nemesis, the Butcher.

"I really hoped I would never see you again." Brian's voice sounded as bitter as he felt.

"What are you bitching about?" The Butcher replied as he sat down opposite the Inspector. "I paid you well for the information you gave me. It's just business, Brian."

"Maybe it is for you. But I am risking my job and my pension."

"Your pension is safe enough. I'm not going to tell anybody about our little business arrangement...Unless I have to."

"It's been weeks though. I thought you'd left the country."

"I come. I go. It depends on my business."

"So, what do you want from me this time?"

"Nothing that's gonna get you in any trouble. I just need to know what's happening with the investigations into the explosion in the desert."

"What explosion?"

"Oh come on...it's been in all the papers. The Nuclear testing grounds."

"That's got nothing to do with Darwin Police. That will be a Federal investigation. I can't help you with that."

"Well, you're going to have to speak to someone at Federal Headquarters then, aren't you."

"I can't do that. An enquiry from me would look really suspicious. I don't have any jurisdictional crossover with those sorts of investigations."

"Well I'm sure you'll come up with some excuse Brian. And while you're talking to them, you can find out about that plane that crashed in the sea off Adelaide."

"A plane crash. Why you are interested in that?"

"Now, now, Brian. You know the rules. I ask *you* questions. Then you give me the answers and I give you some money towards your fat pension fund. Got it?"

"I really don't think I can get information like that."

"Well in that case, you've got a big problem haven't you, Brian. A problem which I will give you exactly two days to sort out. I want to be out of Darwin after that. So best you get busy and talk to your friends in the Federal building."

"It's not as easy as you think..." Brian replied as he watched the Butcher stand up.

"Just do it, Brian. You really don't want to let me down. There are a lot worse things that can happen to you than just going to prison for corruption. Maybe your young daughter would like to meet me in a dark alley one night?" The Butcher told him as he turned and calmly strode along the footway and disappeared into the early morning crowd.

The Butcher allowed himself a rare smile as he walked away from the Inspector. Before he had been forced to close down Khan's Australian operations so abruptly, he had made good use of the Inspector's high-level access to many of the Australian Police's computerised information systems. He wasn't sure if those access levels would allow the corrupt officer to get the information he needed but it saved him time and effort to try the Inspector first. And if he didn't get the information requested, the Butcher decided that he would have some fun destroying the Inspector's career and family before they sent him off to Federal prison. In fact, he told himself, he might even do that anyway while he was here this time. Like most professional criminals, he didn't like bent coppers.

As was often the case the information that Khan had instructed him to obtain was rarely easy to come by, even for a man with his contacts and abilities and right now the Butcher preferred to spend his valuable time tracking down his jade statues and silver bars.

On his way to return to the top floor of the multi-story car park where his hire car awaited him, he used a deliberately circuitous route as he always did. His standard security procedures were probably unnecessary today but paranoia in his line of business, had kept him alive and successful for many years. Once he reached the top of the car park he had a clear view of the entire floor and slowly scanned the assorted vehicles parked there. He preferred to use the top floors, less cars meant less pedestrians which in turn allowed easier risk assessment, permitting lower threat levels. The top floor also had an added benefit for a man trying to remain anonymous. Fewer closed circuit TV cameras.

Using the car's remote control, he unlocked the car automatically disabling the factory fitted alarm from the maximum possible distance, whilst standing behind a thick concrete pillar. He approached the car and quickly walked around the exterior of the car, checking that the thin pieces of adhesive tape he had attached were still intact on all doors, hood and trunk. He had already checked the wheel arches as he circled the car, so a quick glance underneath completed his checks.

Slipping behind the steering wheel he started the engine and began the descent to the ground floor. As he followed the circular ramp down to the exit, he reassessed the problem of finding the secret island again. He was replaying his casual conversation with the helpful secretary from the orangutan charity, when out of the blue a solution occurred to him. If he couldn't arrange for a personal invitation to the island, he would have to persuade one of the real VIPs to tell him the location after they returned from their trip. Obviously, he needed to know who was going to visit the island, so he dialled the charity once again.

"Bonn Thakkrani Charity office, how can I help?"

"Hello, my name is Phillips" the Butcher told her. "Ben Phillips. I'm an independent TV producer. I'm planning on doing a story on imperilled species and want to include the Indonesian apes in the show. I don't have airtime for a complete segment on them, but it would be really helpful if you could put me in touch with one of the VIPs that are going to visit the island. I want to interview them, before and after the visit, to assess the relative change in their attitude to preservation. If you get that angle?"

"Oh, right. Yes, that sounds like a great idea. Would you be identifying our charity in the show?"

"If that was Ok with you, definitely."

"Publicity is great for us, you see. Spreading the word, so to speak."

"I completely understand." the Butcher replied as he smiled to himself. "If you could email me the list for the next trip..."

"We've only got four guests so far, but I can certainly send you those names."

Ten minutes later the Butcher's phone chimed as the email from the charity arrived. He scanned through the document but was disappointed to find there wasn't a VIP from Australia on the list. "But New Zealand isn't too far" he thought when he saw the last VIPs address in Auckland. "I can do a quick flight over there using my new passport and be back here in time to meet Brian again."

Khan was expecting the Butcher to report on his progress in three days' time, when he was due to submit his usual weekly report to Khan's headquarters. As long as Brian came up with his information by then, he could then spend most of the following week concentrating on his own business. Maybe he would fly back to Indonesia to have another little chat with Jasmine, or maybe he would let her sweat a little longer, before putting an end to her useless life.

Chapter 21

Colombo

In the vast candlelit cavern, which had been carved out of the mountain eons ago, the Goddess' statue towered behind the Master. He was in the process of dealing with the three men who had kidnapped Bonn from the spa.

"The Night of the Goddess is almost upon us." The Master reminded them slowly, allowing his booming voice to echo around the lofty cavern. "Your incompetence is an insult to the Goddess."

"We had no choice Master" one of the men stammered.

"You had no choice? No choice about leaving one of your brothers at the scene of a murder and kidnapping?"

"The woman was carrying a gun and a covert radio set." The second thuggee tried to explain. "She must have been some sort of security guard."

"As soon as she failed to answer the radio, the others would have responded." The first thuggee added.

"So, you ran away! You left the body of your sworn brother to be discovered by the police?"

"We couldn't carry him and the girl with us." The second thuggee suggested

"Do you agree with them?" The Master asked the third man.

"I do not know, Master. Your instruction to take a rich tourist from the spa should have gone smoothly. But the security guard reacted so quickly and violently that she had killed Rashid before we could overcome her. I am sure that she wasn't alone and if her colleagues had responded in the same manner..."

"Excuses" the Master spat back at him. "You are cowards."

"We should not have left him behind, Master..." the third man said quietly.

"I had a vision last night, soon after you had returned to the cavern. The Goddess spoke to me about your failure and your cowardice. And now you will be judged by Her, in the presence of your Brothers. Prepare yourselves."

The three men hastily exchanged nervous glances, before removing all their clothing and then taking several steps forward to stand at the feet of the obsidian statue of their Goddess. The twenty other members of the cult who were observing the trial, had formed in a loose arc behind them, also facing their Goddess.

"Blindfold them." The Master instructed the acolyte standing next to him. At his bidding the man approached each of them and slipped a thick length of cloth over their heads to cover their eyes and then knotted it in place.

As soon as the blindfolds were in place the cult members began to chance in unison. "The Goddess is all seeing. The Goddess is all knowing. The Goddess judges the weak. The Goddess punishes the guilty."

As the echoes of the chanting died away the Master's voice once more filled the cavern. "Adopt the prayer position and prepare yourselves" he told the three men.

The men slowly raised their arms to chest height, their palms facing the ceiling, about a foot apart. "The Veil of the Goddess'" The Master instructed and the acolyte carefully draped a white piece of cloth across the open palms of each of those to be tested. The muslin cloths had been pulled from a bowl of perfumed water, by the acolyte and small droplets dripped from the ends onto the polished volcanic floor.

As the acolyte stepped back to stand beside the Master, the voices of the cult members once again rose as one, to repeat the ancient chant.

As their voices died away for the second time, the Master picked up two sets of elaborately decorated, solid silver tongs, from the altar beside him. He took five paces across the temple floor to a smouldering brazier next to the statue, which was glowing red hot. Handling the tongs with long practiced ease, he selected two of the large pebbles that had been arranged on top of the brazier and which now glowed with yellow/red heat. He swivelled around, holding the tongs before him as he approached the first of the three kidnappers. He paused theatrically and then dropped one of the super-heated stones into each of his palms. As he did so the witnesses loudly repeated their mythical chant.

"The Goddess is all seeing. The Goddess is all knowing. The Goddess judges the weak. The Goddess punishes the guilty."

Initially, as the stones touched the ceremonial cloth there was a puff of herbal scented steam, then as the heat of the stone burned through the cloth to reach the flesh beneath the smoke changed colour and the pleasant aromatic smell was replaced with the unmistakable odour of burning flesh. The man's arms trembled as the pain raced up his arms but no sound came from his mouth.

As soon as the last word of the chant had been spoken the Master calmly removed the stones from the man's hands with the tongs and said, "The Goddess' eyes have seen your innocence. Give praise to Her forgiveness."

The man sank slowly to his knees and then prostrated himself full length before the Goddess.

The Master stepped around him and selected two new stones from the brazier and repeated testing process with the second follower. As the skin of his palms burned away, the pain of holding the burning stones was evident on his face but once again he made no sound and passed the test.

The third man in the line began to tremble noticeably while his two companions lay on the floor next to him. The Master once more lowered two stones from the brazier onto the outstretched hands. But this time before the chant was even half completed, the man screamed aloud and dropped the stones to the floor.

The chanting stopped immediately and a deathly silence settled across the chamber.

"You have defiled the Eyes of the Goddess." The Master's voice boomed out.

"Please master forgive me. I am weak, Master. I could not bear the pain."

"You have been judged by the Goddess. In this, the week of dedication to Her, your sin cannot be forgiven."

The Master kicked the two men laying on the floor and said "Get up. Quickly." Once they had regained their feet and stood on either side of the condemned man. "Hold him." he ordered them. They took a firm grip of the condemned man's arms as he began to tremble violently. "Put him on the floor" The Master ordered, his voice like ice in the silence of the chamber.

"Master...I beg your forgiveness...the Goddess" the man pleaded, as the two men forced him first onto his knees and then twisting his arms up and back, onto his stomach at the feet of the statue.

"Do not speak Her name" the Master snapped. "Stretch out his arms" he ordered the two followers.

"Master...please" the man mumbled.

The Master once again turned around and approached the small altar behind him and selected a large curved knife. The handle was made of solid gold and inlaid with several large precious stones above a wickedly honed steel blade. The ornate knife was only ever used by the Master and only when the cult were carrying out the ceremony for blood sacrifices.

"Take off his blindfold." The Master insisted as he returned to stand over the man.

"You go to serve our Goddess." He intoned as the blindfold was ripped from the man's head. "May you serve her more faithfully in death than you did in life." Then bending slightly at the waist, he slashed the knife rapidly back and forth, repeatedly slicing deep into the man's upturned forearms with the curved blade. As his lifeblood gushed out to soak the floor before the Goddess, the glassy eyed cult members who were watching intently, began to slowly chant another of their religious intonations.

"The Goddess demands a gift. We give a gift willingly. The Goddess demands a life. We give a life willingly. She is mighty. She is the soul taker. She guides and guards us. She will live forever. She is the Undying One."

As the last of the victim's thick red blood pumped from the pulsing wounds to join the large pool surrounding him, his heart finally gave out and his rigidly flexed body relaxed in the grip of his captors.

"The Goddess is satisfied with our sacrifice" the Master declared as he gazed down at the lifeless form. "His body will remain before Her to remind all of you that Her will must be done at all times. When full darkness arrives, you may leave her presence and return to your homes. In two days' time, we will *all* be together, to dedicate ourselves to Her for the following year, as She demands of us."

The Master replaced the blade on the altar and with the acolyte trailing in his wake he strode away from the dead body and his awe-struck followers.

Chapter 22

The Tracker

"Okay, so now you've got us here, what have you two got planned to do next?" Sam asked.
"When he got back yesterday, Ben described me what we would find." Stan replied slowly.
"And what have we found?" Sam asked as she nervously looked over the edge of the ravine.
"It's exactly as he described it. You see, it's got those old ropes attached to the huge boulder back there. As an immovable anchor for the bridge. And if you look down there, you can see where the rope bridge hangs over the edge... Just be careful Sam." Stan advised, as she craned her neck to look down.
"I am being careful" she insisted without feeling it.
"Can you see those wooden slats? That would have been the floor of the bridge across the gorge, before the kidnappers cut it." Ben pointed out.
"And this is the climbing rope that you talked about? Sam asked as she examined the brightly coloured cord.
"That's a recent addition." Stan told them. "I would guess they put it in as reinforcing for the main load carrying rope. That's that thick one on top. Which looks like it's been here for years. It might have been the kidnappers, as part of their escape preparations or just the locals who use this bridge from time to time. There's no way of knowing really."

"I guess the Police will have figured most of that out themselves when they were here earlier though. Why are *we* here? Really?" Sam asked suspiciously.

"To follow the trail" Ben replied unhelpfully.

"On the other side." Stan added.

"But I still can't see how we are going to get across to the other side." Sam said

"Which is exactly what the kidnappers intended any one following them, to think." Ben replied.

"Which is where I come in, I suppose." Stan said with a grin.

"Now you've seen the ravine, what's your plan Stan?" Ben asked.

"I'm going to use their climbing rope to rappel down the face on this side of the ravine. Down to that wide ledge down there on the right. It looks fairly stable."

"Where? I can't see a wide ledge down there." Sam insisted as she squinted her eyes against the sun's glare.

"Look straight down the old ropes. It's there, on the right, just before the last of the slats from the footbridge. See it? Stan replied.

"Your joking." Sam replied as her eyes made out the rock feature he was referring to. "You can't call that a wide ledge. It looks about 6 inches across from here." Sam sounded as shocked as she felt.

"Oh, that's more than enough." Stan replied confidently. "I will make my way along the ledge, to the outcropping at the far end. That's a pinch point, where the ravine closes up over there. I bet the water races through there in the rainy season...that would make it a lot more challenging."

"I'm glad it's not raining then..." Sam suggested as she stared at the strange formation.

"Let's move along to get a better look at it" Stan told them as he walked along the edge of the ravine to stand directly above the pinch point.

"And then what?" Ben asked as his eyes followed the route Stan was describing.

"I can jump across the gap at this point. It can't be more than about eight feet. Then just climb up the other side.

"Just leap across a sixty foot drop and then climb up a sheer cliff on the other side. That's your great plan?" Sam asked bluntly. "And when you fall down the ravine and die, who gets to tell your parents? Me or Ben?"

"You don't have to be so dramatic, Sam." He replied defensively. "I'm not going to fall. I will be tied onto the climbing rope. It will be perfectly safe. You know how strong those ropes are. You could hang an elephant from one of them. Trust me."

"You tell him, Ben. He will listen to you."

"I think he's right." Ben replied simply.

"You boys are both mad." She replied huffily. "I should have realised sooner."

"And then what?" Ben asked.

"Then I will pull the rope bridge back up into position, so you two can walk across. Simple. If you're okay with that Sam?"

"You're trying to make it sound easier than it is. I'm not stupid you know."

"I know that Sam. Just relax and we will all be on the other side before you know it."

Sam watched carefully as Stan approached the edge of the ravine and picked up the climbing rope. He looped the rope through a carabiner on his belt that Sam had not noticed previously. "I never leave home without a few useful pieces of equipment, Sam." He said as he noticed her looking at him strangely.

"You never know when they're gonna come in handy, do you?" she replied.

"I'll see you both on the other side." He replied as he stepped backwards over the edge and began to lower himself into the ravine.

Ben and Sam watched as he quickly reached the small ledge and without pausing carefully edged along it to the far end of the narrow point of the ravine. Sam became more concerned when she suddenly noticed that the climbing rope Stan was using was now pulled taut.

"The rope's not long enough" she told Ben, as Stan reached the full extent of the rope.

"I should have thought of that..." Ben replied helplessly.

They watched in silence as Stan then calmly untied the rope from his waist and gripped the far end in his teeth. He paused for one breath and then leaped across the chasm to the far wall, a gap of at least eight feet.

Sam's mouth dropped open but no sound escaped as she saw Stan grip the rock face on the other side of the ravine with both hands whilst his feet scrabbled to find a tiny outcropping to stand upon.

"He's amazing." Ben said admiringly.

"He's terrifying." Sam replied.

"Spiderman himself couldn't have done it any better." Ben insisted.

"He makes me nervous too."

They watched for a further ten minutes as Stan slowly but surely climbed back up the far side of the ravine. Eventually with a sigh of relief from Sam, he heaved himself over the edge of the far side onto flat ground.

He took the climbing rope out of his mouth and shouted across a gap "Told you it would be easy didn't I."

"You didn't tell us you were planning to take the rope off." Ben replied.

"I didn't know I was going to either" he admitted. "But I didn't have a choice."

"Well don't just stand there, pull up the rope bridge so we can get across too."

"I've got to find something to attach it to first. And the microlight cord is going to be perfect for that."

"Microlight cord? Sam asked. "What does he mean?"

"I hadn't thought about that. They cut the rope at the other end remember? Ben replied as he considered the problem. "So now it won't be long enough to attach on the other side."

"So?"

"Like Stan said. He will be able to use the microlight cord as a tether, to broach the gap between the rope bridge and the support on the far side."

"Microlight cord, Ben? Sam insisted.

"Stan borrowed it. In case of emergencies..."

"There goes my Dad's deposit again..."

"Oh right of course. I hadn't thought of that. We will have to drop it off later..."

"Boys!" Sam exclaimed as she watched Stan unravelling the cord.

"Stan's an expert with knots. He will have us across in no time."

Twenty minutes later Ben was proven correct as he and Sam cautiously made their way across the jerry-rigged rope bridge to the far side of the ravine.

"Well I've done my bit." Stan said with a grin as they joined him at the far support post. "Now it's your turn Ben."

"Indeed, it is. And luckily the Police haven't been here to trample over everything."

"Can you pick up the trail again?" Sam asked as Ben began to scan the ground.

"I don't think this rope bridge has been used much over the last few days. So the footprints of the kidnappers are still as clear as day. Come on, they went this way."

Stan and Sam both looked down at the sandy surface on which they stood and once again wondered how Ben did what he did.

"Don't follow me too closely" he warned them from the tree line. "Just in case I need to backtrack. But keep me in sight. I don't want you getting lost."

Bent slightly at the waist, he slowly made his way forward again onto a small game trail which passed between two of the largest trees, which were standing like sentinels over the repaired footbridge.

Progress through the thick jungle was slow but steady as they gradually climbed further up the mountain. As Ben diligently followed the trail, his eyes constantly roamed left and right taking in his surroundings and every tiny clue as to the direction kidnappers had carried Bonn.

After more than an hour of working their way through unmarked jungle paths, the trees gradually died away and they found themselves at the edge of an expanse of exposed volcanic plain.

Ben stopped in his tracks and silently motioned for the others to join him.

"Following them through the jungle was fairly straightforward." He explained once they were standing next to him. "But this volcanic rock makes things much harder."

"So what are you going to do?" Sam asked.

"I'm going to see where the trail leads to next." Ben replied simply.

"You think that you can follow them across that." Stan asked incredulously, as he looked at the rocky ground ahead.

"It won't be easy, so I will have to go much more slowly if I want to avoid losing the trail. But yes, I think I can. Why don't you two wait here and take a rest. You will be able to see me easily enough. Just stay here amongst the trees, where no one will see you."

"But if the kidnappers are watching, they will see you straightaway." Sam pointed out. "There's no cover out there at all."

"That's a risk I will just have to take."

"I vote we come with you." Stan said immediately. "If they see you, we're all in trouble."

"You can't leave us here in the jungle. What if we get attacked by a tiger." Sam asked.

"There haven't been tigers in this jungle for 50 years." Ben replied disdainfully.

"Okay, then snakes or spiders. There's plenty of them here. It's not safe to just leave us. And you are supposed to be the responsible one..." Sam raised her eyebrows challenging Ben to disagree with her.

"You're impossible Sam Ascanio. I suppose it's a risk worth taking. Then if they do see us, they might think we're just lost tourists...If we're lucky."

The next hour passed slowly as Ben roamed further out across the rock-strewn mountainside towards a towering cliff on the far side. Every so often, he would pause and waive for Stan and Sam to join him to reassure them he was still on the trail.

"Do you think we're getting any closer to finding where they went." Sam asked as they stood close together in the lee of the cliff.

"There doesn't seem to be very much up here." Stan offered. "I thought we would have found another road, or even a village."

"There's no sign of civilisation or habitation from miles around, which made it simpler to follow the trail." Ben replied

"So where have they taken her to. You couldn't get a vehicle over that uneven ground, even if you wanted to."

"Maybe they used horses." Sam suggested. "You can take ponies across this landscape without too much problem. Did you see any signs of that Ben?"

"No, I haven't seen any indication that they used horses. Horses inevitably leave easy tracks to follow. Even on ground as hard as this."

"Can we take a break for five minutes." Sam asked. "That sun is getting really hot now. This is a good shady spot for a rest."

"It won't hurt to take a seat for five minutes." Ben replied as the three of them sank to the ground with their backs against the wall. I should have thought to bring more water with us. Stupid really."

"You can't think of everything Ben." Sam replied. "I'll be fine, if I can just sit here for a minute to cool down a bit."

"If we weren't out in the middle of nowhere, I would swear I can hear singing." Stan said as he leaned back against the rock face.

"You're hallucinating..." Ben replied. "I knew we hadn't drunk enough water..."

"No. I can hear it too." Sam interrupted him. "It's more like chanting. The same sound over and over again..."

"And it's coming from the rock." Stan said, as he pressed his ear to the wall.

"Chanting?" Ben asked as he also pressed his ear to the wall.

"Those are definitely human voices." Sam insisted.

"Coming from the other side of this wall." Stan said.

"But that's inside the mountain." Ben insisted.

"Maybe there's a cave on the other side?" Sam asked.

"I think it's stopped" Stan pointed out with his ear still pressed to the wall.

"Maybe it's the kidnappers. It would make sense that it's them." Sam whispered.

"Why them?" Ben asked.

"We haven't seen anyone else around here. You followed three of them all the way here. It makes sense, doesn't it?"

"Maybe we've found their secret hideaway." Ben whispered as he realised the danger they might be in.

"Don't jump to conclusions yet Stan. But if you're right they are bound to have lookouts nearby. You two stay here, I will try to find the entrance to the cave. It shouldn't be far."

"I don't want to be left here." Sam insisted. "I think we should all stick together."

"So do I" Stan hissed.

"Okay. But I need to stay five paces ahead of you. Make sure you don't make a sound."

Moving slowly in single file, the three friends inched their way along the face of the cliff. Two minutes later, Ben found a long narrow archway carved into the mountainside. They slipped into the deep shadows and carefully followed the natural crevice as it wound deeper into the face of the cliff. But after 10 minutes carefully searching the sides of the crevice, much to their surprise and disappointment, they found no cave entrance, or any sign of the kidnappers inside.

"I still can't hear the singing." Stan said as he pressed his ear to the wall.

"Either they stopped completely or we just can't hear them from this spot." Sam suggested as she copied Stan's actions.

"Do you think they saw us." Stan asked looking around.

"If they had seen us I am sure we would have known by now." Ben tried to reassure them. "But I don't think we should push our luck. Let's go back to the hotel now and tell the police what we found."

"But what have we found? Sam asked in a whisper. "Really?"

"We found the kidnappers trail again and followed it to this mountainside. And we heard chanting coming from inside. I think that's enough for them to come up here and do a proper search. Don't you? Ben asked.

"I suppose you're right. That should be enough... Sam replied clearly unconvinced.

"It might have been enough but I think this will clinch it." Stan announced as he pointed out a polished area, sunk into the mountain face just inches from where he had put his ear to the wall.

"The infinity sign." Ben gasped as he followed Stan's indication.

"Somebody has carved that into the rock face with a lot of care." Stan replied. "It's got to be the sign of the cult. I am willing to bet this is where the Goddess is."

"And probably Bonn too." Sam added.

"I think we should go right now." Ben insisted. "We've pushed our luck far too far already."

Chapter 23

Colombo

The atmosphere in the large room at the beachside hotel was tense.

Even though there were no uniform officers to be seen anywhere, at Ong's insistence, the local Chief of Police had set up an Operations Room in one of the hotel's conference rooms. From there the Police would manage the complex operation to ensure Bonn's safe return. The Chief of Detectives, Sadeeb Deburwani had been assigned the case and Ong was tensely reminding him of his requirement to keep the police involvement in Bonn's kidnapping, a closely guarded secret.

"I've been told that kidnappers almost always insist that the Police are not informed or involved in any way. And that they ask for the family and friends of the victim to deal with them directly instead." Ong said as his eyes locked onto Sadeeb's own.

"That is often one of the demands." Sadeeb replied carefully. "Which is why we are now keeping a very low profile in and around your hotel. You won't see any police cars or uniformed officers nearby. We don't know if the kidnappers have the ability to keep you under observation. But just be sure..."

"But what about all the Police activity at the spa? Surely they could have seen all of that?"

"Easily explained as being part of our standard response to a murder scene. But by moving our operational base to the hotel, the kidnapping can be dealt with as a distinct entity. Thereby maintaining your cloak of secrecy, until we get a chance to arrest the perpetrators."

"Once my daughter is safely returned..."

"I understand your concerns Mr Thakkrani" Sadeeb reassured him. "Bonn's safety is our first priority. I can assure you that we are used to maintaining absolute discretion in these matters. My officers and I, have dealt with several of these situations over the last few years. We will get your daughter back for you, safe and sound."

"As I told your Chief. Money is no object. Whatever you need to get her back safely, staff, equipment or support, you will have it."

"These incidents have to run their usual course, Mr Thakkrani..."

"Well this incident is not usual for me and your Chief has assured me that this matter is now *the* top priority for his force. Didn't he make that clear to you?"

"Yes of course, Mr Thakkrani. I completely understand and agree. I just meant that these situations have a certain track they must follow."

"My security team all have experience dealing with critical incidents like this. If they can be of any assistance to you...?

"I appreciate your offer. But currently, I feel that we have more than enough resources to deal with the incident."

"So, what happens next? What are you actually doing?"

"My detectives are following up all possible leads from the scene and also talking to their informants. Forensic examiners have made a thorough search of the spa and at the rope bridge crossing. Kidnappers often make simple mistakes. We have had some notable successes in the last two years."

"But I assume you haven't caught all of them...?"

"Not all. No. But you need to understand that there are often unusual or extenuating circumstance..."

As they were speaking, one of the local taxis was searching for a parking space near the forecourt of the hotel. Having reversed into one of the few remaining spaces, the driver got out, locked the door and walked into the lobby.

He approached the Reception desk and said to the clerk standing there. "Have you got a guest by the name of Thakkrani staying here at the hotel?

"I'm not at liberty to reveal the names of our guests" she replied as she tapped on her computer. "What is this about?"

"I was asked to deliver this envelope to Mr. Thakkrani, at precisely 10am." The driver once again checked his wristwatch. "That's right now" he added urgently.

"I will have to speak to my Manager. Please take a seat over there." She said pointing to one of the nearby chairs.

A few minutes later, Ong appeared in the lobby and after a few words with the receptionist he approached the taxi driver. "I understand that you have an envelope for me?"

"Are you Mr Thakkrani?"

"Yes I am. The envelope?"

"Yes, here it is. I was told to give it to you at exactly 10am. I was here on time."

"Who told you to deliver it?" Ong asked as he slowly examined the outside of the plain envelope.

"A man in the city centre. He didn't give a name. He said he was a friend of yours. He gave me 50 dollars to deliver it. Told me that you were expecting it."

"Yes, that's fine. Thank you. Can you just stay there? I may have a reply for you."

"A reply? But I don't..."

Ong left the slightly confused taxi driver standing in the lobby. He then approached the Sadeeb, who was standing on the opposite side of the lobby, from where he had watched the exchange with the taxi driver.

"I assume this will be the note we were expecting?" Ong asked him. "The taxi driver said a random guy in the city centre paid him to deliver it here, at 10am exactly. I told him to wait, in case I need to send a reply."

"I think you're right. It's an easy, safe way for them to get it to you, as a first contact. But I need to take this through to the operations room to be opened. I don't want to risk losing any forensics. One of my men outside will get the details of the taxi so that we can track him down again if we need to. But I already suspect that he won't be able to tell us anything more than he told you. It's a simple but clever way for the kidnappers to deliver their ransom demands."

"You've seen this method before?" Ong asked.

"It's one of the methods they use. Not specific enough to identify any particular gang that we've encountered before though. Let's get this envelope opened and see what they have to say. In the meantime, it's probably best if you tell the driver you don't need him to wait after all..."

Back in the operations room one of the forensic team carefully sliced open the envelope with a scalpel knife and then using a pair of tweezers, extracted the single piece of folded notepaper inside. As he unfolded the sheet of paper, they saw that it did indeed hold the expected ransom note.

The message was made up from pieces of newspaper clippings, stuck to the surface of the paper.

The officer read the note aloud for the benefit of those in the room.

Thakkrani
we have your daughter.
100,000 US Dollars will get her back.
No police. Or she dies.
Ring this number at 10:15 am. for further instructions
919804568

"It's almost 10:15 now." Ong pointed out as everyone considered the instructions.

"They don't want to give you time to think about it." Sadeeb informed him. "Fairly standard again."

"So, what do I do?" Ong asked.

"In the first instance..." Sadeeb advised him. "You are going to ring the number they provided. We can listen in to the call on the other extension and record it. First thing is too see what they have to say. try to keep them talking. The more they say the more we know. If it's long enough we may be able to triangulate their location too."

"But what do I say to keep them on?" Ong asked.

"It depends what they say to you, we will try to help you with the responses if we can but we also want to make it sound as natural as possible."

"What about the money? I will need time to get that many dollars together. I doubt if the local bank even carries that much American currency."

"If true, it will give us more time to check them down."

"If they've done this before, they should realise that's a lot of dollars, shouldn't they? And that I will need time to get it together?"

"I would say yes to both of your questions. Lastly, if you do get the chance, you should ask for proof that Bonn still alive."

"Still alive?"

"It's an obvious question to ask. And I want you to sound as passive and helpful as possible. I want to make the kidnappers relax. To make them think that they are in charge."

"Okay. I can understand that."

"And then once we find out exactly what they want to do next, we can come up with a plan on how we will respond."

"I'm going to pay them the money and get my daughter back. That's how we will respond. I don't really care about you catching them in the first instance."

"Naturally. Getting Bonn back safely is our only priority too. But managing the payment of the ransom, to ensure you get your daughter back, can be a tricky operation."

"I'm going to completely cooperate with their requests. Whatever they want me to do, that's what we're going to do. I don't want you to spook them."

"Let's see what they have to say first. It's almost time for you to call them." The detective said as he glanced at his wristwatch "Use that phone over there. Please Mr Thakkrani. It's for the best. Trust me."

Ong picked up the telephone on the desk and dialled the number written on the ransom note. The telephone rang and rang before eventually it was picked up.

"Hello" a male voice said.

"This is Ong Thakkrani. I got your note."

"Don't talk. Just listen." The voice replied. "If you want your daughter back in one piece you will do exactly as I ask. The money should be in small bills, nothing larger than a $50 note. Once we have it, you will get your daughter back. You have 5 hours to get the money together. Don't involve the police or I will know. Once I have the money you will get another note at your hotel to tell you where she will be. Understood?

"Yes. I understand. But I will need more time to get that much American currency."

"You don't have more time. Your daughter tells me that you are a very rich man so just get the money. Because if I don't have the money by 3pm, you will never see your daughter again. You got that. Gone! And remember no police. You've been warned." And the phone line went dead.

"I didn't get the chance to ask about her being alive" Ong complained as he turned to speak to the detective. "Should I ring him back?"

"No. I think you need to stick to his rules at the moment."

"But five hours?" Ong asked.

"I can speak to the bank for you. Provided you've got that much available in your account?" The detective replied.

"I can call my bank right now, to transfer the money immediately." Ong stated blandly. "I'm more concerned that they've got enough US dollars locally to cover it."

"I'm sure they can make the necessary arrangements. They can probably get the money in from other branches if they have to."

"Did you trace the call? Lawrence asked from where he was seated.

"Our telephone system is antiquated." the detective replied with a shrug. "It's an analogue system which makes tracing calls much more complicated and time-consuming. I'm afraid it's fairly common knowledge now that everyone watches CSI and similar police programs."

"They probably used a mobile phone." Lawrence suggested. "Can you trace the owner of the number he gave us?"

"If it is a landline number, we can trace that down fairly quickly. But I agree with you, it's more likely to be a mobile, which will have been bought for cash at one of the numerous supermarkets that sell them by the dozen every week." The detective explained. "Effectively making the purchaser untraceable. It's called a burner phone. They will dispose of it as soon as this matter is concluded."

"You just used the word 'they'," Lawrence pointed out. "But the caller only referred to himself. Do you think this might be a one-man operation? Now the other one is dead at the spa?"

"From what we saw at the scene, I would say virtually impossible. But I won't exclude it completely at this point. I want to keep all options open."

"If there's nothing else I can do." Ong interrupted. "I need to telephone my bank. Lawrence can have a word outside please."

Lawrence followed Ong out of the incident room and along the corridor towards Ong's suite where the rest of his protection team was waiting for them. Ong explained about the ransom note and the phone call with the kidnapper to them.

"What do you make of the call?" Ong asked Lawrence as he paced around his suite. "He sounded very confident, I didn't get the sense that he was nervous at all. And you picked up on the use of *me* rather than *we* or *us*."

"So maybe it is this professional killer that attacked James McLeod? He's had enough time to get here from Darwin." Lawrence replied.

"I'm not so sure, Boss." Dan said slowly. "If it is him, why didn't he ask for the silver bars or the jade statues. Surely that's what he's after now? And only asking for 100,000 dollars? He must know that you are worth a lot more than that, by now."

"Maybe he will change the plan tomorrow." Roger suggested. "Some kidnappers want to try to confuse the process, just in case the police are involved. Try to keep all the arrangements last-minute, to confound any possible countermoves by us. This professional killer would know how to manipulate the process to suit himself."

"Yes, that's my experience too" Lawrence replied. "But this would be different. If this killer wants the silver or the statues he would know that you would need time to get them here. By delaying the time he asks for them, he makes the whole process even longer, which increases his risk of being caught."

"So, even allowing for the *me* and *us* point, you are leaning more towards the thuggee gang being responsible?" Ong asked.

"A thuggee cult who worship an ancient goddess" Dan asked. "That sounds much more dangerous to me. I would rather be dealing with the rational professional, than a group of religious fanatics."

"Is it possible that they are working together?" Roger asked. "Whoever is behind it, they are utterly ruthless and willing to kill or die to get what they want, as our Sandy found out. It certainly sounds like this professional who attacked McCloud and his friends."

"He may be working with them to get what he really wants, but I would say that the tattoo on the dead body points to them being our most likely suspects." Lawrence replied.

"And once we've handed over the ransom money, the killer will then ask for the silver and statues? Keeps us off-balance and he gets what he wants..." Roger suggested.

"So we should plan for this taking longer than 24hrs" Dan added. "The Police resources are going to be stretched."

"Which would also work to the advantage of the kidnapper." Lawrence pointed out.

"Whoever is behind this." Ong replied slowly. "Be assured, that once I have my daughter safely back, I will use all of my considerable resources to find out who is responsible for taking her and causing Sandy's death. And they will pay the penalty for that. On that you have my word. Roger...I want you to find the driver who delivered the note and get a full description of the man who gave it to him. The we can compare that to the description McCloud gave us. If this killer is on the island, I want to know about it."

Everyone fell quiet as they considered Ong's words, until finally Lawrence broke the silence. "I told Joseph that I would call him if we had any update. So, if you don't mind, I will do that now."

"Please put the call on the loudspeaker Lawrence." Ong replied. "I want to hear what Joseph and Bob think of the situation too. I trust their advice and guidance more than Deburwani. He has a slightly different agenda than us."

"I tend to agree Sir. Let's see what they have to say" Lawrence added as he dialled the number.

"Hello Larry. Good to hear from you." Joseph said. "We should be with you very soon. Any update for us?"

"You're on speakerphone, Joseph. And Ong is right next to me. We just got a ransom note and also spoke to the kidnapper. Or, at least someone speaking on their behalf."

Lawrence and Ong quickly outlined the latest situation and then paused to give Joseph and Bob time to assess what they had been told.

As they were waiting, there was a loud hammering on the door to Ong's suite and they could hear voices shouting from the other side.

"Can you go and see who that is Lawrence." Ong asked.

As soon as Lawrence opened the door, Ben, Sam and Stan rushed into the room.

"We found them." Sam said proudly as soon as she came into the room.

"Them?" Lawrence asked as he held his hand up in front of her.

"The kidnappers." Stan replied proudly as he stood next to her. "We followed them from the ravine. It's the cult of the goddess. We've found their headquarters."

"Tell me that you didn't take them with you, Ben." Ong voice reflected his exasperation.

"I didn't intend to..." Ben began.

"You knew he was going to try to find the trail? Sam asked, her surprise obvious in her voice.

"You're much too young for such a dangerous task" Ong explained as he looked from one to the other.

"We had to help." Stan explained. "She's our friend."

"And nobody saw us..." Sam added.

"I did try to leave them behind, once Stan had got us across the ravine." Ben replied obviously embarrassed.

"What's happening" Bob's voice asked from the speaker phone.

"Is that you Mr Dalton?" Stan asked.

"Yes, I'm with Joseph on the jet. We should be with you shortly. Ong was just updating us when you burst in!"

"So, if I may continue...It seems that your daughter's friends have done what the Police couldn't." Ong replied.

"What do you mean?" Bob asked.

"The Police gave up on the ravine when they went there at dawn this morning." Ong explained loudly. "I wasn't sure if the police were up to the task of tracking the kidnappers anyway and I don't believe in putting all my eggs in one basket. So I sent Ben up there, to see if he could get across and follow them again. But I didn't tell him to take Sam and Stan with him."

"But it sounds like your plan worked, doesn't it?" Bob replied. "Tell us exactly what happened Ben."

"We went back to the ravine. Where I lost the trail yesterday." Ben replied gratefully. "Stan somehow managed to climb across to the other side. It was amazing to watch him doing it. To be honest, I would never have managed that climb myself, Mr Thakkrani."

"I've heard about Stan's skills on the island..." Ong replied.

"And then he followed their trail again." Sam said proudly. "All the way up the mountain. Even across a boulder field. Then Stan heard them singing."

"Singing?" Bob asked. "On the mountain? I don't follow."

"When we got to the cliffs, I sat down for a rest and heard the chanting. At first I thought I was imagining it."

"Stan's got really good hearing." Sam added. "But just at that moment the wind died down and I could hear the voices too."

"I couldn't make out the words. But it was definitely human voices." Stan added.

"The chanting convinced me that there could be an entrance nearby." Ben told them.

"I always knew that Ben would track them down." Sam said.

"Having followed them that far." Ben continued. "I was determined to find an entrance or a cave. I assumed that I would find some hidden entrance into the mountain which the kidnappers had used, so I began to follow the rock face along."

"Then we found a fissure in the rock." Sam said.

"It was barely wide enough for me to squeeze through." Ben explained. "It went into the rock for fifteen or twenty yards and then became too narrow for us to go any further."

"But we didn't find any obvious entrance." Stan added.

"That was when I found the infinity symbol carved into the rock." Stan said.

"An infinity symbol?" Ong asked.

"Just like the cult's tattoo" Stan replied.

"It wasn't obvious until the angle of the sun shifted and you could just make out the carved emblem." Ben pointed out.

"It was just like the tattoo on the murderer at the spa." Sam reminded them. "The same sign of the thuggee cult, that Izi and Laura found on the web."

"That finally convinced me that we had found the right place." Ben added. "So, we came straight back to report to you."

"That's fantastic news." Ong said. "Obviously, I disapprove of the others going with you but you seem to have survived regardless."

"What do we do now?" Sam asked.

"*We* aren't going to do anything" Ong said sternly. "This is a job for the professionals now. Lawrence? What do you think?"

"Well that's a lot more information than we had before. But it's not definite proof that the goddess cult behind the kidnapping, or that Bonn is being held inside the mountain."

"Are you going to tell the police about this?" Bob's voice asked.

"I don't think so at this point." Ong replied. "For two reasons. Firstly, what Ben and the others discovered **is** not really proof of anything. And secondly, I'm not sure I fully trust the police yet. Particularly, as the kidnapper said he will know if we tell the Police. I think it's best if we keep this just between us at the moment."

"I have to agree." Joseph said. "I also think we need to make sure that we have our own resources ready to go, if necessary."

"We'll be ready." Lawrence reassured him. "One of the guys will pick you and Bob up at the airport."

"I will call you when we we're on final approach." Joseph replied. "That should give you twenty minutes warning."

"Once you and Bob arrive, we will all meet in my suite." Ong insisted. "By then I want to hear ideas about all our options."

Chapter 24

Johannesburg, Republic of South Africa

Jannie and his two protectors had arrived at the orphanage under cover of darkness, the previous evening. They were all tired, hungry and covered in dust. Nonetheless, Theo Johnson, who had managed the orphanage since its inception, welcomed all three of them with open arms.

"I'm afraid you've missed dinner." He advised them, as they each took a seat in his cramped office. "But I'm sure there's some leftovers in the kitchen, which you are more than welcome to. I'm afraid it won't be anything fancy."

"Whatever you have will be gratefully accepted" White replied. "We haven't eaten anything for more than eight hours and Jannie's stomach has been grumbling for most of that time."

"I'm a growing lad." Jannie replied with a smile. "So, I burn a lot of calories."

"I don't suppose you allow beer on the premises, do you?" Smith asked as he looked around the office.

"Only for very special occasions." Theo replied as he stood up and walked across to the small refrigerator which was noisily buzzing in the corner. "But since this is a very special occasion, I hope you like lager..." he added with a grin.

"Lager will be perfect. And gratefully accepted." Smith replied.

"Yes!" Jannie added.

"Just a soda for you, my boy. I only bend the rules so far." Theo replied shaking his head.

"A soda? For a very special occasion? But Theo..." Jannie complained.

"Now you're back, you need to set an example to the other boys." Theo explained as he handed out the drinks. "You know how some of them look up to you."

"But they are all asleep by now. Jannie countered.

"I'm sure some of them will wake up when you go into the dormitory. Funnily enough, I heard some of the boys talking about you this afternoon. You made a big impression on them while you were here. And I have told them about some of your stories since you left. You're turning into some sort of hero around here."

"You told them about me?" Jannie asked.

"You were here long enough to understand how they feel. Even with my best intentions I can't promise all of them that they will have a fantastic life once they leave here. The older boys know that life out there in the city is tough. You're one of the lucky ones. You must realise that? With Mr Prinsloo's help and guidance, you have managed to achieve what most of them dream of. You can't blame them for looking at your life and wishing it was theirs."

"I suppose so. I never really thought of it like that. I do know that I've been really lucky, with all the places I've been and all the interesting people I've met. Like Mr Smith and Mr White here. And of course, all my new friends at the CEA School."

"Exactly. And I also heard that you can now fly million pound airplanes?"

"Who told you about that? I only passed a few days ago..."

"Oh, you'd be surprised by what I hear. Just because you're far away doesn't mean I don't keep an eye on you. I like to keep an eye on all my old boys when I can."

"I'm sure the ones here keep you very busy." White said. "Mr Prinsloo and Owen speak very highly of you and your work here."

"That's very kind of them. We still get new arrivals every month. It's a big city with lots of orphans. I try to take as many as I can and we have expanded considerably with Mr. Prinsloo's help. In fact, we've got another dormitory now, Jannie. It was only completed last month. We needed it, that's for sure. That allows us another twenty beds but they are almost full already.

"I assume some of the guys I know are still here? Jannie asked.

"I'm sorry to admit that most of them are actually still here. Four of your friends left for jobs as apprentices with Prinsloo Industries. They are all training to be electrical engineers. Another couple moved out last month to live in the city, having found jobs for themselves. But the rest are still here. So, after you finish your light supper with Mr Smith and Mr White, there's a bed waiting for you in your old dormitory."

"Just like old times. I will try to sneak in so as not to disturb anyone."

"Somehow, I think that's going to be unlikely." Theo replied. "But for now, let's get you all something to eat."

"I think we could all do with a shower too, if that's not too much trouble?" White asked.

"There's always plenty of hot water. The showers are at the end of the dormitory."

An hour later having finished their simple but filling meal, Jannie made his way to his sleeping quarters leaving Smith and White talking to Theo in the orphanage's small dining room.

The following morning, Jannie woke early to see the sun rising over his favourite city. He quickly washed and dressed and crept out of the dormitory to get a better view of the sunrise. As he closed the door behind him, a flickering movement drew his eyes to his buggy which had been parked overnight on the orphanage's open forecourt. He walked slowly across to the brightly coloured vehicle to find out what had been stuck beneath the wiper blade on the windscreen. The single sheet of paper was flapping gently in the early morning breeze which is what had caught his attention. Carefully slipping the paper from beneath the wiper he read the four words printed across it.

WE HAVE NOT FORGOTTEN

As he gazed at the note, his eyes kept running backwards and forwards across the message, he failed to hear the silent approach of Mr Smith.
"What have you got there?" he asked quietly as he appeared at Jannie's side.
"It seems they haven't forgotten me after all." Jannie answered shakily.
"The Takers?" Smith asked.
"It has to be them. And I have only been here one night. So much for all the secrecy!"

"The secrecy was essential, Jannie. I can assure you. Unlikely as it sounds, I assume that someone saw us arriving late last night. It was a calculated risk. You coming back here I mean. But it seems we've been unlucky; Owens latest intelligence reports weren't as useful as we had hoped."

"So, what do I do now?"

"The first thing to do is to eat a hearty breakfast. Then I need to discuss this message with Theo and Mr White. And probably Owen too."

"Eat breakfast? Don't you think we should just get away as fast as possible?"

"There's no point rushing into anything. They aren't going to try anything here. Once we've all discussed it we will decide what to do next. Let's go over to the kitchen and get ourselves a good meal. It may be the last one we have for a little while."

Jannie's face and posture showed the surprise he felt at Mr Smith's calm response. It took a few moments standing at the side of his buggy before he stepped forward to follow Smith towards the kitchen.

On the other side of the city, in a room at the back of a smoky bar, the Takers leader, Rhino, was feeling very pleased with himself. He hadn't expected to ever see Jannie and his instantly recognisable buggy in Johannesburg ever again. But even so, he had insisted that one of his gang did a drive-by of the orphanage at least once every 24 hours. It was a complete surprise when one of his gang nervously woke him at 5am this morning, to report that he'd seen the buggy at the orphanage again. Rhino immediately told the man to return and leave a note on the windscreen so that

Jannie would be afraid. He wanted Jannie to know that the Takers gang and Rhino in particular, would never forgive his insult to their reputation, even after all these months. He enjoyed the thought that Jannie would spend the day wondering when his life would end. He also instructed the man to keep observation at the orphanage until Rhino could get there himself.

Rhino also hoped that his success in finally tracking down Jannie's whereabouts would reinstate his personal reputation with Mr Abdul Khan. Khan was the only man he had ever feared, even more so since his henchman, the huge Russian named Bol had torn his index finger from his hand. Rhino unconsciously rubbed the scarred stump, as he recalled his first meeting with Bol.

Rhino was under no misconception as to what would happen if he failed Khan again. He had no intention of contacting Khan directly ever again. He would comply with Bol's explicit contact instructions to the letter. Pulling on a pair of baggy jeans and a designer T-shirt, he made his way out of the bar and climbed into his own BMW saloon.

The drive to the central post office, through the early morning traffic, took almost an hour but this was a call that he had to make himself. Bol's instructions on how to contact him in an emergency were very specific. Having parked his car nearby he strode into the post office the moment they opened the doors and he approached the long line of telephones which were set along one wall. Selecting one at random he punched the buttons in the long sequence he had been required to memorise. There was a long pause and then a series of clicks as the connections were made.

"You have reached Phase One Constructions." A mechanical voice told him. "Please leave your message and one of our operators will contact you shortly."

Rhino recognised the expected response and repeated the phrase that Bol had told him to use. "This is John Bergstrom. I would like to place an order with my area salesman. He can call me at home." Rhino then hung up the receiver and strode quickly back out of the building. Bol had told him to expect a response on the burner phone which he had given him, within 24 hours. As he drove off in his car, Rhino was smiling to himself as he imagined how he would be rewarded for his clever work. He was also looking forward to extracting his revenge on Jannie after all this time. It would give him a great deal of pleasure. He had waited a long time for this opportunity and he hoped that Bol and Mr Khan would allow him to deal with this matter personally. But for now, all he had to do was make sure Jannie didn't slip through his fingers before he heard back from Bol to tell him what to do next.

PART FOUR

Chapter 25

Colombo

As soon as Bob and Joseph had cleared customs at Colombo's airport, the car brought them straight to the hotel, where they found Ong and the others waiting for them in his villa. After brief introductions, everyone sat down to discuss their options.

"Every kidnapping is a unique police operation because there are so many variables and usually a number of different agencies involved." Joseph explained. "Which means our response plan needs to be flexible enough to cope with that."

"You told us that the best that we can hope for is that the people who have Bonn have done it before. Why?" Ong asked.

"I've found that the more experienced they are, the more assured they are and therefore the safer Bonn will be. Nervous kidnappers make the whole process much more dangerous, as far as the victim is concerned."

"Well so far they seem pretty well organised." Lawrence replied.

"Which is more than you can say for the Police" Roger told them. "They didn't even bother to check the far side of the ravine."

"Maybe they don't have a tracker like Ben" Sam suggested.

"I'm not sure about the other Police resources either." Ong added. "Even tracing the phone call seems beyond them."

"It's a poor country, Ong" Bob pointed out. "Upgrading technology is expensive as you know."

"What about a hostage rescue team?" Joseph asked. "With the number of kidnappings they say they have dealt with..."

"They don't have one, is the simple answer." Lawrence replied.

"I've been speaking to Owen Strasser about that." Bob told them. "His specialist operations team dealt with our kidnapping in Venezuela without police assistance. Owen told me that outside of the US or Europe, police forces often lack the appropriate training or equipment to manage effective hostage recovery."

"I'm really hoping it won't come to that Bob." Ong replied. "I'm going to pay the ransom money and get my little girl back. Once she's safe, I will worry about dealing with the man or men behind it, in my own time."

"I think the simplest and easiest solution is often the best." Bob replied.

"I would like to keep the other option on the table though." Joseph insisted. "Flexible response, remember...I don't suppose Owen's team is available to help us if we do need them?"

"I did ask him about that" Bob replied. "Just in case. But he told me that the team is deployed elsewhere at the moment and it would take him several days to get them here."

"We will have to rely on the resources that we have here then." Ong said. "Which doesn't appear to be a very attractive option according to what you are telling me."

"Even a last resort, is better than no resort." Joseph insisted. "Plus, we have our team, who all have experience and training to deal with the current situation."

"It's been a long time since any of us crashed through a door Joseph" Roger pointed out.

"I realise that." Joseph replied. "And no refresher training since then either. So normally I wouldn't ask any of you to do it again. But if we absolutely had no other choice..."

The next moment there was a loud knocking at the door. As Joseph was already standing he strode over and opened the door to find Sadeeb Deburwani standing outside.

"Has something happened?" Joseph asked.

"I need to have a private word with Mr Thakkrani." The detective replied as he stepped into the room.

"I'm still waiting for the ransom cash to be picked up from bank." Ong replied.

"I understand that." The detective replied. "But I have something to tell you. And only you."

"I trust everyone here" Ong replied immediately.

"I have to insist..." the detective replied sternly.

"We can all wait outside on the balcony if that suits you" Bob suggested to the detective when he recognised the intransigence of his stance.

"I appreciate that Bob." Ong replied.

"Thank you. It will only take a few minutes" the detective said and visibly relaxed his posture.

Everyone stood up and quickly walked outside through the open patio doors. Joseph was the last one through and he closed the doors silently behind him.

"All right detective." Ong began. "What you want to ask me about?"

"I'm not going to ask you anything, Mr Thakkrani. I'm here to tell you about something that happened in city last night."

"Okay. I'm listening."

"Around nine o'clock last night, there was an attempted robbery not very far from your hotel."

"I'm sure you get a lot of those." Ong replied impatiently. "But I don't see why you wanted everyone to leave to tell me that...or how that's relevant to my daughter."

"Please let me finish and I think you'll see it is very much of interest to you."

"I hope so..."

"Apparently three men attacked an elderly Japanese man in the street. Or at least, they tried to attack him. I say that because it turns out that their intended victim is actually a martial arts expert. An 8th Dan black belt. A Master. He is quite famous in Japan. Consequently, in less than a minute, the three attackers were either disabled or unconscious on the pavement.

"I'm sorry" Ong replied. "I'm still not with you."

"The victim called the police and when the officers arrived to deal with the incident they discovered that the attackers all bore the same tattooed symbol of the goddess in their armpits."

"The thuggee cult?"

"Exactly. My officers arrcstcd the three attackers and took them to our central police station. The officer in charge there then called me. I've left standing instructions at every police station that I should be informed personally, day or night, if any incident occurs involving the cult members. To be honest, I had thought my instruction would be unlikely to achieve anything, since none of them had ever been arrested before."

"Didn't you say the attackers were injured? Surely they should have been taken to the hospital?" Ong asked.

"Indeed they were, but the rules are different in my country. They can be more...flexible than they are in other places."

"It sounds like that."

"My instructions were very clear that any cult members should also be held incognito. I didn't want anyone else to know that we had taken them into custody before my officers from my office had a chance to interview them."

"Incognito? Surely even here the suspects have rights? If you're going to prosecute them for the robbery, their lawyers will probably want to exclude any evidence you obtain."

"I will worry about that once we have safely recovered your daughter."

"And you thought that these suspects could help achieve that? My understanding of these religious cults is that members refuse to say anything when the authorities asked them questions."

"The officers in my team are very persuasive Mr Thakkrani. And the methods we employ tend to be more effective than you may be used to."

"Are you going to tell me that they knew something about Bonn's whereabouts?"

"One of them knew about a young girl who was kidnapped yesterday and was being held by their boss. He's some kind of religious shaman, who has visions. The cult members believe he actually speaks to their goddess."

"I'm still not sure I understand how that helps us."

"There's more. It took a long time to get everything out of them but my officers have been interviewing them *vigorously* for more than 12 hours now. My chief interrogator has just handed me a file, which contains all the information they managed to get out of the suspects. It's very helpful. At that point, I decided to share the information with you."

"I still don't see how this helps. If they are in your custody they can't be involved in the negotiation about my daughter."

"That's true. None of them were actually involved in the operation to kidnap her. But we now know for sure exactly who we are dealing with. Their boss. Which is a big step forward. Plus, they were able to give me a good description of the caverns inside the mountain where she will be being held. They also explained in great detail how to find and open the entrance to those caverns. Which we will need if we have to mount an operation to rescue her."

"But I've already made it abundantly clear to you that I'm going to pay them the ransom, detective."

"Indeed you have and I agree that that is the safest and best option. But I believe in keeping my options open and if the situation changes and we need to go into the caverns, the knowledge we now have will be invaluable."

"Why didn't you tell me this in your operations room? Or even in front of my team?"

"I'm going to be totally candid with you, Mr Thakkrani. I sorry to have to tell you that I can't trust everybody on my team. I don't know who it is, but someone within my part of the organisation has been leaking information over the last two years. One of the cult prisoners actually confirmed my suspicions. Even though he didn't know exactly where the information came from within the police, it was common knowledge within his cult, that their boss was being helped by someone in the city's police."

"That might explain why none of them has ever been arrested" Ong suggested.

"It might. Lastly, they told us that they will be having a big ceremony tomorrow something they do once a year, when every member of the cult is commanded to attend."

"Giving you the chance to round them all up in one go, I assume?"

"Possibly. But my priority is getting your daughter back first."

"You've given me a lot to think about. You appreciate that I will have to discuss it with Mr Dalton and Joseph, even if I have to keep the details of what you just told me between us two."

"I would certainly appreciate that."

"But it doesn't change my decision to pay them the ransom and get my daughter back. That's my *only* objective. Until she is safely back with me, I won't jeopardise that."

"I totally understand and agree, as does my Boss. Hopefully the ransom money will arrive soon. It must almost be time for the kidnappers to contact you again."

"It's on its way from the bank right now." Ong reassured him as they both stood up. "But I want your word that you won't jeopardise the ransom payment by trying to arrest the culprits."

"You have it. The safe return of your daughter is the first priority I can assure you. With the information that my interrogator has discovered we will have more than enough to organise a raid into the cavern any time after they have returned her.

"What you decide to do after my daughter is safe, is entirely up to you detective. I will of course assist you in any way possible but only once she is back with me."

"I can't ask any more than that Mr Thakkrani" the detective said and then left the room.

Ong approached the patio doors and sliding them open invited just Bob and Joseph back into the room to tell them what the detective had said.

"I'm not really that surprised." Bob informed them when Ong had finished speaking. "I'm sure the cops here earn very poor wages, which leaves them open to offers of cash in return for information. It's the same the world over."

"I've seen it in many of the countries we visit." Joseph added.

"Which is why I want you to keep this just between the three of us at the moment." Ong insisted. "I'm sure Tracey and the youngsters are better off not knowing the moment."

"I can give my team an outline of what we now know without giving them the details." Joseph said thoughtfully.

"I agree" Bob said. "And at least we now know that McCloud's psycho killer isn't behind this."

"So it seems" Ong replied as the telephone began to ring. "Hello?" Ong asked as he picked up the phone and listened for a moment. "Yes, thank you. Please send them along to my room."

"The money?" Bob asked.

"With only a few minutes to spare." Ong replied as he looked at his watch.

"I will have to call my team in now to brief them. We might have to move fast." Joseph suggested.

"Leave the youngsters outside though" Ong instructed him. "I haven't got time to deal with all their questions right now."

Chapter 26

Colombo

"What do you think is going on?" Laura quietly asked the others as they sat together on the patio. "It's nearly three o'clock."

"I told you." Izi replied insistently. "I just saw the money arrive."

"Technically, you just saw two men walking along the corridor carrying briefcases." Stan pointed out.

"Which were chained to their wrists." Izi reminded him. "They even looked like security guards to me. Who else would wear a suit in this heat?"

"And you assume they were heading to this villa." Ben added.

"I bet the money is inside by now." Izi told them.

"If Ong ever invites us back inside we could find out for ourselves." Laura replied.

"Let's accept Izi is correct." Sam interrupted. "Now the money is here, they can hand it over and they will let Bonn go. Isn't that the way it usually works?"

"If you believe what you see on television I guess so." Ben replied. "But since we've been cut out of the communication loop, guessing is the best we can do."

"I don't know why they won't let us help. We did find the cult's headquarters." Sam said.

"I don't mean any disrespect to anyone." Ben replied. "But this is a matter for the professionals, regardless how close we feel to Bonn. How would we feel if we did something that resulted in her death?"

"We all know that, Ben." Laura replied. "But I feel so useless just sitting here. I'm sure you guys all feel the same really."

"Waiting is always the hard part." Ben replied. "I had to learn to be patient in my job in the Reserve. Game poachers are nervous by nature, they know the harsh penalties they will receive if they get caught, which makes them extra cautious."

"And you think these kidnappers will be the same?" Stan asked. "I guess they are all facing the death penalty, if they get caught."

"That's what I think" Ben replied as he nodded slowly.

"Do you think the police will try to arrest them? When they pick up the ransom money, I mean? Izi asked.

"Again, if you believe what you see on the television, I would have to say no..." Laura told her. "They will wait until Bonn is safe and then arrest them later."

"Which is exactly what the kidnappers will want to avoid." Ben said. "At any cost."

"But the first step is handing over the ransom money." Stan reminded them.

"And now we know that's arrived in the hotel, the handover can take place." Izi insisted.

"If the money has arrived... Stand replied with a shrug.

As the teens were discussing the arrival of the ransom money, another taxi driver was approaching the hotel reception desk.

Lawrence, who had positioned himself on one of the lobby sofas, noted that the taxi driver was carrying a large envelope. He watched the man with interest and depressing the switch in his hand and whispered. "Taxi driver at the front desk."

"I've got a delivery for one of your guests" the taxi driver said to the receptionist. "A Mr Thakkrani?"

"Wait there one moment and I will page him."

Moments later Ong arrived at the front desk to take possession of the envelope. He returned to the Operations room, where he was met by Deburwani who was waiting with Bob and Joseph.

"May I?" The detective asked and held out his hand. Taking the envelope from Ong he carefully sliced open the flap and peered inside. Then stepping over to a table, he emptied the contents out on the surface. A small mobile phone skidded across the surface and small piece of paper followed it. Using a Biro, the detective turned the piece of paper over to reveal the words on the other side.

Call the number in the phone, at 3 PM exactly.

"Another layer to stop you tracing the calls." Bob suggested as they all leaned in to read the note.

"Bought for cash at some out-of-the-way supermarket." Joseph added.

"And I anticipate he won't stay on the phone very long either." The detective said. "They are taking all the expected precautions so far."

"It's one minute to three." Ong reminded them. "I hope it's already charged." He added as he picked up the phone and switched it on.

"Have you got the money?" The voice asked when Ong had dialled the number.

"Yes, it's all here. Just as you asked."

"Write this down." The voice directed. "134, Church street. It's a coffee shop. There's a concrete bench right outside. Put the money in a sports holdall and leave it under the bench at 4pm exactly. Don't tell the police or you'll never see your daughter again. Got that?"

"Yes, I understand. I will find it." Ong replied.

"And NO POLICE"

"Of course. I understand completely. No police." Ong reassured the voice. "But what about my daughter? Will she be in the coffee shop?"

"Not so fast Mr Big Shot. I haven't finished. You will bring the money yourself. I know exactly what you look like. Once I've got the money and I'm far away, I will call you on this phone to tell you where you can collect her from. Any funny business and you will never hear from me again. Or your daughter. Got it?"

"Far away? Are you leaving the country?" Ong asked.

"That's got nothing to do with you."

"But when will you call me?"

"Same time tomorrow. Once I am free and clear. You will have your little girl back for dinnertime." And then the line went silent.

Ong stood thinking for a few moments holding the phone in front of him.

"I know that area quite well" Deburwani said. "It's a pedestrian precinct, so he won't be coming by car."

"Twenty-four hours between receiving the ransom and giving Bonn back.... I don't like that at all" Bob pointed out.

"And he might be out of the country?" Joseph asked. "This guy is super cautious."

"Are we sure it's the cult?" Bob asked. "Even with what you just briefed us about, Ong?"

"I think we still stick with that scenario for now Bob" Ong replied before turning back to the detective. "It sounds like the kidnapper will be watching for me to deliver the money. In a sports bag."

"It will be difficult to hide a tracking device in a sports bag." The detective said. "I would have been happier if he'd left the money in the briefcases the bank used."

"I'm sure he was thinking the same thing." Joseph suggested.

"No tracking devices." Ong insisted. "And no surveillance team trying to follow him afterwards. I'm going to do exactly as he has asked. Then, once I have Bonn back, you can arrest all of them."

"I think you're taking a big risk, Mr Thakkrani." the detective replied.

"Possibly. But that's what I'm going to do anyway."

"We need to get a sports bag" Joseph said.

"There's one in my suite," Ong replied. "We need to update my team, detective. I will be ready to leave in ten minutes." Ong told him before turning on his heel and walking out of the room with Bob and Joseph trailing behind him.

"He may have been very honest with you about his interrogation techniques and the leak within his own team, but I still don't trust him completely." Bob admitted as they walked towards the suite.

"He has more than one agenda." Joseph replied. "Cops are the same the world over. Catching the bad guy will always be their top priority. Victims always come second place."

"My Bonn will not become a victim of a police agenda." Ong said sternly as they entered his suite. Get the sports bag from the wardrobe over there and put the money inside. I don't want to be late at the delivery point."

"The kidnapper is probably already in position." Bob pointed out. "Hence the short timeframe. He will be watching the street very carefully for any unusual activity now that he's told us where to drop the money. At least that's what I would be doing, if I was running this operation."

"Let's hope you're right Bob." Ong replied. "The more professional they are, the safer Bonn is. As Joseph pointed out."

Chapter 27

Khan

Abdul Khan was sitting in his ultra-secure clean room, buried twenty feet below his luxury villa in the Libyan desert a few miles outside Tripoli. A rare smile creased his usually hard features as he read the report held in his hand. "My patience has paid off once again." He thought to himself.

Ever since that fateful day more a than a year ago, when the Takers had first encountered Jannie Pietersen in Johannesburg, that name had been 'red flagged' in all of Khan's complex array of computer systems. The report he was now reading with such interest, had been generated automatically when the supercomputer had run its nightly enquiry. During that covert search of many of the world's government computer systems, the red flag had been activated by the RSA's border control system.

Khan slowly nodded to himself as he read the details before him. He grudgingly acknowledged that slipping across the border into South Africa from Zaire, would normally have been the perfect choice. Especially if you wanted to do so without that entry appearing on any computer system. And you didn't want to run the risk of me finding you again did you Jannie. He thought to himself. But your cautiousness didn't protect you this time, did it. You need to be smarter than that, if you want to avoid me.

As he gazed further down the page, one of his technicians had added an explanation as to the source of the data.

Many of the border posts between Zaire and RSA have still to be equipped with live computer terminals. Consequently, the daily data is collected manually by the border guards and then transferred overnight to a central data point where it is then input into the border control database. The records in this database may therefore have a minimum of 24 hours of time delay.

24 hours? Khan's smile disappeared. You could be a long way from the border by now couldn't you, young man? He ran his finger over a large-scale map which was spread across his desk. The satellite printout of the countryside south of that particular border crossing had been appended to the report by one his far-sighted technicians. Surely you aren't thinking of heading back to Jo'Burg? Or perhaps you think you can hide in plain sight? Did you decide that all on your own, or is Prinsloo still watching over you?

Standing up from his desk, Khan made his way out of his secure room and into the main computer control centre to speak to his manager.

Thrusting a copy of the report in front of the manager Khan said. "I want to know the names of everyone who passed through that border control point on that day. And I want to know as soon as possible."

The manager quickly scanned the report and replied. "I would need to amend the overnight search, in order to extract that data."

"I need the data sooner than that. Do it now and let me know the minute you get the result."

"Yes sir, of course."

"Encrypt it and send it to my office upstairs as soon as you have the information" Khan ordered before he turned and walked towards the elevator, which would take him to the villa above.

Less than an hour later, a message flashed up on Khan's computer. As he opened it he saw it was from his manager.

The data in relation to that particular border crossing shows only six people listed as crossing during the 24-hour period specified. This number is uncharacteristic of the usual data and should be treated with some sensitivity. I also note the passport number data, which is a mandatory field, is missing from those six entries. This is also unusual. I conclude two possibilities, either the data was not collected or recorded in the first place by the border control staff, or the data entry centre operative failed to key in the data.

Utter incompetence. Khan muttered to himself. Without the passport numbers the names became almost irrelevant, as crosschecking using the names alone would produce hundreds or even thousands of results from the data held on his supercomputers. As Khan's eyes scanned the short list, he immediately noted that only two of them appeared to be non-African in origin.

Mr Andy Smith
Mr Thomas White

I wonder if those two are your travelling companions, Pietersen? Khan asked himself. Surely you wouldn't be foolish enough to travel back alone? Perhaps they are some sort of mercenary bodyguards bought and paid for by your rich benefactor? No way to run background checks on them with the details provided. Those probably are not their real names anyway, he decided. But such men would be easy enough to pick up in Zaire, since the country is a safe haven for them. Yes, two bodyguards would be inconspicuous enough. But do you really think that two poorly paid mercs will be enough to keep him safe from me, Prinsloo?

Khan rocked back in his chair and considered the most efficient way to track down Jannie's current whereabouts. Although South Africa is a vast country, thanks to millions of pounds spent on the police and military, many of their computer systems were now fully integrated, making life much simpler for Khan's own computers to steal the data. If Jannie interacted with the police or army in any way, Khan's data centre would receive the data almost instantaneously. And because of the red flag on Jannie, Khan would be informed immediately after. But where are you heading? Khan looked at the map again. Durban or Cape Town were most likely...definitely not Johannesburg. He wouldn't be that stupid...

But just to be sure, he would have the Takers keep an eye on the orphanage where Jannie had spent many of his years. He opened up a new email on his desktop and typed a brief message to Bol, who had been tasked with keeping in touch with Rhino.

Jannie Pietersen may be returning to Johannesburg. Instruct Rhino to watch for him and inform you if he is seen. Reinforce my instruction that he takes no independent action in this matter.

K

As he pressed the send button, Khan suddenly questioned his own decision-making. 'Why didn't I just send the Butcher to South Africa to manage this?' The answer came back almost immediately. 'Because something doesn't feel right.' His instincts had been right all his life and now those instincts were tingling. The more he thought about it, he realised that the Butcher's reports had subtly changed over the last few months, particularly since he disposed of the Australian problems. 'I need some solid intelligence. I will send Craig Dunlop to find out what the Butcher is really up to. He can start today, while I sort out Pietersen myself.'

Thousands of miles away, the Butcher was blissfully unaware of his boss' growing concerns. He was also sitting in front of a laptop, typing up his carefully worded, weekly report to Khan.

My police informant has reassured me that the federal investigations into the plane crash and the explosion at the mine are getting nowhere. They have recently decided that the location of the plane means its recovery is impractical. The mine tunnels are completely inaccessible without months of expensive and dangerous construction work which neither government wishes to fund. The investigations will continue nonetheless to reassure public opinion. Currently they have discovered no obvious indications of criminal activity. Their efforts to trace the owners of the plane and the mining company have drawn complete blanks. My

informant will continue to monitor the ongoing investigations and report back to me weekly.
I will remain in Australia pending further assignment.

The Butcher read over the report and congratulated himself upon it before he pushed the send button. In view of the continuing Federal investigations, he had decided not to turn Brian in to authorities or make a personal visit to any of his family members. Yet. Now that I've kept Khan happy, I can get on with the important business, he thought to himself.

When he had visited his underworld contact in Darwin to collect his new passport a few days before, he had taken a calculated risk.

"There's something else you can do for me, while I'm here" the Butcher had told the boss.

"Sure. What do you need?"

"I want you to keep your ears open out for anything about antique jade statues being offered for sale."

"Stolen, I assume?" the boss asked with a grin.

"Obviously! I'm not going to pay retail prices for them." The Butcher didn't really like to involve other people in his search for them but, as planned, the request hadn't provoked any unexpected reaction from the boss.

"No problem." The boss replied. He was happy to be able to keep someone with the Butcher's fearsome reputation, happy. Plus, he knew that he would make a fat commission in the middle of any deal he organised. So, everyone benefitted.

Once he had completed his business with the underworld boss, the Butcher had found an Internet cafe in the city centre where he continued his research into the Black Marlin and her famous owner, Ong Thakkrani.

As he scrolled through the web pages, he was once again amazed that his searches revealed so much data about the subjects that he was interested in. His own personal details were recorded almost nowhere and that was the way he preferred to keep it. Anonymity had huge benefits to a man in his profession, but even so he couldn't understand why other people would allow so much of the personal information to be freely available on the World Wide Web. One of his professional mentors had long ago taught him an immutable truth, that in his particular line of work, knowledge was power.

Using standard search engines, combined with his inquisitive mind, he was able to amass a considerably detailed profile on the Black Marlin and both Ong and his only daughter, Bonn. He also found more information about the charitable organisation she now headed up and many of the details of the orangutan sanctuary which the charity was supporting. He was disappointed to find that none of his searches came up with even the slightest clue as to the most critical piece of information. The exact location of the sanctuary. But thanks to the charity's overly helpful secretary, he still had his list of VIPs who had been selected for the next visit to the mysterious island.

Now that the good Inspector was happily working for him again and he had updated Khan, he felt he had time to try out his new passport to flit over to New Zealand to see the VIP in Auckland. He smiled grimly to himself as he looked forward to that particular conversation.

Chapter 28

Colombo

The atmosphere in Ong's villa was tense. The 24-hour deadline, which the kidnapper had given to return Bonn to her father, had just passed without them hearing anything from the kidnapper.

Bob, Joseph and Lawrence were all standing close to the patio doors, listening quietly as the Sadeeb Deburwani tried to explain his situation to Ong.

"As I explained to you yesterday" the detective explained. "The fact that the pickup point was a pedestrian precinct and very busy at that time of day made police action very difficult."

"There wasn't supposed to be any police action. Remember?" Ong replied through gritted teeth. "I made it very clear to you that I had intended to pay them the ransom and get my daughter back. Whatever you wanted to do, in terms of arresting and prosecuting the kidnappers, was supposed to happen after she was safe. That was what you agreed, wasn't it?"

"My men were instructed not to interfere with the ransom collection in any way. Mr Thakkrani. I'm sure that the kidnapper was totally unaware of their presence. But you have to understand that photographs and video recording of them collecting the ransom, would be very helpful in any future prosecution."

"This is incredible" Ong's angry voice replied. "You told me yesterday that you have a leak in your operation. By initiating this observation process, you could have tipped off the kidnappers. Maybe that's why I haven't heard from them. have you thought about that?"

"That's totally impossible. The officers that I used are not part of my team at all. I deliberately brought them in from a unit in the far north of Sri Lanka. I am positive that they could have no connection with the cult."

"And what did you actually discover? That was worth risking my daughter's life for? Ong asked. "Joseph warned me not to trust you."

"Less than a minute after you left the cash under the bench, a man on a motorised wheelchair, picked up the sports bag and wove his way through the crowd."

"So, you can identify one of them at least..." Bob interrupted abruptly.

"The man wore a large straw hat, which totally obscured his face. And a baggy long sleeved shirt which confused his shape and skin colour. Unfortunately, the photographers were using a first-floor window to take their shots and the raised position, combined with the hat made a face shot impossible. So, no, I can't identify him."

"Unbelievable." Ong snapped. "I wonder if he saw them taking his photo?"

"I was told that he never looked up once during the pickup. So definitely not."

"What about the motorised wheelchair?" Lawrence asked. "I haven't seen many of them in the streets around here, can you trace him through that?"

"I've got officers doing precisely that right now, but so far to no avail."

"So now what?" Ong asked. "The twenty-four hours he had to deliver Bonn has passed and he hasn't contacted me. In the meantime, he's had a whole day to escape the country with or without Bonn."

"I'm afraid I have to agree with you." The detective replied sadly. "The time for waiting has now passed. Direct action is required."

"What do you mean by that?" Ong asked.

"Everything that we know for sure, indicates that Bonn was kidnapped by members of the goddess' cult. The three robbery suspects have given us a fair amount of information describing the main cavern and the various tunnels that riddle the mountain. They also told us that today is a special day for their leader and the Goddess."

"Why is today special?" Joseph asked.

"It's the only time that all the members of the cult are obliged to attend the ceremony. It's an annual event apparently."

"At which point, someone is going to notice that three of their members are missing." Bob pointed out.

"Another reason I have to act today." The detective admitted. "Since none of them have ever been captured before, their existence has always remained an urban myth. I have been chasing ghosts and rumours from more than five years, trying to get to the bottom of all the crimes I suspect they have been involved in."

"So, what are you going to about Bonn?" Ong asked as he stepped closer to the detective.

"I don't know why they didn't hand her back to you. But the chances are that she is being held inside the mountain. If we can burst in, before they realise that we have, then we can rescue her and roundup every member of the cult at the same time."

"But if you suspect there are around hundred members, you can't possibly expect to overcome them with the specialist manpower that you have available." Joseph pointed out. "I've been involved in plenty of police raids during my time in London. I know how difficult an operation like this will be with such a small team."

"Even if you are positive that Bonn was being held inside the mountain, you can't be sure exactly where." Ong pointed out. "The way you described it to me, there are a dozen possible places she could be in that maze of tunnels."

"Where would you begin to look?" Lawrence sounded as frustrated as he felt.

"The way the robbery suspects described it, the mountain is riddled with interconnecting passageways and numerous small caverns. We expect most of them to be in the main chamber for the ceremony. That's a huge cavern, where the statue of the goddess is. And it's the first place you come to after the entrance tunnel."

"Which is where you will make most of your arrests, I'm sure" Joseph explained. "But do you really expect Bonn to be held in there too?

"That wouldn't make any sense. Surely?" Bob asked. "I would have thought that you would keep a prisoner in a small space? Easier to maintain security of them that way."

"In normal circumstances, I would agree with you, Bob, but I have reason to believe that Bonn will be in the main cavern, around the time the sun sets tonight." The detective replied.

"That's very specific." Joseph pointed out. "Too specific actually...Why would you say that."

"I'm sorry to have to tell you this Mr. Thakkrani, but I now think the kidnappers never intended to give your daughter back."

"Really! And when exactly did you have this sudden inspiration?" Ong asked as his temper rose again.

"As I told you before my interrogators are very good. Even after the robbery suspects had told us all about their Goddess, the Master and given descriptions of the mountain hideaway, my chief interrogator felt they were still holding something back. They were avoiding something about the big ceremony tonight."

"I don't like the way you're dragging this out." Bob interrupted. "Just tell us what you know."

"An hour ago, my chief interrogator finally got one of them to tell him why today was so different. Once a year, at this special ceremony, the cult make a live sacrifice to the goddess."

"You mean Bonn, don't you?"

"I think it's highly likely. The guy told us that on this particular night, his Goddess demands the blood of a child to be offered up to her. So unless they have taken another young woman, which hasn't yet been reported to the Police, I'm afraid Bonn is in mortal danger."

"But the ransom demand?" Ong asked. "I did everything they asked."

"It's possible that they never intended to give her back. Whether you paid the ransom or not."

"Then you've got to go in there right now and get her back." Ong insisted.

"I agree. I have spent the hour, since my interrogator gave me the information, issuing the relevant orders. The SWAT team will lead the raid and gain us access into the mountain. They will use explosives if necessary."

"How many men in your SWAT team? Joseph asked.

"Twelve."

"That won't be enough. Who else are you going to use? Joseph asked.

"I have a tactical squad of twenty uniformed officers attached to my branch. They've all been trained in rapid entry and search techniques."

"What about the informant in your squad?" Bob asked. "Aren't you worried about him tipping off the cult."

"As far as everyone outside of this room is concerned, the raid is being mounted against a drugs laboratory that has been discovered in the jungle north of the city. I won't tell them the exact location, or where we are really going to until we get there. I plan on being in the lead vehicle.

"So, thirty two of you? You don't have enough officers to do what you need to do." Joseph pointed out. You said there could be up to a hundred of them in there. If they all turn up for the ceremony. It's clear that you need my team as well. We can be responsible for finding and protecting Bonn."

"I can't take civilians on a police raid of this magnitude. There is bound to be heavy resistance. I can't be sure and I suspect we will have to use firearms.

And all of my team are licensed to carry firearms in your country. And we all do. It would be one less thing for you to have to worry about and also give you half a dozen extra on your team. All of whom are trained bodyguards. What do you say?"

"It's out of the question."

"You could deputise all of them as constables." Bob pointed out. "It's been done before."

"Do I need to speak to your Chief?" Ong asked. "I don't want to put more pressure on you, but this is my daughter's life you're talking about."

"Deputise them...that's something I hadn't considered." Sadeeb replied slowly as he reassessed his options. "I would need to speak to the Chief myself. Deputising foreign nationals to join an armed raid...That sort of decision is political, so he would have to sign off on it."

"I suggest that you get on the phone and ask him." Ong insisted. "It will be dark soon."

"You're right. If you will excuse me for a moment..." the detective replied and walked out of the villa.

"I'm going to ring his Chief too" Ong announced as he walked towards his bedroom to use the phone. "To make sure he understands the benefits of using your team Joseph."

"How did you know they've deputised civilians before?" Joseph asked Bob as soon as Ong's door closed behind him.

"You're not the only one who has experience of police operations." Bob replied. "So, when I realised how short of trained staff they are, I thought I would do some research into how they run things in Colombo. You would be surprised what they've been involved in over the last few years."

"Do you think the Chief will agree to our plan."

"I think in view of Ong's financial position, there's a good chance. As you know, Joseph...Money talks."

"And the detective really needs the extra manpower, even if he won't admit that out loud. My guys could swing the odds significantly in his favour."

"They will the need to make a decision quickly. As Ong said, it's going to be dark soon."

"I think we are going to need Ben's help on this too. He's the only one who can show us where this fissure is. We don't have time to waste, searching for it ourselves."

"Agreed. I guess they will have to swear Ben in as a constable as well then. We'd better go find him and tell him what's going on."

As Joseph opened the door, he almost fell over Izi, who was standing right outside, along with all the others.

"We want to know what's going on" Izi informed him.

Laura strolled past an open-mouthed Joseph and stepped into the room. "We know something is happening Dad. That detective who just left, looked really worried. He was talking to himself too. Why aren't you telling us what's happening? We are all involved in this."

"You can't just burst in here... Joseph started to say.

"Actually, I think you had better all come in." Ong replied as he came out of his bedroom.

"My daughter hates secrets." Bob muttered to Lawrence.

"I heard that!" Laura replied as she dropped herself in the middle of one of the sofas. "You know that Bonn's our best friend. We've all been involved in trying to find her."

"We even found the secret hideaway." Stan pointed out.

"It was mainly Ben." Sam corrected him. "But Stan got across the crevasse and we both heard the chanting."

"Which means we are entitled to know what you're up to" Laura insisted.

"I understand all of that." Ong replied. "And I'm very grateful to all of you for your help but this is a police operation, which we are trying to keep very secret. For Bonn's sake."

"We've all kept secrets before and some of us have even survived being kidnapped ourselves." Laura pointed out.

"You're all amazing people." Bob replied. "And of course we trust you. I think Ong, we should tell them what's been going on. Don't you?"

"Yes, you're right Bob." Ong replied after a moment's thought. "Why doesn't everybody sit down and we will tell you everything we now know."

They all found themselves seats and then fixed their attention on Ong as he outlined the events of the previous twenty-four hours and the proposed plan to rescue Bonn from the cavern.

"But we're going to need you to show us exactly where the fissure is Ben." Joseph added as Ong finished speaking. "Do you think you can manage that? Even in the dark?

"I'm fairly sure that I can." Ben replied.

At that point, there was a knock at the door and when Joseph opened it, Sadeeb Deburwani was waiting outside. "What are you doing here?" He asked as he surveyed the group.

"I decided that they needed to know what we were doing to rescue Bonn." Ong replied. "Have you spoken to your Chief?"

"Errr... Yes" Sadeeb replied as he looked around the group. "After he had spoken to you apparently."

"I thought it wise" Ong told him.

"He's approved the whole operation, including swearing-in Joseph and his team as constables. But...I thought we'd agreed to keep this all between us?"

"I know Bonn's friends won't whisper a word of this to anybody, until Bonn is safely back with us."

"Absolutely." Laura instantly replied and her friends nodded their agreement.

"And Ben is going to lead you straight to the fissure." Izi announced.

The detective's face plainly demonstrated his opinion of the recent events but he simply shrugged and then said. "We will definitely need him. I've been looking at the satellite images we have of the area, to try to identify the fissure myself. But the images are simply too grainy to be able to see the location you found. So I'm glad that you've already volunteered Ben."

"I want to help as much as I can." Ben replied modestly

"I appreciate that." Sadeeb said. "And I've also got some more information about that infinity sign. The one Stan found in the rock face."

"More information?" Bob asked.

"I just got another call from my officers who are... interviewing those robbers that I told you about?" Sadeeb replied. "It seems that the symbol that Stan found was deliberately carved onto the flat surface, so that it points in the direction of the entrance. They also told us how to find the trigger that releases the door to gain access into the mountain."

"I couldn't find the door." Ben reminded them.

"That's hardly surprising Ben. The original builders went to a lot of trouble to conceal it. Even the trigger is very well hidden, so that no one would find that either." Sadeeb informed him. "They put the trigger on a ledge just at the point where the fissure becomes too narrow to go any further. They described it as being about eight feet up the wall, on the right-hand side, where there is a small outcropping. It's flat and polished, with another of the infinity signs carved into it. By pressing a finger into each half of the figure eight and pushing downwards, it releases the locking mechanism and the hidden door swings inwards."

"That sounds like something from an Indiana Jones film." Stan pointed out.

"I agree with you, Stan." Sadeeb replied. "But unfortunately, we won't find out if it's all true until we get there."

"What are you going to do if you can't find the button or it doesn't work? Ong asked.

"In that case, the SWAT team will have to blow the door open with explosives."

"Which will remove the element of surprise." Joseph pointed out. "Which will thereby increase the risk to Bonn."

"We better hope the button works then." Stan replied.

"Of course it will." Izi snapped back at him. "We're always lucky."

"But keep your fingers crossed too" Bob told her. "We are going to need all the luck we can get."

"I need to start getting things organised. If you will excuse me, I need to get back to the Ops Room"

As soon as Deburwani had left the suite, Stan asked a question. "I'm sure we are doing the right thing, but one detail is bothering me."

"What?" Ben asked.

"You've only heard one voice on the phone, the taxi drivers who bring the envelopes have only spoken to one man and the guy who picked up the ransom money was alone as far as we know..."

"Just one man..." Ben replied thoughtfully.

"If it wasn't for what Deburwani told us, about the information he was getting about the cult, we would still be considering the guy from McCloud's boat!" Lawrence said in a rush.

"That's what I thought too." Stan replied. "Which means that he's still got Bonn somewhere and the girl in their temple might be someone else entirely."

"No!" Ong replied. "The Police would have heard about another girl going missing..."

"Not if she was a street walker, or a homeless person." Stan pointed out.

"If that's the case we are nowhere..." Ong sounded frustrated.

"We have to go on the best information that we have" Joseph said firmly. "Most of what we know points to the cult having Bonn. And that she's alive and being held in the cult's cavern. We need to get her back in the next few hours."

"Joseph is right" Lawrence said.

"We've got things to get ready too" Bob told them. "Which means we've got to get moving."

Chapter 29

Johannesburg

As soon as he read the email from Khan, instructing him to put Rhino on alert for Jannie, Bol wasted no time in dialling the burner phone which he had provided to Rhino at their last meeting.

"Perfect timing." Rhino said as he answered the phone. "I've been waiting for you to call."

"I've got a message for you from the Boss." Bol replied without acknowledging Rhino's comment. "He wants you to keep an eye on the orphanage again. Just in case the buggy turns up there."

"That's why I wanted to talk to you." Rhino replied.

"What are you talking about?"

"The buggy. It's here."

"Where?"

"In Jo'Burg."

"How do you know that?" Bol's voice showed the anger that had begun to build inside him.

"My guys have been keeping an eye on the orphanage for me."

"Why would they be doing that?"

"I thought it would be a really good idea."

"You, thought it would be a really good idea?"

"I used my initiative." Rhino replied proudly.

"Are you that stupid? You just don't get it, do you. I made it perfectly clear to you last time we met. *You don't decide anything.* If it relates to Mr K's business you tell me and I will tell you what to do. That's it. No exceptions."

"I thought I was doing a good thing..."

"I don't pay you to think, I don't need you to think, I don't even want you to think. Do I need to come and tell you personally?"

"No, no. I get it. Totally. I don't do anything unless you tell me to. It's clear."

"It better be. Now tell me exactly what you've done, so I can work out how much trouble you've caused."

"It's like I said. One of my guys saw the buggy outside the orphanage. It's right in the middle of Jo'Burg."

"I know where it is! What did he see...? Bol's heavy Russian accent echoed down the phone line.

"He told me that the buggy was there, so I went to the Post Office like you told me and then I waited for you to call me. I didn't want to ring the boss myself."

"Well you've learnt one lesson anyway. Is that everything you've got to tell me."

"Err...We saw it there early hours of this morning."

"Okay. So now *I'm* telling *you* to do something. Get one of your boys over there, right now and keep an eye on the orphanage and the buggy. Do nothing else...just watch it. Am I clear?"

"Yes, totally."

"I will ring you back, with further instructions."

Before Rhino had a chance to respond, the phone clicked off and he was listening to silence. "He thinks he's so important but he's just another hired gun like me." He thought to himself. "Probably best that I didn't tell him about leaving the note on the windscreen. Especially as there was no harm done..."

Bol sat in his comfortable Moscow apartment looking at the phone in his hand shaking his head. "Why do I always have to work with such idiots" he said aloud. "Mr K is not going to be happy with Rhino."

He flipped opened his ultra-secure laptop and looked at the screen trying to decide how best to word the email, to show himself in the best possible light. If someone was going to take the fall for Rhinos bad decisions, it wasn't going to be him.

Contact made with SA. Vehicle has already been seen at the expected location. Observation initiated. Awaiting further instructions.

Concise and to the point, just the way he likes it. Bol thought and then pressed the send button.

Rhino was still sitting in his office, fuming over the way Bol had spoken to him. Eventually he picked up his other phone and dialled the number of the gang member who was watching the orphanage for him.

"It's me" Rhino snapped when the call was answered. "Is it still there?"

"Yeah hasn't moved an inch. No sign of the kid either."

"Well, stick with it. If it moves I want to know straight away. And don't lose it or you'll be sorry."

"Got it Boss. I'm all over this."

"I will ring you in a couple of hours just to be sure. Just DONT LOSE IT."

Inside the orphanage office, Theo and White were discussing possible options for Jannie's next safe location with Johann Prinsloo, on the office's speakerphone.

"The buggy must have been the problem" Theo suggested. "There's not another one like it anywhere around here."

"It was a risk we agreed to take" Johann told them. "We won't be using it anymore, that's for sure."

"And Jannie loved the drive down here" White added.

"What if they try to hurt him while he's still here?" Theo asked. "I've got a lot of other boys to think about..."

"We've got that covered, Theo" White reassured him. "These Takers are cowards and bullies. They won't try an all-out assault on the orphanage."

"Maybe not in the daylight..." Theo added.

"Either way, you'll be out of there by tonight" Johann reminded them.

"Once they've taken off that extra tank, I think it's best if you guys pack up and leave." Theo suggested.

"Jannie will be leaving soon to go to your friend's garage to do just that." White reminded him. "Shouldn't take more than an hour, at most."

"That's the plan" Johann replied. "Anyway, I will talk to all of you later on then. I need to talk to Owen now."

Outside, on the forecourt of the orphanage, Jannie was dressed in his favourite bright red T shirt and cut-off jeans. He had spent lunchtime telling the other boys about another one of his adventures but he had work to do now. The extra fuel tank, that had been fitted for the long journey cross-country, now needed to be removed. The plan was to go to a nearby garage, which was on an industrial site a few blocks from the orphanage. Since the garage was less than a couple of miles from the orphanage, Smith had agreed that the drive there wouldn't be a problem. As long as it was done in daylight.

As he swung his leg over the buggy's door, he unexpectedly caught sight of a lone figure standing just outside the gates to the orphanage. The man was looking straight at him. The man slowly grinned at him and at the same time raised the front of his crumpled football shirt. Jannie could see the metal handle of a hand gun poking from the top of his jeans. The grinning man casually dropped his shirt back into place and then slowly drew his forefinger across his neck.

Jannie recognised the implied threat on his life and unusually for him, totally lost his cool. He turned the ignition key and his faithful engine burst immediately into life. Stamping on the accelerator, the buggy's fat rear wheels spun in the dirt, spraying small stones in all directions. The buggy leapt forward and raced towards the orphanage gates and the over-confident Taker who had threatened him. Jannie angrily drove straight at the startled gang member who barely had time to throw himself out of the way of the flying buggy. As Jannie passed through the gates into the road beyond, he braked hard and swung left onto the roadway to stop side-on. Breathing hard, heart pumping, he swung around in his seat to watch the reaction of the gang member.

The Taker's quick reactions had barely saved him from being mowed down by the buggy and Jannie watched as he then ran a few feet to an American muscle car that was parked at the curb and jump into the driver's seat.

The folly of his actions suddenly dawned on Jannie and he decided to put as much distance between himself and the

Taker's car as fast as possible. He put the buggy back into gear and once again floored the accelerator. As he sped a few hundred yards along the road, his escape plan was short lived, when the first traffic light he came to turned red just before he arrived. He found himself stuck behind a large truck which was piled high with plastic barrels. A brief glance in his rear-view mirror showed him that the Taker's car was fast approaching the stop light too. He knew he was trapped and what would happen next. He knew only too well that out here on the streets, the Taker could virtually do what he wanted and nobody would lift a finger to help him. He realised that he was cut off from Mr. White in the orphanage, with the Taker directly between him and there. His only other choice was the garage, where he had an appointment with the owner, who was a very good friend of Theo. Hopefully, like most business owners in Jo'Burg, he would be armed and Jannie would be safe there until Mr's Smith and White could reach him.

His decision reached, he dropped the clutch and swung the steering wheel hard over. The buggy's soft tyres made easy work of climbing the curb and then driving across the footpath, around the corner and onto the crossroad beyond. He hoped that the Taker's heavy vehicle would not be able to do the same. Fish-tailing onto the roadway again, he accelerated along the new road, which led straight to the garage on the industrial site. And safety.

The Taker was only fifty yards away when he saw Jannie bounce up onto the curb and turn the corner. Initially he braked hard as he approached the red light but as Rhino's strict instructions rang through his memory he changed his mind. Swerving onto the wrong side of the road, he floored the accelerator and pressed down on his horn as he raced towards the oncoming vehicles. He scrapped along the side of one car and fishtailed into another as his muscle car swung into the crossroads with all four tyres screaming. As he straightened the steering wheel, he saw Jannie's buggy accelerating away from him. Pulling his Magnum handgun from his belt, he fired off four rounds at the fleeing vehicle in an attempt to stop or slow Jannie's escape.

Jannie heard the tell-tale sounds from behind him and glanced briefly over his shoulder to see the Taker shooting at him. One of the rounds struck the tank behind him with a clang and then ricocheted skywards and he heard another as it passed close over his head. Swinging his head forwards again he saw the huge warehouses ahead of him, which marked the industrial estate where he hoped he would be safe. His accelerator was jammed to the floor, as his trusty buggy bounced along the poorly maintained road surface, engine roaring as he hurtled towards the garage. He knew it would be a close call as the Taker's car was much faster than his and would soon close the hundred-yard gap he had opened up. As the corner raced up, he yanked hard on the steering wheel and the buggy screamed around the first warehouse and into the industrial estate in a haze of tyre smoke.

Inside his apartment in Moscow, Bol was in the process of doing another set of one hundred press-ups, when his secure laptop chirped loudly to let him know that he had received an email. Picking up a small hand towel he calmly wiped the sweat from his hands and arms as he crossed to his desk and opened the laptop.

He was very surprised to find a response from Khan.

I want you and a full team on the ground in SA. ASAP. Pick up Subject and deliver him to me undamaged. Anticipate armed personal protection.

Bol re-read the brief instruction and quickly assessed the relevant timeframes and time zones. Obtaining the services of an experienced snatch squad would not be difficult for him, in fact he already knew the team he would use, if they were available. He had worked with them on several occasions in Africa and they were all ruthlessly efficient. Weapons were now easily obtained in all the major cities of South Africa, so they could pick up the necessary armaments on arrival. Jannie's personal protection, whoever they were, would easily be overcome by Bol's lethal team. The one part of Khan's message that bothered him was the ASAP condition. He doubted that he would find many direct flights from Moscow to Johannesburg, so he would be hard pressed to be on the ground in less than 24 hours. His experience so far with Khan, told him that he would not consider a response of 24 hours to be ASAP. And he was also absolutely sure that he did not want to get on the wrong side of Khan. Ever.

As he quickly combed the Internet for a suitable early flight, he simultaneously dialled a number from memory into his phone, to initiate contact with the snatch squad. He had a lot to do before his flight left Moscow. "I wonder if Rhino will be pleased to see me again?" he thought to himself grimly, as his call finally began to ring at the other end.

In Johannesburg, Rhino had problems of his own. The gang member that he had instructed to keep an eye on the orphanage, had called him a few minutes ago, with a garbled message to say he was chasing the buggy away from the orphanage. But he had not heard from him since. For the fifth time, he punched the redial on his phone to call his gang member back.

"He's crashed the car boss." The gang member said as soon as he answered the phone.

"He crashed into your car?"

"No boss. He crashed *his* car. I was following him just like you told me to. But he was driving like a lunatic. Then he lost control and crashed into a petrol tanker."

"So, you've got him now then?"

"No there was an explosion and a fire."

"You let him get away from you? You idiot. I told you this was important!"

"No, he didn't get away..."

"So where is he then?"

"He's dead boss."

"What? No, no. He can't be dead." Rhino replied, as he quickly remembered Bol's careful instructions.

"He is. I saw him burning up in the car, boss. Then I had to back off. There's Fire Brigade and cops everywhere now."

"Maybe they pulled him out alive?"

"Impossible. They can't even get close. It's an inferno." The gang member replied, quietly pleased with his use of the word.

"Why would it burst into flame?

"I think I may have shot that big petrol tank on the back."

"You were shooting at him?"

"I didn't want him to get away boss. That buggy is real fast. He was driving like some sort of race driver. And you said to make sure he doesn't get away..."

"I told you to follow him. Not shoot him." Rhino's thoughts went into overdrive as he thought about the conversation he would have to have with Bol. How was he going to explain how one of his men had just shot and killed the kid they were supposed to be watching?

"Stay right where you are. I'm coming out there to look myself. Where exactly are you?"

"You know the big industrial area, about two miles west from the orphanage? The one with the big car repair place..."

"Yeah, yeah. I know it. I will be there in twenty minutes. Don't move."

"Just look for the smoke..." he replied, but the phone line was already dead.

Fifteen minutes later, Rhino arrived near the scene of the crash. Police had cordoned off the road approaching the industrial site and he had to force his way through the gathering crowd. As he passed two men in greasy overalls, one of them said. "I saw the whole thing. Scariest thing I've ever seen." Rhino stopped behind them and casually lit a cigarette, as he listened to their conversation.

"I wish I'd had my phone handy to record it." The second man replied.

"It happened too fast. The kid must have been doing forty or fifty when he came around the corner."

"It would have been better for him if he had turned it over..."

"Those sand buggies won't flip, no matter how fast you're going."

"But it did skid...sideways with the tyres screaming...straight into that tanker."

"And boom. Like a bomb had gone off..."

"When that heat wave hit us...thought I'd lost my eyebrows."

"The driver didn't have a chance..."

"At least it was quick. Imagine being stuck there, in those flames..."

At that point, Rhino caught sight of his gang member through the crowd. He was standing right beside the Police cordon tape looking up the street. Leaving the two mechanics to their conversation, Rhino approached him and pulled him into a nearby alleyway between two of the warehouses.

"Tell me exactly what you did and what happened. Miss nothing out. Pretend your life depends on giving me all the details...coz it does."

"Yes. Sure boss. I was doing like you told me to. Just watching the orphanage and the buggy. I saw the kid come out and get into the buggy and he saw me at the same time. Then he tried to run me over for no reason and drove off down the road. I only just managed to catch him coz he got stuck at a red traffic light."

"So why were you shooting at him?"

"That was later. He jumped the light and raced up here towards the industrial units. I nearly lost him at the red light but I was just following him, like you told me to. But then he started to shoot at me. I'm lucky to be alive."

Rhino frowned. He didn't believe what he was hearing. "So you shot back at him?"

"I didn't have a choice boss. If he had killed me, we wouldn't know where he went to. Would we?"

"And then he crashed?"

"I think I probably managed to wing him. As it turned that corner over, to go around that warehouse unit there, he must have lost control and skidded into the petrol tanker."

"So, you didn't see him skid?

"I was just a couple of seconds behind him. Like I said, he was driving like a lunatic. Then, as I turned the corner, I saw him stuck in his buggy, jammed half under the tanker and then bam...it all just burst into flames.

"And you're sure he didn't escape?"

"I guess he must've been knocked unconscious in the crash. He was slumped in his seat. I saw him clear as day for about a second before the whole thing blew up. He burned up right before my eyes."

"Shit!" Rhino spat loudly as he considered Bol's simple directive to do nothing but observe the orphanage. He stood for a few seconds staring at his gang member, before he turned on his heel and walked back towards his car. How the hell am I going to get out of this? he asked himself, once again rubbing the scar on his hand.

Chapter 30

Colombo

Two hours later, Joseph and his team were bumping along in the back of a commercial delivery truck, which the Chief of Detectives had commandeered from one of the city's transport companies. Each of them now wore a top-grade Kevlar vest beneath the dark coloured overalls which the Police had provided for them. The protective equipment was uncomfortable in the evening's tropical heat but the cooling breeze flowing through the canvas sides of the truck, provided some temporary respite.

After Deburwani had completed the comprehensive and well-managed briefing for the upcoming raid, Joseph and his team had clambered into the rear of the truck and dropped themselves onto the wooden floor. Then, just before they had left the headquarters building the detective had taken the last available place in the lorry.

"Good briefing" Joseph told him. "Your guys seemed to be taking in all the details."

"Including the misdirection as to the raid's final destination." Lawrence added.

"They will find out soon enough" Deburwani replied tensely.

"They won't like it when they find out you lied to them." Joseph pointed.

"I don't expect to be liked, Mr Stein. Simply obeyed. Once we alight near the cavern they will each get a copy of the rough sketch of the cavern. That will be all they really need to do their job."

"Makes life much more complicated when you don't know who can trust" Lawrence pointed out.

"My men will do their jobs. And I will be leading them from the front." Deburwani replied and the men fell into an awkward silence.

The route out of the city and then into the countryside took them over an assortment of road surfaces but the last 10 minutes had been continuously marked with regular bounces as the road surface quality rapidly deteriorated as they cleared the tree line. As the trucks climbed ever higher, the headlights of the two vehicles following them winked out in accordance with the raid's briefing. The drivers all now relied solely on the night vision goggles they wore to follow the dark road.

"How much longer do you think?" Joseph asked Deburwani.

He glanced at his wristwatch before replying. "I estimate that we are almost at the drop off point. Five more minutes max."

"I've been thinking about your briefing. I can understand why you glossed over the point, but we are still likely to be heavily outnumbered if all of the cult members turn up as they are supposed to. Why didn't your Chief give you more officers?"

"It can't be helped. I can't use the local cops for this. They just don't have the training for it and would be more trouble than they are worth. I'm satisfied that the addition of your team swings the odds in our favour."

"Maybe, but I think we need to give Ben a side arm too. He may be younger than us but even from the little he has told me it's clear that he has kept his nerve under fire. Gun battles against poachers in the Congo, is a kill or be killed situation."

"I think it's going to be the same sort of situation in the caverns tonight." Deburwani replied grimly.

"Another steady shot working with our team might just make the difference between success and failure."

"You make a good case Joseph." Deburwani replied. "As soon as we arrive at the drop off point and he gets out from the driver's cab, I will ask him if he wants to help us inside the cavern. I know the SWAT team all carry a spare Glock 9mm, in addition to their machine pistols. I'm sure he can handle one of those."

"I know he will agree to help. I spoke to him about it when I gave him his night vision goggles, just before he got in the passenger seat, up front."

A few minutes later, the three vehicles pulled off the road and as the engines died the occupants jumped down from the trucks to stand in a silent mass in front of the lead vehicle. The night sky was moonless and covered in thick clouds so the men could barely make out the figure of their boss as he stood in the centre of the group and began to speak.

"Now we are on scene, I'm going to tell you what we are really doing tonight." Deburwani began in a soft voice. "Put on your goggles and look at these sketches of the target location..."

"Last minute change of plan, boss?" the cynical and long serving Sergeant in charge of the SWAT team asked as he looked at his map.

"Tonight, we are going to save a young girls life..." he replied and then outlined his actual objective of the raid. He finished the update by saying. "Once Ben has led us to the secret door, I will lead the SWAT team through it to the corridor beyond and then into the main cavern. Joseph and his team will find the girl and protect her from harm. The rest of us deal with the thuggees. Any questions?"

"Are we authorised to use deadly force?" the Sergeant asked.

"As soon as we enter the temple, you can assume that your lives are at risk. Shoot first, questions later. I don't want to be explaining the raid to any widows in the morning...Do your final checks now."

Deburwani then had a brief conversation with the Sergeant and relieved him of his pistol.

"Joseph has reassured me that you are steady in a fire fight Ben and we could really do with your help inside too. Do you know how to use one of these? He asked before showing him the pistol.

"I've had more experience with a rifle." Ben admitted. "But I'm pretty good with a pistol too."

"In that case, this is yours to use during the raid. That's if you want to come with us of course."

"I had no intention of staying outside during the fight." Ben replied honestly.

"Good. We need all the help we can get. We better get going it's probably going to take us at least thirty minutes to get back up to the cliff where you found the fissure. You can find it, can't you?"

"The landscape obviously looks different, approaching it from this side I mean. We came from the opposite direction last time. From the ravine side."

"Before the briefing, you told me that you could cut across the trail from here though."

"That's my plan. Once I pickup our previous bearing, I'm sure I can lead you straight to the point where we found the fissure."

"Lead on then. The SWAT team and I will be right behind you."

"Not too close though, remember? Just in case I need to backtrack. As long as they give me twenty yards' lead, that should be more than enough."

Deep inside the mountain, the Master was preparing himself for the annual ceremony which was about to begin. He had spent most of the day meditating in an effort to allow the Goddess to speak to him and let Her will be known.

"Is everything prepared?" The Master asked, as his teenaged acolyte entered the small antechamber. The room had been carved into the solid volcanic rock many years ago to act as the Master's private sanctum. It was hidden immediately behind the towering statue of the Goddess which dominated the main cavern.

"We are *almost* ready Master."

"Almost? The moon is going to rise in less than ten minutes. You should have *everything* prepared by now."

"My own tasks are all complete, Master. And the sacrificial virgin awaits your pleasure. But I am still awaiting three of our members to arrive in the chamber..."

"Who dares to be late for the Goddess on this most holy of nights?"

"The two Bashirs from the lake village and their cousin, Raj, Master."

"I sent on a mission to the city last night. They should have been here hours ago with the spoils."

"I suspect that they have returned to their drug den, Master. My father told me they were all still using heroin, Master."

"Your father should be more careful with his words. Their addiction problems were before they committed themselves to the Goddess. They understand that She demands complete obedience."

"Yes Master. It is true. We all understand that she watches over us at all times."

"Instruct the gatekeeper, that when they arrive he should keep them waiting at the entrance. I will deal with them after the sacrifice. The Goddess may speak to me during the ceremony and tell me what she wishes to be done with them."

"I will tell him, Master. Immediately. It shall be as you command." The acolyte bowed deeply and backed out of the room. Once outside he climbed the steep stairs behind the Goddess and then sprinted through the twisting corridors to speak to the guard who watched the outside door to the caverns. He knew he would barely have enough time to pass on the Master's message and be back in time for the start of the ceremony.

Ben's eyesight and skills seemed undiminished in the almost total darkness and he soon led the heavily armed raiding party unerringly to the fissure in the mountain.

"This is the place." Ben whispered to Deburwani, who had stopped right behind him.

"Amazing. With the clouds and the lack of moonlight I wouldn't have thought it possible" He replied.

"No chance of them seeing us either." Joseph said quietly as he joined them.

"Let's hope we can find the trigger then." Deburwani hissed before turning slightly to speak to the sergeant leading the SWAT team. "This is the place. I will be in front to open the door. As soon as it swings inwards, you and your men will be the first through the door. There will be someone on the other side. He is your first target. Try to take him out as silently as possible. I don't want to warn the others in there."

"He's all mine." the sergeant replied sternly.

"Consider everyone on the other side of the door to be armed and dangerous." Deburwani reminded him. "I expect to encounter up to a hundred suspects."

"Then we've got our work cut out for us, haven't we Sir?"

"Follow me. It shouldn't be very far along."

One by one the members of the SWAT team disappeared into the utter darkness of the fissure. The tight confines and silence of the night meant that the hard surface contours could be heard gently scraping on their flame retardant overalls and body armour, as they followed their leader.

It had been agreed that Joseph and his team, including Ben, would be next into the fissure, with the remaining police officers bringing up the rear. Their role included securing the entrance doorway, to prevent any of the suspects escaping that way.

The silence in the fissure was suddenly interrupted by a loud crack and a long scraping sound.

"We're in" echoed back to Joseph's team as the message was passed from man to man in front of them.

"Follow them." Joseph whispered to his team who were now bunched behind him in the fissure. "We have to get in fast."

As Joseph slid further along he found a section of the wall had moved inwards, revealing a slight glow beyond.

Following a few steps behind the last of the SWAT team he stepped through the doorway to find himself in a large space on the other side. As he paused there, he could clearly hear the sounds of many voices chanting. He also noticed a body was slumped on the floor to one side of the space, with two bullet wounds in its chest. A wickedly sharp jungle machete lay close to an outstretched arm.

"I didn't hear any gunshots." Lawrence whispered to Joseph as he saw the body too.

"Noise suppressors" he whispered back. "I noticed the SWAT guys had fitted them onto their machine guns. Come on we need to find Bonn. Follow me." He added before moving forward again towards the tunnel entrance on the other side of the entrance room, hard on the heels of Deburwani and his SWAT team.

Chapter 31

Johannesburg

Theo's old office phone rang loudly and insistently on the desk. He approached it slowly expecting it to be one of the care workers offering him yet another boy in need of his care and protection.
"Hello this is Theo."
"Theo, it's Cliff. From the garage."
"Oh, hi Cliff. How are you?"
"I'm fine. But I'm going to have to cancel your appointment this afternoon."
"Really? That's going to create a big problem for me. It's really short notice too. Are you sure you can't fit me in?"
"Oh, I could easily fit you in. The problem is that the police have shut off the entire site. So our clients can't get to us. We've had a big fire here see. Apparently, a car crashed into a petrol tanker, on the corner. You can probably even see the smoke from the fire from where you are."
"Okay Cliff. Well thanks for calling. Saved an unnecessary trip. I don't suppose you know anyone else who can take the buggy today? I really need it sorted out this afternoon..."
"Since I've let you down, I will make a few phone calls and ring you right back. Once again, sorry Theo."
"Hope to hear from you soon then..."
Theo hung up the phone and wondered what to do. This was going to cause a major problem. As he walked towards his office door he glanced out the window and realised for the

first time that the buggy wasn't parked out front. He stopped mid stride as a terrible thought entered his mind.

'That industrial site can't be very busy at this time of day. If Jannie had left a bit early to take the buggy there....'

He increased his pace and made his way across the forecourt and into the kitchen area to ask Mr White if Jannie had spoken to him about his plans.

In his Moscow apartment, Bol had completed his urgent travel arrangements and organised for the snatch squad to meet him in Johannesburg. He glanced at his watch and calculated the time difference between Moscow and Johannesburg. He decided it was a good time to ring Rhino for an update.

"This is Bol." He said as Rhino answered the phone. "Have you followed my orders?"

"Yes of course." Rhino answered nervously.

"I will be there myself in less than 24 hours. Even you should be able to keep an eye on it until then."

"You're coming here?"

"Is the car still at the orphanage?" Bol ignored Rhino's question.

"Err... No, it's gone."

"Don't tell me that you've lost it already? You're supposed to be keeping it under constant observation, that's all you had to do."

"No I haven't lost it. There was an accident..."

"You're making no sense you idiot. Tell me what you've done."

"The kid drove it out of the orphanage about an hour ago. My guy followed him like you told us, but the kid crashed into a petrol tanker. And it blew up.

"He just happened to crash? Did your man do something stupid? Did he scare the kid?"

"No nothing. He was just following him."

"So it crashed...? Where is the kid now? Do you grab him against my totally clear instructions?"

"No. He didn't get out of the buggy. The whole thing caught fire. My man saw the whole thing. It was a big ball of flame."

"Are you telling me the kid is dead?"

"Yeah. Must be burnt to a crisp. No way he could have got out alive from that."

"Your man saw him burning?"

"Yeah, he was right there watching the whole thing. Until the cops turned up. The kid's gone."

"So the police are dealing with it now?"

"There's dozens of them. All over the place. They don't usually deal with car crashes but fires always draw big crowds here."

"I don't care about that. Find out everything you can. Can I trust you to do that?"

"I've got good contacts in the police..."

"I will call you when I arrive." Bol switched off the phone without saying another word to Rhino.

"Could this get any worse?" Bol asked aloud. Khan would not be happy with this news. He knew that Khan wanted the boy unharmed. He had made that very clear in the email. So reporting him as dead, was not going to go down well. This felt like somebody had made a mistake. And he knew exactly how Khan dealt with mistakes. Someone would pay for this mistake and he didn't want to be that someone.

Once again flipping open his laptop he quickly tapped in an email to Khan.

SA Subject involved in car crash. Reported as dead. Instructions?

Bol was not sure how often Khan read his emails, as he often had to wait several hours and sometimes even a whole day before receiving a response. He glanced at his wristwatch. His flight was leaving in less than two hours and he was sure that Khan would have new instructions for him in view of what Rhino had reported.

As he was considering his options his cell phone began to vibrate on the desk in front of him. There was no caller ID on the phone but he answered anyway. A high-pitched tone came from the speaker followed by a voice he knew well. "I am scrambled you may speak freely."

"I've just spoken to Rhino." Bol replied. "The kid drove his buggy straight into a petrol tanker which burst into flame. He didn't get out."

"Witnesses?" Khan asked calmly.

"One of Rhino's men saw the whole thing. Rhino said there's no doubt."

"I wouldn't trust Rhino to go to the toilet on his own. He has made one mistake too many. I want *you* to deal with this matter now."

"My flights to Jo Berg are already booked. I will be there tomorrow."

"If the kid is dead I want proof. I don't care how you get it. I want a full autopsy report and a copy of the original police report before someone has the chance to tamper with them."
"What about Rhino? Do you want me to deal with him?"
"No. I will deal with him myself. It will be my pleasure. I will call you in 24 hours for an update."

Chapter 32

Colombo

As Joseph and his team rushed away from the entrance door to the caverns, they entered a dimly lit corridor, with flickering oil lamps hanging from the walls every 15 or 20 yards. After seeing the deadly machete with which the entry guardian had been armed, all of them were now held their pistols in their hands, ready for immediate use, should one of the cult members attack them.

Joseph followed close behind the Chief of Detectives, who in turn was following close behind the SWAT team. The rubber soled boots which the team all wore, made no sound as they sped along the twisting corridor which sloped steeply downwards as they moved ever closer to the sounds of the chanting voices, deeper inside the mountain.

After they had passed by a dozen of the lamps, Ben noticed that the sound of the voices had grown noticeably louder. Joseph's team stopped moving and Dan, the man in front of Ben, raised his clenched fist to tell him to stop. Ben repeated the gesture to the officers behind him which brought them all to a halt.

At the head of the column, the SWAT Sergeant now found himself at the head of a long set of steps, leading down into the main cavern. The smoky space was also illuminated by dozens of the same oil lamps which lined the corridor. By their flickering light, he could make out dozens of the cult members who filled the flat area in the centre of the cavern.

The men's repetitive chants were echoing back from the high ceiling.

Deburwani made his way to the head of the column and the Sergeant whispered in his ear. "I estimate 50 or 60 of them down there. No visible weapons."

"Those men are kidnappers and murderers. Assume there are knives and machetes nearby. If it's a choice between them or us them you have authority to shoot."

"Understood Boss." The Sergeant then waved each of his men forward and whispered in their ears as the detective waited nearby. Each man silently nodded before descending the steep steps into the cavern. In the poor light, their matte black clothing and painted faces made them virtually invisible against the black rock of the cavern. They moved smoothly using the natural outcroppings to cover their approach. The loud chanting would cover even the small noises they made as they took up their positions.

As the Sergeant followed the last of his men down the stairs, Deburwani waited to speak to Joseph. As he stopped to observe the cavern, he whispered to the detective. "Have you seen Bonn?"

"Not yet. But we know that there's lots of alcoves and caves all over this mountain."

"We need to find her before the shooting starts." Joseph reminded him.

As soon he finished speaking, one of the cult members caught sight of the SWAT team and shouted. "Intruders."

His voice was initially drowned out by the chanting of his brothers and it took a few more seconds before his frantic waving and screaming was noticed by the rest of the cult.

The SWAT team however, made good use of those precious seconds and moved forward and fanned out across the floor of the cavern. Joseph and his team also recognised they had been discovered and rushed down the other set of steps to cover the far side of the cavern, with their guns raised.

Joseph had only gone a few steps across the floor, when the change of perspective allowed him to see around the tall stone column in front of him. From his new position, he could see Bonn's diminutive figure spread-eagled on the floor. At the same moment, he saw the Master standing above her with his back to him. He also noticed the large knife that the Master was holding aloft.

The Master's attention was drawn towards the members of the SWAT team as they rapidly approached from his left side. His body stiffened and seemed to pause only briefly before making a decision. He swung his head back to look down at Bonn and then the sacrificial knife swung towards his intended victim, who lay helpless at his feet.

The Master's actions were swift and they caught Joseph slightly off guard. But his years of rigorous training took over his conscious mind and his pistol snapped out in front of him and two shots rang out in the chamber.

The two bullets struck the master between the shoulder blades at almost the same instant and his slender body was thrown sideways and forwards to land to one side of Bonn. The shots also initiated a scene of bedlam in the cavern as the cult members realised they were under attack and that their Master was already down.

Some of them snatched up a weapon and rushed to attack the SWAT team, who were moving towards them. Others stood dumbfounded, eyes transfixed on the figure of the Master who lay bleeding next to their intended victim. Many of them simply turned and disappeared out of the other side of the cavern into the tunnels there.

The SWAT team reacted calmly and efficiently to meet the sudden rush of attackers. The suppressors on their machine guns spat out a deadly volley hitting every one of the initial attackers, who were knocked backwards by the hail of bullets to slump to the floor wounded or dead. The rest of the detective's team had also rushed into the cavern to support SWAT and as they fanned out, the cult members who remained in the chamber lost their tactical advantage.

Joseph led his team forward to where Bonn lay and they formed a protective ring around her. He quickly examined her for serious injuries. Although she was unresponsive, he found no major injuries other than minor cuts and bruises.

Ben who had been just a step behind Joseph down the stairs was now standing over him, his eyes constantly scanning the surrounding battle. Joseph gently scooped up Bonn in his arms and stood next to Ben. "You and I are taking Bonn out of here." Joseph said.

Ben nodded silently without taking his eyes from the thuggees.

"We're moving" Joseph shouted aloud to the rest of his team. With Lawrence at the front, the team retraced their steps back to the exit tunnel, maintaining a protective cordon around the limp form of the unconscious Bonn.

As they reached the relative safety of the tunnel, Joseph stopped and said to Ben. "You need to lead us back to the trucks. I put a First Aid kit in the back of our one, which will sort out the injuries that I can see. I can't do much more until we can get her to a hospital."

"What do you want us to do?" Lawrence asked.

"Looks like the police can deal with the thuggees. But I told Deburwani we would help, so I want you and the others to block this tunnel and make sure no one follows us or escapes this way. As soon as things settle down, meet me back at the truck."

"Judging by what I heard, it won't take long." Lawrence replied.

"I think you're right. I will get the drivers to turn on all their headlights so that you can find us quickly. As soon as we can, I want to get Bonn to hospital to get her checked over properly. I think she's been drugged."

"No one's getting through us here. See you in five." Lawrence reassured him.

"Come on Ben, we're leaving."

Ben took the lead as the three of them quickly made their way back up the corridor to the entrance door. Nodding at the Police officer posted there they slipped through the stone door into the fresh air. As they exited from the fissure, the clouds had blown away and the moon had risen high above them to cast a guiding light back to where the trucks were parked.

It was almost thirty minutes later, when Lawrence and the rest of his team returned to the truck.

"How is she?" Lawrence asked, as they all climbed into the back of the truck to join Ben and Joseph.

"She's still out of it" Joseph replied. "But she seems fine."

"Shall I tell the driver to get going to the hospital now?" Roger asked.

"Absolutely" Joseph replied. "Can you jump in the front? And tell him to put his foot down."

As Roger scrambled from the rear of the truck, the rest of the team took up their previous positions with Lawrence next to Joseph. "All secure in the cavern?" he asked.

"Pretty much. Your detective friend understood that we had to get back to hospital and the SWAT team and the rest of his men had things all under control really quickly."

"Did they have to kill many more suspects?" Ben asked.

"Initially they continued to fight like crazy men, so yes, I think they shot another six or ten during the first few minutes. One of the SWAT team actually got a nasty cut from one of those machetes. But then a lot of them ran away and when the rest saw the number of cops pouring into the cavern, it seemed to take the fight right out of them."

"What did you do then?" Ben asked.

"It took another ten or fifteen minutes to get the plastic ties on all of them. Me and the team stood guard over those ones, while the cops started to search the rest of the cavern. That's why we took so long getting back."

"I still find it amazing that a gang like can operate near a modern city." Ben said as the truck began its bouncy ride back towards the city.

"It's just like rats hiding in the sewers." Joscph replied looking down at Bonn again.

"I bet you didn't even notice the Goddess, did you? Lawrence asked.

"The goddess?" Ben asked.

"That guy you shot, with the knife. He was standing right in front of it. A figure of their Goddess had been carved out of the rock. A foot taller than any man. We could see it clearly once we went back down into the chamber. Deburwani was right. It looks like they were going to sacrifice Bonn to their Goddess in that ceremony.

"We got there just in the nick of time." Joseph replied.

"I saw you shoot that guy when he was swinging the knife at Bonn." Ben said. "You've got fantastic reactions."

"I just did it automatically, Ben. I don't feel good about killing a man. But he was going to use that knife on Bonn. So I had no choice."

"You saved her life, Boss. No doubt about what he intended to do. It was a clean shoot. I'm sure the police will see it exactly the same way."

"I guess...But Bonn's safe and that's the end of it for now." Joseph replied as they all looked at the sleeping figure lying on the bench next to him.

"Once the Police had everything under control, I walked back down to the centre of the chamber where they had put Bonn. My eyes were fully adjusted to the reduced light by then of course and I noticed that there were dark brown stains all over the floor, right in front of the statue. It looked just like dried blood, Joseph. I don't think Bonn was going to be the first sacrifice they've made there."

"The blood of other innocent victims no doubt, murdered in the name of some weird deity..." Joseph suggested.

"Why do these old Indian religions always have to involve human sacrifice?" Ben asked.

"It still happens in other countries too." Joseph told him. "Actually, I think I read something about sacrificial murders in Congo not that long ago, Ben."

"People killing innocent victims..." Ben said sadly.

"That's still not the end of the story though, Joseph. Would you believe that they also had hundreds of jade statues, just like the ones found in Australia?"

"Jade statues? What do you mean?" Ben asked.

"They were all around the Goddess statue. I didn't really notice them at first. But once I had time to look around a bit, I realised that they'd been placed on every flat surface in the cavern. They were positioned so that they were all looking at the statue. As I was standing right in front of it, I started to feel a bit strange actually..."

"That's not like you, Lawrence." Joseph replied with a frown.

"The longer I stood there." Lawrence replied slowly. "The more I felt like the statue was looking right at me too. Even though there weren't any eyes. Those empty sockets actually made it even worse."

"You've got another horror story to tell your children." Joseph said trying to lighten the atmosphere.

"If I ever have children, I won't be telling them about that statue, I can assure you of that."

"What are they going to do with the cult members?" Ben asked.

"I heard the detective calling his Chief, to tell him all about the raid and call up reinforcements to take them all back to Colombo. I'm sure there are going to be medals all round after things settle down."

"I rang Ong to tell him about it too. He's going to meet us at the hospital."

"I'm still surprised that he didn't insist on coming on the raid himself."

"He almost did" Joseph replied. "I had to convince him to stay at the hotel just in case we had it totally wrong and the kidnapper called him there."

"Even so..." Lawrence said.

"I did have Bob on my side too. It was really him who finally managed to convince Ong to stay by telling him about what his own experience in Caracas when Laura was taken."

"It worked out for the best" Ben replied. "And once she's been checked over properly in the hospital, I'm sure she will be fine."

Chapter 33

Two days later

Bob Dalton was visiting the private hospital in Colombo where Bonn had been taken after she had been rescued from the cavern. Her father who had been waiting for the truck as it arrived, had refused to leave her side since then.

"I need to talk to you privately." Bob whispered to Ong as he sat beside his peacefully sleeping daughter.

"I've booked the room opposite for my use too." Ong replied. Glancing adoringly at Bonn's sleeping form, he slowly stood up and said. "Follow me." He walked slowly out of the room, across the empty corridor and into the other room, closely followed by Bob, who was carrying a large manila folder.

Ong selected a seat that had a clear view of the door to his daughter's room and also the armed police officer who was posted right outside.

Once the two men had settled themselves into their seats, Bob said "I understand that she is getting better now?"

"The drugs they pumped into her are almost out of her system now, so she's sleeping naturally. The cuts and bruising she sustained are only superficial. So, if the doctor gives the all clear on his rounds today, I will be taking her home to Thailand later tonight."

"That's excellent news."

"It is but that's only half the solution. Once she wakes up, they tell me that she's going to need all my emotional support and probably the best counsellors that money can buy."

"She's been through a lot. But hopefully she won't remember too much about what happened. Having been drugged most the time, I mean."

"I'm optimistic that will be the case but only time will tell. The other good thing, so they tell me, is that she is young and strong which will help with the healing process."

"I'm sure they're right."

"I assume you also want to talk to me about the file that you're gripping so tightly in your hand?"

"It's a copy of the Police file. Obviously, it's still early days in their investigation and there are so many crimes involved. But our friend the Chief of Detectives and his team, have been working day and night on the case."

"And what has he found out so far?"

"Much of his original supposition about the gang, looks to have been correct. The bloodstains which covered the floor of the cavern, in front of the goddess statue, come from at least a dozen different victims. The lab technicians have also had to work round the clock trying to get the forensics done."

"A dozen human sacrifices..."

"It could be even more. Some of the samples taken are too old and contaminated to be analysed fully."

"It must have been going on for years."

"Looks that way. The detectives are trying to identify potential victims. Going through all the outstanding missing-persons files, trying to match any possibles with the DNA analysis they've done so far."

"I guess that won't be easy. I doubt many people have DNA records around here."

"True. But they are trying anyway."

Ong stood up to look through the window at his daughter again and then said "I don't wish to rush you Bob, but my time is limited. I have to ask...have you found out anything about the statues Lawrence described. Are they the rest of the missing army?"

"The detective showed me one of the ones they recovered. They look very similar to the description that you gave me. And since there are exactly 500 of them, I would say yes. Probably. But how they got hold of them...

"Not so clear?"

"The cult members who finally agreed to be interviewed, knew almost nothing about the history of the statues. They all say that the Jade Guardians, as they call them, have been there forever. Just like the statue of their blood thirsty goddess. The Master preached to them that the Guardians protected the Goddess from evil spirits or some such mumbo jumbo.

"So, they can't be any real help to us...."

"I don't think so. Our best hope of finding out the real history, ended when Joseph shot the Master."

"Thereby saving my daughter's life."

"Indeed, he did. Nevertheless, it seems that he would have been our best chance, if we could have asked him."

"Have they managed to recover all the statues from the scene yet?"

"They did that this morning as soon as the CSI people had finished their examination."

"500 of them exactly. It has to be the ones we are looking for, from the bank, Bob."

"But how would a criminal gang get hold of them? The bank would have reported it, if they'd being stolen. And there's no record of that happening..."

"Maybe they kept it quiet because they didn't want bad publicity..."

"I'm sure the British Government would have insisted. Those statues must be worth a fortune. It would have been impossible to make an insurance claim without a police report."

"But there isn't a police report, so we are back at square one. Any other theories?"

"We have to assume that somehow they stole them from the bank vault but since Blackman Brothers didn't want the publicity they didn't tell anyone."

"And the British Government, or whoever they sold them to, didn't get told either?"

"It's the only thing that makes sense. It's been a hundred years. Maybe the last owners are dead?"

"Do the police have any leads on ownership?" Ong asked.

"I doubt anyone will be able to help with ownership. Where would they start. I assume you don't want me to tell them what we know?"

"Definitely not. We've already given more than enough help to them."

"So now what happens?"

"If they can't find the current owner, as criminal proceeds recovered by the police, I'm hoping they will eventually go to public auction. Many months from now probably, when all the fuss around their discovery has died down. Then, with any luck I'll be able to buy them without too much competition."

"I assume you will send someone here, to buy them anonymously?"

"I intend to keep my usual low profile, Bob. Better all round that way. Any other news for me? I don't like leaving Bonn for too long. When she wakes up I have to be there beside her."

"Well, things are settling down pretty much as we discussed. Sam's parents arrived from Darwin yesterday and Izi's mother is here too. I left them all together at the hotel. They were trying to organise a trip up into the mountains, for some well-deserved rest and relaxation.

"And Stan?"

"His father, Spencer? He should be able to get here by tomorrow. He works for Prinsloo Industries, so I spoke to Johann to get him here asap."

"And his mother?"

"She's a doctor. Apparently, she's working in the middle of nowhere, dealing with an outbreak of Ebola and she's impossible to reach."

"It still sounds strange to me. He *is* their only child. There's no way I would let Bonn wander all over the world with her young friends the way that Stan does."

"Me neither." Bob agreed. "But it's different with girls and their dads isn't it!"

"What about Ben? I know you told me he'd been involved in some serious encounters with poachers, but even so..."

"It seems absolutely fine. He and Stan are actually talking about trying to do some climbing while they are here together."

"I really need Ben back at the sanctuary to finish off his work there. Maybe he could take Stan with him since his parents are so busy with their work."
"I guess they will talk to Spencer when he gets here then. And saying that, I had better be getting back. Tracey made it clear that I was expected to be on their road trip."

Twenty minutes later, Bob arrived by taxi back at his hotel, to find Tracey and the others all waiting impatiently for him.
"I'm sorry I'm late everybody." Bob told them as he climbed into the minibus. But I wanted to check on Bonn before we left for the day."
"Don't try and get my sympathy Bob Dalton." Tracey told him. "We've been waiting ages."
"I'm only ten minutes late." He replied sheepishly.
"You tell him Tracey." Stan insisted whilst grinning broadly.
"Keeping taxis waiting isn't cheap you know, Dad..." Laura added, which caused everyone in the bus to laugh.
"Hello Bob." A strange voice said from half way down the bus.
"Who's that?" He asked.
"Esther. I'm Stan's Mum. We only managed to get here just before you turned up." She replied. "So, it was lucky you were late or we would have missed the party entirely."
"*We* only just managed...? Bob asked, even more confused.
"I'm here too" Spencer Ogenko's voice replied and a hand waved above the seats halfway down the bus. "Apparently when you asked Mr Prinsloo to get us here asap, he took your request literally. He sent a private jet to pick us up."
"When I eventually got Spencer's message to contact him urgently and I heard about what had happened, I threatened

to resign if my boss didn't allow me to take some time off." Esther told him as the bus began to move off.

"Perfect timing then. Because I hear that we're headed to a beautiful spot in the mountains." Bob informed them.

"Nicely ducked, Bob" Tracey said as she elbowed him in the ribs.

"How is Bonn?" Sam asked.

"She's sleeping normally now." Bob told them. "Her Doctor is due to give her a final check this afternoon and then Ong will take her back home to Thailand."

"Will we get a chance to speak to her before she leaves?" Izi asked.

"I'm not sure" Bob replied. "I think Ong is more concerned about getting her home."

"You did all speak to her yesterday" Tracey reminded them.

"But only for a few minutes each..." Sam replied.

"She needs rest and relaxation more than chit chat" Ben suggested.

"For once, you are probably right" Stan told him pointedly.

"The sooner we all get back to normal, the better for everyone." Bob insisted.

"What *you* mean, is back to work as normal" Tracey insisted.

It took almost an hour and a few wrong turns before their well-meaning guide and driver found the small beach at the side of the lake high up on the backside of the mountain, which Sam and Ben had described to him, following their microlight flight.

Once they had waived the driver off, with strict instructions to pick them up again just before sunset, Ben led the group along the small path and onto the black sand of the volcanic beach at the side of the fresh water lake.

"Well it was certainly worth all the effort." Bob admitted as he looked at the amazing view as the others arranged the chairs and towels they had brought with them.

"I bet no one's been here ever before." Izi suggested.

"I really don't think it's that isolated." Laura pointed out. "We're only an hour or so from Colombo. It's hardly a pacific island."

"Don't be such a wet blanket. We certainly have the whole place to ourselves today." Sam said as she slipped off her shoes.

"I've come up with a great idea for my family business, Mr Dalton." Izi said as she dropped into her beach chair next to Bob. "After all our work recently, I've decided that we should all set up private detective agency."

"A what? Bob asked.

"We've all been really good at solving all sorts of mysteries this last year." Izi continued. "And I've decided that since we all make such a successful team, we could do it professionally in the future. What do you think?"

"That's a great idea!" Sam said. "I could fly our private plane..."

"There's a world of difference between that and flying your microlight" her father, Christopher, pointed out.

"Ben could be the tracker. To find missing people" Izi continued with her plan. "And Laura is getting really good doing research on computers, so she can help doing that."

"I take after my father." Laura said proudly. "And don't forget that you did really well too, Izi."

"What about me?" Stan asked. "What could I do. I'm not much of a detective..."

"Well apart from climbing up the outside of buildings like Spiderman whenever we needed you to burglarise somewhere, you also happen to be the world's best computer hacker." Ben reminded him.

"Hardly the world's *best*..." Stan replied modestly.

"Don't forget Jannie..." Sam insisted.

"I haven't! He's our professional driver" Izi said proudly. "If we need to chase anyone, I mean."

"You would need a very big sign to put all your names on. Wouldn't you?" Spencer advised her.

"I've got a solution for that too." Izi said proudly. "We simply use all of our initials. The sign would read...'J. Bliss Investigations'."

"That's really clever, Izi. Solves the problem and it's a catchy name too. You've obviously put a lot of thought into this." Bob said.

"It's a shame Jannie's not here with us. It's been ages since we've all been together in the same place, at the same time." Sam said.

"I bet he's going to be disappointed when he hears that he wasn't here to help rescue Bonn." Ben said.

"I'm sure he's having his own adventure somewhere." Laura replied. "He's been all over the world. Probably more than the rest of us put together. Mr Prinsloo keeps finding him great places for work experience."

"It's also to keep him safe, remember." Bob reminded her.

"And he gets to work with Owen all the time too" Stan sounded envious.

"So do you, Stan Ogenko." Esther reminded him. "He gave you that super computer to play with..."

"I wasn't playing with it, Mum." He replied. "That was real work experience too."

"That's enough talking about work and business" Laura insisted. "Everybody get their snorkels ready." She added as she picked up a pair of scuba fins.

"Last one in, is a rotten coconut." Izi shouted as she jumped up and ran giggling towards the crystal-clear water, carrying her snorkel equipment in both hands.

"But I'm not ready yet." Laura shouted after her.

"If she finds the plane wreck first I will not be happy." Sam said, as she desperately searched for her diving mask, in her brightly coloured beach bag.

"Don't worry Sam." Ben reassured her calmly as he stood at the water's edge. "Even though we told everyone all about the sunken plane, it seems to me that she's swimming in totally the wrong direction."

"Less haste, more speed, eh Ben?" Sam replied as she finally got her gear together.

Thirty minutes later the teens were all sitting on the beach towels with disappointed looks on their faces.

"I can't believe we didn't find it." Izi said breaking the thoughtful silence. "We've looked everywhere."

"It seems that J. Bliss Investigations fell at the first hurdle..." Ben replied.

"Are you sure this is the right part of the lake? Stan asked as he looked from Sam to Ben.

"I'm *fairly* sure." Ben replied.

"Fairly sure?" Laura asked. "We got all excited about this..."

"It's difficult to be totally sure, Laura. Trust me, the world looks really different when you're flying above it." Sam admitted.

"And there *is* a lot of water out there" Bob added.

"It was probably just a trick of the light" Tracey suggested. "It would have been very improbable to find a small plane up here in the middle of nowhere..."

"I think you've all had too many adventures lately" Christopher said

"Why don't you all just relax for a while and get your breath back." Tracey suggested. "It's going to be a lovely day and we've got plenty of time here. You can all go out again in a little while if you're really convinced, Ben. Then, while you're doing that, Bob is going to cook us all one of his fabulous barbecue lunches."

"I will give you a hand with that" Christopher offered.

"And me" Spencer added. "Everybody loves a barbeque."

"And to finish the day, I've organised a Chinese restaurant for all of us." Tracey added. "And you will be pleased to hear that it's karaoke night too."

"Perfect. I love karaoke." Laura informed them.

"I haven't done that for ages." Izi replied.

"That doesn't include us boys, does it?" Ben asked.

"Of course it does." Tracey replied. "Bob is giving prizes to the best singers so everybody will have to join in."

Chapter 34

Tripoli

Abdul Khan was sitting in his secure room, reviewing the email which Bol had just sent to him.

Jo'Burg update:
Visited scene of crash. Checked damage to vehicles. Interviewed gang member. Facts appear as reported.
In view of Rhino's recent failings, I then used my own contacts to obtain the original copies of the reports, which I have attached.
Awaiting further directions.

Although he had not had the pleasure of despatching Prinsloo's precious orphan himself, a grim smile of satisfaction was spread across his face, as he then read the first of the attachments to Bol's report.
It contained details of an autopsy, which the pathologist had recently carried out on behalf of the Johannesburg Police.

Summary
Examination of teenage male involved in a road traffic accident.
Identity confirmed as Jannie Pietersen by next of kin. Dental records concur.
Subject is of mixed race, 5'8" tall, medium build, weighing approx. 130 lbs.

Subject has suffered 100% burns to the skin surface. No other major injuries.
Blood tests negative for intoxicants or poisons.

Cause of death:
Full break of the spinal cord between vertebrae three and four, consistent with rapid deceleration occurring when subject's vehicle collided with stationary object.

'So he didn't burn to death after all.' Khan thought to himself. 'Pity really. I was hoping the kid would have suffered more. Then his uncle's punishment would have been even more gratifying, since I assume he has also read this report by now.'

As he considered Johann's pain, Khan scanned through the next attachment.

The report identified the highly-qualified accident investigator, who in accordance with the Police protocols for collisions involving fatalities, had performed a complex physical examination of the scene and used various mathematical formulae and taken numerous photographs, to calculate the forces involved. Khan skipped through the bulk of the surprisingly detailed police report, to reach the summary page.

The investigator had drawn the conclusion that the primary cause of the accident was that the victim's vehicle had been travelling at excessive speed. When the vehicle turned the 90-degree corner, it induced a flat skid. Poor driver response had then caused the vehicle to fishtail twice, leaving indicative skid marks on the flat, dry concrete road surface. The vehicle, still in the driver induced skid, had then collided with an unattended, stationary tanker, causing the explosion and subsequent fire.

The investigator assigned no blame on the tanker driver, who had apparently been in the process of calling the local police about his brakes seizing, when the collision occurred. The investigator's subsequent examination of the burnt remains of the tanker confirmed the driver's submission, that his brakes had seized and that he was therefore physically unable to move the vehicle from its location.

A thought suddenly occurred to Khan, who sat back in his seat with a frown creasing his forehead. It was highly unusual to get the two reports completed so quickly and anomalies like that always bothered Khan's ever-cautious mind. He knew only too well that South Africa's bureaucracy was usually notoriously slow and inefficient. 'Something was different here.' Khan knew. 'I wonder if Prinsloo had been pushing for the abnormally rapid investigation and report? He was bound to have been curious as so who killed his little friend. I have no doubt that Prinsloo would have all the right contacts to achieve that result in his own city. That explains it.'

Dropping the report back onto his desk, Khan smiled to himself as he considered the implications. 'Finally, your good luck ran out, didn't it, Jannie? I knew it would. I just had to be patient. And I'm very good at that. For a year, I've had you chased all over the world and yet you meet your end at home. Almost poetic, really.' He allowed himself several moments of gloating, as he considered the grief and guilt that Prinsloo would now be suffering. 'Long may it continue.'

Khan hadn't finished with Prinsloo yet though. He had plans to crush his excessive business ambitions too and bring him completely to his knees. But that final victory would wait for another day.

Khan's compartmentalised intellect then turned to other business, as he picked up another page of his comprehensive computer printout. He swiftly read through the numerous, abbreviated reports which may have been of interest to him. Having read carefully through most of them without any particular interest, he soon reached the final page.

Colombo, Sri Lanka: Major police incident. Up to 100 gang members arrested for multiple counts of murder and kidnap.

Khan stopped reading the report as his anger grew. 'Why am I reading this nonsense?' He thought to himself, 'Somebody has clearly set the search parameters incorrectly. And that somebody would pay for their incompetence. My time is too valuable to have to read irrelevant data.' His hand was reaching for the phone, when his eyes automatically read the next line on the report.

Hostage Thakkrani found alive. Property recovered: 500 jade statues

Khan's hand paused in mid-air and another rare smile crossed his face. Sometimes, I really do get lucky. He recognised the name immediately. Thakkrani was one of his main competitors for his legal business in Asia. If his daughter had been kidnapped, he would inevitably be distracted, meaning that this was a perfect time to press the advantage and organise his destruction. Khan would need to contact the chairman of Asia Resources to initiate the relevant response.

The last, single line item, had been automatically connected to the previous report.

Darwin, Australia: Request for all information relating to antique jade statues

'That can't be a coincidence' he decided and rose from his desk and left the secure room, to speak to the data centre's manager.

"The last item on my daily report...get me the details. Now."

"Yes, Sir." The manager opened up the daily report and quickly tracked down the relevant source data. He quickly formatted the information and pressed the print option on his keyboard. Khan ripped it off the printer and returned to his office.

The intelligence report identified the source as being one of the many dubious, but useful, characters working in Khan's vast criminal network. The man, who worked as a 'fence' for valuable art work, had reported an enquiry from Australia to be on the lookout for antique jade statues.

Under normal circumstances, Khan would have taken no notice of such low-level criminality but something in the back of his mind told him that in view of the connection with Thakkrani, it deserved further investigation. Confidentially, of course. He would task Craig Dunlop with tracking down the source of this request as soon as he had finished his enquiries into the Butcher.

Settling back in his comfortable office chair, Khan closed his eyes and breathed a long sigh.

Chapter 35

Johannesburg

It felt like the rain had been falling continuously for two days. The ground beneath their feet was so soft, it made sucking noises as they made their way across the vast cemetery. Braamfontein cemetery contained many of the last three generations of the population of the booming city. It was also the location of the family plot which now also contained the remains of Johann's recently departed father.

Owen, Johann and Theo had followed the hearse which contained Jannie's coffin, in Johann's glistening-black Mercedes limousine. As they had passed through the ornate entrance gate the three men fell silent. The driver followed the brick paved road, as it wound between the massed gravestones towards the Prinsloo burial plot. Eventually, the elegant vehicle slid silently to a stop behind the hearse and the driver stepped from the car. He walked to the rear of the vehicle driver and as his passengers stepped out into the rain, he handed each of them an umbrella.

The three men had spoken only briefly in the car following the funeral service, which had taken place in an almost empty church. But as they walked towards the graveside, following the dark oak coffin and it's four pallbearers, Theo broke the silence.

"I can't believe he's gone, Johann. He was so young..."

"I feel the same." Johann replied. "Much too young. He had a bright future with me."

"He would have done you proud. No doubt about it. As soon as you told me that the Takers had given up on him. I knew he was going to do something special..."

"I had big plans for him."

"He had just passed his test to fly the Predator, too."

"He had many skills, Theo. You did an amazing job with him."

Owen silently trudged two steps behind them, deep in his own thoughts as the rain drummed incessantly on his black umbrella. He was starring ahead through the rain at the scene ahead of them.

Jannie's grave, like many of those in the cemetery, had been impersonally excavated by a JCB backhoe, which was now parked amongst a small stand of trees nearby. The mechanical behemoth stood like a sentinel, as a stark reminder of the mundane inevitability of death which had claimed another victim.

After the backhoe had completed its work, a large, green plastic awning had been erected over the newly dug grave in an attempt to preventing it from filling with the torrential rain. As the pallbearers carefully made their way across the slippery grass and into the protective shadow of the awning, a lightning bolt lit up the sky to be followed by an ear-splitting roll of thunder. The four men carefully manoeuvred the coffin onto the plain wooden supports which had been placed across the grave.

The Reverend, who had earlier led the church service, positioned himself at the head of the coffin and waited silently as the pallbearers retreated to the cover of the nearby trees. Theo, Owen and Johann stood shoulder to shoulder on one side, heads bowed as they each said a silent prayer as the rain fell in torrents around them.

Drawing a breath, the Reverend began to deliver the speech which he had given hundreds of times before. However, the three mourners could barely hear them, through the constant drumming of the rain on the awning. Finally, the Reverend fell silent and at that moment the grey day was lit up by a long series of nearby lightning strikes, immediately followed by another massive roll of thunder.

All four of them turned and looked out towards the grey, cloud filled sky to watch spellbound as the lightning bolts continued to rain down on the city centre for several minutes. As they watched the spectacular light show, they failed to notice the stranger walking towards the graveside who was carrying a large commemorative wreath.

As the stranger ducked under the awning, and stopped to stand next to the Reverend, he asked. "I'm sorry...Is This the Pietersen funeral?"

"Yes, it is." The Reverend replied automatically, his surprise was obvious. "But this is purely a private service."

Owen took a few moments to respond to the stranger's arrival before he took three steps to stand right in front of the stranger and said. "This is a Family Only service. What are you doing here?"

"I'm sorry, Mister. I'm just delivering a wreath. It should have been here before you arrived. Really, I should've been here half an hour ago. But with this rain...well, I'm late."

"Who sent you here?" Owen asked.

"My boss at the florist. Look, I don't mean any disrespect, Mister. I just deliver them. Wherever the customers want them to go. That's just my job. I'm really sorry I'm late. or disturbed the Service..."

"What customer?" Johann asked as he joined the group.

"Pietersen" the stranger replied.

"Not the funeral. I mean who sent the wreath?" Johann insisted.

"Erm... I don't know. You would have to ask my boss. I just deliver them. Look, I don't want to get in trouble. It was just the traffic...in this weather."

"Is there a card?" Owen asked as he took the wreath from the stranger's hand to examine it.

"I...err...think so" the stranger's quivering voice revealed the nerves he was now suffering from.

Owen quickly found the simple white card which was pinned to the wreath. He read the card and then ripped it off the wreath and handed it to Johann without comment.

"And then there were none" Johann read aloud. He also noted the large letter K written on the reverse of the card when he turned it over.

"I don't understand?" Theo said.

"It looks like our efforts to keep the funeral a secret were ineffective." Johann replied, half to himself.

"Look, I'm not sure what I've done wrong but I have to get going." The delivery man informed them. "I've got other deliveries in the van... Please don't complain to my boss. I need this job."

"No, we won't. No harm done here. Off you go." Owen told him as he watched Johann for his reaction.

As the delivery man scuttled away, the Reverend asked them. "Do any of you gentlemen have any last words?"

Johann moved to stand closer to the coffin and looking down replied. "Rest in peace young man. You will be sorely missed." Then looking back over his shoulder to the Revered he added. "Let's get this over with." The Reverend lifted his hand and waved to the pallbearers, to return to the graveside. A few minutes later, the four pallbearers had lowered Jannie's coffin into the grave and taken up a position on the opposite side of the grave to the three mourners.

"Ashes to Ashes and Dust to Dust." The Reverend said as he threw a handful of damp earth on top of the coffin to complete the ceremony. "I will leave you gentlemen now, with your thoughts and my best wishes. May God be with you." He added before stepping out into the rain and returning to his own vehicle parked nearby.

"Who sent the wreath? Theo asked.

"I don't want to discuss it here." Johann replied as he put up his umbrella again. "Let's get back to the car."

The three men left the pallbearers to their work and trudged back to where the limousine was awaiting them. The driver had seen them coming and took their umbrellas from them as they resumed their seats in the rear of the vehicle.

"We are going to ruin your carpet, Johann. Theo said as the rain water dripped from their clothing.

"I will worry about that another day" he replied. "Let's have a look at that card again, Owen."

Johann re-examined both sides of the message without gaining any further information.

"It has to be Khan." Owen insisted as the car moved off.

"The same man that you suspected of being behind the Takers all this time?" Theo asked.

"We think so, Theo" Johann replied. "Owen and I can't prove it, but we feel certain he was the one. And now somebody has put a lot of effort into finding out about the funeral too. We didn't tell anybody about it."

"Not even his friends." Theo reminded them.

"After what happened to Bonn" Johann replied. "Bob Dalton agreed that there was no benefit to telling them right now. They've been through enough recently."

"And if Khan *is* still watching us, that might even have put them in some danger too." Owen pointed out. "He has gone to extreme ends to chase Jannie all over the world. Who knows what he wants next?"

"I'm glad I didn't get any of the boys from the orphanage to come along then." Theo added.

"Surely he must be satisfied by now?" Johann insisted.

"I'm not banking on that, JP. We can't be sure that he's not going to come after you now." Owen reminded him.

"I don't suppose there's any way to be sure..." Johann replied sadly.

"I know you feel uncomfortable doing it, but at least in the short term I think you need to accept my recommendation for round-the-clock protection."

"I suppose you're right Owen. Khan is obviously a man looking for some sort of revenge. And the death of Jannie obviously wasn't enough for him. I don't intend to underestimate his capabilities or his drive ever again."

Watch out for Book 6 of The Adventures of 6ix….